MW00423624

Tides of Blue

Tides of Blue

SHARON BRUBAKER

Tivshe
Publishing

This is a work of fiction. Names, characters, places, events and incidents are either the products of the author's imagination or used in a fictitious manner. Any resemblance to actual persons, living or deceased, or actual events is purely coincidental.

Copyright © 2022 by Sharon Brubaker

All rights reserved.

No part of this book may be reproduced in any form or by any electronic or mechanical means, including information storage and retrieval systems, without permission in writing from the author, except by reviewers, who may quote brief passages in a review.

Library of Congress Control Number 2022917229

Paperback ISBN 978-1-954175-66-2
Hardback ISBN 978-1-954175-67-9

Distributed by Tivshe Publishing
Printed in the United States of America

Cover design by Dark Queen Designs

Visit www.tivshepublishing.com

Acknowledgments

As always, thank you to my family. You are incredible!

Many thanks to my wonderful friends and beta-readers Alice, Barbara, Linda, Peggy, MaryBeth, Roxann, Shauna, Sonia, and Sue.

Thank you to Linda Roller, The Liberty Bookshop in Avis, PA for writing camp and research adventures!

A special thanks to Roxann and Steve Williams for opening up the world at NASGA.

Many thanks to the Kent County Maryland Historical Society.

Many thanks to NASGA – the North American Sea Glass Association (https://seaglassassociation.org/), its board members, members, vendors, and visitors.

Thank you, Laura Minker, for introducing me to the world of vintage carousels.

Thank you, Ralph Watkins, Shirley Hess-Phillips, and George Wilbur, for your insight and information.

A special thanks to Alice Lundgren for her support.

And very special thanks to Jodi Jackola of Tivshe Publishing for helping make dreams come true.

Author's Note:

Sea glass and beach glass are nearly one and the same. The glass is usually dumped in the water or at the shoreline where the glass is found and smoothed by sand and the water's erosive action until these broken pieces possess a silky, smooth finish. Small, pitted marks in the shape of the letter "C" also indicate sea glass. It takes between twenty and one hundred years for the shiny glass to change to the silky, sanded appearance prized by collectors. Sea glass originates from the ocean. Beach glass originates in freshwater areas. Due to PH differences in water, sea glass from freshwater sources is usually not as frosted as sea glass, so sea glass is considered the jewel of the sea and is prized by collectors. The colors of glass are ranked by rarity. Finding pieces of sea glass makes one wonder where it came from, what type of glass, and the history behind each piece. Some are treasured; some are tossed back into the water to further perfect into a jewel, sometimes referred to as 'mermaid's tears.' The sea glass we find holds echoes from the past. There is a story that lies within those echoes.

One

ANNA GRACE – 1860

Anyone who has picked up a piece of sea glass has touched history and touched other lives.

Anna Grace and Tyrone stared at Augustus's lifeless body. In death, he looked at peace and free from pain. In death, his face showed a vestige of his youth.

"It is done," she whispered as she stared from Augustus to the small, cobalt blue glass bottle on the nightstand.

"Yes, missus," Tyrone agreed, and he bowed his head.

There were no other words. After a moment of silence, he reached for the bottle, but Anna Grace's hand stopped him.

"I'll take it," she told him rigidly as her hand reached for the small, uncorked bottle, innocently standing guard by the cup drained of liquid.

She picked up the bottle, cradling it in her hand, wanting to keep it. She wanted it safe, as it was one of the last things Josiah had touched. But Anna Grace knew she had to be rid of it.

Tears pricked at her eyes. They weren't tears of mourning for Augustus but rather tears of relief. She turned to look up at

Tyrone's impassive face with one tear trickling down the side of her face, then wiped it away quickly while Tyrone averted his eyes.

"We're free now, Tyrone. Free," she stated steadfastly.

"Yes, Missus," he answered, turning to look at her. There was a glimmer of hope in his eyes.

"A mercy killing," Anna Grace asserted quietly.

"Yes, missus," he agreed.

He wouldn't meet her eyes now, so she looked down then quietly left the bedchamber with the bottle clutched tightly in her hand. Anna Grace swung the large, heavy front door open, stepping deliberately down the steps and onto the path that led to the small wharf that jutted out into the Sassafras River. A sharp, little wind tore at her hair, tearing it from the pins Pansy had carefully used to lock down her tresses earlier that day.

She felt no remorse in having given Augustus the last of the colchicine. What he had done to Sadie with Mr. Reece was unconscionable. What he had said about Josiah was cruel. She would no longer be a victim of his rages, belt, and rape. She was numb, knowing the poison in the bottle had caused Augustus's demise. Would it be considered murder or self-defense? She didn't know. She did know the Colchicine in that bottle was her ticket to freedom.

Anna Grace stared at the small bottle in her hand. It gleamed brightly in the rays of the setting sun. She thought of Sadie. She thought of Josiah. She thought of herself. Then, she smiled a triumphant smile and tossed the small, cobalt blue ridged bottle as far out into the river as she could. The sunlight caught it mid-arc, and briefly, the bottle glittered brightly, looking as though it had wings before it dropped into the muddy river.

As the bottle struck the water, the bottle gave a little "plop-plop" sound before sinking below the surface. River water filled the bottle as it sank deeper and deeper until finally resting on the sand and silty mud. The bottle lay nestled in the muddy, sandy bottom of the river, oblivious to the commotion happening above.

Now, the bottle was at the mercy of time and tides. Minutes turned to hours. Hours turned to days. Days turned to weeks. Weeks turned to months. Months turned to years. The small, ridged, cobalt bottle lay apart from life above the water. Occasionally, the bottom of a boat created a wake, and the bottle swayed gently back and forth in its cradle of sand and mud. The daily tidal pull, along with storms, and creatures, moved the cobalt blue bottle in an infinitesimal march down the river and to the bay. The silty mud and sand wore away the sharp ridges on the bottle, caressing it and wearing them down to silky, sandy nubs. Crabs darted. Fish swam by. Occasionally a fish lipped the ridges finding rather quickly that the bottle was not food.

Many years passed before the bottle met the Chesapeake Bay. Waves heaved, and whitecaps roiled as if it were a violent sea. The watery chaos churned, and the tiny bottle struck a rock. A tiny chip emerged, turning into a fissure. Like hoar frost, the fissures created a lacy effect of a network of tiny cracks. As minutes turned to hours, hours into days, days into weeks, and weeks into years, the fissures deepened into a beautiful pattern.

Eventually, through time and tides, the bottle cracked into several pieces, large and small. The pieces formed a dense heap on the murky bottom of the Chesapeake Bay. Sunlight did not pierce the water to show its blue beauty, leaving the pieces as dark as the rocks. They were as dark as the blue of the depths of the night sky. The sand and silty mud caressed each piece turning the glossy, smooth, shiny pieces into satiny treasures. The pieces loosened from their resting place, drifting and bumping along. Small "C" shapes adorned the cobalt treasures like a brooch on a beautiful dress.

As the years passed, the tides took the pieces out into the bay and onto neighboring shores. The small, blue pieces drifted apart, moving away from the whole shards becoming part of other stories yet to be told.

Two

BETH – PRESENT DAY

Sea glass is often regarded as a symbol of renewal.

Y ou stupid bitch!" Mike shouted with such vehemence that spittle flew out in small drops with the mean words. "You're a selfish bitch! Did you know that? What were you thinking? You knew we had plans! Now you've ruined everything."

Beth cowed as a hailstorm of expletives and insults continued to spew from his mouth. The verbal abuse was nothing new. He always seemed to find fault in everything she did. This time, Beth had agreed to work a different shift to help a colleague on her floor at the hospital. It wasn't a crime, but Mike didn't like changes to his plans. He didn't like it when she failed to consult him before making any changes to *his* plans. As a hospital administrator, he was anal about his job and everything else in his life. Mike liked control.

His ire could be raised by something as simple as folding his clothing incorrectly or placing the herbs and spices out of alphabetical order. Lately, his anger and rage seemed to be increasing exponentially.

Eventually, the shouting subsided to words hissed in seething anger. Beth stood silently, shoulders drooping as his foul words swept around her like a tyrannical wind. Once again, each ugly word seeped into her skin like drops of rain, each one causing her confidence to dwindle. She sank under the storm of words, slumping into the old couch and hunching her shoulders.

"I'm sorry," Beth whispered. She doubted if her apology would have any effect.

"Sorry," Mike hissed in disgust.

He turned on his heel and strode out, slamming the door behind him. His eyes flashed, and she saw a hard look in them that sent fear into her. Mike hadn't hit her, but the 'yet' seemed to whisper in her head like a fragment of a song. And it was an ugly song that reverberated in her head and would not go away. Her breath hitched tenuously after his tirade. She always held her breath when he spewed his poison as if she was waiting for a blow. He was beginning to frighten her, and she wanted to escape. It was in that instant that Beth realized she could escape if she tried.

The question was, 'could' she escape? Beth had heard of safe houses for women, where they changed their names and found a new identity. Posters of the organization that helped women find safety were posted at the hospital where she worked. Beth had jotted down the number and torn up the scrap of paper several times, not knowing what to do. She questioned herself constantly. Was it abuse when he didn't hit her? She doubted herself over and over again. Fear and self-loathing were becoming her close companions.

As the days and weeks went by after Mike's recent outburst, Beth daydreamed of a life away from him. Was it possible? She wasn't certain, but his complaints and rages made her feel claustrophobic, as though she couldn't breathe.

Finally, Beth came to the realization that she didn't want to live this way. She decided that she didn't need to live in fear anymore and resolved to pull herself away from Mike in degrees.

She would escape. And so, she began to devise a plan. She could begin a new life somewhere new. But where? The possibility enticed her, but she knew she needed to be careful planning her escape from Mike.

That night, Beth pulled herself to the very edge of the bed, turning her back on Mike. She blocked his snores with a pillow and stared into the darkness with burning eyes until she fell asleep. Mentally, she berated herself, wondering what she had ever seen in Mike. At this point, any feelings she had for him crumbled into dust. Disgust was the only thing left. She was bereft of any love of him.

Her plan of escape was inadvertently helped by her nursing supervisor, Mary. The hospital, as always, was short-staffed, and Mary asked Beth to work nights for a month.

The night shift offered Beth the opportunity to work on her plan. Because Mike was always snooping on her phone and email, she set up a new email account that she only accessed at work. Then she found an old road atlas and looked for potential areas to move to, ones she knew had employment areas She wanted to go somewhere different from the mountainous region of Eagle Heights, but she didn't want to go to the city. She wanted to leave Pennsylvania, so she looked south to the Chesapeake Bay area. The upper part of the bay was central to a number of hospitals in both northern Maryland and the northern Delaware area. Her plan was to drive to the area, find a place to live, and then begin applying to the hospitals. This area would give her the option of several hospitals between the Baltimore to Philadelphia corridor.

With her new schedule, Beth would get home when Mike was leaving for the hospital. They were two veritable ships passing in the night. She would sleep a few hours and get up in the late afternoon to prepare dinner and prepare for work, trying her best to be the model girlfriend and not arouse any suspicions from Mike. At first, he'd grumbled and complained about the change in her schedule. These thoughts he shared at home, but not with anyone at the hospital. She didn't know what bad blood lay between Mike and Mary, but there was something about Mike's expression of possible shame and the way Mary pursed her lips when Mike came on the floor that made Beth wonder if something happened in the past. Had it happened with Mary, or with one of the nurses? She didn't know, but he was certainly cowed around her nursing administrator.

Her friends and family continued to tease her and look expectantly at her left hand, planning a future for her and Mike with engagement, marriage, and babies. At one point that had been a possibility, but now it made Beth ill to think about any kind of future with Mike. She kowtowed and spoiled Mike, keeping a fake smile pasted on her face. Beth was still worried, but he seemed mollified for the moment, his criticisms abating for the most part. She worked hard to keep it that way.

Eventually, Beth turned away, no longer able to tolerate their talk of her future. They read her silence as another sign that her relationship was deepening with Mike. In reality, her nerves were on edge. She couldn't eat and lost weight, something Mike noticed and for which praised. Beth gritted her teeth. And she waited.

A month passed. She was certain that if she didn't leave soon, she wouldn't leave at all. She was terrified Mike would discover her plans, and she wanted to be far away from him before he did. Pulling together the fraying edges of her courage, she took a day off, packed up her things, and withdrew every penny from her bank account. She texted her mom to say she was going away for a few days and drove down the road, away from the snowy Pennsylvania mountains to Maryland's gray and rain-swept Eastern shore.

After a grueling five-hour drive, Beth settled into a hotel near the head of the Chesapeake Bay. Exhausted in body and spirit, she fell asleep for nearly a day. When she awoke, Beth looked at the pale late winter sunshine squeezing itself around the edges of the heavy curtains, pushing light into the room. Beth lay on the bed, assessing her situation. She had done it. It was, literally, the dawn of a new day. It was the beginning of her new life, far away from Mike. She was determined to build the foundation of her new life.

She felt like one of the fiddlehead ferns emerging in this early spring weather. She had been so tense, curled up, and afraid to stretch living with Mike. Beth looked at area apartments, but nothing in a complex appealed to her. It took a few days, but she found a cabin to live in south of Kingstown and right on the water. Beth was enchanted with the little cabin, and the price was right.

The little cabin was nestled in overgrown grass perched at the top of the bay. From the yard, she could look north to the small town of North Bay, across the water to another waterside community, and south, where the bay opened up into a vista of water and sky. The neighborhood was tiny, and the homes small and well cared for. They screamed summer, even on this chilly day with windchimes tinkling in the wind and yard décor that flaunted flip-flops and sunflowers. They remained flaunting memories of bright summer days as the late winter winds blew. The majority of the homes were summer cabins, but a few had cars parked in the driveway, so there were some neighbors that lived year-round. There was something about the place that made her feel safely tucked away, far away from Mike, but still close enough to civilization that she could find a job.

The little cabin came furnished with sagging, well-worn furniture. Beth spruced up the home with colorful curtains and new linens. It was a shabby-chic theme that would work for the time being.

Beth loathed submitting employment applications and narrowed her job search to a few local hospitals. Settled in the little cabin, Beth applied for substitute nursing positions. The closest was a small cottage hospital that was in transition to be absorbed into a larger hospital system. They hired her almost immediately. The work was good, the commute was short. It seemed everything was going in her favor, and eventually, Beth began to settle in, embracing her situation and, in time, quelling the fear that still harbored deep inside. Thus far, Mike hadn't tried to find her. She hoped beyond hope, that Mike would convince himself that she was the crazy one to leave. She hoped he would forget all about her.

Three

ᕮᐧᐧᕭ

ANNA GRACE – 1860

Cornflower Blue glass is slightly lighter in shade than cobalt blue glass.

It was the quintessential summer's day. In the sweltering heat of an Eastern Shore summer, a small, light breeze from the bay lazily freshened the air that was heavy, hot, and very, very humid. It seemed to Anna Grace that they lived at the end of the world on this plantation, for all of its bucolic beauty.

Despite the summer heat, butterflies danced gaily in the neighboring meadow. Dragonflies buzzed from the river and over the plantation fields. They hovered near Anna Grace when she was outside of the main house, sometimes landing on her. She brushed away the insane thought that the dragonflies were wise ones, knowing her thoughts. Quietly, off in the distance, the songs of the slaves blended melodically with the songs of nature. Bees buzzed; birds twittered. There was even the sound of distant cows mooing.

The sky was a clear, cerulean blue. It was the blue that waxed poetic in novels and poems about skies and eyes. Once upon a time, in the not-too-distant past, Augustus had told Anna Grace that her eyes were as blue as a clear, summer's day. He had wooed her and convinced her father that he loved her.

She laughed a bitter little laugh at the memory.

The light breeze from the river gently billowed the lace curtains at the tall windows of the large, brick house that overlooked the river and the plantation fields. It was a picture-perfect scene of country bliss. Who would imagine the dark seed of nastiness that lay within?

Anna Grace Cadwallader stood at one of the open windows. Her maid, Pansy, was pulling on her corset. She pulled steadily, and as gently as possible. Anna Grace winced in pain and gave an involuntary moan as the young woman tugged at the laces. The corset covered the bruised ribs lined with long welts from lashes. She kept her back stiff, and her hands trembled as she reached to grab the soft, white, pine of the windowsill. She dug her nails in and held on as Pansy pulled and tugged at the corset, pulling at the wounds. Pansy hissed in sympathy.

"I'm so sorry, Missus," Pansy apologized to her mistress, her voice barely audible.

Anna Grace had been born into faltering privilege. Here she was the mistress of a large plantation, but only by default. She had been sold, by her father, to the highest bidder, for her young body. Bought and sold. The monies from her sale had bolstered her father's flagging merchant business. In turn, Anna Grace had been married and shuttled off from Philadelphia to the far reaches of the Eastern Shore of Maryland, a life foreign to her Quaker faith, which taught that everyone was equal. She could only pray that her father had her best interests in mind with the decision. Since her mother had died, Anna Grace's well-being had been his responsibility. She didn't know if that had been the case, and she didn't have the courage to ask him, but it was what she preferred to think. The alternative was too painful to imagine. She didn't know if she would ever see him again, but she wrote him weekly, keeping her letters light and general. And she never told her father how abusive Augustus truly was. She didn't want to add that guilt to the grief he still carried for her mother.

At first, her husband, Augustus Cadwallader, had been kind and solicitous. He had been especially solicitous in convincing Anna Grace's father that he would be the finest choice for his only daughter's hand. Augustus could charm people. He had a twinkle in his eye, and his suave speech enchanted anyone who would listen. Anna Grace had been charmed as well.

Now, she saw through the veneer of his smile and the forgery of his twinkling eyes. She knew now that his smile wasn't genuine, that the twinkle was rather a cold and calculating glitter that filled his gaze. When he forced himself on her, she kept her eyes closed, performing her wifely duties, relieved when his heaving and grunting came to an end, and he rolled off her. Not only did his thick, portly body repulse her, but he was cruel and abusive. The beatings began when it became clear that she couldn't bear him a child. In turn, his manhood drained, and, unable to perform, he would slam his flaccid member into her over and over. She tried not to cry out, but she lay bruised and sometimes bloody when it was over. He would go away then, relieving her of her embarrassment and misery.

As Pansy tugged harder on the corset, Anna Grace thought back to the prior night. Augustus had come to her bed, once again unable to perform, yet he had slammed into her until she had groaned, in pain, but not in passion. Taking no notice, he had continued thrusting at her further until he'd ended his futile efforts.

Gasping to catch her breath, against her usual reserve, she opened her eyes, seeing dismay and fear on Augustus's face. She thought she'd even seen a trace of a tear.

In a moment of compassion and pity for the man she loathed, Anna Grace had put her hand to his face, cupping his cheek in her hand. For just a moment, he had softened.

In an instant, Augustus slapped her hand away and struck her cheek. The fear she'd seen earlier was now replaced with anger.

"Bitch!" he'd cried before he'd rolled her over roughly.

She had cowered in fear, curling into a fetal position. Augustus had struck her before, and she knew what was coming. Anticipating more blows, she curled up more tightly. It wouldn't do her any good to protest. Protestations only seemed to drive him to beat her harder. She had learned to be as quiet as possible, so she had stayed quiet and squeezed her eyes shut. Anna Grace had grasped the sheets tightly with one hand, white-knuckled, as though the sheets were a life preserver. Her other arm she had used to cover her face, her fist over her ear. She had bitten her lip and waited, listening as Augustus pulled his belt from his pants. Within seconds, the belt met her skin, Augustus striking her over and over again with it. Her thin, cotton nightgown offered no protection, tearing apart to expose her back and buttocks to the belt's wicked sting. She had thought she should pray to survive another beating, but prayer seemed futile. She'd felt bereft from God and everyone.

The question, why, had echoed in her mind with each blow, question blotting out the foul names he was calling her. With each anticipated blow, she'd held her breath, her mind blank in the haze of pain as she'd waited for the blows to stop.

Eventually, they did stop. Anna Grace had wondered for a moment if she had stopped breathing altogether. Her chest ached, so she tried to take a quiet, silent breath. She wasn't dead. Not this time. With a minuscule movement, she'd raised her fist from her ear to listen carefully.

The floor had creaked, and she'd heard a heavy movement. Augustus was trying to leave the room quietly. She'd heard him pick up something from the floor, then swear softly before she'd heard the door creak open and then close. Augustus had called to someone in the hallway, likely his manservant, and walked heavily toward his room. Anna Grace had let out a small sigh, tendered with a sob. She'd known it wouldn't do any good to cry. Still, a few tears had come as she'd hiccoughed softly.

Slowly, she'd begun to uncurl like a fiddlehead fern in the spring. First, she'd uncurled her fists and stretched her fingers. Then, she'd started to stretch out her foot and one leg, stopping when she'd heard the door open. She'd remained frozen, not moving a millimeter. Fear had enveloped her once again, her breath constricting again. Had Augustus returned? Would he hurt her more? She'd closed her eyes and waited.

A soft voice had broken through Anna Grace's fear, and she'd heard Pansy's soft voice cajoling her, "Missus, it's me. Missus, let me see. Let me see what that bad 'un has done to you."

Pansy's soft hands had touched her and lifted her bloodied, torn nightgown from her body. Anna Grace had whimpered, and Pansy had hissed. A tear had leaked from her eye, but Anna Grace didn't have the strength to wipe it away.

"He's a bad 'un, Missus," Pansy had repeated. "He shouldn't treat you like this. It ain't your fault, the way he is. He brought it on hisself. He brought it on hisself, with all of his evilness."

"Oh, Pansy," a strangled whisper had left Anna Grace's lips as she'd winced in pain.

Her hand had slowly uncurled and reached around, and Pansy had taken it in her strong, brown fingers. Pansy had then let go of her hand and taken to the ministering of her back as she told Anna Grace of the long stripes, decorated with glistening drops of bright, red blood that highlighted shimmering, long threads of silvery scars, shining testaments to past beatings. Pansy's breath had come out in a hiss before Anna Grace had heard Pansy dip a cloth in water and wring it out. The cool, soft, wet cloth had touched Anna Grace's skin, and she'd gasped at the cool and burning. It had lasted a few moments and then began to feel better. The shock and pain from the beating had left Anna Grace exhausted. Pansy had helped her into a new nightgown and then brought a tisane to help the pain and help her sleep as she had in times past. Anna Grace's hands had shaken so badly that she couldn't hold the fragile teacup, so Pansy had taken her hands and held them around Anna Grace's trembling ones, lifting the cup to Anna Grace's lips. She'd smelled peppermint and chamomile as well as another scent that Anna Grace hadn't recognized. It was slightly bitter, but she knew the tisane would do her good. She'd taken a hesitant sip, wrinkling her nose at the bitterness.

"Come now, Missus," Pansy had said gently. "This tea will do you good. Drink it down now."

With Pansy's help, Anna Grace had clutched the cup in her hands, drinking the tisane steadily until there wasn't a drop left in the cup. Pansy had taken the cup and set it on a small table by the bed, then helped her lie down on her stomach. She'd pulled a sheet and quilt over Anna Grace's body, then crooned, "Hush-a-bye, don't you cry. Go to sleep, little lady," and patted her hair gently. Pansy had changed the words from baby to a lady for Anna Grace, who had loved the song about the horses. It had made her smile, thinking of the freedom of horses cantering across a meadow.

The involuntary cry of pain when Pansy gave the final tug to the corset jerked her from the memory of the abuse.

"I'm sorry, missus," Pansy apologized again.

"It's all right Pansy," she said, straightening her back as well as she could without passing out from the pain. She had a full day ahead of her, and Augustus would be unhappy if she didn't attend to her duties, no matter what condition the previous night's abuse had dealt her.

Four

JOSIAH – 1860

Brown sea glass is a very common glass for beer and whiskey bottles dating from the late 19th century to the present.

I t was hot and sticky. Josiah pushed himself up from his overflowing desk, tugging at his brocade waistcoat as he went over to the window that overlooked the harbor in Baltimore. You couldn't really call the small wisp of air that teased him through the window in this early morning light a breeze. Josiah wrinkled his nose at the smell it brought in. The wharf held the stink of the ages, but it was nothing unusual. He stared out at the ships creaking in the change of tides, their masts wobbling oh-so-slightly. Glancing back at his brimming desk, he felt like groaning, just like the wooden ships that creaked and groaned at the wharf.

This wasn't the life Josiah had imagined. This was the life he had inherited when his parents had died from the yellow fever epidemic that had cursed the city. He had been far away at St. John's College, studying the classics, when he'd received the news of their death.

He knew it had always been his father's greatest wish that he run the import-export business. His father had built a thriving business of imports and exports in Baltimore's Fells Point. Their family's sturdy brick warehouse was large and comprised two floors of storage. It hugged the wharf but was adjacent to the railroad. His father had been a brilliant businessman with a vision of the future.

When Josiah was a boy, his father would bring him to the warehouse and let him gambol along the wharf. One of his favorite sailors, Big Red, a brawny, red-headed sailor, would swing him high in the air. Josiah would screech in delight and terror as Big Red swung him out over the water and back. Big Red had taken Josiah onto the ship, where Josiah explored every corner in his excitement. Josiah had loved watching the sailors clamber up the ropes to the masts and sails. They seemed to be going right into the sky. What he didn't like was the hold where it was smelly and dark, and he'd often heard the rats and mice scuttle about.

As he'd grown, his father had assigned him to work in the warehouse, starting the lowliest job and working his way to the management of the business. His father had preached frequently to him that a business owner needed to know every inch of their business and be able to do any of the jobs required. Josiah had seen his father on several occasions take off his dress coat, roll up his sleeves, and jump in to help the dock hands move merchandise in the warehouse. It wasn't something most business owners would do, but he had a suspicion his father rather enjoyed it. Josiah liked the physical labor assigned to him as well. There was a sense of accomplishment in the tasks when they were completed.

Now, he was alone and running his father's business. Spending his days totting up numbers, coddling suppliers, wooing customers, writing letters, and inspecting ships and warehouses, rather than reading the classics and having discussions on philosophy. He often daydreamed that if his father were still alive, he might have chosen to be a scholar or enter the clergy. His father's untimely death had thwarted thoughts of alternate careers. His respect for his father swelled more each day as he assumed the responsibility of running the family business, and he fervently wished he could keep his father's dream alive and thriving.

Josiah glanced back at his desk. It was a snowstorm of papers, rounding themselves out in a mountain at the top and sliding down to a level snowy field covering the polished walnut desk that gleamed where papers did not grace it. The morning sun lit up the papers so that they glowed, reminding Josiah of his uncompleted work. He tugged at his red-gold mop of hair. This pile of work would need to wait until his return from his trip to locate additional tobacco to export.

Josiah glanced out the window and wondered about the weather. The stillness and humidity did not bode well for his next piece of business. He was due to travel across the bay and up the river to make nice with Augustus Cadwallader with the goal of enticing him to sell his tobacco crop. He disliked Augustus and his pomp and crassness. He had also heard stories that he chose not to believe about Augustus's character. Josiah liked to think of the best in people.

Nevertheless, Augustus had a reputation. Josiah had a reputation too, or rather his father had had a reputation, of being a fair and honest merchant. He hoped in his heart to live up to the reputation his father had built with the business. Turning from the window, he sat down at the desk with a sigh, trying to organize what he could, knowing he needed to find a secretary, a man who would be his right hand in business matters. He wished that Abraham, his manservant of Mulatto origin, could be his secretary. Things like that were just not done. Still, he would think about giving Abraham more responsibility. Maybe, just maybe, in the coming years, people of color would all be free. Mr. Lincoln thought so, and that gave Josiah hope in this country. He pulled the necessary papers he would need to take on today's trip to the Cadwallader plantation.

Not long after, Abraham knocked at the office door with three succinct raps. Josiah looked up from his desk. Abraham nodded to him without a word. It was time. Josiah left without a glance back at the mound of papers and headed out the door, following Abraham to the boat that would take him to Augustus Cadwallader's plantation.

Josiah stood with Abraham in the bow of the ship, breathing in the fresh air and leaving behind the stink of Baltimore as they sailed across the bay to the Sassafras River. The boat picked up wind in its sails, and it flew across the water that was as smooth as glass. The bow of the boat cut a neat slice in the water as it traversed across the bay. The trees on the Eastern shore were backlit with golden sun that glowed above the horizon. It was quite beautiful. Their trip to the Sassafras River was assisted by the incoming tide that pushed the boat, as if in anticipation, toward their destination.

Hours later, Josiah and Abraham arrived at a small wharf where they transferred their belongings from the sloop to a shallop at a rickety, wooden wharf. He marveled at the green country on this side of the bay. It was so different from the brick and stone of Baltimore. The air smelled sweet compared to the stink of the city along the harbor's edge. The sound of the waves on the shore was a soothing backdrop of noise from the clang and clatter of the city streets. The city had its own kind of music, but the sounds on this quiet Eastern shore of the bay was like a fugue compared to the symphony in the city.

Josiah didn't want to spend one extra moment in the

company of Augustus Cadwallader and had written ahead for accommodations at a nearby inn. There were a few other plantations his father had established business with, and he would check on their upcoming crops as well. It would be a week or more until he could return to his overflowing desk.

Josiah shook off the trepidation he had about meeting with Augustus Cadwallader. A new day had dawned, and he hoped it would bring good things. He also knew proprieties must be adhered to. He had learned protocol in business dealings with his father. This was his chance to practice what he'd learned to woo and discuss a business transaction that would benefit both parties.

The shallop they rode in up the Sassafras River was a sturdy, small boat. It wended its way up the river at a slow pace and gave Josiah time to think of his upcoming meetings with the plantation owners. He had learned much from his father and felt he had a decent grasp on the business at hand.

There was an abundance of wildlife as they sailed up the Sassafras. Heron squawked in protest and raised their huge, blue-grey wings into the air. They glided above. He had marveled at the terns that dove straight into the water on their sail from Baltimore but now marveled more at the cormorants and their sleek feathers as they dove underwater. It didn't seem natural for a bird to swim underwater, but there it was. The buzz from the insects alongside the river filled the air with a symphony that Josiah did not usually hear in the city. He could even hear a variety of small creatures rustling in the greenery alongside the river. It lulled him, and his mind drifted.

Josiah woke from his daydream when the captain of the small boat docked at a small wharf that jutted out into the river. He looked around. Ahead he saw a cove and glimpsed creamy, yellow water lilies. Fields were beyond the copse of trees lining the river, and he could hear the songs of the slaves as they worked hard in the fields. At the wharf, a small, well-worn dirt road, packed solid by the years of travelers traipsing the path led up a hill to where Josiah assumed the Cadwallader plantation house would be. Abraham took their bags and placed them on the wharf, handing Josiah a well-worn carpet and leather valise that held his papers. The captain of the shallop tipped his hat and turned his boat to return to his dock at the bay.

Josiah and Abraham looked at the road, pausing a moment to stretch and get their legs used to dry land. As they walked up the hill from the wharf, Josiah was impressed with the tall, brick structure that appeared. It was a handsome house that overlooked a cove teeming with lemony-yellow waterlilies in the Sassafras River. The scent of the flowers wafted toward the house mixing with the green smell of the vegetation surrounding them. It was a glorious spot. He stopped to take a breath and stare at the vista. Josiah fervently hoped that Augustus appreciated the peacefulness of the setting. Envy tinged his thoughts.

Abraham went on ahead with the bags. He rounded the house and went to the back to the servant's entrance. He would need to complete the details for horses to travel to the inn this evening.

Josiah walked to the front of the house, passing by a formal knot of a garden with boxwood, where he wrinkled his nose at the boxwood's sharp scent. There was a tall, imposing door with a heavy, circular, brass knocker. He raised the knocker and let it fall sharply, and the sound reverberated from the door, into the house. Moments later, a distinguished gentleman opened the door that swung smoothly inside on its hinges. Josiah introduced himself. The gentleman nodded and led him to the parlor.

Augustus Cadwallader did not rise when Josiah arrived. Instead, he sat king-like in a wing-backed chair with his foot bandaged and propped on a stool. Josiah suspected Augustus was in significant pain by the lines on his face and the grimace when he shifted to sit up taller to greet Josiah. All the better, his meeting would be short and sweet. He would be polite, get to the point about the tobacco and make his excuses about dinner.

Josiah sat uncomfortably in the chair opposite Augustus. The chair deemed for Josiah was overstuffed and brocaded. The seat tipped him forward, and it was uncomfortable as he had to perch on the edge. He learned the distinguished servant's name was Tyrone and gratefully accepted an iced mint julep served to him on a small, shiny, silver tray. The talk went well, and they focused on the business at hand, discussing the upcoming tobacco harvest and sale. Even though Augustus was wily, Josiah thought they'd made a fair deal. They had returned to small talk when *she* walked into the room. Josiah was stunned. He had heard that Augustus had wed but hadn't a clue about the wife.

Anna Grace Cadwallader seemed to glide into the room. Josiah thought she held herself somewhat stiffly, but not unfriendly. She was young and quite beautiful. The yellow, silk gown she wore was embroidered with sprigs of delicate flowers. It mirrored the honey-gold of her hair twisted and braided into a goddess-like vision.

Josiah barely heard Augustus say, "Mr. Bryant, may I present my wife." Augustus paused in the introduction as the barest hint of derision laced his tone, "Mistress Anna Grace Cadwallader."

Josiah Bryant took a gallant step toward Anna Grace, bowed, and took her gloved hand. He raised it to his lips and gave it a gentle kiss. He felt and heard Anna Grace catch her breath. His lips buzzed with unexpected pleasure and desire.

"My pleasure, Mistress Cadwallader," he greeted her in a light tenor. "I can now believe the rumors are true. The finest flower on the Eastern Shore lives here. Josiah Bryant, at your service."

As Josiah stood from his bow, their eyes met for a moment. Anna Grace seemed to falter when he gazed into her eyes. He wondered if she might faint, and tightened his firm grip to keep her steady.

Augustus made a noise that startled them both from their

reverie of gazes held a moment too long. Anna Grace tore her gaze away from Josiah and looked nervously at Augustus. Augustus's approving glance had changed to one of cold steel. The lines around his mouth tightened. His eyes took on a dangerous glint. Anna Grace tugged at her hand, and Josiah reluctantly let her hand free. What was this about? His compliment was not untoward. Puzzled, Josiah stood until Anna Grace was seated, then he returned to his own chair. Anna Grace sat in the armless ladies' chair where her skirts spread around her demurely. Josiah thought she sat oddly as if the movement of sitting was painful. Her posture puzzled him. It was with reluctance that he pulled his gaze from her face.

He turned to Augustus and said in a light, teasing tone, "You have been unfair, sir! You have been unfair to keep this lovely lady squirreled away on this plantation. You should bring her to Baltimore! She would be the toast of the city."

Anna Grace blushed at the compliment. Augustus snorted. His face sneered at his wife, and she looked at the floor. Augustus Cadwallader, in Josiah's opinion, was a cad.

Anna Grace looked up, and with a nervous tremor, she greeted Josiah, "Welcome, Mr. Bryant." Her low, quiet voice was filled with honey.

He looked into her eyes again. Once again, he held the glance a moment too long. Anna Grace swiftly averted her gaze to Augustus. Josiah understood, giving her an imperceptible nod.

"What brings you to our fair shores, Mr. Bryant?" Anna Grace asked him in a light, conversational tone.

"Tobacco, Ma'am," he told her. "I have a warehouse in Baltimore. I ship the bulk of the cured tobacco to England in exchange for goods that I sell to merchants in Baltimore and Philadelphia."

Anna Grace looked at him in surprise.

"My father is a merchant in Philadelphia, sir. He has a mercantile," she informed him.

"You must give me his address, then," Josiah insisted. "The

next time I am in the city, I shall stop by and tell him I met his lovely daughter and how well she is faring. I will let him know she is the fair mistress of this plantation."

Anna Grace blushed prettily with a rosy hue blooming on her cheeks. She looked as though she was unused to the kind and flattering attention. She looked down at her hands, neatly folded in her lap but clenched them as Augustus grunted again, rather rudely

Before she could reply, Tyrone announced dinner. There had not been a moment to make an excuse to leave earlier as he had planned. Now, Josiah was grateful. Dinner would bring a few more moments in Anna Grace's company. They all stood. Augustus leaned heavily on Tyrone as he led him to the dining room, and Josiah proffered Anna Grace his arm. She took it lightly. A buzz of energy between them sparked. She gasped, and he put his other hand over hers to lead her to the table. Reluctantly he let go to pull out the chair for her. There was a fragment of a moment when her eyes held his, and he saw raw emotion within. She sat, again, rather stiffly, giving an inadvertent sound as if tightly holding in a cry of pain.

Josiah looked concerned. "Are you unwell?" he asked Anna Grace.

"I am fine, sir," she managed to say quietly.

He stood another moment by her chair, wondering why she would be in pain.

Tyrone now stood by the chair for Josiah and, in a quiet, deep voice stated, "Sir."

Josiah walked to his seat, puzzled by the strange undercurrent of emotion that filled the room. It was like a very strange play. His mind raced, thinking of the literature he had read in college. It wasn't a Shakespearian play, but more like a Greek tragedy. He wondered if he had a part in this play, or if he was just a member of the audience.

The evening sun started to slant toward the western horizon;

its light blazing through the windowpanes in one last hurrah of fire in the sky. The servants lit the tapers on the table and the sideboards. Each bit of candlelight was like a small sun flickering in competition with the larger orb outside, applauded by gathering clouds. Servants began to enter the room with trays laden with food. *And the play continues,* Josiah thought, *scene two, the dinner.*

Five

MATTHEW

Thick shards of sea glass are often from older pieces of glass aged over one hundred years ago.

M atthew squinted across the bay as the bright sunlight pierced his hazel eyes through a hole in the clouds. He scanned the sky. Moments ago, the mackerel sky portended change, and now one patch of sunlight fought for space as the rest of the sky filled with burgeoning dark clouds. It looked like rain but felt like snow as the wind sliced through his coat and hoodie, blowing his shaggy, brown curls around his head and across his face.

Damn it! he thought. He wouldn't have much time. He had worked all night in the warehouse and had snagged a couple of hours of sleep. He had planned to be on the shore at the beginning of low tide but had overslept.

Matthew worked odd jobs to support his true love of creating unique jewelry from the sea glass he harvested from the Chesapeake Bay. He had glassed in lovely places along the Eastern seaboard, but he loved returning to his small home and studio to search his secret beach for sea glass treasures. The nighttime warehouse job was steady and paid well but was exhausting. Sometimes he felt like a lab rat working to get to the prize at the end of the maze. He looked out over the bay and the sky. This was his prize, waking up to the beauty of the beach and the water.

Matthew rented a studio apartment above the garage of a writer who spent the bulk of the year in Florida. The owner permitted Matthew to rent part of the garage area for his studio, too. In this neighborhood that closely abutted the bay's shore, garages weren't really garages for cars. They doubled as laundry areas, storage, and guest houses. His apartment was quite small, but he had a room for a studio and a slice of view of the bay, so it met his needs. His neighborhood residents were an aging, motley crew of artists, writers, photographers, and woodcarvers. Most had retired, but they were understanding of his art. And they liked their solitude. Matthew could almost feel the palpable sigh of relief when their families of children and grandchildren left on Sunday afternoons, and they could return to their peaceful existence of watching the sky, the water, the shore, and the drama of the wildlife. A peaceful, but sociable bunch, he reminded himself. The quiet community would party with sunset soirees with favorite libations handed out liberally to watch the magnificent sunsets. Occasionally, Matthew was invited to join these celebrations as well. Here, they talked easily, drank deeply, and appreciated one another.

As he walked the shoreline, he focused on the pebbly sand beneath his work boots. They scrunched, and he accidentally broke a new piece of green glass, likely from a beer bottle. The wind tore at him again, and he shivered. Picking up the new glass, he tossed it back into the bay to cook, where it would become well sanded and worn enough for him to turn it into a piece of jewelry. It would take twenty to fifty or more years, but he hoped that one day it would wash ashore for him to find again and that his fingers wouldn't be too gnarled to still create something beautiful.

The wind continued to blow in sharp, mean gusts, sending

cold fingers of air down his neck and beneath his sweater. For God's sake, it was March! Where was spring? Hadn't that damned groundhog predicted an early spring? The air had a definite wintry bite. A few snowflakes rained down, but Matthew doggedly trudged on, searching for the perfect piece of glass.

He loved the lovely baubles, bubbles, and well-worn pebbles of glass he found along the New England shorelines on his treks north. He used those for rings, earrings, and pendants. But it was the Chesapeake that always drew him back; the glass here was his favorite. More recently, he'd experimented with cutting out detailed designs using his jewelry saw on the backplate of the bezel setting to enhance the flat glass he'd found on the Chesapeake Bay beaches. The design would gently shine through, and it made the piece reversible. Here on the Chesapeake, he found those younger and larger pieces of bluish-green and white flat glass to showcase the intricacy of his carved designs. They were worn just enough to bezel set without cracking.

With an upcoming show, a few months from now at the Atlantic Sea glass Society, he had his work cut out for him. The show was held in early May to draw the tourists and sea glass lovers to the shore, just before the busy summer tourist season boomed. He always did well, with a bevy of women crowding his booth at the show, delightedly oohing while handing over their dollars and credit cards for his pieces. His goal was to have nearly nine hundred pieces of jewelry ready by then. He had bezel set hundreds of small, stack rings from shards of glass, and had already used nearly all his glass from his New England finds. Now he was focusing on the pendants. The carved, silver pendants took a while, but they were worth every second.

Matthew was lost in thought, planning for the show, when the sun moved behind the clouds again. Just before the last shaft of sunlight hid behind the clouds, he saw a glint of blue. A large glint of blue! His hand brushed away the sand. He couldn't believe his luck! It was a rounded rectangular bottle bottom of cobalt blue glass. This was quite a find! It was well sanded with the classic "C" markings of sea glass. He picked it up and marveled at the color, holding it up to the clouds in the sky. The deep blue glowed in the brief flash of sunlight and turned to a deep, inky blue when the sun hid behind gunmetal-colored clouds.

Already in his mind's eye, Matthew pictured a heavy pendant, bezel-set, attached to a heavy, Viking knit chain. He had recently learned how to knit the wire, feeling like a knight at arms, knitting chain maille as the strands of silver wire created a thick, tubular structure. It was a masculine piece. He gripped it in his hand, grinning wildly at the sky, before plunging it deep into his pocket. This piece was a keeper for himself. He had found similar cobalt blue pieces in Maine a year ago at Roque Bluffs State Park. Sea glass friends had told him it was a good spot for greens and blues. Both were snapped up by buyers at his online shop and at sea glass and Coastal Arts Festivals, where he vended. Now he had a piece of cobalt blue glass for his very own.

Matthew paused a moment, taking in the peace and silence surrounding him. A great blue heron soared overhead with a rusty squawk announcing its arrival. It landed on the shoreline, far away from him. It stood in a few feet of the chilly water, with unquavering concentration, searching for lunch. Its feathers matched the grey-blue sky and water. The heron didn't seem to mind the cold but ruffled its feathers until they were fluffed out, making a downy coat against the chill.

Another piece of good luck, Matthew thought. A great, blue heron was just the thing to carve out of silver for the back of this piece of glass. Matthew always attributed sighting the great birds to good fortune. He shivered. It wouldn't be long now until spring came, and he looked forward to it. But for now, he turned back to his studio, determined to make a hot cup of coffee and take it to his bench where he would use a jeweler's saw, torch, and other tools to create his works of art.

Six

BETH

Sea glass is formed by pieces of glass tossed into a body of water that tumbles in the sand and the grit to become a silken jewel.

Beth strode along the tiny stretch of beach, looking out at the muted gray palette of sky and water. She watched the patterns of wind and water wend their way toward the shore. Small, persistent waves lapped more loudly than usual. The timbre of the waves indicated the tide was turning, and she would need to be careful. It was low tide, but at the tip-top of the Chesapeake Bay, the only accessible beach she had to walk on was narrow and full of pebbles. The waves hit the pebbles and retreated with a satisfying whoosh and rhythm, providing an unobtrusive accompaniment to her thoughts. Once the tide was in, the sand and rocks would disappear under the murky water, and often, the waves would quiet, only the wind and zooming boats stirring them. Dodging the waves was critical as cold, wet feet would only add more angst to her day. It was a complicated dance as she dodged the water and avoided logs and slippery seaweed. Beth carefully stepped over a log resembling a beached whale. There were more logs, like the bleached bones, scattered like pick-up sticks on the shoreline. They were the detritus of winter. Old seaweed clung to the logs emitting an iodine-laced perfume. She wrinkled her nose. It wasn't unpleasant. It was the smell of the Chesapeake Bay.

The March air was raw and cold. It still held vestiges of winter as it blew. It was the cusp of winter and spring that vacillated back and forth by the whim of the gods. Earlier that day, sunshine and mackerel clouds predicted a lovely, springlike day. But March weather couldn't be trusted. Clouds gathered and covered the sun, causing the brief bout of spring warmth to surrender. Now the clouds were moving swiftly across the sky like fuzzy dirigibles. She wrapped her arms around herself, wishing that she had brought gloves and worn a hat or scarf for the millionth time as the chilly air cut through her clothes.

Now, the wind had changed directions, bringing with it the chill from the North. The cold air voraciously erased the earlier remnants of warmth and early spring. The tip of her nose was red, and her hands and ears turned pink with cold. The constant breeze slipped up Beth's coat sleeves and down her neck, causing her to shiver. But she didn't turn back to her house...yet. It was here on this beach that she had finally found peace. She felt safe and far, far away from the horrible memories of Mike or of the possibility of him finding her.

Since birth, her mother had drummed into her that a man would rescue her and take care of her every need. After all, her mother still expected her father to walk through the door after he'd left over twenty years ago. Mike hadn't rescued or taken care of Beth. It had been a dream of a love that had turned into a nightmare. She could blame some of her hesitations to leave Mike earlier on her mother. Filled with embarrassment, she'd never had it in her heart to tell her mother that things weren't going well with Mike. Her mother would likely have told Beth that it was all her fault. And now that she had left, her mother refused to speak with her because Mike was such a "catch." Her mother's archaic beliefs still astonished Beth.

Beth had to make her own way and her own fate. She'd left the comfort of the Appalachian blue ridges for the rocky shores of the Upper Chesapeake. She'd been craving something different in her life, and yet still didn't know what *it* was. Whatever *it* was, she didn't think it involved freezing on the shoreline, and at times, she questioned if it had been a sane decision.

Beth thought of her childhood home in Eagle Heights, Pennsylvania. The town was much larger than Kingstown, Maryland, and a bit larger than North Bay, Maryland. There were stately, brick homes on the side streets and mansions that dated back to the 18th century. The Daughters of the American Revolution was an aging but still vocal group in the town. It was old-fashioned and reminded Beth of times gone by, as if the town had been stuck in the 1950s, with morals and attitudes of a small-town hierarchy. Kingstown was a small, historic town perched at the tip-top of the Chesapeake Bay that had been a busy port for Britain in the early days of the country. It, too, had historic homes and taverns that dated back to the time of the American Revolution. She had read on a historic sign that a British warship had been captured and burned in the Kingstown harbor during the Revolutionary war. Kingstown had once been an active port in Revolutionary times. Even so, Kingston remained a quiet, sleepy place, perfect for someone like herself who wanted to live under the radar.

Beth sometimes wondered if she was pretending at life. The day-to-day stress of nursing sometimes left her feeling drained and devoid of emotions, opposite of the wild roller coaster of emotional peaks of hope and valleys of despair she sometimes felt escaping from Mike and settling into a new life. She looked out over water and sky, and, at that moment, every little thing was all right. She continued to walk and muse, not noticing the clouds gathering ominously in the sky like a menacing villain.

This was home for now. Her cottage was outside the town

limits on a point of land that stuck into the bay like a small fist. It was a beautiful setting, healing in its quiet, natural setting. She looked up from the beach at the water, the trees, and the sky. Even with all of the angst over Mike, Beth had never felt so settled in a place. She was like a little pebble on the beach, buried deep in the sand. No matter how big the storm, the waves, or the tide, she would stay rooted on the beach. She loved the little cottage. She loved the view. And, she was happy with her job. It was fear of Mike that was still a fly in the ointment.

Daydreaming, Beth didn't pay attention to where she was walking and stepped on a piece of driftwood that cracked with a loud snapping sound. Startled, a great blue heron belted out a rusty, "Krack, craw, Krack" of annoyance. The huge wings took off with a great whoosh of sound. The heron soared into the sky with its powerful wings, its gangly, ungainly legs, and feet trailing behind. Beth watched. She sucked in a breath and held it as she focused on the heron. It was like a teenager, she thought, head-strong, sure of itself, pumping wings and flying free. Inside, it stood on stalks of legs, bumbling its way as it moved through life. Beth realized it wasn't how the heron felt, but how she felt. Right now, she felt unsteady in her life –bumping and bumbling along as she traversed this new life in Maryland. She had no idea what her future held. It felt as fragile as the gangly legs of the heron. The heron represented freedom. A large part of her could breathe more easily with the freedom of being away from Mike. She could stretch her wings and be free from his criticisms and consternation from her mother. Beth grinned as the heron flew away from her shoreline. She watched the smote of blue-grey as the majestic bird flew across the bay to the other shore.

Beth sighed, noticing how the incoming tide had eaten away the remaining sand at her feet. She would soon need to leave the beach for the grassy hillock at the edge. The sun came briefly through a break in the clouds, lighting up the shore and the glossy, wet rocks of quartz pebbles, serpentine, and brownish-red concretions. Broken glass lay nestled in the rocks and on the sand. Clear, brown, and green glass, likely from beverage bottles of boaters, adorned portions of the beach like jagged, bright ornaments. The glass pieces shone brightly in the sand and in the sun. Beth spotted a frosted white piece sticking out of the sand and picked it up. The sand had worn the glass to a silky texture of a worry stone. She rubbed at it absently, now focused on continuing the treasure hunt. A lavender shard lay in the rocks at the edge of the water. It was one of the largest pieces of sea glass she had ever seen. She snatched it up before a wave came to take it back into the bay.

Beth felt like the gangly heron on long legs as she picked her way along the beach, her tongue between her teeth. She was now searching in earnest for sea glass to put in her pockets. It had become a habit to pick up the glass. It now filled jars and bowls in her small cottage, along with interesting pieces of driftwood that decorated the flat surfaces and windowsills. Finding the glass was like finding a beautiful treasure. Every shard had a mystery to be solved with its origin.

Something caught her eye. There was a glint of blue in the water, so tiny that for a moment, she thought it was a trick of the light. She gasped in delight, not believing what she'd spied in the water. She wanted to look closer, but an oncoming wave was fast approaching. Beth rushed forward, not caring if her feet became wet. She knew that cobalt blue glass was a rare find. It was small. It looked old. The chilly water encircled her fingers as she reached for the prize in the shallows, trying to beat the wave before the glass was watched back out to the bay. As if alive, the wave lapped up, wetting her jacket's sleeve. She let out a brief expletive as she shivered, but her fingers curled around the small piece of glass with success! She pulled her hand out of the water and dried the glass off on her coat, then blew on her icy fingers to warm them as she dropped the small piece of blue glass in the palm of her other hand. Beth's numb fingers tingled in the cold, and nervy shocks danced in her palm. Her skin burned from the cold as it reddened quickly A cold burn was so much worse than a sunburn. She was frozen, but she wanted to look at her prize before she ventured back to the cottage.

She gasped. The tiny, blue, coffee-bean piece of glass that was nestled in her palm was perfect. It was beautiful. She couldn't believe her luck! It looked old as it was well sanded and a deep, deep, cobalt blue. Beth curled her fingers tightly around her palm and did a little happy dance of joy on her find.

Reality struck her. Her feet were wet. Her arm was wet. A mixture of rain and snow suddenly pelted down without warning. The weather was an insult to her joy in finding the piece of blue glass. The snowflakes quickly became a memory as a mixture of rain and ice bombarded her. Cold, real cold, seeped beyond her coat, past her skin, and down to her bones as her hair grew. Her treasure hunting was over for this day. Beth didn't mind. She had her prize and made her way on the remaining small slice of beach to the grassy shoreline which edged her cottage.

Making a beeline for the cottage's kitchen, she pulled a small bowl out of the cupboard, then emptied her palm and pockets, listening to the satisfying clatter as it fell into the bowl. Next, she peeled out of her wet things and left them in a heap near the washing machine. Freezing, with goosebumps popping up all over her body, she jogged from the kitchen to the small bathroom and turned on the heater before jumping into the shower. The hot spray of water burned her cold skin at first. Beth allowed the flurry of water to soak her head and warm her bones. Leaving the shower was another matter. Once the water was turned off, her warm, wet cocoon was gone. Hesitantly, she stepped onto the chilly floor of her bathroom, and goosebumps returned immediately. Her small electric heater chugged away, sending out some heat but not enough to combat the chill of the warmth evaporating from her skin. Hurriedly, Beth toweled off. Beth ran to the bedroom to don cozy sweatpants and sweatshirt before heading to the main room and the wood stove.

The cottage's main area was an open concept, with a small living area of white-washed pine paneling for a living and dining space and a tiny kitchen tucked into the rear. The bedroom and bathroom were off to one side as if an afterthought. The cottage didn't have central heat but instead had a woodstove on the wall opposite the brief hallway to the bathroom and bedroom. It heated the main rooms nicely. The bedroom and bathroom were chilly, but Beth had portable heaters plugged in for warmth. She opened the door to the wood stove. Coals lay glowing in a heap. She blew gently, trying to get a small flame to start. She teased the fire with junk mail, and it caught with a whoosh. She smiled. Who needed a shredder for documents when one had a woodstove? She added a few small sticks of wood and a small log to keep the fire going.

Beth went to the kitchen to put the kettle on. When the kettle whistled impatiently, Beth made a large mug of tea and, balancing the mug and basket of glass, pulled a small, worn upholstered chair closer to the wood stove, eager to look at the shards she had found that day.

She sifted through the glass, looking for the blue piece, having difficulty finding it among the shards. Momentary panic seized Beth before she saw the blue piece hidden by a larger piece of dark, brown glass. Carefully, she pulled it from the bowl and looked at it. Very tenderly, Beth touched it with her finger. There was something about this piece that drew her heart. It captivated her as it sang silently in the palm of her hand. Beth wondered where it could have come from. What was its history? It didn't seem to fit the cobalt blue of a Noxzema jar or bromide bottle. It looked older than that. The blue was deeper than more contemporary jars. She rubbed a fingernail over the glass. It was like a tiny worry stone.

Seven

ANNA GRACE – 1860

When sea glass is tumbled from wind and weather, it takes on a white, matte sheen known as 'frosting.'

Tyrone placed a low bowl of crab bisque in front of her, drawing her gaze from Josiah to the moment at hand. Tyrone's gloved hand brushed lightly and briefly on Anna Grace's arm. *It is a warning,* she thought. She looked up to see Augustus watching her. Her palms were sweaty. She carefully tugged her gloves from her hands and laid them aside. Surreptitiously Anna Grace wiped her hands on the skirt of her gown. She was grateful to Tyrone. She would be careful.

"Thank you, Tyrone," Anna Grace whispered softly.

He nodded in response. They didn't need words. Tyrone stood behind Augustus's chair.

Anna Grace picked up her spoon. *Matilde has outdone herself,* she thought. Aromas of sherry, cream, and crab wafted to her nose as she lifted her spoon to taste the creamy soup—lumps of snowy, white crab nestled in the creamy soup base. A well-roasted herbed chicken, new potatoes with butter, and a cucumber and corn salad followed the soup.

Anna Grace felt her corset tighten dangerously. She could only pick at her food and take a few bites due to its constrictions, so she moved her food distractedly around the plate. She wanted to know more about Josiah, but she didn't want to encourage Augustus' wrath. She kept stealing surreptitious glances at Josiah. He seemed so familiar to her, as if she had met him on a previous occasion. But that wasn't possible. She had never seen the man before in her life, and here she felt she had a connection to him, a bond that she couldn't explain, especially when their eyes met. It was so unexpected, yet so wonderful!

"Can you tell us about yourself, Mr. Bryant?" she asked, careful of her words. She glanced at Augustus, who seemed to approve. Anna Grace's shoulders relaxed a trifle.

Josiah took a sip of wine and looked across the table at her.

"Yes, Mistress Cadwallader. I lost my parents to the yellow fever epidemic in Baltimore a few years ago and have taken over my father's warehouse business as I was their only child. Prior to that, I was studying in Annapolis, at St. John's College. The fever took them quickly, and I must say, I did not expect to take over the family business so soon, and without my parents at the helm," he finished.

Emotion glazed his face, and he took another sip of wine. Anna Grace knew about loss as well. She had sorely missed her mother since her death and was homesick for her father.

"I am so sorry for your loss, Mr. Bryant," she told him sympathetically and with all the honesty and caring she could muster, as her voice caught in her throat. Emotion nearly overtook her as she thought of her own, dear, mother.

Josiah cleared his throat lightly. "I thank you, Mistress," he replied to her.

The conversation lagged. Augustus had not offered any condolences. He turned the conversation to politics. Anna Grace was aware that these were troubled times. She looked up when she noticed a tense tone fill Josiah's voice.

"So, you will continue to keep your darkies as property?" he asked Augustus following a conversation regarding the Union and Confederacy emerging in America.

"Of course, sir!" Augustus answered, annoyance in his tone. "I can't run a plantation like this without my slaves! If I freed them, I would be bankrupt."

She noticed Tyrone stiffen, ever so slightly, at Augustus's words. She heard Josiah take a breath and hesitate, as though calming down. He took a bite of food, and it looked to Anna Grace that he was thinking of what he wanted to say. He swallowed and cleared his throat.

When she looked out the dining room window, she saw that clouds had gathered. The beautiful day had darkened with threatening clouds swirling in the sky. She heard a low rumble of thunder off in the distance. Heat lightning danced behind the clouds.

"Sir," Josiah queried carefully, "are you aware that many of your neighbors are freeing their slaves?"

Augustus's face turned purple. He made a derisive tone before shouting, "Bah! Damn Yankees!"

He pounded the table with his fist so hard that the delicate china bounced and clinked. Anna Grace reached for her wine glass to keep it from spilling. She had barely sipped at the wine, and the contents of the glass swayed dangerously within the confines of the cut crystal.

Augustus had jerked his gouty foot in his rant and now groaned in pain. He looked at Josiah and narrowed his eyes.

"And you, sir!" he snapped. "You said you would bring some medicine from Baltimore in our correspondence."

"My apologies, sir. I believe it is in my bag. Could someone bring my valise to me?" Josiah asked Augustus, but truly aiming the question at Tyrone.

Tyrone nodded and exited silently. Dessert was brought in, a lovely, light sponge cake, but Anna Grace could only manage a bite.

Tyrone returned with a good-sized carpet bag. It was deep red with leather handles. He sat it next to Josiah on another chair.

"Thank you, very much," Josiah thanked Tyrone.

Tyrone nodded and gave a deferential bow. But he smiled at Josiah, quick and sure. Anna Grace felt certain that he liked their guest.

Josiah rifled through the bag, searching for something. Finally, he pulled out a small, ridged, blue bottle, and handed it to Augustus.

"It's Colchicine," Josiah explained. "An excellent medicine for gout, made from the autumn crocus."

"I have not heard of such a thing," Anna Grace remarked.

"It has been a long-used remedy. I am surprised your local doctor did not know of it," Josiah answered.

"The doctor has not been here," Anna Grace informed him. "Augustus would not have it."

Augustus didn't say thank you but barked to Tyrone to bring him some brandy. Tyrone returned quickly with the decanter and glasses. First, he proffered the brandy to Josiah, who, in turn, waved his hand.

"Perhaps, later," Josiah told Tyrone. "Thank you."

Tyrone poured brandy into a glass and handed it to Augustus, who splashed a good amount of medicine into the brandy and drank it in one gulp. Josiah's eyes grew wide as Augustus belched loudly after guzzling the mixture. Anna Grace caught Josiah's eye and saw a hint of amusement. His lips twitched, and she had to look down to avoid the giggle that was rising in her throat.

Josiah turned away, as well. From her periphery, she saw him glance out of the window and frown. Anna Grace lifted her head toward the window, noticing the billowing, dark clouds on the horizon and streaks of lightning illuminating the sky. There was a faint rumble, like drums, off in the distance.

"It looks like the weather has taken a nasty turn," Josiah commented. "Unfortunately, I must take leave of you and try to get to my next destination before the storm. I don't fancy sleeping out in a rainstorm."

Anna Grace tried to hide her disappointment, then, looking at Augustus for approval, with butterflies in her stomach, she offered, "Sir, I believe we could assist you with accommodations."

Augustus's face was one of stone, and she wasn't sure how to read him. Had she gone too far? Would she pay for her offering? Her nerves felt frayed to the breaking point with constant worry if she offended him or not. Her fingernails dug into the lacy tablecloth with tension.

"Thank you, dear lady, but I must be off this evening," Josiah said hastily. "I thank you for your hospitality."

He turned to Tyrone and asked that his horses be quickly readied for travel. Tyrone bowed again and left the room to make arrangements as Josiah then turned to Augustus, commenting, "I will be in touch with you, sir, regarding the contract and payment for the tobacco harvest."

Tyrone returned, giving Josiah a nod, and Anna Grace knew that look. It was a sign for Josiah to go. He returned the nod and stood as Augustus tried to stand. He groaned in pain and then returned to his chair.

Anna Grace's heart raced when she heard Josiah ask Augustus, "With your infirmity, would you permit your lady to walk me out?"

Augustus winced in pain again and nodded his head. Josiah offered his arm. It felt so natural when she put her arm through his as if it were a daily occurrence. She savored the moment as they walked to the door and exited the steps to the gravel drive in front of the house. Anna Grace noticed a young man of mulatto origin, holding the reins of two horses. It must have been Josiah's traveling companion. The thunder continued to rumble distantly, and the heat lightning that lit the sky had grown closer.

Josiah released her arm and turned to face Anna Grace. The small breeze that had blown into her window earlier in the day had kicked up to an eddy of a breeze that swirled around them, drawing them closer.

The wind loosened the curls from the braids of her elaborate hairstyle. It tugged at her skirts, and they swayed gently like a bell in the breeze. Josiah's hair lifted into large wavy sections showing his chiseled cheekbones hugged by his muttonchops. His whiskey-colored eyes bore into hers. They seemed to hold questions, but he didn't speak. Anna Grace was at a loss for words as well. Her heart skipped a beat when she looked up at him. She felt breathless. She now understood what it meant when she read of swooning in her novels. She felt like that now. She swayed, and he grasped her arm. There was so much to say and so little time. She wondered what Josiah might think of her if she asked him to take her away from this place. Would he be shocked? Or would he understand after his brief encounter with Augustus. Anna Grace's stomach tied itself in knots.

The thunder crackled closer now, ominous and threatening. The heat lightning lit the sky through a thick bank of clouds, now overhead. Rain threatened to spill upon them as her emotions swelled. She wasn't sure what to make of the feelings, but she was content to let them be, enjoying something besides the pain and weariness she was used to carrying.

He took her hand and bent over to kiss it, his lips lingering before he withdrew them and retreated to his horse.

"Thank you for the lovely evening, Mrs. Cadwallader," he told Anna Grace his voice quiet, yet full of emotion.

Anna Grace knew needed to respond for etiquette's sake, but she couldn't. Her mind whirled with a myriad of thoughts. She wanted Josiah to stay and wondered if he was feeling the same way. She'd felt a connection. Had he? She thought she saw it in his eyes before she dropped her eyes to the ground. She moved a bit of the gravel with the toe of her slipper, and a tear leaked from her eye, traversing down her cheek.

"The wind is kicking up a lot of dust," Josiah observed gently.

He pulled a silk handkerchief from his pocket and dabbed at Anna Grace's eye. He wiped a second tear that leaked out. More tears threatened to spill from her eyes. She was as puzzled as he was, thinking only that it was the connection she felt to him that led her to mourn his leave-taking.

And what must he think of her, crying as she stood to say goodbye? She wanted to clutch at Josiah and beg for him to take her away. His kindness pierced her heart, and she felt desperate to tell someone of Augustus. She wanted a means of escape. There was something about Josiah that assured Anna Grace that he would help her if he could. She could see it in his eyes. It was something more than his kind gestures and words. Was this cupid's dart? She wanted him to hold her in his arms and tell her everything would be all right. She wanted to be with Josiah and not with Augustus. But, what an insane thought after just meeting the man. Her sensibilities needed to return.

"I'm sorry," she whispered, thinking her words were lost to the wind.

"Oh, dear lady, there's no need to apologize," Josiah murmured. "I am sorry I must take my leave of you. If time would permit, I believe we would have much to say to one another."

"We would. You have no idea, sir," she murmured. "I wish...I wish..."

But her words were lost to a growl of thunder, and the moment was lost. Anna Grace recovered her emotions.

"I am so glad you were able to come this evening. I hope you can make it back to this little corner of the world, Mr. Bryant," Anna Grace shakily responded, taking in a small, sharp breath to formally observe the proprieties. She bit her lower lip, controlling the emotions that welled within her.

. Josiah took his hand and lifted up her chin so he could look directly into her eyes, now brimming with unshed tears that threatened to spill onto her cheeks.

"Dear lady," his voice was thick with emotion as he replied, "I must go."

Anna Grace could only nod. She watched him take a set of reins, the young man giving him a leg up on the horse. Josiah glanced back to her before setting the horse at a pace to go down the long drive to the main road. Her eyes followed him and the swinging lantern down the darkening road.

Anna Grace's eyes burned as she focused on the two retreating riders. She watched the darkening road, even after the riders disappeared, hoping beyond hope that Josiah would change his mind and return to the plantation to spend the night with the approaching wicked weather. Minutes passed, and she remained alone in the wind. A raindrop hit her hand and then two, but still, she didn't turn to go inside. She felt as if someone had scooped out her insides, and she was as hollow as the clay pipe Augustus smoked on occasion. She wanted to run after them. Wanted Josiah to return. She wanted. She yearned. She wished with all of her heart. The road remained dark, and the hoofbeats became silent. Now there was nothing but darkness on the road.

Goosebumps raised up on her arms, and she shivered violently with the heavy rain that began to fall. She pulled her hands, which had been clutching the fabric of her dress, over her head to protect herself.

Miserable, she turned to go inside, only to find Pansy waiting for her just inside the door.

"Pansy!" she cried as one who had been startled from a dream. "What are you doing here?"

"Waiting for you, Ma'am," Pansy retorted. "I was 'bout to come to get you. I was afraid you might get struck by lightning."

"I'm all right," Anna Grace claimed stoutly.

"No, you're not," Pansy argued with her mistress. Her eyes flashed at Anna Grace with intent.

Anna Grace shook her head slightly. It was never good to argue with Pansy. She was always right. At least, she thought she was always right. It made Anna Grace smile for a moment. But the smile disappeared when she glanced toward the living room and then the dining room. Anna Grace put a warning hand on Pansy.

"Where's the Master?" she whispered.

"Already gone to bed," Pansy informed Anna Grace. "His gout was too much for him. He shouldn't be eating those rich foods. Matilde should know better," she finished slyly.

She shot Pansy a look of wonderment. Was Matilde making rich foods as revenge against Augustus? Realization washed over her, and Anna Grace hid a giggle behind her hand as she picked up her skirts and tiptoed upstairs. She knew Pansy would never admit it, but she *always* caught a glint of humor and satisfaction in Pansy's eyes when she talked about Augustus and his gout. Anna Grace had to wonder who else shared the secret besides Matilde, Pansy, and herself. Tyrone?

When Anna Grace reached her room, Pansy helped her with her evening ablutions. She re-dressed Anna Grace's wounds and helped her into another voluminous nightdress. Pansy gently unbraided the elaborate coiffure she'd created earlier and combed and brushed it until it shone brightly in the candlelight of the room. Then she braided Anna Grace's hair into two, long braids instead of one, fearing one would slap her on her injured back.

While Pansy assisted her, she commented on Josiah, "That Mr. Bryant is one fine looking fellow."

"Yes, he is," Anna Grace agreed, dreamily tugging at her braids

"Will he be returning, Missus?" Pansy asked coyly.

"I certainly hope so," Anna Grace said in something above a whisper, and louder, "I think so, to do business with Augustus."

"That's just fine, Missus," Pansy replied in a teasing tone.

Anna Grace was dreamy for a minute. She thought of Josiah. Her thoughts and emotions filled her. She wanted to keep all of her thoughts and emotions about Josiah in a secret place in her heart that fluttered wildly when she thought of his whiskey-colored eyes, his red-gold curls, and his neat mutton chops. What if he had stayed? He would have been just a few steps away. The thought sent her mind whirling and her heart beating madly.

Carefully, Pansy patted her shoulder. Anna Grace smiled. Pansy knew what she'd been thinking.

"Thank you, Pansy," Anna Grace told her as Pansy helped her to bed.

"You have pleasant dreams, Missus," Pansy told her gravely.

Pansy blew out the candles in the room, one by one, then took the remaining candle and left the room.

If Anna Grace could have tossed and turned with her stricken back, she would have. Her mind was a myriad of emotions. She could not sleep. Her mind buzzed with the emotions she'd felt for Josiah. She wondered if he'd shared those emotions too. She thought he had, but her only real experience with a man was with Augustus. Her sheltered upbringing kept her from experiencing anything but glances shared with girlfriends at the handsome young men at meeting. Those poor boys! They would giggle incessantly, surely embarrassing the boys. Now, she was experiencing desire for the first time in her life. She wondered if she could trust her emotions from Josiah or if he was a rake or a scoundrel. Was it even possible to have a connection with someone you just met? Was she only seeking someone who would save her from Augustus? Her thoughts whirled with questions.

Anna Grace had wanted to run after Josiah, begging him to take her away from Augustus and the world she lived in. Longing, as well as fear, had frozen her to the driveway. She felt more and more like a slave as each day passed. She pushed thoughts of Augustus and her current situation out of her mind and focused on remembering Josiah.

She loved how he had combed his curly hair into a wave across the front of his head. It was rich and full and bronzy-red. Some of it had threatened to come loose from the neat swoop and dangle on his forehead. His mutton chops were neatly groomed and brushed against the dimple in his cheek. And those eyes! She could look into his eyes forever. Her thoughts tossed about like the winds from the storm tossed the trees. Thunder shook the house, and lightning rent the skies lighting up the room in intervals. At one point, Anna Grace pulled the sheet over her head, thinking the house would come down around them. In the distance, she heard a sound, a loud crack, a yawning sound, and then a loud crash. A tree must have fallen. She wondered where it fell and listened for voices to see if anyone was rushing to take care of the tree. All was quiet, except for the storm that rumbled on and on and on, the thunder and lightning pushing away from the plantation like waves on the shore. A hard, steady rain fell. Anna Grace drifted off to sleep to the soothing music of the falling rain, holding the thought of Josiah close to her heart.

Her dreams were filled with desire for Josiah Bryant. His hands were touching her and his mouth was kissing her, kind and gentle compared to Augustus. The tingling from his touch reached a pinnacle so that she cried out. She woke herself, whispering Josiah's name. Her body was on fire with desire and, at the same time, languid from the zenith of climax as she slid back to reality. Newly awake, Anna Grace was surprised that Josiah wasn't in bed beside her. She looked around the room, searching for him. She felt the bed for a warm spot and an indentation in the bed.

It wasn't there. Josiah wasn't there. It had only been a dream. Her mood went from elation to sadness. The dream had been so very, very real. She lay back, reliving the dream in her mind, and held it closely in her heart.

Eight

JOSIAH - 1860

Most gray sea glass has been created when the clear glass has reacted to light. Additives such as magnesium can give gray sea glass a gray-green or gray-blue hue.

Josiah and Abraham settled into the room at the inn. Abraham fell asleep easily, but Josiah couldn't stop thinking of Anna Grace and her sad eyes. They haunted him. Some inner sense told him she needed rescue. He tossed and turned, thinking about her. There was something about her that rocked him to his very core. The creeks and groans of the old inn were alien night sounds that didn't soothe his thoughts or help him sleep.

A clear and fresh day dawned after the rainstorm, and it was then that Josiah finally fell asleep for a few hours. Abraham woke him mid-morning, and after breakfasting, he brought the horses around. They set off to complete their business at neighboring plantations on the second day of their journey. The rain had left the world sparkling, and it was a pleasure to ride among the many fields of tall tobacco plants. After meeting with the other two plantation owners, Josiah was weary, but confident that he had secured enough tobacco to make successful trades.

Josiah returned home to his parent's townhouse in Fells Point after three days on the road. The townhouse seemed to echo emptily as he walked through the halls. He ran his hand along the paneled walls and sighed. Abraham, always quiet, eyed Josiah. He made a brief comment that Josiah might need a draft to raise his spirits and prevent illness. Josiah would have none of it.

"Early to bed tonight and work tomorrow," Josiah insisted stoutly. "Work is the best cure for any ailment. And with that, I will say good night."

Josiah slowly went up the stairs and into his room, shutting the door firmly behind him, leaving Abraham watching him from the bottom of the stairs.

Josiah sat in a comfortable wing-back chair in his room and leaned his head back against the brocade. It felt cool and comfortable. He placed his feet on the small stool in front of the chair and drifted into thoughts about the business. His trip had been successful. He still wondered about Cadwallader, but other plantation owners, Marsh and Cox, appeared to be men of good character. Their business had been tied up in only two days. Josiah would speak with his attorney tomorrow and get the contracts expedited.

But, he had to think about Cadwallader. He didn't trust him and wondered how he could guarantee Cadwallader would follow through on his word. Perhaps frequent trips, as his schedule would allow, to check on the tobacco crop. If he did this, he could see Anna Grace as well. Josiah clenched his fist in excitement. It could work. He could state in the contract that if Cadwallader didn't agree to frequent inspections by Josiah or Abraham, their contract would be null and void. Josiah could only imagine how purple Augustus's face would be when he read those lines in the contract. He was gleeful at the thought and retired to bed a happier man than he'd been earlier that day, the anticipation of forcing Cadwallader's hand and of seeing Anna Grace on his mind. When Josiah returned to the warehouse the next day, he inspected the activity that had taken place in his absence. Satisfied with the inspection, he trudged up the stairs to his office. The window had been closed while they were gone, and it felt stale. The smell of ink and paper gave a scholarly scent to the other smells that drifted through the boards from the warehouse below. Josiah opened the window to permit a breeze to blow through. It riffled the papers stacked upon his overflowing desk. The sunlight was filtered with dust motes and shone through the window in a plank of golden light. It was quite warm in his office, and Josiah took off his overcoat, placing it on a hook on the wall before he rolled up his sleeves, ready to greet the work that awaited him.

Josiah tugged at his hair as he scanned the untidy office. Burgeoning respect grew for his father exponentially. How had his father kept up with the correspondence? The business itself? Josiah now knew why his father had spent long hours at work and in his study at home. Running a business occupied the majority of his thoughts day and night.

For the most part, the plantation owners had extended their sympathies and commented favorably on previous business with his father. It was clear to Josiah that some plantation owners were hesitant to deal with him due to his age and lack of experience in the trade. Fortunately, the owners knew it was a better risk to stay with Josiah and his company rather than risk finding new trade in uncertain times. The sales calls had been necessary to cajole the owners into keeping their business with his firm. He had tried his best to be cordial and jovial, assuring the plantation owners that he had grown up in his father's shadow and had been under his tutelage for most of his life.

The current unrest and talk of civil war were discussed quietly after dinners over cigars, whiskey, or brandy. Maryland was a border state between the burgeoning Confederacy and those crying for the emancipation of slaves. The state of Maryland was in a quandary on which side to take. He had heard rumors that the state was leaning toward emancipation, but some of the plantation owners were adamant about continuing to keep slaves to run their plantations. Josiah was careful in his comments but assured the plantation owners that their products would be safe. He didn't expect any altercations or blockades of the port. It was the beginning of the undercurrents of potential civil war. Fear and discontent gripped the nation.

His mind turned back to the present, and Josiah looked at the pile of paperwork with dismay. The floor of the office creaked, and he whirled around. There was Abraham.

The man is as quiet as a damn cat slinking around, Josiah thought.

Josiah had not heard the door open. But then, he had been in his own world of despair looking at the huge pile of correspondence, invoices, and bills and wasn't surprised he hadn't noticed Abraham enter the room.

"Look at this, Abraham!" he shouted and waved a hand at the snowstorm of papers. "What can I do?"

Abraham looked at Josiah, at the papers, and back at Josiah again before answering, "I think I have an idea."

Without another word, Abraham left the office as quietly as he'd come in, leaving Josiah with his mouth gaping in surprise. A few minutes passed before he heard voices, bumps, and a few unsavory words. It sounded like large men carrying something bulky up the stairs to the office. Abraham gave a brief, sharp knock at the office door and opened it before Josiah could respond. He motioned the people in the hallway to enter the office.

Four men carrying sawhorses entered, and Abraham pointed to where they should be set up. Next four more men carrying large sheets of wood were directed by Abraham to lay them on the sawhorses making a very long, make-shift table. Lastly, a young boy in raggedy clothes came through the door, nodded politely to Josiah, and deposited a half dozen bricks on the table.

Josiah's mouth dropped open. He had the wherewithal to say thank you and nodded to each of the men, and the raggedy boy, pulled some coins from his pocket to give to each of them. . They tipped their hats and exited the office.

Meanwhile, Abraham was busy transferring the piles from the desk to the long, makeshift table. Josiah made suggestions to Abraham on how to organize the papers, separating the invoices from the contracts. Amongst the papers, Abraham pulled out a letter.

"Sir," he said distinctly, causing Josiah to pause in his sorting.

Abraham held out the letter, and Josiah took it. He looked at it, not recognizing the feminine handwriting. Puzzled, he opened the letter, discovering that it was from Anna Grace Cadwallader. He read the few lines quickly and looked back at Abraham.

"It's from Mistress Cadwallader. Apparently, her cad of a husband needs more of the Colchicine. The man must be drinking it! He finished the bottle in the three days while we were gone. She's sent a letter, asking for more!"

"Are you going to send more?" Abraham asked.

"I suppose. First, I need to talk with the apothecary," Josiah replied. "Since we missed her messenger, we could essentially take the medicine and the contract to the Cadwallader plantation in the next few days and dispatch the other contracts as well. Cadwallader wanted partial payment, and I agreed."

Abraham looked at him sharply, "Was that a good idea?"

Josiah paused and returned Abraham's look, "To be honest, I'm thinking not, but with the new constraints in the contract where I'll be checking the harvest, it will not be as much of a risk."

They were interrupted by shouts below that drew their attention to the window. A schooner was pulling up to the wharf and unloading its contents into the warehouse. Its tall masts danced high above the ship and were at eye-level with Josiah and Abraham.

"We had better go see what this ship is bringing in. I'm expecting coffee, sugar, and molasses. And then, I must see the attorney and the apothecary as soon as possible," Josiah spoke his schedule aloud.

Abraham and Josiah left the office, still in disarray. Josiah looked back briefly and shook his head.

"There's never enough time," he muttered and followed Abraham out the door.

Nine

MATTHEW

Clear glass bottles from the 1800's changed to pale lavender when exposed to sunlight due to the glass being made with manganese.

The bitter wind, pelting rain, and unexpected cold showers of snow drove Matthew back to his home and studio. Inside, he deposited his treasures on the counter so that he could quickly peel out of his damp clothes. Even his feet felt damp when he took off his work boots. Sweatpants, sweatshirts, thick socks, and warm, sheepskin slippers were the beginning to getting him warm again. He toweled the weather from his long auburn curls and tied them back with an elastic band. Next, Matthew made a steaming cup of coffee and sat down on the old couch to look out the window. This building looked like a two-story garage, charming with wrought iron hinges and handles on the street-view doors. Inside, his living space was light and ultra-modern. The creamy, white walls soaked in every shred of light from the skylights and wall of windows that faced the bay. The couch sagged, but Matthew propped himself on pillows and looked out. It continued to rain and snow, but he saw a slice of blue on the southwestern horizon. It always fascinated him to see the wall of clouds give way to the blue sky. Weather watching from this spot had become a passion. He translated some of what he saw in the sky, the clouds, and the stars into his jewelry by twisting wire, forging the metal, and setting the stones and glass.

Matthew sipped at his piping hot coffee, slightly burning his tongue. After his foray to the freezing beach, he didn't care. His hands were wrapped tightly around the toasty mug, warming his frigid fingers. The hot liquid seared his esophagus and settled in his stomach, where the warmth seemed to expand into his limbs. The caffeine gave his tired brain a slight buzz.

Warmed a bit, he gathered his treasures from the morning and brought them to the coffee table. He picked up his sketchbook, pencil, and eraser along with a piece of glass. After holding the treasured glass in his hand for a minute or two, Matthew usually had an idea of what he would make from it. Sometimes a brief flash of insight would come when he found the glass on the beach. Other times the design would come as he touched the softened edges. It was magical the way he could see the finished piece of jewelry when he picked up the shard.

After he'd thought about it for a few minutes, Matthew felt inspired. He needed to get the design in his head down on paper so that he could work out the mechanics of creating the pieces of jewelry. He made a rough set of sketches and made notes on the gauges of silver or copper sheet and wire for each piece Afterwards, he took the glass fragments to the kitchen and dropped them in the dishwasher's silverware basket. The dishwasher would clean and sanitize them, something he liked to do before he created a piece. Dishwasher running, he went to his workbench. Matthew loaded his jeweler's saw with a new blade, turned on the pickle, and refreshed the water in the quenching bowl. He laid his tools out after he ran a damp cloth to clear any debris. His torch was ready, and his safety glasses were on.

Matthew knew he wanted to fold form a leaf shape and solder long prongs to hold a piece of green glass onto a pin for the one large piece of green glass. He cut a piece of copper and used a bone folder to smooth it down tightly, then cut half a leaf shape leaving the center of the leaf where the fold in the metal was. Now, the work began. Pulling out his special hammers, Matthew pounded and pounded along the edge of the fold. He annealed the metal, turning it red-hot before letting it cool. He repeated this process over and over until the metal seemed to magically curve on its own, the leaf taking shape. Finally, he used an oyster knife to separate the fold and tapped gently here and there until he was satisfied with the leaf shape. Next, Matthew used a screw-driver end and mallet to create texture on the leaf before he soldered a pin back and long prongs whose ends were balled. The balled ends of the prongs Matthew rested on the bench block and pounded flat. It would give the piece a modern flair. Finally, he swabbed on the patina, let it sit, and wiped off the bulk so the dark areas would highlight the forging and texture on the piece of metal.

Matthew loved working with silver, but he thought he loved copper even more. It had such earthy character, particularly after the forging process. He marveled at the indentations, the color striations, and how it all came together.

Matthew listened. The dishwasher had not finished its cycle. He was so tired that it wasn't safe for him to work with flame, so he curled up on his bed to take a nap. He could finish the pin before he went to work that evening.

Ten

BETH

Sometimes, the small islands on the Chesapeake Bay hold secret caches of sea glass.

Beth woke with a start when her phone's alarm jangled with a horrid, jarring sound. She jerked awake and sat bolt upright. The fire had burned down, and there was a slight chill in the room. Glowing coals showed through the wood-stove window. She rubbed her eyes and scratched her head which was still slightly damp from her shower earlier that day. She would need to hurry a little to get to work on time.

Beth opened the door to the woodstove, blew on the coals, and added kindling. Slowly, the kindling caught, and Beth added a larger log to the flame. Closing the door, she jogged to her room to put on her uniform. She returned to the kitchen and threw a couple of things together for her lunch and breaks. She grabbed a plastic Ziplock bag and dumped a few of her day's treasures inside. Her friend and colleague Marsha would be working the shift with her tonight. Marsha had been the one to hook her on sea glass hunting, and Beth was excited to share her finds.

Double-checking the fire in the woodstove, Beth stacked in

one final log. She prayed it would last through the night and that the cottage would be warm when she came home from the hospital. She was working the evening shift from seven at night until seven in the morning, and returning to a cold home was not an appealing thought.

Next, she put on her warm, quilted coat, and wrapped a scarf around her head before snagging the canvas tote bag that held her lunch, snacks, and the sea glass. Her car sputtered in the cold, damp air. Beth felt bad that she didn't have a nice garage for her little car. She patted the dashboard and verbally coaxed it to life before driving the ten miles to her job.

The sun was quickly making an exit from the horizon. Vestiges of color streaked the sky as dusk and dark fell quickly. Beth could see it in her rearview mirror as she drove toward the hospital.

Technically, their glass was bay glass since it was found on the shores of the Chesapeake Bay. Marsha would be quick to correct her. She was an aficionado of sea glass and bay glass. Marsha had opened an entirely new world to Beth. Her enthusiasm for the topic radiated through her and compelled Beth to begin picking up shards on the little beach outside her cottage. Marsha waxed on about collectors and groups on social media. She raved about the upcoming sea glass convention in a few months. Beth knew she would like some of her finds from today. Fingers crossed that the patients would be stable, and Marsha and Beth could get their paperwork completed promptly so they could snag a break to talk about sea glass.

The small hospital where she worked as a cottage hospital recently taken over by a larger hospital corporation. Her substitute job had turned into a full-time position. She had always been happy with the hospital and liked the feel of it. She hoped that the larger corporation wouldn't make it a cold place where people were numbers and not names. Everyone seemed to know one another at this hospital, not only the caregivers but the patients as well. It was the beauty of living in a community with a lot of small towns.

There was, however, benefit to a larger hospital corporation, it had provided funds to complete a recent renovation shortly before Beth moved to the area. Instead of clinical glaring white, gray, and toothpaste green, the hospital had added industrial laminated wooden floors, soft greens and blues with botanical patterns, copper fixtures, and tiling on the walls. The copper was naturally anti-microbial, so it served two purposes in the hospital. Beth took the stairs up to the third floor, huffing only a little on the last set of stairs.

She reached the landing and entered the door to the third floor, where she deposited her coat in her locker and took her lunch bag and bag of glass to the break room. Beth worked with a team on the short stay unit, where patients stayed for observation before returning home or moving to another floor. The many beeping machines blended to create an odd type of music as she exited the staircase and came to the main desk. She greeted everyone at the desk with a cheery hello, made her way to a computer station, and then tucked her bag under the desk. Marsha either wasn't at work yet or had arrived early and was in a patient's room.

Sherry, another RN, had her tongue between her teeth and was focused on her typing. She tore her eyes away for a moment and told Beth she would update her on patients as soon as she finished her report. Beth logged into the computer and began to review patient files. They had their garden variety of ailments. She noticed that Mrs. Crites had returned. She was an elderly woman who complained of chest pain frequently at her assisted living home. It was typical for her to be brought to the emergency room and then to Beth's floor for observation. As far as Beth could tell, all the tests were negative for any heart-related issues. She personally thought Mrs. Crites demanded to go to the emergency room for a bit of extra attention. Beth would stop in and see how she was doing.

The majority of the patients on the short stay unit were preoperative and post-operative prep patients. The team of nurses would make sure the patients were comfortable and showed no signs of acute care needs. The short-stay unit usually exited patients within twelve hours. Beth noticed that a few of the patients would be going home this evening as she finished reviewing the cases.

Marsha came in at the very last minute, explaining, "Sorry, sorry, sorry! Believe it or not, I hit traffic!"

Traffic in this area usually meant farm equipment, the exodus of cars from Aberdeen Proving Ground, or an interstate accident.

"Bad accident on I-95," Marsha said grimly. "They needed the 'jaws of life.' The ER will be busy this evening."

Sherry nodded to Marsha, logged off, stood, and stretched. She gave Marsha and Beth an overview of the patients on their floor. None of the patients seemed acute. A couple were very needy, but for the most part, Sherry informed them, they should have a quiet night.

"That's fantastic news," Marsha said. Marsha had spied Beth's Ziplock bag of treasures and winked at her. "A quiet night would be nice for a change."

"So, don't go and jinx it!" Beth returned just as the bells rang for patients needing assistance.

"That's my cue to go," Sherry told them as she almost ran to get her things.

Beth looked at Marsha and suggested, "You take one, and I'll do the other before we do introductions and vitals?"

"Sounds good," Marsha said and went to get the vital signs monitor, the machine that took temperatures, blood pressure, and oxygen rate.

Beth took the other vital signs monitor and began her rounds.

First, she stopped in at Mrs. Crites' room. She needed to use the bathroom, so Beth assisted her and recorded her vitals.

She made rounds to all of her patients, checking vitals, and having brief conversations with each. All were stable, but one gentleman, Mr. Shaw, worried her. He'd been running a low-grade fever since his surgery, and his eyes were a little glassy. Beth put in a message to the physician on call to give Mr. Shaw medicine. She knew the doctor would not be making rounds until much later.

Beth, Marsha, the LPNs, and aides worked together like an orchestrated ballet. They answered questions, took vitals, and administered medicine, and comfort. It was after midnight when the floor quieted down, and Marsha, the lead RN, sent the LPNs and aides to a well-deserved break. She sat down next to Beth, who was working speedily on the computer, entering data for each patient's hospital and insurance companies.

"I think nursing has become more paper-oriented than people-oriented," Beth complained to Marsha.

"Take a little break, hon, and show me your treasures," Marsha told her.

With a grin, Beth pulled out her Ziplock bag. She showed Marsha a thick piece of white glass, a thick piece of pale blue, a young piece of green glass, and some smaller shards.

Marsha admired her finds, fingering each shard. Finally, she looked up and saw Beth grinning at her.

"What are you smiling at? You look like the Cheshire cat," Marsha commented.

"Close your eyes and hold out your hand," Beth teased.

Beth placed the small, cobalt blue, coffee bean-shaped shard in Marsha's palm.

"Open your eyes," Beth told her friend.

Marsha opened her eyes, looked at her palm, and sucked in her breath.

"Oh, Beth!" she breathed as she turned it over and over in

hand, "it's gorgeous! How did you find it? Where did you find it?"

Beth relayed her story of glassing earlier that day in the freezing rain and snow squall. She told Marsha of diving into the bay to grasp the coffee bean-shaped piece of cobalt blue.

"This," Beth said, holding out the thick piece of light blue, well-sanded glass, "is likely from an old Coca-Cola bottle. See the curve?"

Beth nodded.

"I don't know about the white. I suspect this piece is from the bottom of a bottle. It's quite a hefty piece. Now, this," Marsha continued, sucking in her breath, and focusing on the cobalt blue piece again, "I think might just be from a Victorian poison bottle."

"Really?" Beth was impressed. "How can you tell?"

"The color," Marsha told Beth matter-of-factly. "It's a deeper blue than the Noxzema glass or Phillip's Milk of Magnesia bottles. And," she paused for dramatic effect, "there's a tiny, worn ridge off the center of this shard."

"I felt that!" Beth exclaimed. "I didn't know what it could be. It's been like a worry stone. I keep running my finger over and over it, wondering about the differentiation in the glass. And it looked old to me."

Marsha nodded. A buzzer beeped, and Marsha glanced up at the board.

"Your friend," she said with a bit of sarcasm.

"Who?" Beth asked.

"Mrs. Crites," groaned Marsha.

Beth gave a tiny sigh but stood up. "Don't worry, I'll go," she told Marsha.

She checked on Mrs. Crites, helped her to the bathroom again, and checked on Mr. Shaw. He still had a concerning fever, and Beth was anxious for the doctor to arrive. She hoped he would arrive soon.

When she got back to the nurses' station, he was sitting and reading through charts. She reported Mr. Shaw's fever, and he went to his room immediately. The doctor quickly ordered a fever reducer and an increase in fluids. Beth followed through immediately. The other patients were copacetic.

Marsha had accompanied the doctor on his rounds but was ensconced on her computer when Beth returned from assisting Mr. Shaw. The weary doctor left the floor. Marsha tore her eyes away from the screen, and her fingers stopped typing.

"You really need to plan on coming to the ASGS Festival with me in May. You could get your blue shard identified. You could probably ask one of the artisans to make it into a sweet little ring or a pendant."

"I don't know if I could get the time off. I'm still fairly new here," Beth commented.

"Look," Marsha insisted, "you could work Thursday night into Friday morning. You could shift your hours so that you have Friday and Saturday off. I could drive to the conference, and we would be home in time for your shift on Sunday night. Easy-peasy."

"Let me think about it."

"Don't think too long. Hotel rooms fill up quickly," Marsha warned.

They both turned back to their respective computer screens, inputting data before their next patient checks. The night was quiet. Patient monitors beeped in a regular rhythm with fortunately no buzzers pulling them away from the nurses' station. The night dragged in infinitesimal increments. It stretched and pulled like bubblegum. In many ways, Beth hoped it would continue to stretch and not have a pop of surprise like a bubble blowing with an emergency. Beth tried not to look at the time, but her cold trek glassing and a brief nap were making her more tired than usual. She yawned a huge, gaping yawn.

"Don't start!" Marsha snapped at her.

"I know, I know," she moaned.

Beth stood and stretched before she announced, "I'm going on a walk-about to check on the patients and then get a cup of coffee. I need a screen break. Would you like a cup, too?"

Marsha shook her head, "I'm all right at the moment."

When Beth returned, Marsha took a quick break. Beth looked around and then guiltily logged on to her email. With all of the trouble with Mike, she'd bought a burner phone, communicating solely with her family via email. They didn't understand how Mike really was. She sent a quick email to say she was fine. Once she clicked send, another email popped up in her inbox. It was from Mike. Beth's hand trembled. Should she read it or just delete the damned thing?

She clicked to open the email. There was a one-word message in the body of the email.

Gotcha.

Now her hand really shook, and the feeling of icy water raced down her back. Beth heard Marsha's footsteps. Quickly, she logged off her email and switch the screen back to the patient input data.

"I checked Mr. Shaw. His fever is down."

Marsha gave Beth a sharp look. Beth had clenched her hands under the desk, twisting them. She knew she looked guilty, so tried to shake her head and smile at the same time.

"I'm fine. I'm just tired, I think," Beth lied to Marsha.

"Okay..." Marsha trailed off, unsure and giving Beth a sideways glance.

Fortunately, Mrs. Crites' bell rang. Beth jumped up quickly.

"I'll go," she said as animatedly as she could, before practically racing down the hall.

As time marched toward morning, Beth and Marsha were busy administering medicine, checking IV's, and monitoring vitals. They worked steadily and then worked on updating the paperwork for each patient. Beth was relieved when it was time to go home. She made a showy deal of yawning broadly and loudly.

"I'm heading home as soon as I can. I'll see you tonight," Beth told Marsha. She ran out before Marsha could question her more. She was sure Marsha had sensed something was wrong, but she didn't need to know what it was.

Once she was in her car, Beth let her emotions get the better of her. How did he get her new email? What did Mike's message mean? *Gotcha.* Fear niggled in her stomach as if a little lizard was running around inside. Her hands shook, and she gripped the steering wheel hard to stop them from shaking so she could drive home.

Eleven

ANNA GRACE – 1860

Jade green glass has been popular for bottles from the 1860s until today. If you find a jade green piece with bubbles inside, it's certainly an older piece of glass.

Anna Grace watched Tyrone leave. She didn't know why her hands were trembling, but they trembled slightly. She wiped them on her dress and belatedly looked to make sure ink had not stained her hands or her dress. She picked up *Pride and Prejudice* before she made her way upstairs to sit with Augustus. She stopped by her room first to grab her mending, thinking she could work on it as well.

Anna Grace went down the hallway to Augustus's room. Quietly, she opened the door so that the hinges would not squeak. She looked and listened. There was soft snoring from the bed. Opening the door wider, she stepped inside. The room reeked of feces and sweat. The smell was overpowering, and it turned Anna Grace's stomach. She walked quickly to the window and slid it open as quietly as she could, then went to the second window and did the same. Skirting the room, Anna Grace, stayed as far from

Augustus as she could. At the window, she perched on the sill and breathed in the fresh air.

She watched Augustus as he slept. He didn't look as terrifying in this state. The harsh lines on his face were softened. His double chin lay flat against his neck. His breathing was deep, and his snoring was soft and steady. He still did not smile, even in sleep. Anna Grace wondered what had turned Augustus into such a mean man. He had alluded that his parents had been harsh taskmasters and stoic. Had they been the cause of his unending rage? Augustus stirred a little, still sleeping. Even in this soft, harmless state, she still did not like him.

Anna Grace looked at the bedside table where the small, cobalt, blue bottle had been. Tyrone had told Pansy that Augustus was taking the medicine without care. Pansy had then told Anna Grace. She wondered if the medicine had caused dysentery. She wasn't familiar with Colchicine and didn't know if it were a side effect. She wished he would permit a doctor to come to the house. Apparently, not believing in doctors was another leftover from his childhood and his parent's beliefs. He made a noise, something between a grunt and a cough, then moved in the bed, turning over onto his side. Quietly, she tiptoed to the chair close to the window, opened her book, and started to read. The words seemed to dance in front of her eyes, and she stared at them, not comprehending. She couldn't concentrate on reading when every nerve was poised for a sound from the bed.

Anna Grace pulled out her mending, and with tiny, careful stitches, she began mending part of the never-ending pile of stockings and breeches. The afternoon sun was sharp in the window when Tyrone returned. Thankfully, Augustus was still asleep. She wondered if it was the medicine, the brandy, or the weakness keeping him asleep. Perhaps, it was a combination of all three. Whatever it was, she gladly gave up her post to Tyrone. He smiled his thanks to her, and she nodded her return before slipping out the door with her things. She placed the book and mending in her room, then quietly went downstairs and outside.

It was still quite warm, but the drier air made the summer's day pleasant. Anna Grace walked down to the small wharf on the property. The sun glinted off the water, and a jumping fish startled her. It was low tide. The water had pulled back from the shoreline to reveal a skirting of deep, reddish mud. Under the trees at the river's edge, the shade offered a modicum of coolness in contrast to the summer sun. The heat felt good to Anna Grace, like melting butter sinking into her skin and down to her bones. she wondered how the river water would feel on her bare toes, but she didn't dare take her stockings and shoes off for fear a boat might come sailing by.

She stayed for a few minutes more before she turned back toward the house. When she came to the top of the hill, she saw Pansy rushing toward her.

"Lordy, Missus! Where have you been?" Pansy scolded. "The Master's up and asking for you. I've been searching high and low and couldn't find you. I'll tell you, Missus; I am glad I found you! I was scared to go back to the Master to tell him you were missing!"

Pansy said it all in a rush, and Anna Grace listened carefully to the story. She paled with the thought of Augustus being up and about again. Their freedom vanished with his mobility.

"Hurry, Missus," Pansy urged.

They hurried up the remainder of the incline to the front of the house. The sun had started its afternoon descent. What had felt like warm butter several minutes ago now shot daggers of light into Anna Grace's eyes. She put a hand up to her forehead to block some of the glare and felt beads of sweat gather on her brow. This heat was intense. She wondered how the slaves stood it, day after day, working in the fields in this hot sun.

When they reached the house, Anna Grace put a hand on Pansy's arm.

"Just a minute," she said, "I need to catch my breath."

Pansy watched her mistress carefully.

"Go on, Missus. No good is gonna' come from you waiting out here."

She gave Pansy a sharp look at her wise words before answering, "You're right, Pansy."

Anna Grace took a steadying breath as she put her hand on the large, decorative, brass doorknob. She turned the handle and opened the door. The cool duskiness of the house's interior compared with the sun's intensity blinded Anna Grace for a minute. She stood, in the silent, cooler foyer, staring up the stairs until her vision cleared. Then she walked quietly and slowly up the stairs and stood outside of Augustus's door. She raised her hand and knocked softly. Tyrone answered the door immediately.

Anna Grace hesitated before stepping inside, but Tyrone gave her an encouraging smile. Augustus was sitting up in bed, and the room smelled much fresher.

"Greetings, wife," Augustus addressed her.

She wondered why he couldn't say her name. It had always bothered her.

"Greetings, husband. Are you feeling better?" she asked, returning the impersonal salutation.

"Much better, thank you," he told her.

There was an uncomfortable silence that followed for a few minutes. Anna Grace squeezed her hands tightly together as she and Augustus looked at one another, both at a loss for words. She was worried she had committed yet another transgression and was grateful Augustus couldn't reach her from the bed. She remained, still as a statue, just out of reach from Augustus, wondering at his silence. She didn't have anything to say to him, small talk would have filled the air with prattle, not substance. So, she maintained her silence. Tyrone gently cleared his throat and looked pointedly at Augustus.

Augustus looked sheepish. He cleared his throat before talking.

"Thank you, wife. I understand you nursed me through this illness. Also, you wrote to Mr. Bryant for more medicine. I thank you," he stated formerly.

Tyrone looked satisfied. Anna Grace was tongue-tied.

Finally, she answered, her tone filled with surprise, "You are welcome, husband. Charles went to Baltimore with the letter and the bottle to be refilled. He should return either late tomorrow or the next day."

He nodded. "Charles is a good man."

"Will you be coming downstairs for dinner?" she asked.

He paused before telling her, "I think I will have a tray in my room. I trust that tomorrow, I will be able to join you."

Nodding, she replied, "I understand, husband. Rest well."

Anna Grace then left Augustus's bedroom. When the door was closed, she unclenched her hands. She was relieved; one more night of freedom. She thought that she might ask Matilde to make her a picnic to celebrate her brief bout of freedom.

It was only a short distance from the house to the kitchen. Anna Grace could feel the heat emanating from the low, brick building before she reached it. Matilde had the ovens fired up. On the long table, Anna Grace could see biscuits on a tray and pie dough in pans. One of the younger slaves was shelling lima beans, and another was cutting corn from the cob. It looked to be the makings of succotash. They peered up shyly at Anna Grace when she walked in. They were different children than had been there the last time she'd visited the kitchen.

Even with the heat of the fire and the ovens, Matilde was a happy soul. She hummed away while she cooked. Anna Grace waited as Matilde made another stir or two, then stepped back from the fire. She looked inquiringly at Anna Grace, who delivered her message that Augustus would eat in his room that evening. Matilde answered, "Yes, Missus," before turning back to the fire. Anna Grace understood that the fire wasn't anything to ignore, having heard of so many women who had been maimed or died by kitchen fires.

She had planned to tell of her idea for a picnic dinner, but then she felt the thought selfish. Matilde worked so hard and had spent hours making this dinner. She didn't want to insult her by not eating it.

"I'm looking forward to dinner, Matilde," she said instead. "It smells divine."

Matilde smiled her thanks and turned back to the dinner. Anna Grace soberly walked out of the kitchen, unsure where to go. Finally, she went to the cove that skirted the front lawn of the house. It was a small inlet from the river, filled with waterlilies. At the beginning of the month, the cove was a sea of pale-yellow blooms topping green lily pads. They looked like small stars floating in the water. In the recent heavy heat, the blooms wilted to small, brown mounds riding atop the lily pads. A pathway of green filled the cove. Dragonflies darted all around her. Frogs croaked in the shallows in a lazy chorus of sounds that filled the afternoon.

Anna Grace stared at the water. She imagined her messenger, Charles, on the steamboat to Baltimore. How exciting this trip must be for him! She could almost imagine the wind in his face as he watched the Eastern shoreline disappear and the other shoreline rise in the distance. She wondered about Baltimore. Was it like Philadelphia? Going to the docks had been forbidden by her parents, but she remembered going once, when she was quite small, with her father. It had been hurley-burley of activity! It was so noisy! It smelled! There were rats freely skittering about the wharf. Would Charles be able to find Josiah Bryant in the bustle of Baltimore's busy docks? Her thoughts slipped to Josiah, her hands nervously clutching at her skirt. What would he think of her letter? Had it been wrong of her to send it? Should she have said more? She stared at the water, her thoughts going from joyful to pensive.

A dragonfly landed on her arm, and she looked at its transparent wings, electric blue body, and huge eyes. Anna Grace stood frozen to the spot, watching the insect. It took its front leg and licked it, then cleaned its eyes. Anna Grace held her breath. In a moment, it took off again, darting over the water and landing in various spots. She could see the small ripples in the still water of the cove. Turning back toward the house, her mind stayed on the insect. She was astounded by the insect's behavior and how it had landed on her sleeve. She knew it didn't make sense in her ordered world, but the thought that her mother might be communicating with her raced momentarily through her mind. She missed her mother immensely, and wished she were here to talk with. She often wondered if her mother were still alive, would she have agreed to the marriage of her daughter to Augustus? Would things have been different? Glancing back at the water, she spotted the dragonfly hovering above the water. Had it been her mother's spirit? If so, what had she been trying to say?

She turned back toward the house only to spy Pansy running toward her for the second time that day. She was out of breath, and Anna Grace grew concerned.

"Oh, no, Pansy!" she cried, startled from her thoughts. "Is everything all right?"

Pansy huffed and puffed a minute before answering, "Yes, Missus. Dinner is ready. You'd best come to the dining room."

"Thank you, Pansy," Anna Grace said a bit irritably. "Time got away from me while my thoughts went a-wandering. I was on my way."

Anna Grace felt as whiny as a small child, not wanting to come in from play. It was a pleasure to be away from the house for a few minutes. She pouted but followed Pansy's swift steps towards the front door.

The late afternoon sun felt heavy. It seemed to fill everything up to the brim with heat and emotion. Her skirts felt burdensome as her latent, irritable thoughts as she walked swiftly to her waiting dinner.

As she ate her dinner alone, Anna Grace tried to sort out her feelings which were conflicted at the moment. She was missing her mother. She was still angry with her father for selling her off to Augustus. She was slightly jealous of Charles having the opportunity to see Josiah. And, although the thought was quite wicked, she was sad that Augustus had recuperated from this bout of gout. She had enjoyed her taste of freedom. Augustus had been ill with gout in the past, but not quite so ill to keep him down as he had been in the last twenty-four hours.

Pansy came to take her plates, pulling her from her thoughts.

"What's amiss, Missus?" she asked Anna Grace, noticing her dour expression.

"Nothing to worry about, Pansy," Anna Grace told her, trying to smile. "I have some melancholy thoughts I must shake off."

"Hmm..." muttered Pansy. "No use fretting, it will be what it will be. But I think everything will turn out all right."

Anna Grace forced a small smile. "Thank you, Pansy. I am glad you feel that way. I hope so. I can't help but feel we're on the verge of a huge storm. I don't know why." She shivered, despite the summer's heat.

"Go on upstairs, Missus," Pansy ordered. "I'll be there in a minute."

Anna Grace stood up from the table. It was still light enough to read without a candle for a bit. She would put on her nightclothes and continue to read her book in the comfort of her bed. She nodded to Pansy on her way out of the dining room and headed upstairs to begin her evening ablutions.

Anna Grace started to undress but needed to stop to wait for Pansy to assist with the corset. While she waited, she combed and brushed her hair with gentle, even strokes. Pansy finally came to the bedroom. She was unusually silent.

Finally, Anna Grace said, "Please don't take my willy-nilly, melancholy thoughts to heart, Pansy."

"No, Ma'am," Pansy told her.

But Pansy still didn't smile.

"Is everything all right, Pansy?" Anna Grace asked.

"Yes, Missus. Don't you worry."

"The Master?"

"Resting in bed," Pansy answered.

There was still something off with Pansy's tone and stance. She looked at Pansy quizzically, but the woman was unusually stoic. Pansy put her hair into braids for the night, and Anna Grace decided to let it go, for now, climbing into bed with her book.

"Good night, Pansy," she said, feeling more settled.

Pansy picked up the last few things in the room, then turned to Anna Grace and finally smiled.

"Good night, Missus."

When Pansy left, Anna Grace picked up her book. She read about Elizabeth, her family's troubles, and Mr. Darcy until she fell asleep.

Twelve

JOSIAH – 1860

Amber-brown sea glass is quite common. It has been used for beverage bottles since the mid-1850s.

It was a return to business as usual for Josiah. He sorted through his piles of papers, signed contracts, and checked on the activities of the imports and exports in the warehouse. It was all copacetic, and Josiah was satisfied. When Abraham brought him a tray mid-day, Josiah approached Abraham with the possibility of becoming his secretary. Abraham had been shocked at the possibility, but also concerned about the ramifications if anyone found out that a colored was doing the job that was perceived as a white man's job. Josiah didn't care, and he'd told Abraham so, stressing that he trusted Abraham and offering him a salary increase.

"Things in this country are changing. Mr. Lincoln will see to that! I would like to set you up for a comfortable life," Josiah had insisted when he'd talked with Abraham.

Abraham had said he would think about it, and they'd worked in companionable silence for the bulk of the day after

Josiah had pleaded with Abraham to help him organize some of the papers.

When the sun was slipping away from the window, Josiah laid down his pen and rubbed his tired eyes.

"Go home. Tomorrow is another day," he told Abraham, who slipped out the door after a quick good night.

Josiah surveyed their progress. The snowstorm of papers had dwindled to neat piles with Anna Grace's letter at the very top. He would discuss the delivery of the medicine and contracts with Abraham tomorrow. He stood, stretching his legs and back.

Finally, Josiah picked up his hat and locked the door to his office. He made his way home on streets that were now quiet. As he walked from the wharves, through the merchants' area, to townhomes that neatly lined the streets, Josiah greeted the lamp-lighters lighting the streetlamps along the way. He tipped his hat to each and wished them a good evening.

He walked up to his brick townhome, which towered three stories high. It wasn't ostentatious, but quite comfortable with its red brick façade, white marble steps, and glossy black painted door with a beautiful transom window above. He unlocked the door and stepped inside the rich walnut-paneled hallway. Josiah walked down the hallway, leaving his hat on the table mid-way. He had sent a message to his cook that he would be working late. Usually, she left something warm in the kitchen.

His footfalls echoed in the silence of the house. Josiah went to the kitchen and pulled out a meat pie from the warming oven. It smelled divine, and he realized he hadn't eaten much that day. He sat at the table, slowly eating the savory pie, thinking that not so long ago, he would have had dinner with his parents in the dining room. The house felt cold and empty to Josiah. It should have been filled with laughter and activity. He should have married by now, he knew this, but the business had kept him too busy of late. After meeting Anna Grace, there would be no one who would come close to what he imagined life would be with her. Cupid's dart had speared him, and now he felt lost and alone. He wondered if she felt the same and knew, as propriety demanded, that he would never, ever have the chance to be with her.

Why did the world work this way? His simple life wasn't what he wanted anymore. He couldn't get Anna Grace out of his head or his heart. And he didn't want to settle for second best for another woman. It wouldn't be fair to either of them if his heart was with Anna Grace. It was a quandary he couldn't resolve in the immediate future.

In the meantime, the meat pie had turned cold, and he didn't want any more. He placed a plate on top of the remaining pie. When he put it in the larder, he spied a crock of pickles and took one out, grabbing a handful of soda crackers and an amber-brown bottle of beer to accompany it. These he took to his room which was lit by the warm light of gas lamps. Josiah had been delighted when his father had upgraded to gas lighting in the household. His father liked new inventions and was always improving the house, sometimes to his mother's dismay, with the latest and greatest technology. He and his father were like small boys, always amused by the little "pop" sound as the gas lamp was turned on or off. He thought of his father with a smile as he made his way up the heavy, polished, wooden stairs, turning the gas lights off with a pop that ridiculously pleased him.

When Josiah crawled into bed, between the smooth and crisp linen sheets, he thought again of Anna Grace. He decided he would fulfill her request for more Colchicine for Augustus. He would personally take the medicine and the contract for the tobacco to the Cadwallader plantation. He would speak to Abraham in the morning and begin to make plans. Settling back on the feather pillows, Josiah felt certain that seeing Anna Grace again would quell his romantic ideals of her when he faced the hard thrust of reality. He couldn't be in love with her. It was a figment of his lonely heart from the loss of his parents and his lonely life.

Thirteen

ANNA GRACE – 1860

Some collectors love the purity of common, white sea glass. Others are fascinated with the many shades of gray.

Anna Grace found Augustus sitting in the dining room the next morning. He was feeling better and spouting off orders like a general going to war between large bites of an enormous breakfast of eggs, biscuits, ham, sausage, grits, and potatoes. Tyrone nodded as Augustus spouted orders and then left to execute some of the plans, nodding to Anna Grace as he left.

"Greetings, wife," Augustus said when she entered the room with a quiet swish of her petticoats.

"Greetings, husband," she answered as she sat at the table.

Augustus nodded at her greeting but continued to eat, ignoring her presence. She poured tea and took some eggs and a biscuit from the table's covered serving dishes. She tried not to look at Augustus while he ate. He was a pig, shoveling food into his mouth and often talked while the food was still partially chewed. It sickened her. He ate enough for three men. She ate slowly and carefully, in the antithesis of Augustus's actions.

Augustus finished and abruptly stood up to go. He winced when he placed weight on his foot and grabbed the chair for support.

She looked up and saw his face twinging with pain.

"Gout still?" she asked.

Augustus could only nod.

He limped out of the dining room, and Anna Grace returned to her breakfast, thinking about her day. She considered assisting with harvesting herbs in the kitchen garden to dry for winter storage or continuing with the never-ending piles of mending. She trusted Matilde and seldom interfered in the responsibility of meal planning.

Her mind churned with another idea as she thought of sweet little Sadie, whom she had met in the kitchen. The majority of the slaves had no education, and she thought perhaps it would be good to start a small school. She would need to speak with Matilde and Pansy about her idea before she approached Augustus.

Determined, Anna Grace went to the kitchen garden. Matilde and two children were pulling weeds. Sadie was not one of them. Anna Grace smiled at these children.

"Matilde, do you have a moment?" Anna Grace asked.

"Certainly, Missus," Matilde answered, standing from her weeding of the garden.

Suddenly, Anna Grace was tongue-tied. She looked at the children and then looked at her feet. Anna Grace looked back at the children again, regaining her determination. They deserved to learn to read. They deserved to be able to write their names and do sums.

"Matilde, I was thinking of a school for the children. I wondered if I could begin to teach them their letters, to write their names, and some basic sums. What do you think?" Anna Grace asked.

Matilde stood and looked stunned, and her shoulders stiffened. Her usually animated face was suddenly stoic. Anna Grace couldn't read Matilde's emotions. Had she crossed some sort of line? She looked inquiringly at Matilde for an answer.

"I believe it's a wonderful idea, Missus," Matilde answered slowly, "but I doubt the Master would approve."

"I know," Anna Grace said gravely, "but perhaps I could begin by teaching one or two. Like, Sadie, for instance, when she's working with you. I could help with the kitchen chores and teach Sadie and a couple of the other children to start. There's nothing for him to know. Not at first. I'll figure out a way to bring it up to the Master."

"It's takin' a pretty, big chance to hide it from the Master," Matilde said warily.

"But, worth it," Anna Grace insisted.

Matilde relaxed a moment. A grin crossed her face.

"It is that, Missus. It is that." she chuckled.

"Then, it's settled," Anna Grace said confidently. "We'll begin mid-morning tomorrow. Now, let me get a hat and gloves, and I can help you all with those weeds."

Anna Grace took the hat, gloves, and basket she had used the day prior from the kitchen. She worked alongside the children while Matilde worked on luncheon. The summer sun was getting high in the sky, beating down on them. Anna Grace felt trickles of sweat on her face and down her back. She brushed a few stray hairs off her face and felt a smear of dirt. Her neck was damp. She would need to clean up before luncheon.

Pansy brought fresh water to everyone, and Anna Grace took a great gulp.

"Slowly, Missus or you will get a stomachache," Pansy warned.

Anna Grace nodded. She took off a glove, poured water on her hand, and patted the water on the back of her neck.

"You best get in and clean up for luncheon," Pansy advised. "I'll be in to help you in just a few minutes."

Pansy took the empty glass from her and held out her hand for the basket, gloves, and hat. Anna Grace obliged. She brushed lank, loose tendrils from her face and tucked them over her ears. She winced as she arched and stretched her back. It rubbed the now-healing wounds through the dress, corset, and layers of cotton underthings, a subtle reminder to hurry inside and dress so as to not disturb Augustus' mood.

She looked over the garden as she stepped out of the gate. She was pleased with her work. They'd had a small kitchen garden in the city, but a maid had taken care of it. Living on the plantation was Anna Grace's first experience tending plants. She found she liked it and smiled at the two children running quickly back to the slave quarters for their lunch.

Turning back to the path, she heard a "hello-o-o" echo up the pathway from the wharf. Anna Grace turned to see two figures striding up the path. She stood stock-still as she recognized Josiah and his man. He was back! He had returned much earlier than she had expected.

Anna Grace was beside herself. Conflicting emotions undulated through her. She was thrilled Josiah was back, but she was in such a state. She didn't want Josiah to see her like this, a mess with dirt streaks on her face and on her dress. Her hair! A hand flew up to pat some pieces in place. She bit her lip nervously as she watched them come closer and closer.

Josiah's warm, whiskey-brown eyes found hers as he walked up the path. She couldn't move. It was as though a lifeline caught them and held them in place. Everyone and everything else disappeared.

"Mr. Bryant!" Anna Grace exclaimed after a moment. "This is a surprise!"

"Dear lady," Josiah told her, "I thought I would bring the medicine and the contract for the tobacco. What is that old saying? Kill two birds with one stone?"

He took her hand and held her fingers firmly as he kissed the top of it. The electric sparks coursed through her body as they had before, and she gasped lightly.

She thought she heard him say, "dear lady" again with a sigh as well. Somewhere, off in a distant part of her brain, Anna Grace heard Pansy clear her throat.

"Shall I tell Matilde to prepare another place for luncheon, mistress?" Pansy asked. "Mistress?" she said a bit louder.

Anna Grace felt her attention pulled away from Josiah as slow as molasses in winter. She tore her eyes away from Josiah and slowly turned to Pansy.

Anna Grace stuttered, "Yes, that would be wonderful, Pansy. Please let Matilde know that Mr. Bryant will be joining us for the luncheon. And provide luncheon to his man as well. Also, would you send word to the Master that we have a guest?"

Pansy cocked one eyebrow knowingly at Anna Grace before she answered, "Yes, Missus."

She turned and ushered Josiah's man along to the kitchen, leaving Josiah and Anna Grace standing alone on the gravel path that led to the house. The summer sun glinted off Josiah's hair. She was painfully aware of her appearance, but he didn't seem to notice. Instead, he offered her his arm. She tucked her hand into his arm lightly. It felt so natural to be walking beside him, like a dream with the sun drenching them in warmth and light. Everything seemed filled with light—the grass, the sky, the trees, and even Josiah and herself. Anna Grace couldn't help but think this must be love. It filled her completely, warmly. She was whole when Josiah was close. Everything seemed right in the world. They took their time walking up the gravel path to the house, not speaking.

Anna Grace hesitated at the huge front door of the house. Josiah released her arm and turned to look at her. His eyes searched her eyes for an answer. Anna Grace didn't know what to say. She thought her heart might burst through her corset, it was so filled with love and desire for the man who stood before her.

Unsaid words and emotions filled her eyes instead of her tongue. She wondered if Josiah felt the same. He seemed on the brink of confessing something.

"Dear lady," was all Josiah was able to say when Tyrone opened the door to let them in.

"The Master is waiting in the sitting room," Tyrone informed them.

"If you will excuse me," Anna Grace told the men, "I will become a bit more presentable."

She floated up the stairs, feeling Josiah's eyes on her. She heard his footfalls as he followed Tyrone to the sitting room but felt his gaze on her back.

Safely ensconced in her room, Anna Grace looked into the mirror and groaned at the sight of her dirty face and lank hair. She stood and went to the washbasin, then poured water from the heavy, white, china jug into the matching large, broad bowl set in a wooden base. Off to the side sat a small bar of soap. It was the fine, French-milled soap she had brought from home and her father's mercantile. Its floral scent was light but luscious. The water felt cool and lovely on her face and neck. She cleaned up as best she could, then took down her hair and combed through it until it shone like honey.

Anna Grace stood up and tried to undress. She was a little impatient when Pansy was late coming to her, so she wriggled out of her gown. She washed all of the exposed skin that she could before Pansy, finally, came to the door.

"Sorry, I'm late, Missus," Pansy apologized. "The Master's been barking orders, and everyone's in a tizzy. Everyone's waiting in the sitting room, so we'll get you fixed up right away."

Pansy pulled out a dress of fine, cornflower-blue cotton. The color of the dress matched Anna Grace's eyes. Its trim was sweet with white, eyelet lace. Its modest neckline would make Augustus happy. Pansy helped her into the dress, then sat Anna Grace at the vanity and began combing and pulling her hair into a simple, yet elegant, hairstyle. She rolled Anna Grace's hair smoothly back from her forehead into a large chignon at the back of her neck, adding a decorative comb.

"There you are, Missus. You're as good as new. You'll be needing to keep out of that sun, though. I see a few freckles popping out on your face."

Pansy took a small pot of rice powder and dabbed at Anna Grace's face.

"Oh, not too much, Pansy," Anna Grace said. "I'll sneeze!" And, indeed, she sneezed loudly, not once, but seven times.

"Bless you, Missus. You must have a secret," Pansy said playfully.

"What are you talking about?" Anna Grace asked her more sharply than she intended. She was anxious to get to Josiah.

Pansy recited, "One for sorrow, two for joy, three for a girl, four for a boy," she took a breath and continued, "five for silver, six for gold, seven for a secret, never to be told."

"Oh!" was the only reply Anna Grace could give Pansy.

She blushed, thinking of her secret. Pansy knew her well, and Anna Grace wondered if Pansy had guessed her attraction to Josiah.

"Enjoy your luncheon, Missus," Pansy stated in almost a teasing tone.

"Thank you," she returned, "I will indeed."

She noticed that Pansy had a twinkle in her eye. She knew. So much for secrets.

When Anna Grace made it to the entrance of the sitting room, she could feel the tension. Once again, Augustus was in a filthy mood. He was snapping about something. She could hear it in his voice as she descended the stairs. When she entered the sitting room, Josiah stood up in respect. Belatedly, Jedediah Reece, the plantation manager with whom she rarely interacted, stood up. He looked slightly embarrassed. Anna Grace had never gotten a good feeling about the man. He was a leftover from when

Augustus's parents had run the plantation. Augustus had known him all his life, and he seemed to revere the older man. Their relationship was jovial, but Mr. Reece gave Anna Grace the willies, and she didn't know why. He was older, lanky without being overly tall, and had a gray goatee. He was missing a couple of teeth, so he rarely smiled. She had heard from Pansy that he liked to "have his way" among the slave women. One woman, Cecilia, Pansy had told her, now lived with him in his cottage. Anna Grace thought her unkind feelings of the man were because he was the one who had urged Augustus to marry and produce an heir.

Augustus stayed seated, but he kept his eyes on Josiah's face. His eyes took on the hard glint that Anna Grace did not like. Thankfully, Tyrone came to the door and announced the meal was ready.

Nodding, Anna Grace led the way into the dining room. Josiah and Mr. Reece followed her while Tyrone helped Augustus. Even though he was much better, he still winced in pain as he stood and walked.

Matilde had prepared a Southern feast. She had crispy, fried chicken, cornbread, potatoes, and a piquant cabbage salad. The luncheon was fairly quiet. Anna Grace willed herself not to gaze at Josiah. It was difficult.

Augustus wolfed down several pieces of fried chicken and cornbread spread thickly with butter and honey. Sometimes she wondered if he had ever learned manners. Augustus had told her once that his parents had been quite strict, perhaps, once his parents had passed away, his manners had vanished. After all, it had been almost ten years of eating alone.

"That Matilde is a fine cook," Mr. Reece remarked.

"She certainly is," Anna Grace agreed.

Josiah was wiping his mouth and couldn't answer but nodded in agreement. He turned to Augustus to ask about his gout.

Augustus grunted and spoke, with food still in his mouth. It was disturbing, and Anna Grace looked away.

"Somewhat better," Augustus said. "My right foot is still paining me."

"I brought more medicine for you," Josiah said. "I would recommend taking it in smaller doses. I understand it takes a few weeks to cure gout."

Josiah reached into the inside breast pocket of his suit and pulled out the familiar, ridged, blue bottle. It was full to the brim and corked sturdily with a wax seal. He raised his hand to give it to Tyrone.

"So, a maintenance dose would be recommended?" Anna Grace asked.

"Yes," Josiah replied. "The apothecary mentioned a steady, maintenance dosage only to be increased if the pain is acute. He also said that you must be careful in taking it, as too much is likely toxic."

Anna Grace looked shocked. "Toxic?" she asked. "But the bottle doesn't say "poison" on it." She remembered seeing brown and blue bottles with the word poison clearly embedded in the glass, often accompanied by a skull and crossbones.

"Yes, from what I understand, very much so. You took this last bottle much too quickly," he warned Augustus before turning to Anna Grace. "The ridges on the bottle are meant to state caution in the consumption of the medicine," he explained.

"Faugh!" Augustus groused. "I'm just fine. It helped tremendously. I thank you, sir, but let's finish here and get to our business."

Josiah looked out the window. The sun was heading toward the west.

"Yes. My goal is to catch the remaining boat back to Baltimore," Josiah agreed.

Augustus looked pointedly at Anna Grace. She took the hint.

"If you gentleman will excuse me," she murmured.

She rose to leave the table and dared a glance at Josiah. He stood as well, and raw emotion was in his eyes. Anna Grace nodded to each of the men and left the room. She wanted to speak to Josiah so desperately, but how? She paced back and forth in the foyer. She heard their voices rise and fall. It had been almost an hour since they were talking. She had kept notice of the tall grandfather clock in the foyer that ticked away. Anna Grace wondered what they were discussing. Tiptoeing down the hallway, she stopped and listened. They were arguing over the price of tobacco. Augustus was insisting on payment in full before he delivered the harvest. Josiah wasn't budging. Eventually, Josiah and Augustus agreed that he would give him half the payment today and half when the tobacco came to Baltimore. Josiah said he would come personally to check on the tobacco mid-harvest and see the bales of tobacco loaded onto the steamboat. They agreed. She heard Augustus suggest a toast and send Tyrone to get some whiskey.

Anna Grace tiptoed as quietly as she could back to the foyer. Now what? Josiah would be leaving soon. What could she do?

As if she knew, Pansy appeared at the top of the stairs with a large, woven, straw picture hat with a blue ribbon tied to it and a pair of Anna Grace's gloves. She held the items in one hand, put another on her hip, and raised an eyebrow before descending the stairs.

"I thought you might be wantin' to take a stroll, Missus," Pansy commented.

"Oh, Pansy," Anna Grace replied with a relieved sigh. "Thank you! I believe I will!"

Anna Grace tied on the hat and put on the gloves. She went out the door and pointedly walked on the path that went in front of the dining room windows. She hoped Josiah would take notice. She examined a blooming rosebush and sniffed its luscious fragrance before she continued on the path that led to the wharf. She walked very, very slowly, stopping to gaze every few seconds, listening for the door of the house to open.

Finally, it did. She heard Josiah's farewell and his feet walking swiftly on the gravel path.

Soon, he had caught up with her.

"Dear lady," he said, as he always seemed to.

Anna Grace stopped and turned to him.

"I do have a name," she told him boldly. "It's Anna Grace."

"Anna Grace," Josiah said quietly.

Anna Grace liked the sound of her name coming from him.

"Would you accompany me to the wharf, Anna Grace?" he asked. He said her name softly so that only she could hear.

"Of course, sir."

He held out his arm, and they silently walked away from the house and down the path. When they reached the wharf, Josiah took her hands.

"Dear lady..." he began, then flushed as he corrected himself, "Anna Grace, I will be returning to check on the progress of the tobacco and then later to accompany the tobacco harvest to Baltimore. There is much to say, but it would not be..." he trailed off, seeking the words.

"I understand," Anna Grace told him. She tried to tell him all the thoughts that swirled inside her as she looked into his eyes.

He squeezed her fingers lightly, and she felt as if she could grasp them and hold onto his hands forever. Time seemed to stand still. His gaze seemed to reach inside of her as if his soul spoke to hers.

"When will you return?" she asked finally, coming back to the reality that they were standing on the wharf for a length of measured time. She looked around to see who was there. No one. Thankfully, there was no one from the plantation to report to Augustus that his wife was clutching at the hands of another man.

"In a fortnight. I'll return in a fortnight to check on the tobacco,"

Anna Grace nodded. She wasn't sure of her voice.

They leaned in closer to one another, her breath catching,

heart leaping. She tilted her head up and, for a moment, thought he might kiss her. Butterflies moved inside of her. She closed her eyes in anticipation. This is what she had dreamed of. She heard Josiah take in a breath and felt his hands tighten around hers. He was so close; she felt his breath on her skin. She waited for that exquisite moment for his lips to touch hers.

"Sir!" Josiah's man called. "We need to depart!"

As if cold water had been splashed on them, they pulled apart quickly. She didn't know what to do with her hands, so she clasped them in front of her and looked down at the wharf's old wood.

Josiah nodded in response to his man but still kept his gaze on Anna Grace.

"On my way," he returned to his man, his voice ragged with emotion.

"I'll return," he promised. "I'll return in a fortnight. Until then," Anna Grace told him, not knowing what else to say.

She watched as he boarded the small skiff. His man took the oars and began to row them down the river. Josiah raised one hand in farewell, and Anna Grace raised her hand as well. She watched until they rowed out of sight.

Anna Grace was a welter of emotions as she turned to go up the path to the house. Two weeks. She could look forward to seeing Josiah in two weeks! But, then what? After the tobacco transaction, she likely would not see him, if at all, until a year from now. The lashes on her back were healing, and they itched. It was an unpleasant reminder of her life with Augustus. Gripped with a "devil may care" attitude, she turned back to the water. For a brief moment, she wanted to run down to the riverbanks and call Josiah to take her with him! She looked longingly at the bank of the river, but something inside of her said, "not yet."

Anna Grace stepped into the house. Augustus and Mr. Reece were apparently celebrating. She could hear the sounds of their cackling laughter as she walked down the hallway. She peered in at the two men. The whiskey had begun to take its insidious way with them. They slurred their words and laughed too loudly.

"Did you see the popinjay off?" Augustus asked mockingly.

"Yes," Anna Grace replied, pulling herself up to stand very straight.

A popinjay? Josiah? She didn't believe that for a minute. It was Augustus just being nasty, calling Josiah a dandy.

"Well," Augustus drawled. "We'll see him in a fortnight, and then at the harvest, and then it will be good riddance until next year!"

He laughed raucously at some private joke, and Mr. Reece joined in.

"I'll leave you to your celebration," Anna Grace said primly.

She turned and went to her room to return the hat and gloves. Augustus infuriated her! She stomped her foot in her anger. Augustus was such a nasty, bully of a man, and Mr. Reece wasn't much better. She prayed he would drink himself to sleep so she would be free from him another night. Then she would be free to dream of Josiah until she could see him again.

She went downstairs again to inform Matilde that she would have her dinner on a tray in her room and wandered through the kitchen garden, idly stroking the fragrant herbs.

Two more weeks until Josiah would return. Would she have the courage to speak with him and confess her feelings? Anna Grace didn't know.

Fourteen

ANNA GRACE – 1860

A glassblower uses a long, five-foot pipe to gather molten glass from the 'glory hole.' The glassblower then blows a bubble of hot glass, which he rotates to create a bottle.

Anna Grace spent the rest of the evening in her room, avoiding Augustus. She had finally collapsed on her bed with thoughts of Josiah filling her mind. She wanted to run far away from Augustus and wondered if it was possible. The look in Josiah's eyes had given her hope. Could they run away together? She would need to write to him or capture him alone for a few minutes. Neither option was safe. There seemed to be nowhere safe from Augustus. What she was thinking of doing was scandalous. Divorce was unacceptable in society and adultery against the law. But still, she wondered if had had some of the same thoughts. Would she ever know? Anna Grace hugged her pillow, wondering, and then leaped up to pace the room once again.

There was a knock, and she froze. It was Pansy. Anna Grace stood and looked at her, wild-eyed, her heart thumping from fear it may have been Augustus.

"Now, Missus," Pansy ordered, setting down the tray with Anna Grace's dinner. "You need to sit and settle yourself."

"Oh, Pansy! This is maddening! I think I'm in love, and there's nothing I can do about it!" Anna Grace confessed.

"Right now, you need to sit and eat your dinner. Those men are up to their cups in whiskey, and you don't want to be near them."

"No, I do not!" Anna Grace agreed vehemently.

She sat down to look at the tray. It looked inviting, but she was not hungry.

"What should I do, Pansy?"

Pansy nodded her acknowledgment. "I don't know, Missus. I don't know. I think you gotta' trust in the Lord. He'll put things to rights."

"Maybe," Anna Grace replied.

Anna Grace hadn't thought much about God being here with Augustus. In truth, she thought God had turned on her. She wondered how a good and kind God could put her in place with a man such as Augustus. She often likened Augustus to the devil himself. Something like the devil came over him when he was in a temper, so it seemed plausible.

Anna Grace turned to Pansy and asked, "Were you here when Augustus's parents were alive?"

"No, Missus. I wasn't. Matilde was, though. She said his parents were awful strict. They didn't show any lovin' to the Master when he was little. They had all sorts of rules and didn't spare the rod, not on anyone," she finished darkly.

"That's probably why Augustus is the way he is," Anna Grace ruminated. "I hadn't thought of it before."

"I expect so," Pansy said, keeping a poker face.

Anna Grace looked at her.

"What do you know?" Anna Grace asked Pansy.

"Nuthin'."

"What do you mean, Pansy?" Anna Grace persisted. "You know something, and you're not telling me."

"It's nuthin' for your ears, mistress," Pansy insisted.

"Of course, it's for my ears," Anna Grace began, and then realizing how she sounded, as the high and mighty mistress of the plantation, she stopped while Pansy's eyes went from sharp, jagged pieces of coal to the softer brown she knew.

"I'm sorry, Pansy. Obviously, it's none of my business. But, if I can help you with something, please don't hesitate to come to me, all right?" Reluctantly, she let the matter go. "I think I want to turn in early."

"You should eat a little more of your dinner," Pansy bossed Anna Grace.

"Truly, I'm not hungry," Anna Grace insisted. I just want to go to bed."

"Yes, Missus," Pansy said, acquiescing to her mistress.

"Oh, Pansy! Do you think he feels the way I feel?" Anna Grace asked dreamily as Pansy helped her prepare for bed.

"I expect so from the way he was lookin' at you," Pansy told her. "But, Missus, aren't you getting' ahead of yourself? What about the Master?"

"I know, Pansy," Anna Grace replied soberly. "I'm caught here. I'm a prisoner, and I see no means of escape. And love is sort of an escape, isn't it? If I know he loves me, perhaps I can bear Augustus. Perhaps there's hope." Her voice held a pleading tone.

"Yes, Missus," Pansy agreed seriously.

Anna Grace reached up to stop Pansy's hand from brushing her hair a moment. She looked pleadingly into Pansy's face when she asked, "Do you think I have any chance of escape?"

"I don't know, Missus," Pansy said. "I don't know. I will think about it."

"Thank you, Pansy," she said gratefully.

Anna Grace climbed into the tall four-poster bed. They both heard something crash loudly downstairs. Swearing followed.

"Oh, no," Anna Grace moaned.

"I think he's too much in his cups to pay you a visit," Pansy said. "Tyrone said he's been drinking all afternoon and evening."

"But he's such a mean, mean drunk," Anna Grace replied, and she shuddered.

"Yes, Missus. I think Tyrone will convince him to go to bed. Tyrone wasn't too happy to learn what happened the last time," Pansy confessed.

"So, he's on my side?" Anna Grace asked.

"Yes, Missus. You could put it that way."

Pansy pulled up the sheet and tucked it around her.

She was getting sleepy and said, "You know, you remind me of my mother sometimes."

"Is that so, Missus," Pansy replied.

"I've never asked, Pansy. Do you have children?" Anna Grace asked her, waking a little bit.

Pansy froze. Once again, Anna Grace could feel the tension. She went from sleepy and dreamy to awake, instantly. She put her hand on Pansy's arm.

"What's wrong, Pansy? What happened? What did I say to upset you?"

"My child was taken from me when I was sold," Pansy said softly.

Anna Grace was shocked. She had heard of this but had tried not to believe something like this could happen. Here was Pansy, going on, day by day, not having her child or her husband by her side. This, to her, was crueler than the beatings Augustus gave her. Her eyes filled with tears as she looked at Pansy.

"Oh, Pansy! How can you bear it?"

"Not too well, sometimes," Pansy admitted. "I don't know where my child or my husband is."

"That's horrible!"

They heard another loud sound. It was the sound of heavy footsteps, slowly coming up the stairs. Tyrone could be heard urging Augustus to his room. Anna Grace held her breath. It was obvious that Augustus was quite inebriated by the sound of the footsteps that stumbled every few feet. They heard him bang against the wall, then swear again. They listened as Tyrone continued to help Augustus down the hallway, the sound almost as if he were being dragged like dead weight. His feet hit the floor in a stumbling gait every so often, and the groans of pain echoed through the door.

His gout must be ailing him, again, she thought.

She was hopeful that he would simply pass out in his bed and not even think to come near her. Pansy waited until they had gone past the door and then slipped silently into the hallway. There were a few more groans and moans from Augustus's room, and in a few minutes, all was finally quiet. Anna Grace breathed a sigh of relief.

After Pansy left, Anna Grace remained tense, gripping the sheet up to her chin and squeezing her eyes tightly shut. When the quiet had settled, she opened her eyes and stared at the incoming inky blackness of the night. Her limbs relaxed, and she let go of the death grip on the sheets. She saw stars twinkling in the inky sky and heard a fox forlornly call in the woods to the north of the property. The sound reminded her of a baby, and she shivered, remembering what Pansy had told her. Poor Pansy! How horrible to lose her baby and her husband! It was inhuman how the slaves were treated. She thought back to her life in Philadelphia. It was only whispered, but she had heard of other Quakers helping to smuggle runaway slaves to the North and to freedom. It was all very clandestine, but she had heard rumors.

Pansy's situation was too hard to bear. Anna Grace couldn't think of a way to help her, at least not yet. She wondered how many other slaves on the plantation were in the same predicament, having lost their families. She might write a letter to her father, explaining the situation. Perhaps some of the Quaker Friends had ways to help.

Now her mind wandered instead to Josiah. She wondered what he was doing. Was he thinking about her? He'd be back in Baltimore soon. She'd never been to Baltimore, but she imagined it must be similar to Philadelphia. What was his life like there? Could she run away to Baltimore, to him? What would he think? How could she do something like that? If she went to Josiah, she would be considered an adulteress, something that gave her pause. She didn't know the punishment for such a crime in Maryland. She thought of Nathaniel Hawthorne's *Scarlet Letter*, thinking she would be like Hester Prynne.

Could she run back to her father and explain that Augustus was a brutal man and beat her nearly to death? She didn't know if she could trust him; after all, he had sold her to Augustus in the first place. He would likely tell her it was her duty to return to him.

Her whirling thoughts finally settled, and sleep began to overtake her. The noise of the September chorus of insects provided a soothing backdrop. The air was sweet, and sleep came, bringing dreams.

Anna Grace woke with a start from a terrible nightmare. She felt out of time and out of place. Through the open window, the insect chorus was more subdued. She released her hands that were gripping her bedclothes and wiped the perspiration from her forehead. She had dreamed she was Hester Prynne, the main character of the *Scarlet Letter*, sporting a scarlet "A" for Adulteress on her bosom. Augustus had been the evil Roger Chillingsworth and Josiah the Reverend Arthur Dimmesdale. The child, Pearl, was replaced by a child fathered by Josiah. The child would have her blond hair and his whiskey, brown eyes. She was a child of intelligence, just like the character of Pearl.

The dream had frightened her. If she ran away with Josiah, she was afraid Augustus would come after them, perhaps even try to kill them. He would certainly send the authorities after them.

And then what? She was agitated by her thoughts, and she fumed at her predicament.

An owl hooting in the distance startled her, and she froze, listening carefully. All became calm and quiet again. She relaxed, her breathing rhythmic and deep until, eventually, she fell back to sleep.

Fifteen

BETH

Much of the pink sea glass comes from pink, Depression glass.

Maryland's weather changed on a dime. A warm front moved in overnight, and the vestiges of the remaining cold had disappeared. In its wake, a blanket of heavy fog hugged the ground. Beth had difficulty navigating her car from the parking garage onto the street. She could barely see beyond the car.

Mike's email still shook her, and she gripped the steering wheel tightly. The local radio station said that schools were delayed due to the fog, and she was grateful. When the stop lights looked like iced maraschino cherries, looking out for school buses would have been difficult. Beth drove slowly and carefully home. She tried to see if any cars followed her, but the fog prevented everything except full concentration on driving.

When she arrived at the cottage, she realized she couldn't see the beach a few yards away. She stepped from her car and went inside, then carefully locked the door before collapsing into the chair in front of the wood stove. For a brief moment, she considered putting a chair under it as well.

Now what? This peaceful cottage at the edge of the Chesapeake Bay had always been a safe haven for her, until now. No one understood about Mike. For God's sake, even her mother didn't understand! She still thought Mike was a good "catch." He had a steady job and had given the appearance to everyone that he loved and adored her. The truth of the matter was that he had loved to control her and had been emotionally abusive. His email frightened her. She was sure that he'd sent it purposely, knowing it would freak her out. Shivering, she prayed he didn't know where she lived or worked. His insidious game had gotten under her skin, and she was certain he knew it. This time, she wouldn't let him win at the mental games he played. She had to figure out a way to be safe, not only physically from Mike, but from his mind games. She wondered how he had found her email but knew in her heart that her mom had probably given it to him, wanting to get them back together.

Beth was overtired. Her mind was a muddle. She needed sleep. She was grateful she didn't need to build a fire in the woodstove today with the warmer weather. She turned the space heater on low and cuddled under the blankets, and in moments she was asleep.

But the sleep didn't last. Beth's dreams were disturbed by Mike's leering face. She would wake with a start, remember where she was, and then sleep again. By the time she woke to face the day, she felt as though she had been run over by a truck more than once. Beth stretched, pulling her body this way and that until she was limber.

Rain pelted down with a hard tap, tap, tap that drummed on the roof and on the windows. Beth squinted out the window that was covered in droplets. Gray was everywhere. The rain pelted down in the pewter gray sky that was giving way to darkness.

The day that had started in heavy fog gave way to the warm front that had moved in with a deluge of rain. It was still warmer than it had been for days, but the rain had brought penetrating dampness. Insulation was scarce in the cottage, and the space heater chugged sluggishly as if tired from the effort to do its job and chase away the chill. Beth wished she could crawl back into the soft, warm bed. She felt as though she could sleep for a day and a night and another day.

She needed to wake up. Beth turned on the stove to heat the water for coffee. Next, she peered into the scarily sparse refrigerator. She would need to go grocery shopping as soon as possible, but glancing at the clock on the microwave, she saw that it would have to wait until she got off work in the morning.

Rain slushed around her tires, and her wipers were going as fast as possible as she drove to work. Some idiot in a black truck, with no lights, nearly hit her as it barreled down the highway and passed her. Beth felt her little car hydroplane, and she worked to control it.

"What happened to you?" Marsha greeted her with concern when Beth stepped onto the floor.

"Not sure where to begin," she told Marsha.

She stowed her things and realized she had forgotten to stop to get something to eat. Vending machine dinners were not her favorite. This added to the morass of the day.

"How are you?" she asked her friend as she tucked a stray hair into her ponytail.

Marsha shrugged her shoulder. "Same old stuff. I'm fine." Marsha took a sidelong look at Beth. "Are *you* all right? You really don't look well."

Beth stammered, "I...I didn't sleep well, and then on my way here, an idiot nearly hit me, and I hydroplaned. I'm tired and shaken up. That's all."

She didn't tell Marsha about the email from Mike. As their friendship had grown, she'd started to trust Marsha, but she still had not told her everything about Mike. Now she felt a trifle guilty. Marsha was a good friend. She knew Beth had some kind of history, but she didn't pry. She was letting Beth tell the story in her own time.

When Beth had started working at the hospital, she'd hit it off with Marsha right away. Marsha was at least ten years older than Beth, but something had clicked with them. Beth had visited Marsha's house and met her husband, Harry. After all that had happened with Mike, she was still gun-shy, but she liked to watch Marsha and Harry as they moved around their house together. It was almost like watching a ballet. They were comfortable with each other, they laughed, and they had fun.

Beth turned away from Marsha and began to look over the patient charts. It was a new crop of patients except for Mr. Shaw, who was still battling a fever. Mrs. Crites must have been discharged and returned to the assisted living home.

A room alarm beeped. Beth pushed back from the desk.

"Duty calls," she said, businesslike. "I'll take it."

She grabbed the vitals machine monitor on the way and her clipboard and pen, then headed down the hall. She didn't see Marsha's mouth drop open a little at her untoward abruptness as Beth walked down the corridor.

Their night was fairly quiet, and Beth found herself dozing a little in her seat at the nurses' station. When a patient's room alarm bleeped loudly, Beth woke with a start.

"Oh my!" Beth cried out. "What happened?"

"You fell asleep," Marsha told her. "And, by the way, I'll see what's going on in room 112B. When I get back, we need to talk."

"Okay," Beth said softly.

While Marsha was gone, Beth went to wash her face and make a couple of cups of coffee for Marsha and herself. Starving, she ran her credit card through the vending machine and purchased cheese crackers and cookies.

It was the magic time on the ward when everything was calm. Beth sipped at her coffee, the warmth and caffeine seeping through her. She shared her crackers with Marsha, who had returned. Marsha was patient and waited to see if her friend would say anything. Unsure where to begin, Beth remained silent.

Marsha cleared her throat. The small sound seemed out of place on the quiet ward with beeps and bleeps in a soft background chorus. Beth remained silent.

"We're off tomorrow, Beth. What do you say, after a good night's sleep, that we go glassing and have a girls' day out?" Marsha suggested.

"I can cancel my plans for wild parties then?" Beth returned slyly.

"Well...I guess I'll have to drive if you want to go on a bender tomorrow," Marsha teased. "Look, I'll check the tide tables and pick you up bright and early. We'll have breakfast out, go glassing, and maybe do a bit of shopping and a lot of gabbing. The weather looks perfect. It's set to be sunny. Does that sound good?"

"It does," Beth said, smiling. "It's a date."

Sixteen

MATTHEW

Some of the greatest Sea glass beaches: MacKerricher State Park in Fort Bragg, California; Hawaii Hanapepe Bay Glass Beach in Glass Beach, Kauai; Steklyashka Beach in Vladivostok, Russia, and Seaham, England.

Matthew pulled the blinds down and closed the wooden, louvered shutters across the window. He stumbled to the bed. The recent cup of coffee had not given him the caffeine buzz he'd desired. Working all night, his foray into the brisk weather, and the outpouring of creative energies had left him exhausted.

Matthew closed his eyes. In his mind's eye, he saw several pieces of sea glass and the jewelry he envisioned making for the glass. This resting process was like telling himself a bedtime story. He could switch the visual images of jewelry pieces in his head to create whatever he wanted. The bonus buy was actually creating the pieces when he awoke.

Matthew kept a small journal by his bedside along with a variety of drawing pencils and art erasers. Sometimes, he would take a minute to capture the image in his head and add dimensions. But not today. He was too exhausted. He only wanted to see the pieces in his dreams. Perhaps tomorrow he could draw the pieces. The blue piece intrigued him, and he thought the silhouette of a great, blue heron carved from the bright silver would contrast well with the cobalt blue glass. He wasn't sure if he wanted to carve the figure of the heron standing in the water or flying in the sky. The cobalt blue shard had to be the base of a small bottle, that was possibly Victorian. The shard wasn't the right shape for the bottom of a bromide bottle or a Noxzema jar. For the large, thick, well-frosted white shard, Matthew envisioned a chrysanthemum. The gleaming silver would be simple and exquisite, but the chrysanthemum would be a challenge to carve.

In a few hours, he would need to return to work. He wanted to rest and then complete the piece he'd been working on before he started out the door to his job. Matthew set his alarm, rolled over with a groan, and went to sleep.

He woke to his alarm blaring. Staring at the time, he muttered an expletive. He must have slept through his first alarm. This was his second, his emergency alarm. Matthew had a couple of hours before he needed to leave for work. He stretched, scratched his belly, and made a strong cup of coffee. While the coffee was brewing, he fished the sea glass pieces from the dishwasher and dried them thoroughly. The green piece was older than most of the pieces he'd found on the beach. It was an odd cylindrical piece, fatter on one end. Matthew thought it had likely been a very old bottle stopper. He wondered how old. It was quite possibly from the time of the Revolutionary War or the War of 1812. Settlements in Carpenters Point, Seneca Point, and Kingstown, Maryland, had existed since the 17th and 18th centuries. Kingstown had been a thriving port back in the day. Now, it was a sleepy, little town. He never found much glass on the public beach and wished he knew someone at Carpenter's Point. He had heard that glass and other debris whooshed out of the Susquehanna River and, through currents, ended up on Carpenter's Point beaches. He was grateful that he found glass on his little patch of beach. Further down, all that he usually found were large, iron-filled rocks with interesting shapes. Up his way, there were tubular and tiny bowl-shaped rocks that he'd learned were concretions. He'd made a few pieces into jewelry, and he wanted to explore doing more. The look was very organic, but he imagined some interesting designs. Perhaps, he could make a few and take them to the ASGS Festival to try out the market.

Matthew took the green piece and set it into the leaf pendant, wrapping the flattened prongs around it. The green gleamed against the copper. It was a lovely piece.

Matthew's stomach growled. He couldn't remember the last time he had eaten. He went back to the kitchen to make a second coffee cup and scrambled eggs for a quick egg sandwich with cheese. He took his steaming coffee and his egg sandwich, now cradled in a paper towel, back to the couch.

He loved looking out at the water. The drama of the sky, water, and wildlife never grew old. The heron had returned. It was stalking something on its gangly legs in the shallows. It stopped and waited. Matthew sipped his coffee, watching intently as it dove to grab a small fish and lifted its long neck to swallow it whole. Matthew grinned.

"Bon Appetit!" he said to the heron and raised his mug of coffee in salute.

Matthew turned on the sultry mix of evocative female artists, Bonnie Raitt, Norah Jones, and Sarah McLachlan. He listened as he looked at the water and sky, musing on life and the day. He didn't often dwell on the reasons why he chose to be alone. He liked his solitude. He knew from experience that there weren't too many women who would put up with his work and creative schedule. It was a problem, and yet it wasn't. For the moment, being alone was a small thing to trade for his freedom. The ladies crooned on in melancholy tones.

Matthew ate his sandwich, drained his coffee, and crumpled the paper towel in his hand before he stood to get ready for work.

Seventeen

❧

JOSIAH – 1860

Bubbles in sea glass usually indicate that it is older, hand-blown glass.

Josiah stood on the small boat watching the Cadwallader plantation fade away into the distance. At the last glimpse, he put his hands over his face. What was the saying about the cure being worse than the disease? That was how he felt about seeing Anna Grace again. He'd told himself that seeing her as mistress of the manor would change his mind that she was an available debutante. He thought of Augustus and his disgusting manners. His stomach lurched, not only from the heavy lunch and bumpy ride on the small shallop but from the thought of Anna Grace sharing the cad's bed.

"Sir!" Abraham's voice broke through his thoughts. "Sir," Abraham repeated again, "we're ready to board the packet."

Josiah nodded and mutely followed Abraham off the boat, lost in thought.

Upon his return to Baltimore, Josiah threw himself into his work. He trained Abraham on contracts and completed a mountain of correspondence regarding upcoming shipments. Abraham proved adept, and Josiah found himself giving the man more and more responsibilities. When one of their boats carrying rum and molasses became lost at sea during a hurricane, Josiah wished he was not in business.

His father groomed him for the import and export business, but Josiah's love was for reading. At one point, he had considered becoming a clergyman. He thought of his quiet days of reading at university with longing. Now, he was in the throes of a business crisis, without his father to turn to for advice.

Josiah wondered what his father would do. His father was a decent man and would contact the family members on the crew. Josiah did this and then looked for advice from his father's cronies on what to do with the business.

They advised him to stay the course, and Josiah knew he had to get the tobacco he purchased from the plantations and sell it for a good profit to keep the business going. He had to organize an efficient plan to bring in all of the tobacco and send it on ships across the world. Josiah didn't feel they, no he, had the funds to purchase another ship, but he didn't know if they could make the shipments when they were short by one ship. He worked the math over and over again for measurements of the holds and the tobacco, trying to make it work. He had to figure it out, there was no other option. Now he understood why his father had sported several silvery hairs on his head. This business was all about juggling—juggling so things could fit in neat boxes. Everything needed a place to go so the funds would flow like the tides. He hoped the high tide would flow into the company's bank account, but he had his doubts.

Eventually, Josiah shared his worries with Abraham. Abraham listened carefully as he always did, but he didn't say anything. Abraham was a thinker, he needed time to process, and Josiah knew he would share his thoughts when he had things worked out. Josiah could live with that for now. At least his heart was lighter for confessing his concerns to Abraham.

As he sat at his desk days later, he thought about Anna Grace. He had buried himself in his work, trying not to notice how the minutes crawled toward the time until he could see her again. Not seeing her tortured him as much as seeing her did. He was determined to put her out of his mind and out of his heart. But how? It was a puzzle he had yet to figure out. As things stood now, there was no way for them to be together in the present or likely in the future.

He put his head in his hands. He couldn't think of any good that would come of this. And still, through it all, he wanted to see Anna Grace, wanted her arm in his again, to hear the sound of her voice in his ears.

Eventually, the day came. Abraham and Josiah boarded the steamship to take them to the Cadwallader plantation to complete the deal on the tobacco. Josiah marveled at the technology of the ship. It was a fine day, and he felt like a small boy watching the paddlewheel pull the water around. He loved to watch the splash and feel of the pull of the ship as it sliced through the blue water. He remembered reading long ago that paddle wheels had been around since early Roman times. Funny how inventions like this stayed.

Josiah walked around the deck, enjoying the fine weather. The sunshine seemed to fill the sky, and the clouds were scattered in their lamb tail shape. A change in weather was coming. Josiah held onto the hope that it was a good change. As he walked, he talked about how he would approach Anna Grace.

It was then he smelled sharp smoke. He heard gasps from the crowd and saw the black smoke billowing up toward the sky. Flames erupted, and Josiah ran to help the crew lower the lifeboats to the water. He turned back to help with the bucket brigade rather than get into the lifeboats with the other passengers. As he was grabbing a bucket, he saw the flash. He heard a roar. And then there was an explosion.

Josiah was catapulted from the deck, landing among the

flaming debris in the bay where the water roiled and frothed. He was having a hard time keeping his head above the water, and he struggled, gulping in water and straining to breathe.

His voice came out as a croak as he called Abraham's name. He called over and over and thrashed around the water, avoiding the burning bits of wood that flew from the boat. Ahead, there was a lifeboat. He needed to reach it, but a wave swamped him. Exhausted, Josiah sank under the water. His body became limp, and his chest grew tight. It would be so easy to sink into this soft haven. An image of Anna Grace filled his mind, her eyes seeming to watch him from above the water. He wanted to see her again. Reminding himself that he'd been on his way to see her, he reached toward her eyes, fighting through the water with what remaining strength he had. He reached up and up toward the surface until he found it.

He gasped great breaths of air and was nearly knocked in the head by a large piece of wood. But he was alive, for now. Grasping the wood, he held on for dear life.

Eighteen

ANNA GRACE – 1860

The yellowish, grayish, green citron glass was often used for food containers such as olive oil and wine.

The next few days were long. It seemed to Anna Grace that they passed with an intense slowness and dream-like quality. Anna Grace tried to keep herself busy. Each morning she went to the outdoor kitchen under the ruse of assisting Matilde. There she met Sadie and two other children, Isaac and Sam. They were good children. Anna Grace started with the alphabet, tracing the letters, large and small, into the sand on the kitchen floor. She noticed Matilde was paying attention as well. After she said the name of each letter and gave the accompanying sound, the children copied her. Each child took turns copying the letters in the sand as Anna Grace wondered how she could get slates for each of them. For now, the sand would have to do.

One week passed. Augustus seemed to be very, very busy with Mr. Reece. He was with him from morning until night. Anna Grace assumed they were preparing the tobacco harvest for shipment to Baltimore. In the last month, she had noticed the tobacco hanging in the barns. It turned from the long, large, bright, green leaves to a mustard yellow. The barns were unique to Anna Grace. The longboards on the side could prop open to allow the air to flow through and dry the tobacco leaves. She had never been inside the barns but had watched the tobacco hanging from the distance as she walked about the property.

Augustus no longer joined her for dinner. She sat alone in the dining room each evening, so she started to bring her book with her. Following her dream, she had begun re-reading *The Scarlet Letter*. The plot of adultery seemed to echo through her. She was so very anxious to see Josiah again. More than once in the last week, she had considered writing to him. What she wanted to suggest to him would be scandalous, but she couldn't imagine life without him. She only wanted a few moments alone with him, feeling she would know immediately if he held the same affections as she. One more week. One more long, long week until he was to return.

The weather began to shift. The heat and humidity abated. A cool breeze blew, one that portended cooler autumn weather. Anna Grace felt the change in the air. She could feel a change with Augustus as well. He looked at her in what she thought was an odd way. He'd become extremely reserved around her, barely speaking a word. It puzzled her. More puzzling was the fact that he now left her alone. That in itself was a relief. His gout was acting up again, and he was now using a cane each day. Matilde continued creating rich, sumptuous meals on a daily basis.

It was a bright, cooler afternoon when Anna Grace noticed Sadie wasn't there for lessons. Matilde went to the kitchen garden to cut a few herbs, and Anna Grace asked Isaac and Sam if Sadie was ill. The boys didn't respond, instead looking down at the floor and shifting their feet uncomfortably. Sam was even twisting his hands. What could have happened?

Anna Grace looked at Matilde when she'd returned from the garden. Her usual happy face was grim.

"What's wrong?" Anna Grace asked Matilde. "Is Sadie all right? Is she sick?"

"Boys!" Matilde ordered sharply. "No lesson today."

The boys scurried from the kitchen as fast as they could. They could tell by Matilde's tone that she meant business. Anna Grace watched the boys hurry out the door and disappear down the lane toward the slave quarters, then she whirled to face Matilde.

"What's going on, Matilde?" Anna Grace asked.

"Nastiness," Matilde answered, spitting out the word as though it tasted bitter.

"What do you mean?" Anna Grace asked, growing worried.

"That damned Mr. Reece," Matilde said, tears welling up in her eyes, "He's turned the Master to liking black flesh. They feel they can have their way with anyone at any time."

Anna Grace's stomach turned in knots, hoping what she was hearing wasn't true.

"What? What did they do?" Anna Grace asked, afraid of the answer.

Matilde's eyes were snapping in anger. She spit on the ground, her eyes filling with tears.

"Bastards!" she spat out.

"No, no, no! Not Sadie!" Anna Grace cried out, guessing what Matilde hadn't said.

She thought she would faint. She gripped the edge of the table and held on.

"Oh, Matilde! What can we do? Is Sadie all right?" Anna Grace asked.

"She'll never be right again, Missus," Matilde said with quiet, even, anger. "Her childhood has been stolen from her. They are makin' her their whore."

"Oh, God!" Anna Grace. "Oh, God, no!"

She knew how violated she had felt with Augustus. But Mr.

Reece, too? She raced out of the summer kitchen, doubled over, and promptly lost the breakfast she had ingested a few hours earlier. She knew she had to be strong, so she stood up and returned to the kitchen. She walked to Matilde and took her hands in hers.

"Matilde," Anna Grace ordered. "We need Sadie to be safe. How can we work to help her escape this place? Someone must have a contact. They must!" Anna Grace had a sudden idea. "Mr. Bryant! We can ask him! He wants slaves to be freed. Perhaps he has a contact in Baltimore. I can speak with him this week or slip him a note."

Matilde nodded. Tears were streaming down both their faces. Matilde squeezed Anna Grace's hands.

"You're a good woman, Missus," Matilde managed to say through her tears.

"Just a few more days," she told Matilde. "Perhaps you can tell the men she has her monthlies. Say anything!"

"She's hurting pretty bad," Matilde informed Anna Grace.

Anna Grace closed her eyes. Her hate for Augustus grew. She wasn't sure she could face him. She felt like scratching his face off with her fingernails and screaming and kicking him.

"Let me know if I can do anything. Please," she pleaded to Matilde.

"Thank you, Missus. And now, I have to prepare the richest dinner I have ever made," she said with a saccharin note and bitter smile.

"I'll let you get to your cooking."

Anna Grace racked her brain, thinking through those she knew from the Quaker meetings she had attended. Had any hinted at taking slaves to freedom? She and her father had attended infrequently once her mother had died. She didn't know if her father's lack of faith was due to grief, bitterness, or both. Part of him had died with her mother. He had become a different man, a broken man. Still, she tried to remember some of the names in the congregation. Perhaps, between Josiah and the members in Philadelphia, she could find a safe place for Sadie to live. She walked back to the house to get paper and a pen to write to her father. She would need to figure out what to say to her father, knowing she'd have to be careful in her inquiries.

The door to the study was closed, and Anna Grace heard voices within. It was Mr. Reece and Augustus. Disgusted, she turned away from the door; unable to face them. But as she turned away, Mr. Reece came through the door.

"Excuse me, ma'am," he said, leering at her as he went by, supposedly to the privy. He did his best to lean into her as her skirts took up a substantial amount of room in the hallway.

Anna Grace pressed herself against the wall, her hands against the cool plaster.

"You're quite a lovely little filly," he commented. He chuckled at his own joke.

Anna Grace paled at his comment, but he continued on his way to the privy, leaving her shaken. How she hated that man! She never wanted to be alone with him—ever.

She paced the afternoon away, while Mr. Reece and Augustus were ensconced in the

study, neither leaving. She could not concentrate on reading or mending, so walked down to the river and back, grateful when it was finally time to dress for dinner.

When Pansy opened the door to the bedroom, Anna Grace jumped up from the window seat.

"Oh, Pansy!" she cried when she saw her. "How's Sadie?"

"She's hurtin', Missus," Pansy told Anna Grace. "I sure hope that nice Mr. Bryant can help."

She turned to Pansy to ask, "If you could run away, would you?"

Pansy stopped and stood still. "I don't know, Missus. I just don't know. Part of me definitely wants to be free, but I wish I knew where my husband and child were. I don't want to go until I can have them join me. I fear for my child, Missus. How can my child survive without her mama? And what's happened to my man? He's a feisty one. I worry he's swinging from a hanging tree. If I move on, I'm afraid they wouldn't know where to find me if I escaped," she answered Anna Grace in a worried tone.

She thought Pansy might break down. She could see the emotions behind the mask of Pansy's tight mouth.

"Oh, Pansy," Anna Grace responded in a small voice.

She was having trouble keeping back tears, and Anna Grace put her hand over Pansy's. They both stood there, swallowed up in their grief. Unable to say anything further to comfort Pansy, Anna Grace went down to dinner. She was grateful Mr. Reece hadn't joined them that evening. She avoided eye contact and talk with Augustus, and he took notice.

"What ails you, wife?" he asked her.

"I'm sorry, husband," she said through gritted teeth, not sorry at all, "I am not myself today."

Augustus nodded. "I understand," he said. "My gout is acting up again."

She could hardly believe that he was being civil and attempting a conversation with her. It was then she noticed that he had his foot upon a stool, his cane nearby in the corner. Tyrone seemed to be standing stiffer than ever, and Anna Grace knew why. If she were Tyrone, she would want to strangle Augustus. She stole a glance at him. He seemed to understand and gave a brief nod of his head. He stood behind Augustus so that he took no notice. They ate the remainder of the dinner in silence. Being near Augustus sickened her, and she couldn't eat.

"If you will excuse me, husband, I will retire early," she told him. She turned to Tyrone and said, "Perhaps Pansy can bring a tisane?"

Tyrone nodded and replied, "Yes, Missus."

She stood to go, but before she left, she mentioned to both

men, "Perhaps you should increase the medicine from Mr. Bryant's apothecary this evening."

Deep in her heart, she wished he would drink the entire bottle.

"Thank you, wife. That is a good suggestion," Augustus told her.

She left the bulk of her dinner on her plate and exited the dining room. She returned to her room, where Pansy joined her a few minutes later with a fresh plate of food.

"I couldn't stand to be in the same room with him," she confessed to Pansy. "How can Tyrone serve him? He's disgusting."

"Tyrone knows better than to attack or hurt his Master," Pansy told Anna Grace. "It would mean death for him."

Anna Grace sighed. "I never thought of that."

Pansy stayed with her while she ate and helped her prepare for bed. Before she left, Anna Grace reached for her hand.

"We have to think of something, Pansy," Anna Grace told her. "This cannot go on."

Pansy nodded. She wouldn't confirm or disavow what Anna Grace had said, knowing it was wiser not to say anything.

When Pansy left, Anna Grace tried to relax. Josiah was due in a few days, and she would need a plan on how to talk to him. Finally falling to sleep, she dreamt of speaking with him. Rising peacefully in the morning with him on her mind, her spirit boosted until the reality of the situation settled heavily upon her again. She prayed the days would go quickly, but instead, they crawled by.

The time of Josiah's expected arrival passed, but Josiah didn't come. Anna Grace wondered about the delay. Augustus had not commented about Josiah or the tobacco harvest. When Anna Grace joined Augustus and Mr. Reece for luncheon, the two men were sitting, drinking mint juleps, and acting as gleeful as could be. She was puzzled. They were halfway through their lunch when Augustus turned to Anna Grace slyly.

"That popinjay," he started.

Anna Grace's head flew up, and she stared at Augustus. That was the name he used when he referred to Josiah.

"He never came for the tobacco," he said, continuing to lead her on.

Anna Grace nodded. In her heart, she was miserable. She missed Josiah, and now Augustus was taunting her about him.

"That popinjay was on his way here," Augustus continued, "but the steamboat he was traveling on, caught fire. There were several deaths and missing people. Mr. Bryant was one of them."

She stared at Augustus, unable to respond. She looked at Mr. Reece, and he nodded.

"No word from his warehouse?" Anna Grace asked raggedly after absorbing the initial shock of the news.

"Here!" Augustus crowed. "Here!" He waved a letter in the air.

Mr. Reece and Augustus clinked their mint juleps.

"The letter from his company is mysterious. They stated they couldn't take the tobacco harvest. That's the bad news. The good news is that we already cashed the down payment, and it's ours!" Augustus said gleefully. "So, we're assuming he died in the fire or is missing. That's the rumor."

"How horrible! How horrible to die in a fire!" she cried.

Anna Grace pulled herself up and left the room. She ran down the path to the wharf. It couldn't be true. It couldn't be true!

Anna Grace stared down the river. No one. No one was traveling up or down the river. It was lazy in the afternoon sunshine, glinting like bright, yellow diamonds where the sunshine touched the water. Anna Grace doubled over. She heaved and sobbed. Josiah was gone. What would she do?

How could she survive this? Josiah, Sadie, the cruelty of

Augustus? And what shred of hope did she have? Anna Grace felt she couldn't trust the brilliant sunshine, the sparkling water, or the green of the trees. She didn't feel alive any longer. The grief had torn her heart from her chest. It hurt so badly that she clutched at her chest and crumbled to the ground.

Nineteen

BETH

Ussuri Bay Beach in Russia glistens with sea glass. It was a dumping ground for discarded bottles and other glass and waste from a local porcelain factory.

T here's something about working nights that really knocks your circadian rhythms, Beth thought. She'd belayed her grocery store trip, choosing instead to head home and crawl into bed, not caring nor worrying about Mike for the time being. Sleep was the only thing on her mind.

When she woke a few hours later, she felt much better. She went out to the grocery store and refilled the refrigerator and cupboards with some basic needs. After putting her stores away, Beth went to the water's edge. It was high tide. Little waves lapped at the grassy edge like ruffles on a dress. The water itself looked like two-toned, moiré silk. The light danced on the water, creating diamonds dancing further out in the bay as the afternoon sun started to dip toward the western sky.

Beth was a little sad that she couldn't go glassing this afternoon with the fine, warmer weather, but no matter, she was going tomorrow with Marsha. The weather forecaster had said it was to be in the lower seventies. That would be lovely, even with the still winter-cool edge to the air.

Beth turned to go inside and start dinner. She had picked up a plant-based burger meat package and planned to make a big, juicy cheeseburger loaded with pickles, onions, ketchup, and mustard. There was enough in the package to have leftovers for the next day or two. It only took a moment to stir pub burger seasoning into the plant-based burger. While it cooked on the stove, she prepared the pretzel roll she had purchased at the bakery and added the condiments, cheese, onion, and pickles. Sadly, she had forgotten to pick up a tomato. She poured packaged salad into a large bowl, added some of the onion she had sliced for the burger, and topped it with Ranch dressing. As a treat, she added a bit of extra dried dill weed.

Since she primarily worked nights, an evening at home was a rarity. It was times like this that loneliness assailed her. She worked to put it out of her mind and poured herself a generous glass of red wine.

When the burger was done, she lit a candle on her little table and sat down to eat. She had read somewhere that when alone, it was best to make meals as nice as possible by setting the table. She didn't do this often enough. Usually, standing up in the kitchen to eat or in front of the television were the choices for eating her meal. Tonight, she decided to do something a little different, a meal fit for a queen. Beth bit into the juicy burger and ate the crispy salad. Dill was her favorite herb. She wondered if her landlord would permit her to put in a small herb garden. She made a mental note to ask him. Spring came sooner here in Maryland than in her hometown area in mountainous Pennsylvania, so she could likely plant earlier than if she'd been home. Musing about her potential garden, she cleaned up her dishes and took her wine to the woodstove, where she had built a small fire to keep off the chill that had developed as the sun had set. She pulled out her laptop, thinking she would email her landlord as it was almost too late to put in cool weather crops such as lettuce, radishes, turnips, and spinach. She didn't want to take on peas. If he said it was all right, she would need to pick up seeds and plant them very soon.

She sipped at her wine and emailed her landlord. Another email from Mike pinged in just as she was about to shut down. She didn't need this! Beth took a gulp of her wine and opened the email with a shaky finger. It read *I know where you are.* Beth slammed the laptop shut.

When she picked up her wine to take a drink, her fingers were so shaky that she dropped the glass. It shattered, spilling the wine and spreading shards of glass everywhere. Beth groaned and stood, avoiding the mess, and ran to the kitchen for paper towels. Thankfully, the red wine hadn't gotten on the rug, and it was fairly easy to clean up.

This was so creepy. Mike was creepy. Beth locked her doors and put chairs against them. She didn't know what to do. She sat back down in front of the fire and hugged herself, her mind spinning.

She must have fallen asleep in front of the woodstove as Marsha's knocking woke her up. Beth groaned as the muscles in her neck and body protested sleeping in the position they had been in for the night.

"Coming!" Beth called Marsha. "Coming! Just a minute!"

She ran to the door to move the chair and unlock it, letting Marsha inside.

"You okay, girlfriend?" Marsha asked, noting Beth's disheveled appearance and the chair she was lightly holding onto.

"I fell asleep in the chair last night. Let me throw some clean clothes on and brush my teeth. I'll be ready in a minute."

"Okay, if I make some coffee for us?" Marsha asked, already heading to the kitchen.

"You're an angel!" Beth called over her shoulder as she retreated to the bathroom and then to her bedroom.

She kept her ablutions brief and pulled on jeans, a long-sleeved t-shirt, and a hoodie. Sneakers would probably be the best thing to wear. She went out to the kitchen, sneakers dangling from her hand as Marsha was just finishing the coffee.

"Better?" Marsha asked, handing Beth a cup.

"Now I am," Beth told her. "I think this is a morning for my coffee to need coffee. And to think, last night I felt I was on vacation."

"What happened?" Marsha asked.

It's a long story," Beth replied.

"We have all day," Marsha said, pausing, "If you want to share."

Beth sipped more at her coffee. "I need to think of how and where to begin. Give me a bit to let the caffeine sink in."

"Drink up, then," Marsha said. "We want to get on the road."

Beth drank her coffee and followed Marsha out the door, locking it behind her. They settled into Marsha's car. Marsha was quiet, letting Beth take her time to get her thoughts together.

They drove off the peninsula, driving past the campground and down the wooded lane until they reached the main highway. The trees stood as if waiting for spring. The leaves on the ground looked tired and worn.

"I ran away," Beth blurted out.

"I'm not sure what you mean," Marsha said. "Who or what were you running away from?"

Beth sighed. She knew eventually she would need to tell her story, but she still wasn't comfortable sharing it.

"I ran away from my hometown, my family, and my boyfriend," she admitted to Marsha.

Marsha waited. She didn't ask why instead letting Beth tell it in her own way. She turned south on Route 213. Beth was quiet again.

Finally, Beth said, "No one believed me."

Marsha waited.

"No one believed that Mike wasn't the upstanding, all-around, perfect guy. My family thought he was a good catch. They were pushing us to get married. No one knew or would believe he had another side."

"So...Mike wasn't Mr. Perfect?" Marsha asked. "What guy is? If you didn't want to be with him, so what?"

Beth gave Marsha a baleful look before answering, "He was the golden boy at the hospital where I worked. He was in hospital administration and specialized in marketing. He pulled in some major funding for the hospital. He's Mr. Nice Guy, that everyone loves. But he's not."

"Was he abusive? Did he hurt you?" Marsha asked Beth sharply.

"Not with fists. It was subtle. And he was very, very good at emotional abuse. On the outside, to everyone else, he was the perfect boyfriend. But really, he's a very scary guy."

"How did you meet him?" Marsha asked.

"He came into the ER where I was working. They were doing some kind of photo op for the hospital. I was new, just fresh out of college. We met, and then he swept me off my feet. It was like something out of a romance novel. Boy meets girl—you know the scoop. He brought me flowers, took me to dinner, and wooed my family and me. It was perfect. He snowballed me. I fell in love. But the longer we were in the relationship, the more I doubted him. You see, he made me feel terrible about myself. Things were always my fault. He criticized me daily, whether it was my hair, clothes, or the way I completed something. He worked hard at keeping me away from my family. They thought we were lovey-dovey and exclusive. The truth is he wanted me to stay away from my family and friends unless he chose the time and place," she told Marsha. "And that's just the tip of the iceberg."

"It all sounds gruesome," Marsha commented, her eyes not leaving the road.

"Then, you believe me?" Beth asked her friend.

"Of course!" Marsha insisted.

They were quiet for a few minutes. Emotions overcame Beth, and she stared out the window at the miles of flat fields, an occasional line of trees as a windbreak, and some beautiful farmhouses in various states of repair and disrepair. She had remained stoic telling Marsha about Mike, but now her strength crumpled. She started to sniffle and then cry in earnest. Marsha patted her leg as Beth tried to pull herself together by focusing on the landscape flying past. Marsha chatted on, pointing out the drawbridge when they drove over the Sassafras River. Marsha commented quite favorably on the restaurant at the marina nearby.

As they drove through more small towns and innumerable fields, Beth pulled herself together and shared with Marsha how her mom had favored Mike. He had charmed her with plans of a perfect future.

"It's all so archaic and Stepford wife-ish," Beth shuddered. "Mom dreamed that I could be the perfect suburban wife, eventually give up working, and produce grandchildren, I think."

"Umm, Marsha?" Beth interrupted as Marsha picked up speed when they cleared the small towns. The landscape was now flat and empty as they rolled past fields and signs for upcoming towns.

"Yes?"

"Didn't you say we were going to Tolchester?"

"Yup," Marsha answered. She was keeping an eye on the huge piece of farm equipment that loomed ahead coming in their direction.

"Well, you just passed the road to get there," Beth said as they breezed past the sign.

"I know," Marsha assured Beth, "we're headed to breakfast in Chestertown."

"Oh."

Marsha pulled into a small shopping plaza.

"We're here," she stated simply and nodded to the restaurant. "Evie's Place. It's the best breakfast around."

They walked in to find a seat where it looked like a sea of red-check tablecloths. Marsha led Beth to a booth. Old black and white photos lined the walls.

"Take a look," Marsha suggested. "Those are photos of the park in Tolchester. It was once an amusement park a long, long time ago. There's a marina there now and housing development. I've been able to get us access to the beach. The glass there is amazing!"

Beth took a look at the photos hanging on the wall. There was one of a steamship, of people swimming in old-fashioned bathing suits, and several of various carnival rides. The dates ranged from the early twentieth century to the 1960s. It was a timeline of endless summer happiness.

The waitress came up to them and offered them coffee. Beth and Marsha nodded their heads vigorously at the offer. They looked at the menu which consisted of basic breakfast food. Unsure of what to order, Beth looked around the restaurant and saw that the portions were enormous. The pancake served to the table across from them was as large as a platter.

When the waitress came to take their order, she was patient while Beth toyed with her decision. In the end, she chose eggs, potatoes, and toast, while Marsha went with the French toast. After the waitress left, Beth wrapped her hand around the white china mug that held the steaming, hot coffee, and stared into its depths.

Finally, she said, "Marsha, I feel so very stupid."

Surprised, Marsha responded, "Why?"

In a twisted, guttural sound, Beth answered, "For loving someone that was such a...a shit...a shit to me!"

"But you didn't know, Beth! You didn't know he was a shit. You just wanted someone to love you, and that's not a crime!" Marsha was vehement.

Beth sat up straight up and tears came to her eyes.

"Thank you," she answered in a watery whisper. "I just want a normal life. I want to not be afraid in a relationship or afraid... period. I want to be happy and someday have a good relationship with someone."

The waitress brought their loaded plates, and Beth sniffled.

"Thank you," Marsha told the waitress.

Beth pushed her food around the plate for a few minutes. Eventually, she took a bite. And then another.

Marsha took one bite, and then she looked at Beth with a long, sympathetic look.

"I don't know if I can help," Marsha told Beth. "But I'm here for you."

"Thanks," Beth answered.

After breakfast, Marsha drove to the marina, parked, and led her to the beach. It was fairly deserted. A few intrepid boaters were beginning to prepare their boats for the upcoming season. They walked past a building, still closed for the season, which looked like a small restaurant.

"That's the bar," Marsha explained. "They have great bands. We'll have to come down when the season begins."

Beth didn't answer. Marsha went on ahead, as eager as a child to get to the water's edge.

Beth went more slowly, taking it all in, mesmerized by the sky and water. The sky was a muted blue. The crescent beach between the stone breakwaters was filled with caramel sand and stripes of rocks, shells, and detritus. The waves were gentle.

There were two fishermen on the breakwater, casting their rods. Further down, a guy was sitting cross-legged on the beach. She caught a scrap of music that drifted along the air. Beth was unfamiliar with the instrument. The bell-like music was unique and compelling to listen to, and she had never heard anything like it. She listened again, but the music had stopped. He was packing it up and moving off. She followed the figure with her eyes as he exited the beach.

Marsha was like a young girl. "C'mon!" she called to Beth with sheer delight in her voice. "Come see!"

Marsha looked down, focusing on what she saw on the sand and Beth began to follow suit. Here and there, they picked up glass. It was older than what Beth had found on Carpenter's Point shore. After several minutes of glassing, Beth looked up. She liked this place of sea and sky. There was something special about it. It was a feeling she got sometimes at places. Her grandmother had told her she was sensitive and gifted to be able to feel vibrations from the past.

Beth didn't understand then, and she still didn't, but walking the Tolchester Beach, there seemed to be many voices. Happy voices. She took in a deep breath and let it fill her, like the wind and the sun.

"Wow!" Marsha's crow of delight reached her ears. "It's turquoise, Beth!"

Beth ran to Marsha to look, temporarily displacing her feelings

"Wow, Marsha! That's gorgeous!" Beth exclaimed before resuming her hunt.

They found a handful of aged pieces in whites, greens, and browns. Marsha was positive they were from the early 20th century since they were well-rounded and sanded. They were small, and Marsha told Beth of glass lockets that you could fill with small pieces of sea glass or other things.

A day like she was having with Marsha was just what Beth had needed, the water, the sky, and the sun. Even the clouds. It all came together and fused into something that her soul melded with. It erased most of the uneasiness and outright fear that had enveloped her in the last few days.

Marsha was waiting for her at the end of the beach, where there was a long, stone breakwater. She smiled, her pockets bulging with glass. Beth had found only a few pieces but was happy to be out, just out, and away from home and from the hospital. She walked along the edge of the water where small waves were lapping at the shore. There, just a few inches away, she thought she spied a bit of blue. The water rippled. Perhaps it was a trick of the light. She looked again, unsure of what she was seeing. It had a curve and a gleam. The piece looked dark in the water. Beth thought at first that it might be a piece of black pirate's glass. She had read about pirates on the Chesapeake Bay. Now, that would be a find! The piece of glass was nestled in the sand, but the wave action was loosening it, and she saw it move with the swell and pull from the small waves upon the shore.

She reached down to snatch it before a wave took it away. It was glass in the shape of a circle. It was cobalt blue glass, like the coffee-bean bit she'd found a few days before. Beth held it up to the sky to see the glow. This was an unbelievable prize, the neck of a small bottle.

Marsha came rushing up. "Beth! I've been calling and calling you!" she scolded. And then she saw what Beth was holding. She sucked in her breath, "Oh, Beth! That's amazing! Why it looks a lot like the small, blue piece you found the other day."

"It does, doesn't it," Beth said. "It could be the perfect ring." She put it on her little finger to demonstrate.

"How cool would it be if it were from the same bottle as the other piece of blue?" Marsha asked.

Beth laughed with unabashed scoffing. "That would be a zillion to one chance now, wouldn't it?"

"Trust, Beth. You never know. We'll probably never know, but it is a cool possibility."

Beth looked at the cobalt ring of glass on her little finger. What were the chances it was from the same bottle as her other, small, ridged, cobalt blue piece?

Twenty

MATTHEW

*Amber glass looks very much like brown glass. Look closely under
light to tell the difference.*

The melancholy of the music artists followed Matthew
into work, where he was a picker in a warehouse. It
wasn't a job of joy, but it paid the bills and permitted
him to pursue his art. He and his team oversaw the picking of
items for pallets to go to other stores. They wrapped them up and
sent them off to the waiting semis to take them to the next destination. There was no talking on the floor. They couldn't listen to
music or books. It was sort of an odd competition that was
extremely physical. Working at night, he made a little extra money.
Picking faster brought in more money. More money purchased
more supplies and tools for his creative job. Making jewelry was
the job of his heart. He only wished it could pay the bills, and
then some. Until then, he worked hard in the warehouse, saving
every precious moment of vacation to go to ASGS Festival and
other sea glass Festivals. He led a solitary life, but he was pretty
happy.

The previous year, he'd taken a trip to Maine, staying at Air

BnB's or with vendor friends from the sea glass show. Matthew had wandered beaches and searched for sea glass. It had been great to visit the vendors and their families in their home spaces. They had become family in many ways.

His vendor friends teased him unmercifully about some of the groupies at the sea glass festivals. It was a little scary to have some of the women texting and emailing him constantly, offering him all sorts of delights from culinary to sexual at the festivals and after. Matthew didn't want to get caught up in that nonsense.

He heard a crash and found his pallet had toppled over. This would require rebuilding, and he would lose valuable time on his pick rate this evening. Matthew cursed under his breath and turned to fix the problem. There wasn't much time for daydreaming on this job. Daydream, and you would likely become injured. A colleague had a gruesome accident a few weeks prior and had lost part of a leg when a heavy pallet crashed down on top of him. It had taken them a long time to get the merchandise away from his leg. By the time the paramedics and ambulance had arrived, it was too late, the leg was injured beyond repair. Daydreaming was not a good idea in this place, Matthew reminded himself as he rounded a corner with two full pallets on his glorified forklift. It was quite an ingenious machine, really. He just needed to remember to be careful. He powered through the night, trying to focus on the task at hand and make it through the night.

It was on a whim that Matthew decided to head to Tolchester to go glassing directly after work. He googled low tide on his break, and knew, that if he hurried, he could make it just in time. He left work the moment he clocked out, picked up a drive-thru breakfast, and was on his way. He was tired from working, but with a couple of days off, he felt he could spare the morning, especially if he could snag some good glass.

Matthew had discovered Tolchester by accident when he'd been boating with friends. They had docked at Tolchester to listen to a band at the marina's bar. After a few beers, he'd wandered to the crescent moon-shaped cove just to glance around for glass. He was shocked at the quantity and quality of glass he'd found on the beach. His pocket was heavy by the time he'd returned to the bar.

Boaters were early birds, and there were already a few preparing their boats for the upcoming seasons at the marina by the time he arrived. He parked and studied their industriousness for a moment before grabbing his backpack and heading to the beach. The air held the promise of spring, but there was still a slight chill. His long-sleeved t-shirt and hoodie were perfect layers against the slight breeze.

Early spring was always a good time to go glassing. His grand-father had once told him how streams would purge in the spring, bringing up all kinds of debris from the bottom. He thought that the bay did the same. Everything seemed to go through upheaval in the spring, whether animal, vegetable, or mineral. Perhaps that was why he felt restless. Not out of sorts, really. Just restless. It would be good to get away from work, his studio, and his neigh-borhood for a few hours.

The beach was deserted save for some fisherman at the end of the breakwater. Matthew dropped his backpack on the sand and fished out a small Ziplock bag. He strolled, looking at the tidelines for glass. He was specifically seeking tiny, older pieces of glass that he could place in stack rings. The stack rings were extremely popular at Festivals and online sales. He could make them quickly and charge forty to fifty dollars a ring. He picked through the pebbles and sought the gleam of the glass, still wet from the outgoing tide. Here and there, he found shards. Matthew was careful. He left pieces that wouldn't fit his jewelry line or didn't inspire his creativity. He wandered the beach and back, always surprised at what he'd missed on the first trip down the beach.

Fatigue from working all night crashed in on him. He went back to where his backpack sat in a puddle of sand, sat cross-legged, and stared out at the sky and the water. There was something about this place that he loved. He could almost feel the happy voices of the visitors who had come to the old amusement park for decades.

Matthew pulled out his tongue-drum. He sat it on his lap and struck a couple of notes, then waited for them to dissipate in the air. He meditated for a few minutes, and then he began to tap out a tune that filled the air around him with a mystical sound that blended with the waves of the tide as it sat on the edge of turning.

Matthew had learned about tongue drums the prior year when he was on his trip to Maine. He'd hiked to the Sand Beach at Acadia National Park after hearing that he could find pink sea glass there. He had driven ten hours straight to the park, hoping to find sea glass treasure. After a futile hunt, he'd fallen asleep in the sand and woken to strange, mystical music. Near the trees, he'd found and met Molly and Noah Manafort playing tongue drums. A small crowd had gathered. Noah and Molly had seemed oblivious to the crowd and completely focused on their music. Their music wove in and out together, creating an exquisite music piece. Later, he'd learned that it had all been improvised. They played from their hearts, and it worked. It worked well. When they stopped playing for a few minutes, the crowd dispersed. Matthew had waited for the crowd to clear before he questioned them about the instrument that intrigued him. Molly had handed him one. Matthew had taken the medium mushroom-cap-shaped instrument reverently, as she instructed him to sit and tap out on the drum. As he did, he was surprised to find that his heart felt light, and his chest seemed to open.

Noah and Molly had urged him to jam with them for a few minutes, and Matthew was surprised at how their improvisation flowed and blended into a melody. But, Matthew had started to fade. He'd told them he had driven all night to arrive at Acadia in the morning and had bid them farewell, but not before exchanging their contact information. He'd kept in touch with them ever since. And when he'd returned home, Matthew had immediately ordered the tongue drum Molly suggested. He found it calming and meditative to play, improvising with his moods.

Matthew finished playing his drum with the music washing over the beach and the water. He came out of a trance-like state and saw two women come onto the beach. One was older and eager to get to the water's edge. Matthew could tell they were glassers, too. The other one, a younger woman, had large, soulful eyes that looked out toward the horizon. She was beautiful. Her long hair was braided to the side. Matthew watched her for a minute and saw her visibly relax as she stood looking out at the vista. Her friend called and beckoned her to come to the shoreline for glass. Matthew packed up his drum and headed back to the car, home, and to his bed.

Twenty-One

JOSIAH – 1860

Kelly green glass has been produced since the 1930's.

Josiah clung to the bit of wood that buoyed him. Too weak to call out, he lay his head on the wood and closed his eyes. He thought of what happened and wondered what had gone wrong on the steamboat.

He raised his head up again and looked around. The lifeboat he had seen earlier was long gone. He squinted and thought perhaps he could see it near the shoreline. The steamboat had cracked in two and sunk in the bay. The ensuing wave had pushed him further away from the lifeboat. Josiah looked around for any other survivors clinging to bits of wood like he was. He wondered about Abraham. He knew he couldn't swim.

With a very weak voice, Josiah called, "Help!"

He took a breath and counted to one hundred, then called again. Over and over, he yelled at intervals to no avail. He bobbed in the cool, dark water. It seemed very, very deep here in the middle of the Chesapeake Bay. He closed his eyes for a few minutes, trying to figure out what to do. Josiah thought he should probably try to use the board and kick himself toward a shoreline. If he gave himself breaks and rested in between, he hoped he could make it.

Opening his eyes, he squinted in the light and looked around. Which shore was closer? He wasn't sure, so he chose a spot to aim for, hoping there would be someone there to help him out. As planned, he kicked and rested in a continuous pattern. It was exhausting, but he forced himself on, praying he wouldn't fall asleep as it would bring certain death by drowning.

After what seemed like hours, Josiah made it closer to the shoreline. There were people picnicking on the beach, and he raised a hand weakly.

"Look!" a man shouted. "There's someone there!"

A crowd gathered, and it seemed that everyone was staring at him, but no one came into the water to save him.

Josiah waved his hand and called weakly, "Help!" once again.

It took a while, but eventually, two people got into a small rowboat and made their way toward him. They pulled him over the side of the boat, where he lay like a dead fish, breathing hard as they rowed him back to shore.

Josiah was at the mercy of strangers. Fortunately, they carried him to their farmhouse, where they stripped him of his wet clothes and tucked him into a bed. Josiah's teeth began to chatter, and the women of the house brought blankets and a bed warmer. An older lady brought him a poultice for his chest, and a young girl brought him soup and a small whiskey. Josiah downed both with chattering teeth and then fell into a deep, deep sleep.

He didn't know how long he slept— it could have been hours, or it could have been days —but when he awoke, all he remembered in his waterlogged brain and body were hours of shivering cold followed by bouts of intense heat. He was now very, very hot. He tried to swallow. He tried to call out. But his voice was raspy and weak. When he tried to leave the bed under the weight of blankets and quilts, he found his limbs were not obeying his command to move. They were heavy and sore. He fell partially out of bed with a crash, and he heard feet running toward him. The door burst open, and a man rushed in. The man's mouth dropped open when he found Josiah and most of the bedclothes half on the floor.

"Here now, young man, what are you trying to do?" he asked Josiah.

Josiah just looked at him as the man helped him out of the bedclothes.

"I suspect you'll be needing this," he told Josiah and helped him with the chamber pot that was conveniently under the bed.

While Josiah was relieving himself, the man introduced himself as Richard Fox. Josiah nearly laughed. In his fevered delirium, he thought the man looked nothing like a fox with his dark head of hair, full mutton-chop whiskers, and what looked like a day's growth of beard. The man was tall and well-muscled. He looked more like a bear than a fox.

"We need to get you back to bed. You may still have a fever," Richard observed.

Josiah was still too weak to protest but gave a small nod. He let himself be put back into the bed and get tucked in with the many blankets and quilts. It was the briefest of moments before he slept again.

Josiah awoke much later, his eyes searching the mostly dark room. There was an oil lamp that shone with a steady light. Richard wasn't anywhere to be seen, but a middle-aged woman sat in a chair near the bed.

"You're awake," she stated.

Josiah could only nod. He felt he had a little more strength today and started to throw off some of the quilts and blankets.

"Now, now, let me help you," the lady crooned and helped him by neatly folding the blankets back. She had straight, graying brown hair that was pulled back severely from her face and kind eyes.

She had Josiah sit on the edge of the bed with his feet dangling for a few minutes and then helped him to the chamber pot. His legs did not want to seem to work very well.

"You haven't used them in a few days. Give your legs a chance to remember they're part of your body. You need to be patient."

"And, good morning, I am Lucy Fox. I think you met my husband yesterday," she told him.

Josiah nodded and introduced himself before asking, "How long have I been asleep?"

"Oh, about four days. Your body had to recuperate, and you had a fever," Lucy told Josiah.

His stomach growled, and Lucy Fox chuckled before saying, "You're on your way to feeling better if your stomach is beginning to growl. Let me fetch you something to eat and drink. You rest, and I will be right back."

Josiah sat on the edge of the bed. He was anxious to find out more about what had happened. He had no idea if Abraham was alive or dead. He needed to let someone in Baltimore know that he was alive.

Josiah looked out the window. There was a lightening in the Eastern sky where the horizon went from black to charcoal to a blue rising above a dull orange. He could begin to see well-tended fields about the house and what looked like an orchard. He heard a rooster announce dawn as the sky brightened more, and smelled breakfast cooking. Josiah was surprised at how weak he was and lay back down in the bed with a flop.

He stared about the room. It was a simple, spare bedroom. He was resting in a spindle post bed. There was a matching bureau against one wall and a rocking chair near the fireplace. The windows looked out upon the land, and Josiah could see water in the distance. He shivered inwardly when he looked at the bay. How far had he swum? He didn't see any vestiges of the steamboat, and he didn't know where he was.

The woman returned carrying a tray filled with fresh peaches, eggs, and heartily sliced bread covered in creamery butter. There was a cup of steaming, hot coffee as well. Josiah's mouth watered when she set the tray on the side table.

"Let me help you sit up," she told him.

She propped pillows behind Josiah so that he could sit up comfortably and put the tray on his lap.

"Eat up," she ordered, "but slowly. I hope the food settles all right."

She pulled the rocker closer to the bed and sat down.

"I introduced myself earlier, but I'm not sure you remember. I am Lucy Fox," she reintroduced herself. "My husband and I own this farm and orchard," she told him and nodded out the window to indicate their land.

"I'm Josiah Bryant," he informed her between bites of the soft, fluffy eggs cooked to perfection. "I'm from Baltimore."

"And a survivor!" Lucy pointed out. "You're a very lucky young man to be alive."

"And where am I exactly?" Josiah asked. He couldn't remember where the steamship was in their travels when the explosion had happened.

"Oh!" Lucy replied. "You're at the edge of the Patapsco River, just before the bay. It's called Sparrows Point. That steamboat exploded and caught on fire and sank in over one hundred feet of water in the middle of the river!"

Josiah cringed, thinking of Abraham and wondering where he was.

"How long have I been ill? Have you heard of any other survivors?" Josiah asked, anxious for news.

"Your job was not to die in the last few days. You swam a long way and had a fever. We know there were a couple of lifeboats, but we haven't heard of any other survivors. Are you missing someone?" she asked, curious.

"Yes," Josiah answered solemnly. "My man, Abraham. A mulatto free man. I don't think he could swim."

Lucy Fox grimaced before apologizing, "I'm sorry, I don't

know anything about your man. We can ask my husband when he comes in from the orchard."

"And I have to get word back to my business that I am alive and fairly well," Josiah added anxiously.

"All in good time. You're very weak now. You need to build yourself up," Lucy advised.

And Lucy Fox is correct on that point, Josiah thought. Eating breakfast had exhausted him, and he lay back on the pillows. He had a difficult time keeping his eyes open. He heard Lucy chuckle lightly as she picked up the tray and pulled the covers up over him.

"Rest now, Josiah. We'll help you get word to Baltimore later today. Rest easy," she said.

Josiah barely heard her last words as he fell asleep. He woke sometime in the mid-afternoon. Lucy was no longer in the rocking chair. He looked around, squinting in the bright sunshine that filled the room, washing the walls in shadows and light. Lucy had only put a few quilts on him this time, and he easily folded them back and then sat on the edge of the bed, his legs dangling over the side. His head swam a little, but he waited until it passed before putting his feet on the floor. He remembered what she had said about his body needing to remember how his legs worked. The floor felt cool, but his feet felt numb. He tapped them a little to see if he could get feeling back in them. Pins and needles filled the soles of his feet. He was a little scared to put weight on his feet, fearing a fall as he had a couple of days ago. He stared at his feet, willing them to be all right and able to support his legs, when he heard a light knock at the door. The dark-haired man peered around the corner.

"You're awake!" he stated jovially. "Be careful there. Let me help you. Remember what happened the other day?"

Josiah nodded and permitted Richard to support him as he stood up beside the bed. Once again, his feet did not want to hold him.

"Let's try to walk over to the chair," Richard suggested, firmly holding Josiah around the waist with his arms and guiding him across the room.

It was only a few steps, but it felt like miles to Josiah. A wave of dizziness enveloped him. He swayed and plopped into the rocking chair with a grunt. Richard Fox perched on the edge of the bed and looked him over. Josiah used a hand to palm his face.

"I see you're still as weak as a kitten. We like watching the steamboats going to and from Baltimore. They're a sight to see! But that fire! You'll have to tell me what happened on that river," Richard commented.

Josiah sighed and closed his eyes for a moment before he shared his story. He told Richard how he and Abraham had boarded the steamboat in Baltimore. He described the interior and the exterior and how the wheel worked. It was a marvel. Josiah mentioned smelling smoke and then seeing fire. He told Richard how he helped people get into lifeboats and away from the fire. He remembered hearing an explosion and catapulting into the air before landing in the river among fiery debris. He told him how he couldn't find Abraham, who had been standing near him on the deck, assuming he was blown off the ship as well. The boat had burned quickly, and Josiah told Richard how he'd nearly drowned, and his boots had been sodden, like lead weights. He'd been unable to untie them, so he'd had a choice, to sink in the river like the burning ship, or to use the piece of wood as support and try to get to shore by kicking and resting.

"Undoubtedly, you know the rest," Josiah ended, "since you pulled me out of the water."

"Oh, my," Richard said quietly, listening to Josiah's story. "No wonder you're weak. Between the explosion, the swim, and the shock, it's a wonder. It was a good thing my daughter and her young, strong husband were visiting that day. It was my son-in-law who helped pull you from the water. He helped me bring you up here, too," Richard commented and nodded at the room.

Then he asked, "Are ye hungry?"

Josiah was still a moment. His stomach growled, and he smiled. "I think I am."

"I'll bring you up a tray," Richard told him. "Lucy's cooking us a nice meal. When you get stronger, you can come downstairs. After you've eaten, we can talk about whom you need to contact in Baltimore, and we should get the doc to come out to give you a look over."

Richard left the bedroom, leaving Josiah in the rocking chair. He rocked very slowly, wondering whom he would need to contact in Baltimore. With Abraham gone, he was truly an orphan. There was his housekeeper and his attorney, and his employees, but he was now bereft of family. He supposed he should send word to his housekeeper and attorney first. His attorney could take care of any details.

And then it struck Josiah, the contracts! He had been on his way to the Cadwallader plantation and the others to check on the tobacco. He thought of Anna Grace and wondered if she knew what had happened and if she even cared if he were dead or alive. And that cad of a husband, was he thinking he could get out of their contract? He would see about that! Cadwallader and Reece were ugly, slippery men. He wanted no more dealings with them after this harvest, with the exception of wanting to see Anna Grace again. It was a conundrum.

His thoughts were interrupted by Richard bringing in a tray. Lucy had prepared a lovely dinner of chicken, potatoes, green beans, and biscuits. There was a gorgeous slice of peach pie too. He felt ravenous, and Richard was amused as he downed the meal and quaffed a mug of fresh milk.

"I think that's one of the best meals I have ever tasted," Josiah commented as he looked down at the now empty plates.

Richard chuckled, "I'll let Lucy know. You'll make her blush," Richard teased.

But then he turned serious and asked Josiah, "Whom do you need to contact in Baltimore?"

Josiah asked for paper, a pen, and ink. When Richard took the tray away, Josiah had a moment to think. He wrote brief notes to his housekeeper, attorney, and the one manager at the warehouse to inform them what had happened. He requested his attorney to make arrangements for Josiah to return to Baltimore and to provide some remuneration to the Fox family for saving his life and caring for him. He gave the letters to Richard when he returned and asked for them to be posted.

"I'll take these to town in the morning," he promised Josiah.

Richard dispatched the letters, and Josiah focused on healing while waiting for a return on the correspondence. By the end of the week, he was able to go downstairs to eat with Richard and Lucy. And as the end of the following week approached, he had grown restless and very anxious to return to Baltimore.

His attorney, Robert Stirling, responded to Josiah.

Dear Josiah,

It was a great relief to hear that you are alive and doing well after the horrific steamboat accident on the Patapsco River. Many lives were lost, and several individuals are missing. When we could not locate you amongst the survivors, I'm afraid I assumed the worst until we knew further. After learning of the accident and your possible demise, I sent letters to the plantations with tobacco contracts, effectively canceling the contracts until further notice. No other information was divulged. Your warehouse and import-export business are continuing to run smoothly. I'm afraid I have had no word on your man, Abraham Freeman, but will make inquiries.

Regarding your return to Baltimore, I will personally come to Sparrows Point to bring remuneration to the Fox family and provide a carriage to bring you back to the city. I look forward to seeing you in a few days.

*Again, it is with great relief and happiness to learn that you
are alive and well.*
  Robert Steele,
  Attorney at Law

Josiah read the letter twice and shared the contents with
Richard and Lucy that he would be returning home soon.

Feeling better, Josiah began to help around the farm. He
started with small things, like feeding the chickens and gathering
the eggs. He worked on small carpentry projects with Richard and
began to thoroughly enjoy their simple, quiet life. The hustle and
bustle of Baltimore and his import-export business felt very far
away.

Nevertheless, Josiah was happy to see his attorney when he
arrived at the Fox farm in a smart carriage. But he was also melancholy. Staying with Richard and Lucy had given Josiah a sense of
family that he hadn't realized he missed. When his parents died,
Josiah had not given himself time to grieve. He'd been much too
busy trying to keep his head above water and the business afloat.

He had grown quite fond of Richard and Lucy during his
stay. They were all emotional when he had to take his leave of
them. He pressed upon them to stay in touch and hoped they
would come to Baltimore to visit. He would treat Richard and
Lucy like royalty.

If Attorney Steele noticed his emotions when they got into
the carriage to return to Baltimore, he didn't let it show. Josiah
stared out the window of the carriage at the passing countryside,
not speaking.

Twenty-Two

ANNA GRACE – 1860

Deep red glass is a rare find. In the late 1800's it was often used for stained glass windows and lamps. Later, in the 20th century, red glass was used in headlights and warning lights of vehicles.

Anna Grace had sunk down on her knees, her skirts billowing around her, and cried until she couldn't cry anymore. Pansy and Tyrone found her on the wharf. When they tried to buoy her, her head remained in her hands.

"Come, Missus," Pansy said gently.

"Let me help you, Missus," Tyrone said in his deep baritone.

Anna Grace looked up at Pansy and Tyrone with dull eyes. She barely recognized them in her grief, but let them lead her to the house. They led her through the back door and up the back stairs.

"Where's Augustus?" Anna Grace whispered worriedly. "Where is he?" She looked around in a panic.

"He's with Mr. Reece, Missus," Tyrone said, "too far gone on whiskey to do anyone any harm."

Anna Grace nodded. She felt hollow inside. Her mind was blank. Tyrone left Pansy with Anna Grace, who undressed her.

Her limbs felt frozen and as hard as a small porcelain doll. and she could barely move as Pansy put her in her nightclothes and tucked her to bed.

"I will tell the Master you are under the weather," Pansy promised.

Anna Grace nodded. She was in shock, unable to cry another tear. She lay in bed and watched the sun make its way across the sky and the ceiling in her bedroom. Her eyes burned, and she felt as though she had cauldrons of unshed tears, but she couldn't cry. In her mind, she kept asking herself, *What now?*

Pansy brought in a dinner tray a few hours later. Anna Grace had drifted in and out of sleep. She was still shaky and feeling ill so shook her head at Pansy.

"I'm not hungry," she whispered.

Pansy looked pained. "Missus, you must eat," she insisted.

Anna Grace shook her head and turned away. Pansy put the tray on the dressing table and tiptoed out of the room. When Anna Grace sat up to see where she'd put it, she felt dizzy and nauseous. She let her head fall down heavily on the pillow. At this point, she didn't care if she lived or died.

The next day, she couldn't get out of bed. The day passed in a haze of sleep, tears, and dreams.

Pansy came to her the second day. She spoke sharply to Anna Grace, who lay like a flounder in the bed, staring at the ceiling.

"Missus!" she scolded Anna Grace. "You need to get out of bed! We need to figure out what to do for Sadie. Please, Missus."

Anna Grace turned to look at Pansy. She couldn't talk at that point. She continued to stare blankly. Pansy held out her hand, and Anna Grace looked at it for a moment, then put her hand in Pansy's, who smiled her beautiful smile. Anna Grace couldn't help tearing up once again. Pansy patted her arm in encouragement.

"I know he's deep in your heart, missus," Pansy told her

solemnly, "and there's no one who can take that from you. No one." Her voice was firm.

"It seems you know something about that, Pansy," Anna Grace replied gently.

She put her hand over Pansy's hand, so their fingers intertwined briefly, Anna Grace's porcelain fingers to Pansy's brown sugar ones. They understood one another.

Anna Grace put one leg out of bed, then set her foot on the floor. The reality of the solid floor supported her as she stood. She sighed and teared up again. She had to face the world. This was similar to how she had felt when she'd lost her mother. Pansy tugged a little at Anna Grace's hand, pulling her gently from the bed to the dressing table. She brushed and combed Anna Grace's hair as Anna Grace stared in the mirror at her hollow-eyed self.

Eventually, she found her voice. "How's Sadie?"

"Hurting still, Missus. Those men were nasty to her. She's in about the same shape you've been in. She's curled up in her bed. She won't talk to no one," Pansy told her, sadness filling her voice.

"Can I see her? Can I go to her?" Anna Grace asked in a small voice.

"That might be a good idea, Missus," Pansy told her. "Let's get you ready."

Pansy helped her dress. She had a tray with Anna Grace's favorite tea, cornbread, and biscuits with butter and honey. Fortified with breakfast and a purpose, Anna Grace stepped from her bedroom. She hesitated as she put her foot over the threshold.

"The Master?" Anna Grace asked.

"In bed with gout," Pansy said with satisfaction.

Anna Grace nodded and softly went down the stairs. Pansy led her out of the house and through the slave quarters. People nodded to her as she walked through the small cabins but mostly scattered in her presence. Pansy led her to the next to the last cabin in the row. She knocked gently. A woman came to the door and glanced at Pansy and then at Anna Grace. Her eyes grew wide when she saw Anna Grace. Then they grew hard. Anna Grace was a white woman. She was an enemy to this woman and to her daughter. Anna Grace started to speak to her, but the woman looked down and stuffed a fist in her mouth. Pansy shook her head. Anna Grace went silent. The woman let Anna Grace pass.

"Her mama," Pansy told Anna Grace in a quiet voice.

Pansy led her inside the cabin. It was swept clean. A rocking chair was by the fire. A couple of pots were hung over a small blaze. There were pallets up off the floor. Sadie was curled up in a fetal position on a pallet by the wall. She was turned away from Anna Grace, Pansy, and her mother. She didn't move when they walked in but stayed deathly still. Anna Grace went to her immediately. She sat on the edge of the raised pallet and put her arms around Sadie as best she could.

"Oh, Sadie," she crooned.

She hugged the young girl. And then Anna Grace began to cry. Sadie began to cry, and they cried together. They cried, and they cried. Pansy, overcome with emotion, stepped out of the cabin and stood guard by the door. Anna Grace murmured something to Sadie quietly. She repeated Sadie's name over and over, apologizing. When they had cried themselves out, Anna Grace stood up and wiped her eyes.

She told Sadie that she wanted to get her away from Augustus, but that she didn't know how she could accomplish this, yet. Her voice caught in her throat when she tried to tell Sadie about Josiah.

"You are safe for a few days," Anna Grace told Sadie. "We told the Master that you had your monthlies."

Sadie could only nod in response. Sadie sat up then, and Anna Grace put her arms around her.

"I know exactly how you feel," she told Sadie. "Exactly."

Sadie nodded and looked up at Anna Grace with her huge, brown eyes.

"I hate them," she told Anna Grace in a cool, mature voice.

"I do, too," Anna Grace told her quietly. "Don't worry. We'll think of something."

Anna Grace was worn out again when she returned to the house. Matilde had prepared her something light for luncheon, a chicken salad, and a few fried oysters. Anna Grace picked at her food despite the urging from Pansy. When she had finished luncheon, she looked up at Pansy, telling her, "I am exhausted. I don't even know what to do."

"Yes, Missus," Pansy assured her.

Anna Grace went up to her room, her feet seemed like lead, and her skirts seemed to want to drag her down. She reached her room and lay on top of the coverlet. The bed linens felt cool against her cheek and smelled like sunshine and lavender. She took in the lovely smells, breathing deeply. In a few moments, she was asleep.

When she awoke, dusk was creeping and putting an end to the day. Anna Grace was thinking about the small, cobalt blue bottle on the side of Augustus's bed. Josiah had said it was toxic. She wondered if Augustus was taking the normal dosage or if he had increased it. She went to his room, determined to find out.

When she came to the door of his room, she could hear moans from within. She knocked, and Tyrone answered. His face was grave.

"How is he?" she asked dully.

"Not well," Tyrone answered. "He seems to be quite ill."

"Is he ill from gout or from the medicine?" Anna Grace asked Tyrone.

Tyrone looked at her, eyes wide, shook his head, and then told her, "Mr. Reece is gone, Missus."

"What? What do you mean?" she blurted out, unable to help herself.

Tyrone didn't answer but gestured for her to enter the room. Anna Grace looked at Augustus, lying on the bed. He was gray and looked near death. She picked up the cobalt blue bottle of medicine. It was almost half gone.

Gathering her courage, she asked Augustus, "What happened, husband?"

"He took the money. He took our money," Augustus rasped. "It's all gone. We're in debt, wife. With the money gone, the plantation is gone. We'll never recover."

Anna Grace took this in.

"This is why you're ill?" she asked Augustus. Her voice came out more sharply than she had intended.

Augustus shook his head. He looked gray. It was difficult for him to respond.

"Gout?" she asked.

He just looked at her, his eyes blank in shock, pain, and disbelief

"Can we call the authorities?" Anna Grace asked Augustus.

"Long gone," Augustus rasped. "Never find him."

"Excuse me, Missus. I remember he talked about his dream of going out west to find his fortune when he's had too much to drink," Tyrone interrupted.

Anna Grace paced about the room. Augustus watched her with blank eyes. She went to the window and gazed at the twilight gathering around the plantation. Her mind raced. What would they do? She only had inklings of the finances it took to run a plantation. And, Anna Grace wondered about Augustus's funds. He'd made comment to Josiah that he couldn't run a plantation without the slaves. She also knew Augustus and Mr. Reece were counting on the tobacco harvest profits.

Perhaps she could return to Philadelphia and take Sadie with her? It would be an escape for both of them. Augustus, in his current state, couldn't protest.

"Husband, why don't you let me take Pansy and perhaps another maid, and we'll go to Philadelphia to speak to Papa," she suggested, thinking it would be a good way to sneak Sadie from the plantation. As said, the words, 'escape' was in her thoughts.

Augustus's eyes grew wide and then hardened in the horrible look she knew only too well. "Absolutely not!" he croaked out. He pounded the bed weakly with his fist.

Of course, he protested, it *wouldn't be something under his control,* Anna Grace thought.

But, in this case, perhaps he was right. She thought of Pansy, Tyrone, Matilde, and all of the slave families. She didn't know what August would do when he felt better. She could only imagine his rage and what he would do to satiate it. She didn't like where her thoughts took her. Could she remove Augustus from the situation? Could she take him to Philadelphia? But what would happen to the plantation then? Surely, he had an attorney, perhaps in Chestertown? She would need to seek his advice on what the next steps would be to save or sell the plantation.

"As you wish, husband," Anna Grace returned demurely, but her back was stiff and ramrod straight with determination. "Perhaps when your gout abates, we can discuss this more reasonably. Perhaps you can get away from the plantation long enough to accompany me on the trip? Or perhaps, I can speak with our attorney for his advice, while you are laid up with gout? What's his name? Where is his office located?"

Augustus looked uncomfortable. Besides the pain of gout and the discomfort of his dysentery, she could see a welter of emotions crossing his face. He didn't want to lose control of anything, and here he was, helpless. His body was betraying him. His overseer had betrayed him, and now, she felt, he thought his wife was betraying him with thoughts of taking his control.

Of course, she wanted more control. It was time to stop being a ninny. It was time to grow up and steer the course of her future. The future of the plantation and the lives of the slaves.

At that moment, a small ray of late sunshine pierced the clouds as it set, and the small bottle of Colchicine blazed brightly in the light. Only for a minute, but long enough to give Anna Grace a pause. She looked at the bottle. She looked at Augustus. She remembered what Josiah had said. Could she steer the course of the plantation? She looked at Tyrone, whose eyes met hers. Did she see an imperceptible nod from him?

Augustus's voice was a ragged, stage whisper, "Alfred Beachum. Chestertown. Send for him."

"I will, husband. I will send for Mr. Beachum, and we will seek his advice," Anna Grace told Augustus.

He seemed a trifle relieved.

"But you must be feeling a trifle better to speak with Mr. Beachum. You should take this medicine from Mr. Bryant," Anna Grace ordered.

Tyrone handed her a cut, crystal glass. She splashed some raspberry cordial into it. Then she reached for the small, blue bottle of the Colchicine. Her hand trembled as she held it above the edge of the glass that held the raspberry cordial.

Would this large dose kill Augustus? she thought. Her mind raced. *Could it be considered a mercy killing? Would it be mercy for Augustus from his pain or for all those he abused?* She hesitated, looked at Augustus again, then back at Tyrone.

If she did this, she could return to Philadelphia. Maybe take Sadie with her and introduce her to a new, safer life. She could free her and pay her wages. In fact, she could sell the plantation and free all of the slaves. She could become a part of the Underground Railroad like many other Quakers. She could be part of the cog in the machine that would save black folk. She would have a purpose and help people. Without any further hesitation, Anna Grace poured the remaining colchicine into the glass.

"Here, husband, drink this," she said, handing him the glass.

Tyrone's eyes were wide, but he didn't say a word.

"Good wife," Augustus rasped as he reached for the glass.

Anna Grace's hand faltered at his words. The liquid shook dangerously in the glass as it nearly reached Augustus's hand. She wasn't a good wife. Here, she was about to commit murder. She glanced at Tyrone again. Her back twitched from the most recent blows from Augustus's belt. She thought of Sadie, raped and broken on the pallet in her slave quarters, curled up in grief that no woman should bear.

Tyrone helped Augustus sit up in bed. Anna Grace helped Augustus hold the glass to his lips. He drank it, sputtering when he took a gulp.

"It will help," Anna Grace asserted, feeling terrible about her lie. "Drink it down."

Augustus drank the Colchicine and the cordial, then he lay back in the bed, panting.

"Give it some time," Anna Grace said calmly. "You'll feel much better soon."

As if in a dream, Anna Grace took the small, ridged, cobalt blue bottle in her hand, then she walked down the stairs and to the wharf.

She felt numb. She felt no remorse in giving Augustus the colchicine. What he had done to Sadie with Mr. Reece was unconscionable. Augustus had been a cruel husband. The abuse she'd suffered at his hands was given without remorse. She stared at the bottle in her hand. A wind had picked up, and it blew her hair wildly about her. She felt like a madwoman, but she also felt very, very sane. She stared at the bottle one last time as it sat innocently lying in her hand, gleaming in the last rays of the setting sun. Anna Grace smiled. She thought of Sadie. She thought of Josiah. She thought of herself. Then, she smiled again and tossed the small, cobalt blue ridged bottle as far out into the river as she could. She watched it as it floated for a moment, filled with water, and sank to the bottom of the river.

Anna Grace walked toward the house. The late afternoon sunshine lit the sky in a glorious, rosy backdrop to the plantation house. She knew what she would find. She really didn't care.

Josiah was gone. She had nothing more to lose. She had no remorse. She had only the future.

Tyrone met her at the door. He nodded at her. She knew the unspoken words. She returned his nod and took a deep breath. This was the start of a new chapter in her life. She would free the slaves, sell the plantation, and return to Philadelphia. Beyond that, she didn't know, but she did know that it would begin tomorrow.

The door closed behind her as if closing the door on her old life, leaving an opening for a new life. It beckoned with the last vestiges of the light of the day. It blazed with a promise. Anna Grace knew this in her heart. She silently thanked Josiah for the small, ridged, cobalt blue bottle. It had brought her freedom. She walked up the stairs, smiling.

Twenty-Three

BETH

Seaham, England, is considered the United Kingdom's Sea glass treasure chest.

On the way home, Marsha broached the subject they had avoided talking about all day.

"What happened, Beth? What happened to changing your days off from vacation to something else?" Marsha asked.

Beth sighed. Her eyes strayed out the window, then down to her hands.

She turned to Marsha and said, "Today's been good. Today's been like a vacation."

"And..." Marsha pressed.

"I think Mike knows where I am. I'm terrified, Marsha!" Beth confessed.

"What happened?"

"He sent me a couple of emails. The one said, 'gotcha.' The other email said, 'I know where you are,'" Beth told her.

"Those are threats!" Marsha gasped.

"I know," Beth said. "And the reason I left is because of his

constant and abusive words and criticism. His volatility had esca-
lated to threats. He's scary, and he had convinced me that he had
all the power. He probably still thinks he does."

Marsha was quiet.

"I really, really don't know what to do," Beth said.

"Do you feel safe where you live? Do you need to come and
stay with me?"

"I don't and won't impose on you and your husband, Marsha.
I'll be fine," Beth told her. "I appreciate you listening to me."

"Of course," Marsha said, reaching over to pat Beth's arm.
"Keep me in the loop, okay?"

Beth nodded. They had pulled into the small driveway at the
cottage. The afternoon sun lit the trees in the woods behind the
cottage, and the water had turned gold.

"Thanks, Marsha. It was a lovely day, and thanks for
listening."

Beth got out of the car, and she noticed Marsha waiting for
her to unlock the door and get inside the house before she left.
She plopped down in the upholstered chair that looked out the
window to the water. The sun was coming her way now, making
its path across the sky to set behind her and the cottage. The water
was swathed with golden light. Beth thought about the lovely day
at Tolchester and how it had erased the fear for a short while. She
was relieved she had confided in Marsha. She'd needed to talk with
someone about the situation with Mike.

Mike. A cold spot of fear rumbled in her belly. She remembered the Christmas party. Beth had been so excited about her
ruby red dress. She'd thought Mike would like the plunging neckline and had bought sexy, black lace lingerie to go underneath
adorned with red ribbons, complete with garter and stockings.
She'd had her hair done in an updo with long tendrils escaping
that sparkled with diamante pins. Beth had thought she was beautiful for once, at least before Mike had a chance to destroy the illu-
sion. He had come home and told her she was dressed like a slut

and a whore, saying he wouldn't take her to the party unless she changed. Beth had been crushed. She'd started to cry, and the make-up she'd carefully applied had run down her face. Then he'd called her an ugly name and left for the party without her. That had been only one of the many, many instances of his abuse.

She couldn't confide in her family. Mike had isolated her. He read her texts, emails, and monitored her phone. If he saw anything remiss, he accused her of being unfaithful. He even had his buddies watching her. She couldn't imagine what they thought of her. All of those things, along with the yelling, had made her doubt her sanity. Those were the reasons why she had run away. She thought she had run far enough, but now she wondered. She thought she had taken her fate into her own hands. Now, she wasn't so sure. And he was playing his game again. He was trying to control her again and bring fear back into her life. And he was doing a good job.

Beth went out to the kitchen to pour herself a large glass of red wine. She turned on some music. Norah Jones' sultry voice filled the cottage. She sat back in the upholstered chair to watch the water until dusk fell. And that was when the fear returned. Beth locked the doors and put chairs beneath the door handles. She checked the windows and double-checked all the locks. She sat back in the upholstered chair and sipped her wine. Darkness fell. Norah Jones crooned on. Beth fell asleep and, fortunately, did not remember the nightmares that filled her dreams.

Mike had stopped emailing in the following days. The silence was nearly as disconcerting as his threats had been. Marsha thought that he was being intentional, playing a continual mind game with Beth. Beth wasn't about to disagree.

They had come up with a plan. Marsha had a friend in Philadelphia who agreed to drop cards and letters to Beth's family in a local mailbox so they would be postmarked Philadelphia, Pennsylvania, rather than Maryland. She also sent the woman a small fee to pick up any mail from a post office box and forward it to Beth. Marsha also wanted Beth to subscribe to a company that would turn her computer's IP address into an IP address from another country. Beth thought this was a bit over-the-top, and she'd told Marsha that she read too many murder mysteries. Still, Beth felt she couldn't relax. She kept looking around for any sign of Mike and considered Marsha's suggestion of changing her IP address. The companies that sold the software claimed they could switch the IP address on all of her devices.

The fear was constant, and the precautions were stressful. Beth couldn't eat. She lost weight. And then she binged. Her eyes frequently had dark circles under them because she would wake up at the slightest of noises. Marsha scolded her. Beth continued to berate herself, thinking she should have changed her name. She should have gotten a job in a private physician's office. What had she been thinking? She was feeling as stupid as Mike had repeatedly told her she was.

Two weeks after she had set up the mail ruse, she received another email from Mike. It stated, *So, Beth, you think you can hide in Philadelphia?*

She sighed with relief and texted Marsha immediately.

Marsha called her back and crowed through the phone, "Beth! You're safe! We've stopped some of his crazy-ass craziness."

Beth began to laugh uncontrollably, relief in every chuckle.

"Maybe I can sleep through the night now," Beth agreed.

Her insides danced. She suddenly felt very tired.

"I think I'm going to take a nap," she told Marsha.

"Good girl," Marsha agreed. "See you tonight."

Beth hung up the phone and fell onto her bed. It wasn't more than a minute until she fell into a deep sleep.

When she went to work that night, she and Marsha fist-bumped. Beth didn't want to share any of her personal issues with co-workers, but Stan, the orderly, noticed the fist bump.

"What are you celebrating?" Stan asked them.

Beth blanched. Marsha stumbled but said, "Oh, we were celebrating our sea glass finds this past week."

Stan knew it wasn't the truth. His eyes narrowed, then he shrugged his shoulders. Marsha didn't see Stan's dour expression, but Beth did. She didn't like it. It really wasn't his business. Instead of confronting him, she turned to the night's tasks. Stan pushed the empty gurney to the elevator. She gave him a little wave, hoping the friendliness would outweigh his annoyance.

Stella, the day-shift nurse, was working late, completing her paperwork. She looked tired. Mrs. Lingle, a newer patient was in near critical condition. Her blood pressure was soaring, and atrial fibrillation was peaking in an unpredictable pattern. Stella told Marsha and Beth that the patient was on several medications, but they were watching her carefully. Her husband was with her, and he wasn't belligerent but extremely worried about his wife.

"He's sticking to her like glue," Stella said. "I guess we should all be so lucky in love. I think she should head to the cardiac ward, but I haven't received the okay yet."

"We'll keep a good eye on her," Beth assured Stella.

Stella gave them the rundown on the other patients.

"I'm going to start the introduction rounds and take vitals," Beth said.

Marsha nodded. "See you down the hallway in a few minutes."

Beth first checked on Mrs. Lingle. Stella was right. Mr. Lingle was sitting beside her, looking adoringly, but worriedly at his wife. He held her hand in his. Mrs. Lingle looked gray. Beth glanced up at the monitor. She introduced herself and took the vitals, noting that her blood pressure was still fairly high.

"Have you heard anything from the doctor?" Mr. Lingle asked Beth.

"I just got on shift. Stella, your other nurse, said the doctor had been contacted. I'll contact the doctor again as soon as I return to the nurses' station," Beth assured him. "And I'll check in with you in just a few minutes."

Beth continued working her way down the hall, introducing herself to patients and obtaining vital signs. She heard a cry and a shout for help. It was coming from Mrs. Lingle's room. Beth rushed in. Mrs. Lingle was coding. Beth used her walkie-talkie and called for a crash cart team. Marsha rushed in as Beth started using CPR. The crash cart team rushed in, and Beth moved out of the way to let them work.

Marsha asked Mr. Lingle to step outside. He had completely broken down, wringing his hands, and crying, "no, no, no!"

Beth guided Mr. Lingle to the chair at the computer station, then she heard the unmistakable sound of the heart monitor flatline. One team counted down in warning to administer the electric shock of the automated external defibrillation device. The loud buzz and then silence. The flatline tone again. The team counted down again. Bang! Silence. Flatline noise.

Marsha emerged from the room, her face pale. Mr. Lingle stood up from the chair.

"Mr. Lingle, I'm so very sorry," Marsha began.

"Oh, no," he said in a strangled voice. He stumbled, and Beth caught him by the arm.

"This can't be happening. She was just fine. Why? Why? Why?" he asked, his voice rough with emotion.

"I wish I knew," Beth replied.

Beth had a hard time grasping Mrs. Lingle's death. Her heart ached for Mr. Lingle. Here she was, fighting against someone horrible and uncaring who was healthy and alive. And here the Lingles, who loved and cared for each other, were torn apart. She didn't understand why good people like the Lingle's needed to suffer. It wasn't fair. But, as the old adage went, life wasn't fair. Her struggles with Mike were a testament to the statement. This is when Beth hated her job, seeing people suffer – either the patient, the families, or both. She felt helpless.

"May I sit with her?" he asked.

Marsha peeked in the room. The crash cart team was just exiting. She surveyed Mrs. Lingle's body and the area around the bed before she nodded to Mr. Lingle and to Beth.

"Mr. Lingle, is there someone I can call for you? Can I get you some coffee or tea?" Beth asked him.

The shock was registering, and Beth wasn't sure if Mr. Lingle heard her. "There's no point," he told Beth and Marsha. "We couldn't have children. She was all I had. She was the love of my life. What am I going to do without her?"

Beth watched Mr. Lingle walk into the room with his dead wife. His face was crumpled with sorrow, emotion, and grief. He stood by the bed a moment and then kissed his wife's forehead. He sat down and put his hand on hers and just stared at their two hands, gnarled in age, adorned with thin bands of gold.

Beth returned to the nurses' station subdued. She put a call into the social worker's office and to the pastor on call.

"That poor man," Beth commented to Marsha when she hung up the phone. "What devotion!"

"Rare these days," Marsha replied.

The social worker and pastor came to the floor to assist Mr. Lingle. They led him to a family consultation room where they could discuss arrangements with him and give him what comfort they could. Someone from the morgue came to take care of the body.

Unfortunately, emergencies like Mrs. Lingle put Beth and Marsha behind in their already hectic schedule. They barely said two words to one another all evening. Marsha left promptly at the end of her shift at seven, but Beth stayed to complete paperwork and fill in the next team. Stella was on again, and she sadly told her about Mrs. Lingle. On her drive home, Beth thought about Mr. and Mrs. Lingle. She felt a bit of awe and a bit of envy for them. They had lived and loved well for forty-seven years. Beth knew couples that loved one another and loved well, but Beth couldn't shake the feeling that today, people were impatient with each other. No one wanted to take things slowly anymore. And after her experience with Mike, slow was the only way she wanted to enter and be in a relationship.

It was a relief knowing that Mike thought she was in Philadelphia instead of Maryland. The feeling was almost palpable as she made her way into her house. Mentally and physically exhausted from worry and stress, all Beth wanted to do was sleep. When she went to bed, Beth slept soundly and without worry for the first time in weeks. She woke refreshed and ready to face the day or, albeit, the evening. To treat her newfound luck of throwing Mike off the scent, Beth visited the next town over, North Bay, to a small coffee shop and café near the park. They had luscious lattes and delicious sandwiches.

As she drove to the café, Beth noticed that the world seemed to be celebrating with her. Forsythia was blooming, and daffodils were budding. Crocus popped over people's lawns. Spring was here and would officially be here next week with the spring solstice.

The park was crowded with walkers, joggers, families, and couples. Beth had called ahead for her food, and she was glad she had when she saw the line stretching out the door for seating. Thankfully, the to-go line was separate, and she was able to move through the crowd to pick up her order. As she wended her way through crowded tables, someone else was jostling the myriad of diners. He bumped into her shoulder and nearly knocked her down.

"I'm sorry," a voice said as she rubbed her shoulder.

Beth looked up to see a tallish young man with long, tawny curls and deep, brown eyes. He looked back at her, concerned, and then recognition blossomed in his face.

"You!" he said.

"I'm sorry?" Beth asked, startled. "Do I know you?"

He flushed and looked down before he answered, "No, not

163

really. I think I saw you at Tolchester Beach the other day. I am a glasser, too."

"Oh!" was Beth's only response. "You were playing the instrument? It was beautiful. I've never heard an instrument like that before. What is it?"

He was about to answer, but a nearby gentleman made a rude noise. People around them were growing impatient.

"Oops, sorry," Beth apologized to the man. "Let me get my food," she said to him. "I'll be right back."

The young man was waiting outside, just a few steps away from the door and the porch of the café when Beth returned. She was flushed from pushing her way through the crowd, balancing her drink carrier and paper bag. She didn't know why, but she was happy to see him waiting patiently for her.

"Sorry," she apologized.

"No need," he said. "The rude guy should be the one apologizing. To answer your question, the instrument is a tongue drum. It's ancient in origin, from the Aztecs. There's an African counterpart, too."

"The sound was glorious," Beth said. "And the beach was the perfect place to play it with the water, the sky, the sand, and the sun."

He looked at her, a little surprised.

"Thank you," he said.

The sun was beginning to go down, and the sky was on fire.

"This would be a good time to play, too," Beth murmured, looking at the sky.

"I wish," he commented, "but I need to get to work."

"Me too," Beth replied, "and it would be good if I arrived with the coffee still hot. It was nice talking with you."

"Same here," he returned. "Maybe, I'll see you here again, or in Tolchester."

"Maybe," Beth replied, not sure what else to say.

Twenty-Four

MATTHEW

In northeastern Britain, near Shippersea, eggs of glass slag wash up onto the shore. They're called Dragon's Eggs.

Matthew slept until late. After a bite to eat, he started making stack rings with the small pieces of glass he'd picked up in Tolchester. He set up an assembly line to create the bezels and the ring shanks. He soldered the bezel to the shanks and set the sea glass. It was after midnight when he finished. He put the rings in the tumbler with some steel shot, water, and a few drops of dishwashing liquid. He started the tumbler and listened to its rhythmic whoosh, whoosh, whoosh.

He took out a beer and settled on the couch to look out at the bay. The moon had risen. It was traveling across the glittering, star-filled sky, and the moon sparkled on the water as it made its way across the bay. Darkness danced across the water, rippling with the tide. Black diamonds. That was always what he thought about when he saw the water sparkle like this. Black spinel on steroids. His mind went back to the beach. He remembered the bay and the sky. He remembered the girl with the long, dark braid and the soulful eyes. He wondered who she was.

He drank a second beer and wondered about himself and his life. Molly had chided him, telling him to get "back in the saddle" again. He hadn't listened to her. He didn't know anyone he wanted to be in the saddle with. That was, until today. But it was an impossibility. He didn't have a clue to who she was. He chugged the rest of his beer and went to bed. And he dreamed.

He went to the local café to pick up a coffee before his shift. There she was! The girl with soulful eyes. Their brief conversation intoxicated him, and he was dearth to ask for her phone number.

"Maybe," had been her reply when he commented he might see her again at the cafe. What did that mean? Matthew didn't have time to mull it over because he was running late to work himself. He drove quickly to the warehouse, parked, and jogged across the expansive parking lot inside to where the time clock was waiting, gloating at him. He waved his ID badge, and the chip inside registered his time. He wasn't late, and he was relieved. If they had three late arrivals, the workers could be fired on the spot. He had never been late, but he didn't want to be.

Matthew didn't permit himself to think of the woman from the beach until after his shift. He threw himself into his work, picking items and building pallets for the incoming trucks. Even though the air was cool outside, Matthew worked up a sweat as he raced around the warehouse, trying to beat his own time and his own record. It was a game to him. And it was something he could do since he wasn't permitted to chat with his co-workers while on the floor. Matthew frequently wondered if warehouse workers would one day be replaced by automatons. He felt like a human automaton most days. In his strange streak of humor, he'd even thought of dressing as the tin man from the Wizard of Oz or C3PO from Star Wars. He didn't think his boss would see the humor, however.

Matthew left the next morning, exhausted by his efforts to challenge himself. His superiors were delighted with his numbers which reflected how quickly and accurately he picked items and built pallets. If Matthew was an eye-roller, this would have been the time to do so, but discreetly.

In his car, he released his hair from the elastic band that had held it during his shift. He shook his head like a dog and leaned back. Home. He wanted home, and he wanted to sleep. And he wanted to think about his encounter with that beautiful woman.

Matthew couldn't believe it when he'd seen her at the café. He'd spoken with her but realized he didn't ask her name or for her phone number. By the looks of it, she worked nights as well. He had prattled on about tongue drums. She'd listened, and with interest, but their time had been short. Now, he had to figure out how to see her again and ask her name this time.

A horn beeped loudly at him. Roused from his daydream, he realized he was still at the stoplight, and it had turned green. Matthew waved to the car behind him. They were obviously in a hurry to get somewhere and zoomed passed him at the first chance, glaring at him for good measure.

He didn't care. It always seemed like the people who passed him in annoyance and fury always ended up at the next stoplight along with him. He always chuckled when he saw this, as the impatient drivers never got very far.

Matthew sighed with relief as he turned onto a secondary road that went past the marinas and led to his home. The neighborhood was quiet. There was one runner, two dog walkers, and a cyclist this morning. Everyone waved, but he didn't stop to chat with anyone. They knew he was just getting in from work and likely tired. He pulled into his small driveway and climbed to his second-floor apartment. Matthew dithered about making coffee but decided against it. He settled for a banana and a slice of cheese before he went to bed.

Just before he drifted off to sleep, Matthew thought of the woman. There was definitely something about her that caused his chemistry to fizz. He wondered if she felt anything for him. He wondered if he would ever see her again. Their meetings, at this point, had been serendipitous. How would they meet again? He had no idea.

When he woke later that day, Matthew knew he needed to focus on creating more jewelry for the upcoming sea glass festival He designed and created a bracelet of bezeled sea glass pieces in a flower design. They were attached to a hammered cuff. He worked all day on the bezels, leaving the forging of the cuff for the next day.

His days followed the same pattern of working, sleeping, and making jewelry until his next two-day break arrived. Then he updated his inventory and double-checked everything he needed for the show. He still felt he needed to make more jewelry. He had the room for it if he wanted to take more pieces. The nice thing about jewelry was that the product wasn't overly heavy. He had a small, flat dolly to maneuver his tote boxes into the show. Mary had worked with him to create a lightweight but sturdy backdrop with tall, wooden frames that folded on hinges, fishermen's nets, a banner, and clever, battery-operated, LED light fixtures. He had the fabric for the foldable tables and antique boxes for his locked glass cases to sit upon. A foldable stool completed the ensemble, and he was ready to go. Matthew started stacking the boxes for the displays in a corner of the garage where he could tote them to the car to pack for the festival.

Throughout the week, he drove by the café on his way to work, hoping to catch a glimpse of his mystery woman again, but with no luck. It seemed that she had disappeared into thin air. His only consolation was that she likely lived in the area if she had come to the café before work. He wondered where she lived in North Bay.

Twenty-Five

ANNA GRACE – 1860

Most of the cornflower blue glass comes from milk of magnesia bottles.

Anna Grace was a new woman after Augustus's demise. Her freedom had given her strength. She asked Tyrone to get help to take care of Augustus's body. She dispatched a letter to the attorney, Mr. Beachum, in Chestertown, and asked Pansy if she could enlist some of the women slaves to create a mourning wardrobe as soon as possible.

"Please, no frills and furbelows. I'll be returning to my Quaker home, and we wear plain, simple clothes there. Augustus insisted that I dress differently here. One of my childhood dreams was to not dress plain. He did make that dream come true," Anna Grace told Pansy dreamily, fingering the dresses. "I let my vanity get away with me, I think, with these clothes."

Pansy made an audible scoff. "You're not vain, missus," she insisted.

"Thank you for saying so, Pansy. In the Quaker world, wearing these clothes would make me vain. Quakers pursue their own inner light and reject the world's vanity. Augustus also insisted that I drop the Quaker "thee" and "thou." At first, he was nice about it, but then he ridiculed me when I accidentally dropped in a 'thee' or a 'thou' into the conversation." She sighed as she said this. "Now, I'm used to talking differently. When I go home, it will be like learning a new language."

Anna Grace looked through her clothing and said with dismay, "I'm not sure what to do with all of these clothes! I'll be in mourning dress for two years. I will need to get Quaker clothes tailored again." She turned to Pansy. "Pansy, why don't you distribute the dresses amongst the slave women? Would that be all right?"

"Oh, missus," Pansy breathed. "They would be cherished."

"Good!" Anna Grace replied stoutly. "Then it is done. I am sure you'll figure out how to be fair. That's a huge worry taken away from me. Thank you."

"Yes, missus," Pansy said, but she was distracted. She eyed the beautiful dresses and touched the fine cloth. "Yes, missus," she said again, "thank you."

"Pshaw, I should be thanking you!" Anna Grace told her. "But for now, we have more work to do. "

Anna Grace enlisted assistance in moving her bedroom, the place where Augustus had abused her, to a guest room down the hall.

There was a small graveyard on the plantation. Anna Grace planned to bury Augustus there, beside his parents. Tyrone arranged for a group of men to dig the grave. They also sent for a nearby minister to say a few words. She wanted to keep things as simple as possible. They made arrangements for Augustus to be buried by the end of the week.

A sense of peace and relief embodied the plantation. As far as Anna Grace could tell, everything ran like clockwork. She would need to consult with Mr. Beachum on the ongoing business of the plantation.

He arrived the next day. Mr. Beachum viewed Augustus's

body and shook his head, "All that gluttony," he murmured as he eyed Augustus's portly form on the bed.

Anna Grace remained quiet and hoped she appeared demure in her mourning garb that had been hastily stitched together. She motioned for Mr. Beachum to accompany her to the dining room where Matilde had cooked a superb luncheon.

"Your cook is excellent," Mr. Beachum stated as he wiped his lips after finishing his dessert of a featherlight sponge cake. "Definitely a prize for the plantation."

Anna Grace winced at his remark about Matilde being a 'prize,' thinking he was referring to her slave status, but she demurred and returned, "Thank you. I'll let Matilde know how much you enjoyed the meal."

"What are your plans now, Mistress Cadwallader?" Attorney Beachum asked.

Anna Grace outlined her thoughts of selling the plantation and freeing all the slaves. Mr. Beachum was shocked. He urged Anna Grace to think again. He advised her to send the authorities after Mr. Reece.

"I will agree to send authorities after Mr. Reece. He should be found and prosecuted for what he has done," she replied bitterly. "But, I am resolute on freeing the slaves. I am a Quaker, and I believe all human beings are equal and deserve respect. The slaves on this plantation will be free. I will return to my home in Philadelphia," she stated in a cool tone.

"All right," Mr. Beachum said slowly. "Beg my pardon, Ma'am, I had no idea you were a Quaker."

"My husband did not permit me to use the Quaker mannerisms," she explained. "And there's another matter, if her mother will permit it, I would like to take young Sadie to Philadelphia with me. She can earn wages working in my home until she is comfortable to venture elsewhere, but she will always have a home with me," Anna Grace informed Mr. Beachum before saying thoughtfully, "And, I don't know if it's possible, but can you inquire as to where Pansy's husband and child are? She has been of invaluable service to me, and I would like to do this for her. Perhaps you could take the funds for the search from the sale of the plantation? If she would, I would love for her to come to Philadelphia, too. I suspect it depends on the news we hear about her husband and daughter."

Mr. Beachum nodded. He was busy taking notes on everything Anna Grace had told him.

He looked up at her and asked, "What about the contents of the house?"

"Nothing belongs to me except my clothes and a few books," Anna Grace admitted. "I have no attachment to the household belongings. They can be auctioned or sold with the plantation."

Mr. Beachum continued to busy himself with notes, and Anna Grace looked up at Tyrone. He gave her a subtle nod of approval.

"I believe I have the information in my files, but I will need all the names of the slaves for the writs of freedom. If you could compile a list, I can double-check it against the one that I have at my office. There may have been births or deaths, or perhaps sales and purchases since Mr. Cadwallader presented the list to me. I will also begin making inquiries about potential buyers of the plantation. I'll wait until the funeral is over before parading them here," Mr. Beachum announced.

"Thank you," Anna Grace replied. "I appreciate your sensitivity. Between now and the time for the funeral, I will work on the list of slaves who will need writs of freedom. I will send Charles with the information."

She turned to Tyrone to ask, "Can you please ask Pansy to come in here, Tyrone?"

He nodded and left the room silently, returning a few minutes later with Pansy, who was twisting her apron in her hands in nervousness in front of Mr. Beachum.

Anna Grace addressed her gently, "Pansy, can you please give

Mr. Beachum details on the sale of your husband and daughter? He's going to see if he can find them."

Pansy looked wide-eyed, first at Anna Grace and then at Mr. Beachum. Anna Grace had never seen her look so emotional. She looked torn, as if she wanted to jump for joy but was afraid to do so or wanted to break down and cry. Anna Grace wasn't sure which emotion would lead.

"Go ahead, Pansy," Anna Grace said gently, touching her arm.

Pansy started to stammer at first but found her usual confidence returning and told Mr. Beachum her story. He took notes, nodded, and wrote more notes.

Their discussion wended through the afternoon. When Anna Grace noticed the change in the light at the window, she asked Mr. Beachum if he wanted to stay to have some tea or dinner.

"No, no," he assured her, "I must be getting back to Chestertown. It will be quite late when I arrive, so I must be off as soon as possible. Thank you for your hospitality, Mistress Cadwallader."

Anna Grace turned to Tyrone and asked, "Tyrone, can you let them know Mr. Beachum is ready to return to Chestertown?"

Tyrone nodded, gave a small bow to Mr. Beachum, and turned silently on his heel.

"Thank you so much for coming so quickly," Anna Grace told Mr. Beachum. "You have been invaluable, and I look forward to working with you in the coming weeks."

They stood, and Anna Grace walked him to the front door where his carriage was waiting outside.

"I will be in touch," he told her.

He nodded to her and went to his carriage. Anna Grace watched the carriage carry Mr. Beachum away. He seemed like a nice man, and she still embodied hope that everything would work out.

Pansy's eyes were shining with unshed tears and gratitude when Anna Grace went to her new bedchamber after a quiet dinner.

"Oh, missus!" Pansy cried, "I can't believe that I might be able to find my man and my little one. Thank you! Thank you!"

Anna Grace placed a soft hand in warning on Pansy's arm before stating, "We're going to try, Pansy. I think Attorney Beachum will do his best. I don't know what will become of it. You will be free, but I'm not sure about your family. Whatever happens, please know you will always have a home with me. You are welcome to come to Philadelphia and work for me for wages or find a job on your own. Right now, I can't begin to imagine my life without you in it. You've been..." her words broke off. Anna Grace took a deep breath, "You've been my family here, and you've cared," she said simply. "And, I think you saved my life on more than one occasion from those beatings."

"Oh, missus," Pansy replied, but was unable to go on due to the emotion in her soul. She helped Anna Grace from her garments into her nightgown.

Word had gotten around about Augustus's death, and neighbors began to arrive to give

their condolences. Tyrone had Augustus laid in the parlor in a dark suit. A black wreath was hung upon the door. Mirrors were covered, clocks were stopped, curtains were closed, and windows were draped in black. They had set up chairs, and Anna Grace welcomed curious neighbors and mourners into the house. Matilde made cookies and special funeral biscuits that would be given to guests as they exited the house. The spicy fragrance of the funeral biscuits spread through the house and around the grounds near the kitchen.

As the mourners began to troop through the house and propriety, Anna Grace needed to be the gracious wife in mourning. She wondered how she was to keep up the façade of deep mourning for the required two years after a husband died. She remembered reading somewhere that it was de rigueur for women to embody grief when their husbands died. And, here she was, wanting to dance a jig at her freedom.

Anna Grace had not met many of the neighbors. When she'd first arrived, Augustus kept them off, saying it was their honeymoon. Later, he ignored the social proprieties. He didn't lock her away but kept her from socializing. Anna Grace wondered if he was afraid, she might divulge what a horrible man he was. On their plantation, he was king and bully. She wondered what others thought.

What Anna Grace gleaned from polite, but strained comments from the mourners was that not many of the men from the nearby plantation had respect for Augustus. They didn't like his bullying ways. Some had known him since childhood. They didn't seem surprised to hear about Mr. Reece, either. He was definitely considered a bad sort. One mourner said, 'good riddance to bad rubbish!' But he hoped the authorities would capture Mr. Reece and bring him to justice. No one seemed surprised that Anna Grace wanted to leave Eastern Shore, Maryland.

The funeral was held a few days later and, much to the dismay of some local mourners, Anna Grace kept the funeral small and private. She wasn't sure she could keep up the charade. And, she had a burning desire to go home to Philadelphia. She had written her father about what had happened, and he had replied that he looked forward to her coming home.

The day of the funeral dawned very hot and humid. The air was oppressive and seemed to press down upon her. Anna Grace thought she would choke on any intake of breath. They made a small procession from the house to the graveyard. A few of the slaves carried Augustus's body, wrapped in heavy, waxed canvas, feet first from the house. The minister and Anna Grace followed slowly, with Pansy and Tyrone nearby. Some of the other slaves held back, looking on from a distance.

At the graveside, Anna Grace swayed with dizziness under the heavy mourning clothes and traditional black veil. Pansy held her firmly by her arm, and Anna Grace leaned heavily on her, teetering back and forth. The minister, who did not know Augustus, led the service using general words of mourning.

Anna Grace felt like a fraud, mourning a man she hated. Hysteria bubbled inside her, and she cried out when the first clod of earth hit Augustus's body. The plunk of the dirt was muffled as it hit the canvas, but it was a final, deep sound, signifying the end. She thought she might be going mad, and Anna Grace didn't know if her involuntary cry was from joy, relief, or perhaps a small, soupcon of grief. She didn't know. Pansy turned her away from the grave and nodded to Tyrone. He would take care of the minister, and Pansy would care for Anna Grace.

Pansy led her back to the house, but her steps were heavy and difficult.

"Come on, missus. You can do this," Pansy chanted. "Just a few more steps, missus."

Pansy helped her upstairs to her room, where she loosened the stays. Anna Grace lay on the bed.

"It's over, Pansy. It's finally over!" Anna Grace said and then, in a small voice whispered, "What have I done?"

"You've saved us all, missus," Pansy told her firmly. "There ain't nothin' wrong with stopping evil. And, he and Mr. Reece were evil. Sadie can sleep a little better now. She's still afraid Mr. Reece will come back. Her mama said it was good of you to take her to Philadelphia. She can start a new life there and maybe have a bit of peace. We're watching to see if she's goin' to bear the brat of that evil man."

"Oh!" Anna Grace started in surprise and asked, "I never thought of that. Do you think she's with child?"

"Not if her mama can help it. She's asked 'Tilde to brew her special teas and forced 'em on Sadie. I don't think there's going to be a child," Pansy shared.

"What a relief!" Anna Grace admitted. "Would it help for Sadie to see Augustus' grave? To make it final, I mean."

"It couldn't hurt," Pansy said.

"I would like to rest a little, but after dinner, Sadie and I can walk to the grave. Can you please let her know?" Anna Grace

"Yes, missus, that would be fine," Pansy agreed. "You rest now."

Anna Grace lay in bed, dry-eyed, and unable to sleep. Her thoughts were a little giddy. She wondered how her Mama would react in heaven when she met Augustus. She thought her mama would slap him silly. But then, Augustus wouldn't be in heaven. He would be rotting in hell, and that gave Anna Grace satisfaction. She wondered what her mama thought of Josiah. Perhaps they were looking down on her. Perhaps. And with that thought, she drifted into a nap.

Anna Grace woke a few hours later. She was a little disoriented in the new bedroom, and not used to seeing the angle of the sun through these windows. It was a pretty room, but the furniture was heavy. She longed for the simpler furniture at her home in Philadelphia.

The door to the bedroom opened, startling Anna Grace. It was Pansy, coming in quietly, in case she was still asleep.

"Dinner's ready, missus, if you'll come down," Pansy told her. "And Sadie's ready to go to the grave after you've finished."

"Oh!" Anna Grace responded, wakened from her daydream. "That will be fine, Pansy. Thank you."

Anna Grace got out of bed, and Pansy pulled her stays lightly before putting on a black dress over all of her undergarments. She went down to a solitary dinner. Anna Grace noticed the food was lighter and not as rich as the meals Matilde had created for Augustus. There was a bounty of vegetables from the garden, and Matilde had created a colorful plate of sliced tomatoes with herbs and a light dressing, succotash, and well-roasted chicken thighs. It was delicious, as usual. When she was finished, Anna Grace walked out to the kitchen where Sadie was sharing a similar meal to Anna Grace's at the table with her mother and Matilde.

"Hello, Sadie," Anna Grace said softly. "Are you ready?"

"Yes, ma'am," Sadie answered.

Anna Grace noticed she had a determined look on her face. They walked to the small graveyard and stood before the freshly turned earth at the grave. Sadie stood as still as a statue, staring at Augustus's grave. Out of nowhere, Sadie gave a little stomp of anger and spit on the grave. Anna Grace was taken aback at first, and then she started to giggle.

"Do it again!" she urged Sadie.

And Sadie did. She spat on Augustus's grave three times before she looked solemnly at Anna Grace.

"It's your turn now, missus," Sadie said gravely.

Anna Grace stared at Sadie. The thought hadn't occurred to her.

"Go ahead," Sadie told Anna Grace gently.

Anna Grace threw her head back and spit on Augustus's grave with all her might.

"Again!" Sadie urged, "And again!"

So, Anna Grace spat on Augustus's grave three times. Afterward, she felt immensely better.

"I won't tell no one if you won't," Sadie told Anna Grace slyly.

"I won't tell," Anna Grace replied gravely.

And they walked back to the house together.

Twenty-Six

JOSIAH – 1860

Clorox and medicine bottles were housed in amber brown bottles.

It wasn't as though Josiah had forgotten about Anna Grace. Truth be told, he'd dreamed about her almost every night. But he was occupied solely on keeping his father's business, no his business, afloat. Without Abraham, Josiah had to shoulder more responsibilities. The missing boat, the broken tobacco contracts, and the loss of his cash in the steamboat accident all dwindled his coffers. Josiah worked day and night to put things to rights again. There was still no word on Abraham, and with each day that passed, hope dwindled.

The steam-boat accident became a memory for most people, but for Josiah, there were daily flashbacks of flying from the boat in the explosion, the feeling of drowning, and clutching that piece of wood for hours. He found himself waking up at night, drenched in sweat, and his throat hurting from what he expected was shouting during his dreams. He woke up, clutching a pillow like the piece of wood he'd clung to for hours and hours.

And he felt alone. He felt very alone. Josiah didn't want to be alone any longer. Everyone he had ever cared about was gone. He thought it was time to settle down and to have a family and to have someone who care for him. But whom? Anna Grace Cadwallader haunted his thoughts. And, it was an impossible dream to fulfill since she was married to that cad of a husband. He would need to find someone else.

He had to get Anna Grace out of his system. He didn't know how to do this, except to see her again and rub salt in the wound. With the broken contracts, Josiah needed to play nice with the plantation owners, renew the contracts, and get the harvests back. It might take a lot of bowing and scraping, but it had to be done. He hoped they hadn't sold their harvest to someone else due to the accident. He had to get the tobacco purchased, sold, and exported soon because the busy oyster harvest season would begin in a few weeks. That was one of his busiest times of the year, and one of the most lucrative.

Josiah made arrangements to visit the plantations once again. He also reserved tickets on a steamship to take him across the bay. His heart was in his throat when he stepped on board, and he stayed far from the turning wheel. White-knuckled, his hands gripped the rails as the ship sailed down the Patapsco River. He wished he could signal to the Fox family that he was passing by. He looked longingly at the farm and remembered Mistress Fox's peach pie.

The steamship glided through the water, and eventually, Josiah relaxed a modicum. He sighed a great sigh of relief when the steamboat docked, and he transferred to the shallop that would take him to the Cadwallader plantation up the Sassafras River.

Stepping from the shallop onto the small, wooden wharf, Josiah was once again struck by the peacefulness of the area. The sun was shining, and the birds were singing. He had a better appreciation of these bucolic wonders after spending time on the Fox farm. He breathed deeply, rolled his shoulders, and marched up the path to the house.

He wondered how he would react to seeing Anna Grace Cadwallader again. He didn't relish the time he would need to coerce that cad, Augustus Cadwallader, to rekindle their tobacco deal. Josiah didn't have a doubt that Augustus would demand more money.

As he walked up the path to the house, he didn't notice the fields were quiet. Nor did he notice the stillness surrounding the property. It was only when he came to the large, brass knocker at the front door that he felt something was amiss. He didn't know what it was, but he hesitated before lifting the loud, brass knocker and letting it drop against the door. The sound reverberated through the house. Josiah waited. No one came. He waited another minute and lifted the knocker again, and let it hit the door with a bang. He waited again. Eventually, he heard footsteps that were walking quickly to the door. The large, heavy door swung open, silently. Tyrone stood on the other side, looking more than shocked at Josiah's presence.

"Good morning. It's Tyrone, isn't it?" Josiah inquired, hoping he had the man's name correct.

Tyrone nodded, but still held a vigil at the door, not letting Josiah pass. He almost gaped, but his good manners did not permit him to do so. Josiah was puzzled.

"Are Mr. or Mrs. Cadwallader in?" Josiah asked.

Tyrone still continued to stare at Josiah.

"Tyrone? Is everything all right?" Josiah asked.

"Perhaps you should come in, sir," Tyrone stated.

Tyrone led him inside to the parlor, which stood empty.

"Just one moment, sir," Tyrone stated, and he left Josiah standing just inside the room.

Josiah looked around. There wasn't a stick of furniture to be found. But Tyrone was back in a moment with a chair in hand. He set it down and motioned for Josiah to sit.

Josiah sat, albeit uncomfortably, in the ladderback chair. He looked up at Tyrone questioningly.

"Sir," Tyrone began in his deep voice, "Mr. Cadwallader died unexpectedly a few weeks ago. Mr. Reece ran off with the funds. The plantation has been sold. I'm here, waiting for the new owners."

"And Mistress Cadwallader?" Josiah asked, almost afraid to know the answer.

"She's returned to her father in Philadelphia," Tyrone told him. "In fact, sir, you just missed them by a day."

Josiah let all the information sink in. His ears were filled with the ringing silence of the empty plantation.

"And the slaves?" he asked faintly.

Tyrone stood up straighter and said proudly, "Missus freed everyone."

Josiah's eyes grew big, "Everyone?" he asked.

"Everyone," Tyrone reiterated firmly.

"Good for her!" Josiah quietly cheered.

But now what? How could he get to the other plantations? Where was Anna Grace? And it dawned on him that she was now a widow. She was free of that cad, Augustus! But he had no idea where she was.

"Do you know Mistress Cadwallader's address in Philadelphia?" Josiah asked hopefully.

"No, sir, the attorney in Chestertown knows," he answered quickly.

"And his name is?" Josiah inquired.

"I am really not sure, sir. I'm sorry," Tyrone answered.

Josiah looked around the room, and then at Tyrone, "Is there any way you might have a horse I could borrow? Or I could pay someone to take me to the inn?"

Tyrone thought for a moment before answering, "Jonah is still here. There's a farm cart and a mule that wasn't sold. He could take you to the inn in that."

"That would be excellent. Can you make the arrangements?" Josiah asked.

"Certainly, sir," answered Tyrone. "I'll only be a few minutes."

Josiah sat only for a moment after Tyrone left. He paced the empty room that sounded hollow with his footfalls on the floorboards. He paced over to the windows and back. He paced back and forth and back and forth, wondering how he could find Anna Grace. Not knowing the attorney's name was difficult, but not impossible. It would take time and patience. He also was due to go to Philadelphia. Perhaps this was the time, although the number of mercantile in Philadelphia was daunting, perhaps he could visit his customers and then search out the mercantile that belonged to Anna Grace's father. Tyrone returned.

"Your transportation is ready, sir," he informed Josiah.

Josiah had another idea, and he asked Tyrone, "What are your plans, Tyrone?"

"I'm hoping the new owners will take me on and pay me wages," Tyrone answered. "If not, I guess I'll be moving on."

"I recently lost my man in the steamboat accident," Josiah told him with difficulty. "You might remember Abraham."

Tyrone nodded and commented, "We thought you were both dead."

"Well, I was lucky," Josiah continued. "But I still need assistance. Abraham was free, and I paid him wages. If you're interested, I would like to hire you. It's a position that would require you to be a bit of a valet and also a secretary. There's a bit of travel, and that's difficult with the current political climate if you're dark-skinned. But, you would be with me. I feel I pay well. Why don't you think about it and let me know? I'll be at the inn for two more days." He handed Tyrone his card.

Tyrone couldn't speak but only nodded. He took the card and he finally remembered his speech, "Thank you, sir."

"No, Tyrone, I thank you, especially if you come to work with me," Josiah told him.

Tyrone gave a slight bow. Josiah tipped his hat and went out the door to the waiting cart and donkey. He climbed in, nodding to Jonah, and they started down the road. The cart bounced and rocked, and Josiah thought his head might fall off. It took a while, but they finally made it to the same inn that he and Abraham had stayed at weeks before.

Josiah staggered out of the cart, swaying like a drunk until he got his land legs back from the jostling and bumpy ride. He thanked Jonah and gave him some coins before saying goodbye.

Josiah entered the inn that wasn't overly crowded at this time of day. Smoke hung in small clouds over the few men who sat talking at tables. A few looked up, saw Josiah, gave him an acknowledgment with a nod, and turned back to their companions. The innkeeper greeted him heartily, welcoming Josiah back. He automatically poured a cider and handed it to him as Josiah approached the bar, asking how he had been and if he needed a room.

Josiah quaffed almost half a pint of the cider before he answered the innkeeper. He told him he wanted food and a room for the next two days. The innkeeper inquired if Abraham had joined him, and Josiah had to take a deep pause, reining in his emotions, before explaining to the innkeeper all that had happened since his last visit. The innkeeper, shocked to the core about the explosion on the steamboat, poured Josiah another cider and said 'on the house' quietly so as to not interrupt Josiah's tale. Josiah continued, finding it easy to talk to the innkeeper. Josiah shared what had happened today as well.

"Well, good riddance to bad rubbish, I always say," the innkeeper told Josiah when he mentioned Augustus Cadwallader and Jedediah Reece.

Josiah nodded in agreement. His head was swimming after the heat, the bumpy ride, and now the two mugs of cider. He was grateful to see the innkeeper put down a plate of cornpone and sausage gravy. Josiah dug in right away.

"By the way, I wanted to speak to Mrs. Cadwallader about the harvest. Do you happen to know where she is?" Josiah inquired, being careful of his emotions.

The innkeeper shook his head, "No, sir. Somewhere in Philadelphia, I think. Someone mentioned she had family there. They took a wagon up to the train and went into Philadelphia, I believe."

"They?" Josiah asked.

"Mistress Cadwallader and two negro women," the innkeeper told him.

Josiah nodded, knowing Pansy was likely one of Anna Grace's companions. He didn't know who else would accompany her. Probably one of the slaves she had freed.

"Did you know she freed all her slaves?" Josiah asked the innkeeper.

The innkeeper moved his hand to motion for Josiah to keep his voice down, and he looked around at the patrons of the inn. No one seemed to be taking any interest, and the innkeeper replied sotto voce, "I do indeed! Good woman."

When Josiah finished his meal, he relayed to the innkeeper his needs of a messenger and a horse. He also told him he hoped that Tyrone, from the Cadwallader plantation, may come looking for him for work. He told the innkeeper he had offered Tyrone a job.

The innkeeper nodded. He told Josiah he could use the room he used previously. He assured Josiah he would have a horse available for him when he needed it and would make arrangements for messengers to go to the other plantations with any necessary correspondence.

Josiah wrote brief missives requesting to meet the next day. He sent them off to the plantations with hope in his heart that he could still acquire their harvests.

Twenty-Seven

ANNA GRACE – 1860

Roques Bluff State Park and Fort Popham Beach, Maine, are noted for blue and green sea glass.

Anna Grace was so exhausted she could barely think as they bounced up and down in the buckboard wagon that would take them to the train with their belongings. It was a hot day and dust billowed around them from the dry road as they bounced along. Their driver was cheerful, but not overly talkative. The women didn't talk much either, each caught up in their own thoughts.

Anna Grace worried over the decisions of the past few weeks. Augustus was like a bad nightmare she had put at the back of her mind, but he still haunted her. The responsibilities of selling the plantation and auctioning the contents were daunting. She worried about the freed slaves who had left, one by one, others in groups, to head north to a safer place to live. She had written to her father for information on Quakers who would help her former slaves, and he had sent one of the Quaker Friends to assist. There was still no word on Pansy's husband or daughter. Her maid and friend had become more discouraged each day. Her husband had been sold, bought, and sold a few more times. Apparently, his hot head got him into trouble. Pansy shook her head knowingly when she heard this news.

"My John could never rein in his anger, missus, especially when he saw one of us get mistreated. He's a good man with a good heart. He's a hard worker, too, if they treat 'em right," Pansy stated.

"I'm sure they'll find him, Pansy. We just need to be patient a little longer," Anna Grace told Pansy to what was now becoming a litany.

"Yes, ma'am. I'm trying to keep the faith," Pansy admitted.

Sadie was beside herself to be going on the journey. She was excited and she was scared. Sometimes she clutched at Pansy or Anna Grace who patted her arm.

"Just wait until you see the train!" Anna Grace warned excitedly. "It's loud and huge." She tried to explain what the immense machine was like.

Sadie was terrified of the train and its loud whistle when it pulled into the station. She covered her ears and cowered on the platform. Pansy and Anna Grace practically had to carry her to a seat. Once the journey was on the way, she began to enjoy herself, but still clung to Pansy.

Anna Grace was relieved to reach the city and to get a carriage to her father's house. Her father welcomed them warmly and they settled into the rooms above the mercantile. She returned to her old room, while Pansy and Sadie took rooms on the third floor.

Her father was still a handsome man, tall with a full head of brown hair and mutton chops. He had lost weight, Anna Grace noticed, as his clothes were loose on his thin frame. she suspected he still mourned her mother's death.

He was a successful merchant on Market Street and had made innovations in his general store. He placed price tags on items and had firm prices rather than haggling over purchases. He guaranteed each item he sold. He believed in cash payment and full cash on a return, so, his general store was very popular.

In those first few minutes of greeting, Anna Grace knew everything was not quite all right. It was obvious from looking about the kitchen that her father wasn't eating properly. The house was fairly neat, but very dusty. She would have her work cut out for her to bring it to rights.

She settled her bags into her old room but didn't unpack. Anna Grace removed her bonnet and gloves and laid them carefully on the bureau. She smoothed her skirts and took a deep breath, then she went downstairs to the kitchen. She opened the cupboards only to find they were spare. She wondered what she could cobble together for dinner.

It was then that Anna Grace heard the call from the street, "Come buy my Pepper pot Soup! Spicy and warm, Pepper pot soup!" She had forgotten about the street vendors when she'd lived at the plantation.

Anna Grace went into the store to find her father. He was totting up figures at the register.

"Papa! Papa!" she cried.

It took him a moment, but he looked up at Anna Grace and smiled, "Yes, daughter?" he asked.

"Papa, we'll need dinner. Should thee go and purchase some Pepper pot soup?" Anna Grace asked, remembering to add in the Quaker speech.

"Excellent idea, Anna Grace. Thank thee," her father replied.

He pulled his tall form up from the stool and went to the street to purchase the soup.

Anna Grace bustled back to the kitchen. She would need to get the wood stove going to keep the soup warm. The stove stood, cold and unused in the kitchen. She was having a difficult time getting the fire lit when Pansy and Sadie came down the stairs. Working together, they were able to light the stove.

Anna Grace told Pansy and Sadie about the Pepper pot soup.

She would need to send her Papa out to purchase rolls or bread for them, too. She returned to the store to find her father, followed by the Pepper pot woman, to pour the soup from her kettle into one of their kettles. When he had settled up with the Pepper pot woman and the soup was warming on the cookstove, Anna Grace rummaged around the kitchen and found some cornmeal and flour. She took out a bowl and proceeded to make cornbread.

Pansy put her hands on her hips and cried, "Laws, Missus! When did you learn how to cook?"

Anna Grace laughed a tinkling laugh, "Oh, Pansy! I am not a very good cook, not like Matilde, but I know some rudimentary things. My Mama put a spoon in my hand whenever I was restless. She taught me to cook things to keep me busy and out of trouble. And I'm not the fine lady of the manor here in Philadelphia. I am the daughter of a merchant. But, speaking of Matilde, where did she go?"

"Baltimore, Missus," Sadie spoke up. "She's hoping to get a job as a cook in a fine establishment."

"I hope she knows she can use me as a reference. I've never had finer food than Matilde's," Anna Grace said almost wistfully. Then she asked, "Why Baltimore?"

"There are more free black men and women in Baltimore than anywhere else in the country," Sadie told her stoutly.

"Really? I had no idea," Anna Grace admitted. "Did a lot of the freed slaves go to Baltimore?"

"Yes, missus," Sadie said. "My momma went there too."

Anna Grace, Pansy, and Sadie talked as they cleaned the kitchen. Most of the dirt was dust from disuse, but they scrubbed and polished until the kitchen was clean and tidy again. Anna Grace brought out bowls, plates, and spoons for the dinner. The soup bubbled, and the room was filled with its spicy, warm scent.

"That's a scent from my childhood," Pansy said, breathing in great breaths of the soup's aroma.

"Oh?" Anna Grace asked. "Were you in Philadelphia?"

"No, ma'am. That's a smell straight out of west Africa," Pansy told her.

"Really? That's fascinating!" Anna Grace exclaimed. "It's one of Papa's favorite soups. I have many memories of Pepper pot soup from my childhood."

"What memory is that child?" her father interrupted, coming into the kitchen from the mercantile.

"Pepper pot soup," Anna Grace told him. "Your favorite."

"It is at that," her father stated firmly.

They filled the bowls with the soup and passed the bread around. Anna Grace's father asked them to bow their heads, and each offered up a silent prayer for grace.

Their first evening ended with good conversation and much laughter over the sharing of soup and bread.

Twenty-Eight

JOSIAH – 1860

One of the best ways to find sea glass is to have the sun at your back and to look for sparkles in the sand.

Josiah returned to Baltimore, thankfully with Tyrone by his side. Since Tyrone had no home of his own, Josiah moved him into his townhouse to the former butler's quarters. It was an adjustment for both of them. Tyrone was used to plantation ways and had never been near a city. The hustle, bustle, and noise surprised him constantly, and he was wide-eyed as they traversed the streets between the townhouse and the warehouse. He had a million questions, and Josiah found himself explaining everything as Tyrone accompanied him everywhere. Josiah needed to remember that Tyrone was not Abraham. Abraham had been raised alongside Josiah, soaking in the learning from Josiah's tutors. Tyrone had a rudimentary understanding of letters and numbers, but Josiah would need to work with him, daily, to bring him up to speed. And, he did.

Eventually, Josiah and Tyrone found a rhythm to their days. Tyrone, who had befriended the cook, served Josiah breakfast, and assisted him with his clothing before they walked from the townhouse to the warehouse. Tyrone was learning some of the duties of a secretary to Josiah and Josiah was pleased with his organizational skills and his ideas. The import and export business was new to Tyrone, and his questions provided a different perspective for Josiah. Slowly, Tyrone began to trust Josiah and opened up to him about the ways of Augustus and the plantation. Josiah's low opinion of Augustus plummeted further with the stories..

Tyrone's presence was a daily reminder of Anna Grace. Josiah wondered how Anna Grace was faring. He remembered her honey-colored hair and her beautiful blue eyes that had mirrored his longings for her. He was more determined than ever to get to Philadelphia. He hoped to travel there once the tobacco harvests were settled, and the oyster imports and exports were running smoothly. The Cadwallader plantation harvest was a loss, but Josiah had been able to recoup many of the harvests from the neighboring plantations. Soon the tobacco was resold, and on its way out of the warehouse. The oyster season was now underway with imports from the eastern shores of Maryland to lands beyond. The oysters were one of the largest cash crops of Baltimore's harbor. They were sent to far corners of the globe. Josiah's father had established business with several oystermen on the eastern shore, and most had transferred their loyalties to Josiah. He was fair and paid them well for their efforts. The negotiations and sales of the oysters filled his days and most of Josiah's evenings.

Autumn arrived in full. The winds on the wharf were chillier, portending cooler days ahead. Dried, colored leaves skittered on the cobblestones from the few trees that were in the city. The shorter autumn days brought an early twilight. One evening Josiah and Tyrone were walking back to the townhouse. Tyrone was still fascinated with the men lighting the lamps and slowed to watch at each street corner even after these past few months. Josiah waited for him patiently, understanding the wonder of the gas lamps.

"Are you settling into the city?" Josiah asked Tyrone as they neared his neighborhood.

"Yes, sir," Tyrone answered in his deep voice and a grin. "I am delighted to be here. It's quite different from the plantation, but I'm liking it just fine."

Josiah nodded and grinned back before he announced, "Now that things are under control with the start of the oyster harvest, I would like to visit Philadelphia in the next few weeks. I have business to commence with several mercantile but would also like to find Mrs. Cadwallader."

"I understand, sir. Will I be accompanying you?" Tyrone inquired.

"Yes, of course!" Josiah answered. "I can't imagine how I would get along without you."

Indeed, Tyrone had become invaluable to Josiah. He was impeccable as a valet and was picking up on acting as secretary. Josiah had been working with Tyrone's reading and sums He opened his library to Tyrone, and they had interesting discussions on Thoreau's *Walden* and *The Scarlet Letter*. After reading *Uncle Tom's Cabin*, and discussing it with Tyrone, and hearing stories from him about Mr. Reece and Augustus Cadwallader, Josiah was bound and determined to work with the abolitionist movement in Baltimore. They spent many enjoyable evenings reading and discussing books, and Josiah wasn't so lonely anymore.

Twenty-Nine

BETH

The bottom part of a bottle, where the glass is pushed inward to make the bottle stable, is called a "kick up."

Beth held a smile inside as well as one she shared with the world. With the threat of Mike being far away, she felt she could finally relax. She began to think of the tall, lanky man with long, golden-brown curls and nice eyes. Definitely nice eyes. There was something about him that drew her like a tide to the shore. He seemed nice enough. She knew he was musical, and from their brief conversation at the café, she had learned he worked at night and liked sea glass.

Out of curiosity, Beth made her way to the café to look for him, getting a latte and a sandwich. She repeated this action on several occasions, but he never appeared. She was a trifle disappointed and wished she had learned his name that day.

At work, Marsha pestered her about the upcoming ASGS Festival. They needed to make reservations for rooms as soon as possible. The festival was only a couple of weeks away. When they had some downtime on the floor, they peeked at Airbnb to find a spot. Minutes away from Ocean City, Maryland, where the festival was being held, they found a charming cottage a few blocks from the beach. It had a kitchenette so they could cook instead of going out if they wanted. Beth decided to go, getting excited about the presentations and vendors that Marsha had told her about. Now that she was settling into her cottage, she thought she could decorate a little bit. She also wanted to find a vendor to make a ring for her from the sweet, coffee-bean-shaped, cobalt blue piece of glass she had found a few weeks ago.

The air had warmed considerably, and she discovered that spring was glorious in northern Maryland. It was a perfect combination of warm air and cool nights. Every day brought a new surprise in shades of greens and flowers of all colors. Beth's landlord had given her permission to put in a garden. After a trip to the garden center for a small, raised bed, lots of pots, seeds, potting soil, and tools, Beth prepared her small garden for spring. One of her new pleasures was to pick up a coffee, then tootle to the various Amish farms in nearby Pennsylvania. She found a family-owned plant farm where she felt she could wander forever, planning gardens of all sorts in her mind. Her own small garden was planned primarily for vegetables and herbs. Although warned about frost, Beth felt all right about planting since there hadn't been a frost in weeks. Gardeners at every farm remarked on global warming and the lengthening gardening season. She'd need to return to the plant farm after the festival to pick up more tender plants in May.

Gardening brought Beth peace and joy as she dug, weeded, and planted while listening to the waves on the shore. Boaters had returned to the bay, and the speedboats did not heed the "no-wake" zones or speed limits, creating waves that sounded like the ocean crashing. Gardening tired her out, bringing her good sleep throughout the day, and she woke refreshed to work in the evenings.

Mike and his threats became a distant memory, and Beth decided she was quite happy with her life in Maryland.

On the eve of their departure to the ASGS Festival, Beth's supervisor came to the floor when she came on shift. Pat was a tall woman and a little imposing. Beth had come to respect and admire her nursing decisions, but now, Pat had an odd look on her face. It was somewhere between curiosity, sternness, and worry. She tugged at the white lab coat that she wore over her suit.

"Good evening, Beth," Pat greeted her.

"Hi, Pat!" Beth returned as she straightened up things on the desk to suit herself for her shift.

"Beth, I need to speak with you a moment," Pat said, "in private."

"Okay," Beth replied.

Pat led her to a small conference room. Beth wished Marsha were there, but Marsha had taken a vacation day to rest and prepare for their ASGS Festival trip the next day.

Pat unlocked the door to the conference room and motioned to the table and chairs.

"Have a seat, Beth," she said.

Beth sat, now becoming worried. Her mind raced to the past few weeks. Had she made a grievous error with something? Was the hospital about to do layoffs? She was one of the last hires. She couldn't think of anything that would warrant discipline.

Pat cleared her throat. She watched Beth keenly as if she was trying to make up her mind about something.

"Pat?" Beth asked tentatively. "Have I done something wrong?"

Pat let out an odd laugh. "Oh, no, dear, not anything wrong. At least, I don't think so. We've had an odd situation come up. And I will confess, I've never had it happen before."

"What are you talking about?" Beth asked.

"We've had an inquiry from the police about you," Pat said. "Supposedly, in relation to a case, they're working on."

"What?" Beth replied, shocked at Pat's words.

"Frankly, I was shocked, too. You don't seem like a person to..." her voice trailed off and then continued, "but you never know about people."

"Pat, can you please explain what's going on?" Beth asked again. "What police? Where from? What's the allegation?"

Pat bristled a bit. "The police, from Pennsylvania. I couldn't believe it, and I can't give you the particulars, of course. I just had to come to talk with you and feel things out. I just can't believe what they were saying."

"Pennsylvania? That wouldn't be from Eagle Heights, would it?" Beth asked, now suspicious. Mike. Now Mike was coming after her and her job. He had found her.

"It might be, I would rather not say," Pat told her, looking uncomfortable.

"I am not sure what was said," Beth began, her ire getting the best of her, "but I can assure you that whatever they are accusing me of is not true."

"You left there in a hurry, as I understand, and were fairly desperate for a job a few months ago."

"That's true," Beth agreed. "But it's not for the reasons they stated, I'm sure of that."

"Perhaps you should explain yourself."

Beth sighed. Here it was. Mike had raised his ugly head again. She spilled out her story about Mike and why she had escaped Eagle Heights. Beth told Pat of the emotional abuse and her fears of possibly being on the brink of physical abuse. She also told Pat that she could contact Marsha to corroborate the email threats and the steps they had taken to keep Beth a step ahead of Mike. Now, it seemed, those steps hadn't worked.

Pat sat quietly and listened to Beth. Her hands clenched and unclenched a pen as Beth told her story.

"Beth, I am so very sorry," Pat said, shaking her head. "I believe you, but I also need to protect the hospital. I need to learn more about the allegations from Eagle Heights. I'm so very sorry."

"Am I fired?" Beth asked in a quavering voice.

"No," Pat answered, "let's just say, you're on watch."

"That's so unfair!" Beth expostulated. "I'm innocent! Isn't it our law innocent until proven guilty?"

"I agree," Pat sympathized, "but better that than suspended until further investigation. That's the next step. I wanted to let you know."

"Unfortunately, Mike has power or thinks he has power. It wouldn't surprise me if he falsified records at the hospital. He's high up in the hospital administration. I'm sure he could sweet-talk anyone in personnel to do some dirty work for him. He's a good-looking guy. The girl who works there wouldn't know what hit her. He snowballed me at first. That's what he does. Mr. Charming. He's out to ruin me for getting away from him." She took a breath, trying to maintain her composure. "At least, that's what I suspect. And to think that I thought I had gotten away, that he thought I was in Philadelphia," she ended bitterly.

Pat was quiet for a few moments before she continued. "Beth, there are a few things you can do. I have the name of a women's shelter that will have resources for you. You should likely hire an attorney—"

"What?" Stunned, Beth asked, "Are the allegations that severe?"

Pat nodded. "Just to be on the safe side. Also, I am aware that you and Marsha have a girls' weekend planned. It's probably good that you are heading out of town to relax. In fact, I think that you should take the rest of the night off."

Beth looked at Pat sharply. "Really?"

Pat nodded.

Quietly, Beth asked, "And when I return?"

"Why don't you take an extra day. To get your ducks in a row. You can call the shelter and hire an attorney."

"This is a nightmare," she told Pat in a flat tone.

"But one we'll endeavor to overcome," Pat told her. "If what you told me is true, the truth will come out. Isn't that the old saying?"

Beth nodded, close to tears. Mike was out to destroy her. Fear had returned and now worry, a huge worry, that he would ruin her job and reputation. Damn him!

Beth stood up slowly.

"Get your things and meet me in my office," Pat told Beth. "I'll get you the number for the shelter. It's 24/7, but the director will not be in until tomorrow morning. Ask for Mrs. Jones."

Beth walked like a zombie to her locker, gathered her belongings, and waved wanly to the nurses' station personnel. They looked at her quizzically.

"I'm not feeling very well," Beth told them truthfully. "I need to go home."

Stella had come in to cover Marsha's shift. She nodded sympathetically.

"Take care of yourself," she offered.

Beth nodded but turned away as emotions threatened to overcome her. Beth usually walked the stairs in the hospital, but this time, she took the elevator. There was something about that quiet, small space that offered a place to get oneself together. She sniffed and blew her nose and prayed to the universe that all of this would work out.

She met Pat in her office. Emotions were on the brink, and Beth didn't trust her voice. Pat's eyes looked sorrowful.

"I'm so sorry, Beth. I do believe you, but I am forced to follow protocol. Here are the numbers that I hope will help you."

Pat gave the slip of paper to Beth. Beth nodded and turned.

"See you Tuesday. Chin up. You can do this," Pat advised.

Beth went to her car in the hospital's parking garage. It was fairly dark and a little creepy. She sat for a few minutes, staring at the scrap of paper from Pat. How could Mike do this? What a monster! Knowing she needed to talk, she called Marsha.

"Hey, girl," Marsha greeted, "excited about ASGS Festival?"

"Oh, Marsha," Beth started, and then she broke down at hearing the friendly voice.

"What's going on, Beth?" Marsha asked. "What happened? Are you at work?"

It took Beth a few minutes to calm down, then she told Marsha the whole, sordid story of her conversation with Pat.

"That bastard!" Marsha yelled into the phone. "Oh, Beth! Go home, grab your stuff, and come over here for the night. We'll have a glass of wine and kibbitz about this. Harry knows people. He can help, too. Can't you, Harry?" Marsha asked her husband, who was apparently listening.

By the time Beth went home to gather the remaining things for the weekend and arrived at Marsha's house, Marsha had piled pillows and blankets on the couch and had a glass of wine waiting for her. She gave Beth a huge hug when she came through the door.

"You poor thing!" she told Beth.

Harry took her bags. Frankly, Beth didn't think she could carry them one more step. Marsha led her to the couch and handed her a glass of wine.

"So, basically, Mike has gotten to the hospital personnel and falsified records from your old job?" Marsha asked.

"Easy enough, I suppose, if he chatted up and charmed someone in personnel. He's made up some kind of report or investigation that is completely false," Beth said. "He's the only one I can think of who would want to sully my name. I can't believe this is happening. It's so surreal. And it means that he found me." Beth looked miserably at Harry and Marsha. "Why?" she asked. "Why?"

"Control," Harry said grimly. He grabbed a piece of paper from the coffee table and handed it to her. "Beth, here are the names of a couple of attorneys. I suggest you call first thing Monday morning. Their consultations are likely free. They're both good guys." Harry was an IT guy for the county. He had the skinny on everyone in the area.

She could only nod. Her head spun with all that was happening. "Why" echoed in her head. She felt incredibly stupid. When she had run from Mike, she didn't change her name or get different papers. She went to work in a hospital, just as she had in Pennsylvania. How stupid had that been? Now, he had found her. He was making false accusations that could cost her her job, and from what Pat said, more. Police? What was that all about? She should have paid someone for a false identity and gotten a job with a private doctor. But if she had, she wouldn't have met Marsha. And what a blessing it was to have a friend through this. Beth was inordinately grateful to be away from the hospital, away from her cottage, and going to the ASGS Festival.

"Now, drink up," Marsha said, handing her the generous glass of red wine she previously poured. Beth had put it down when she'd begun talking, too upset to drink.

Beth glanced up at Marsha. She took the brimming glass of wine and sipped.

"More," Marsha ordered.

She complied, but in her state, the few sips went to her head. She put the glass down.

"Beth, you can contact the shelter and find out more information. If it's 24/7, someone should be there on the weekend. You're not the first person to go through this, but that doesn't change the pain that you're experiencing," Marsha said sagely.

Suddenly, Beth was very, very tired.

"I'm sorry," she told Marsha and Harry, "I don't think I can keep my eyes open."

Marsha nodded. "We'll leave you be. A good night's sleep will do wonders. Things will be clearer in the morning."

Beth went to change into her nightclothes while Marsha and

Harry made up the couch. t Beth tumbled into it gratefully when she returned. She could hear their muffled voices upstairs, but it didn't matter. Nothing mattered at that moment, except sleep.

Thirty

ANNA GRACE – 1860

Sea glass can be found in greater abundance around trash dumps and busy ports.

Anna Grace was settling back into Philadelphia. Papa kept her busy in the store, and she took on many of the roles her mama had fulfilled in the mercantile when Anna Grace was growing up. Father re-introduced her to the Meeting, and Anna Grace found she enjoyed the quiet, thoughtful time that was a large part of many meetings. When someone spoke, it gave her much to ponder. She did shy away from any social events, claiming fatigue or mourning. Anna Grace was sure people thought she was mourning Augustus, when, in truth, she was mourning the loss of Josiah.

Thoughts and memories of Josiah drifted through her daydreams and her dreams. She remembered his whiskey-colored eyes looking into hers and the touch of his hand. Both held promises that, unfortunately, could not be kept.

Pansy had taken to the city like a duck to water. She loved the hustle and bustle. She had a talent for negotiating with street vendors for various foods. She continued to help as Anna Grace's lady's maid, but also assisted Anna Grace with household tasks and worked in the mercantile on occasion. Anna Grace was happy to see her stretching her wings and to see her content.

It took a while for Sadie to begin to lose some of her shyness. Anna Grace learned she had quite a talent for using a thread and needle. The mercantile had a small selection of pre-made hats and bonnets. Sadie expertly fixed one that had come apart and Anna Grace noticed how Sadie reverently touched the cloth and ribbons for sale at the mercantile. Sadie would get a dreamy look in her eyes, and Anna Grace wondered if she was making hats in her imagination. One day, she approached Sadie with an idea.

"Would you like to apprentice to a milliner?" Anna Grace asked Sadie.

"Oh, yes, Miss Anna Grace," Sadie told her excitedly. "I have so many ideas!"

"Or, perhaps another thought, do you think you could make hats for the mercantile instead of apprenticing?" Anna Grace asked. "We could provide the materials, and you could make the hats. And certainly, you would receive profits from each had that is sold."

"Oh! Oh! Oh!" Sadie cried when Anna Grace proposed it to her. "That would be a dream come true, Miss Anna Grace. That would be so much better than apprenticing!"

Anna Grace smiled at her enthusiasm. "I will speak to Father immediately then."

And, she did. Sadie set up a space in a spare room of the house to start her little business that began to flourish in a very short time. Sadie's confidence grew leaps and bounds in a short time, and Anna Grace hoped it would keep some of the nightmarish memories of the plantation away.

Thirty-One

MATTHEW

NASGA is the acronym for the North American Sea Glass Association.
www.seaglassassociation.org

Matthew was thrilled to be off work. He loaded his van with his wares and displays, locked the door, and headed on down the road. ASGS Festival was being held in Ocean City, Maryland, this year, at the convention center. It was a lovely venue, and Matthew was eager to see the space. Many of his vendor friends were coming from far away and would be at the convention center on Friday afternoon, setting up their spots. He hoped Molly and Noah might show up. He had talked up the show to them and told them he used the pieces of glass from his trip to Arcadia where he'd met them. Molly texted that her dad wasn't doing too well, so it would be a minor miracle if they could make it.

Matthew turned on his music to near ear-splitting decibels. Carole King, Norah Jones, Tracy Chapman, and his favorite, the soulful Leonard Cohen, filled his car. He sang along to most of the songs. Ocean City was only a couple of hours away. He had the day and felt free as a bird as he zipped down Route 1 in Delaware, moving toward his destination. He had booked the same hotel as several other vendors and stopped to check in and drop his duffle bag before proceeding to the convention center. He stretched and checked out the ocean view. The ocean seemed to go on forever. There were a few brave surfers in wetsuits, riding the whitecaps, but people were walking the boardwalk for the most part. He hoped they would make their way to the Convention Center tomorrow and on Sunday. The bed screamed at Matthew, but he ignored it. There would be time for sleep later. This would be a weekend of little sleep. He turned on a light in the room and left.

Matthew checked in at the convention center. The gorgeous venue had a view of the bay on one side and the ocean on the other. Tall windows, at least twenty feet tall, looked out upon the water. Matthew thought it was like one of those infinity pools, though there was a balcony. The architects were clever in providing gorgeous views from many angles.

He greeted old vendor friends and the board of ASGS Festival. It was good to see everyone, and they hoped to catch up over pizza and beer at the hotel after set-up. Once he'd greeted everyone, Matthew set to work at rolling his display area in on the dolly and then his product. It took a few hours, but by seven that night, it was completed. He threw covers over everything and made his way through the center to talk with old friends, and check out their merchandise, promising to meet for pizza in an hour or so.

As they talked and kibbitzed an hour later, everyone felt it would be a good show. Usually, the ASGS Festival was held in the fall, after the summer crowds had left. This was an experiment, offered by the city, to hold the festival earlier. After a couple of beers and some slices of pizza, Matthew made his excuses to retire to his bed. His friends understood that he usually worked at night, and his near twenty-four-hour arousal had him frayed at the edges. He wanted to be ready for the hordes of visitors the next day.

"See you in the morning," Matthew said as he exited the gathering.

Leaning heavily on the wall in the elevator, he was glad to be back in his hotel. A few guests eyed him warily as the floors ticked by. They were likely thinking he was drunk more than fatigued, but he didn't owe them an explanation, instead offering a good night when the doors opened to his floor. He made his way to his room and finally listened to the bed calling his name.

BETH

Black amethyst glass appears black until a bright light illuminates it. Then you can see a deep, purple color. Black amethyst glass was used for insulators of early light bulbs.

A good night's sleep was exactly what Beth needed. Marsha roused her before dawn and said they should be on their way to Ocean City. Harry was still asleep, and they dressed quietly before exiting the house and getting on the road. Beth offered to pay for meals as Marsha drove. They stopped for breakfast at a famous diner in Smyrna, Delaware, on their way to the festival.

The diner was set up after diners in the 1950s. It was charming to see the individual jukeboxes in the booths. The waitress was dressed in period costume and brought them steaming coffee in heavy, white mugs.

"What'll you have?" she drawled in an affected tone.

Beth wondered if the waitress was speaking in her real voice or if she was putting on an act for tourists. Marsha ordered her favorite, French toast, and Beth ordered eggs, one slice of bacon, and toast. The waitress went up to the window to the short-order cook.

"I need a biddy board for one and two dots and a dash for another," she called to the cook.

Beth and Marsha giggled. Their mood lightened.

"Look, when it comes to a reasonable hour, call the lawyers," Marsha suggested.

"Don't worry, I haven't forgotten," Beth told her. "The worst thing is that I don't even know what I'm being accused of."

Marsha patted her hand, "I know, honey. It's horrible. I wish I had more clout at the hospital or more contacts so that I could find out what was going on."

"But, if it's a *he said vs. she said* thing, Mike will win. He has everyone under his thumb. He's likely threatening someone, no doubt," Beth said darkly.

"Don't say that! You can worry, but I don't recommend it."

"I don't want to lose my job or go to jail for something I didn't do," Beth hissed in an angry whisper.

"I know, Beth. I know. I just don't have answers. We need to go through this one step at a time as frustrating as it is."

The food arrived as the diner was filling up. It was a popular local restaurant for area residents, tourists, and fishermen. Soon it became a bustling hive of activity with silverware clinking and the sounds of thick, china dishes bumping together. There was a line of people waiting out the door for seating. Beth and Marsha finished their breakfast and got back out on the road again.

Beth dozed a little as Marsha drove south. The brilliant spring sunshine filled the car, and when Beth woke with a start at a stoplight, she could see the open sky to her left. The ocean was nearby.

"Almost there. We're in Rehoboth. There are a lot of outlets here if you want to go shopping," Marsha said. "I'm not hungry, but I could do with another cup of coffee. You?"

Beth nodded as she rubbed the sleep from her eyes. "Definitely, more coffee."

The major route through Rehoboth, Delaware, was hugged

by shopping outlets and strip malls on both sides. Restaurants and fast-food places dotted the landscape as well. Marsha drove slowly as if she were looking for something, then suddenly made a sharp right into an older strip mall.

"This is what I was looking for!" Marsha crowed.

The parking lot was packed, and the drive-thru line extended around the building.

"This is on me!" she insisted as they waited their turn.

She drove up to the speaker and ordered coffees and a couple of donuts.

"Just wait until you try these donuts! They're made fresh and are still warm. We're not worrying about calories today! We'll be walking and walking," she told Beth.

"But—" Beth began.

"No, buts!" Marsha interrupted.

Marsha handed Beth a bakery bag and a cup of coffee. She placed her coffee in the drink holder next to the steering wheel. Beth maneuvered to put her coffee down and opened the top to let a little steam escape.

"Donut! Donut! Donut!" Marsha chanted softly, getting silly.

Beth laughed. "Okay, Marsha. It's coming."

Beth reached into the bag to pull out a still-warm donut, glaze melting on top. She put a napkin around it and handed it to Marsha once she pulled out onto the highway.

Marsha took a bite and groaned in pure pleasure.

"What are you waiting for?" she asked, looking at Beth.

Beth took the hint, pulling the still-warm donut from the bag and taking a bite. It practically melted in her mouth.

"Good?" Marsha asked.

Beth nodded; her mouth full.

"Finger-licking good," Marsha said as she licked the leftover glaze from her fingers.

Beth agreed.

Marsha drove them out of Rehoboth. It was only a few miles

to Ocean City. Traffic was heavy. It was a gorgeous spring day, and it seemed as though everyone wanted to come to the beach and enjoy the sunshine and saltwater after a long, chilly winter. Marsha found the convention center and a parking space. The parking lot was filling as they exited the car. She explained to Beth that the center had more than one venue going on at a time. This weekend, she told Beth, there was a home show and an RV show, as well as the ASGS show. Lines were queuing at the door for entry. Beth stretched and looked around. She couldn't see the ocean through the buildings, but Marsha had pointed out where they were north of the Boardwalk by several blocks. Condos and hotels were built upon the spit of land that was Ocean City. Behind the convention center was a small bay.

They paid their admission after a few minutes of standing in line. Volunteers for the sea glass Festival were wearing bright, heathered turquoise t-shirts with the title "Atlantic Sea Glass Society" curled around two waves. A volunteer helped Beth and Marsha put on wristbands that indicated they had purchased a two-day pass and could come and go as they pleased. Other volunteers handed Marsha and Beth programs and pointed to the escalator that would take them to the event.

"We should do that sometime," Marsha said as they walked toward the escalator.

"Do what?" Beth asked distractedly She was looking at the tall, fabric signs about the festival and the soaring structure around them.

"Volunteer at the Atlantic Sea glass Society Festival. It would be fun."

Beth nodded in agreement and put her hand on the rail as they stepped onto the escalator.

When they stepped off, Marsha made a beeline for the ladies' room. Beth stared at the incredibly wide hallway with towering, tinted windows. The effect of the light and the water was spectacular. She moved off to one side but turned around, staring at the muted sunlight pouring through the windows. She saw the bay on one side and distant whitecaps of the Atlantic on the other end. She was momentarily dizzy with happiness and must have stumbled a little. A strong hand caught her elbow.

"Easy there," a kind voice said. "Are you all right?

Beth looked up to see a man in a sea glass festival t-shirt. The eyes behind his glasses looked kind, but worried.

"I'm all right," she said, "I think. This is so beautiful." She gestured to the windows and the water views. "I think I was just overcome by the views."

"All right, if you're sure," the man said. "I can get you some water if you need it. You can sit for a minute to enjoy the view or head out to the balconies for fresh air."

"Thank you," Beth told him gratefully. "I'll be fine."

"Enjoy the Festival," he said, giving her a small salute before he hurried on his way.

Marsha came up as he left. "Are you okay?"

"Yes," Beth assured her. "This is an amazing building, isn't it?"

"I think so," Marsha said and sighed. "If I was a billionaire, I think I would want a place with these expansive windows framing the water."

"I agree. We'll have to remember to buy a lottery ticket on the way home," she suggested playfully.

They both giggled and linked arms as they walked down the long hallway to enter the festival.

The first room they entered was a large, expansive space filled with booths and people. The tall windows were on two sides of the room, filling it with natural light from the west as it faced the bay. People were milling about everywhere.

"Ooh!" Marsha said. "My favorite place. But I want to go to a workshop on antique bottles that starts in about fifteen minutes. Are you interested?"

"Not really," Beth replied, being honest with her friend. "I'll meet you back here in an hour or so?" She knew Marsha had a collection of antique bottles that were used for medicine and also had an interest in Civil War medicine and nursing.

"Okay," Marsha said, "have fun."

She hurried off in the direction of the lecture rooms, a huge smile on her face. Beth looked around. She wasn't sure where to begin. She decided to start on the left-hand side of the vendor area and work her way around before exiting to the balcony when she finished. It was slow going through the vendors. Everything had a sea glass theme, and posters explained the difference between real and fake sea glass. She knew from Marsha that the festival was a stickler for using authentic glass, and Beth was glad for that. She noticed the vendors came from all over the United States. There were even vendors from Europe, England, and Puerto Rico. She hadn't realized this was such a big thing and her knowledge of sea glass was minuscule compared to many of the people attending the show.

Beth bought a book about the history of sea glass around the world, after hearing a vendor talk about different pieces of glass and their origin with another customer. She was also enamored with a window frame with sea glass set in resin. She loved the designs the vendor had to offer but had to think about the price. The window would look lovely and bring light and color into her small cottage. She looked at sea glass ornaments, candles, and house items. They were all beautiful, and Beth wished she had a million dollars to fill her home with sea glass items. She picked up two keychains with mermaids and sea glass attached from a mermaid-themed vendor, intent on giving one of the keychains to Marsha. The vendor was tall and lithe and looked like a mermaid herself. Or, at least what Beth imagined a mermaid looked like.

Beth continued through the vendors, looking at the jewelry. She wanted to find someone who would make her cobalt blue piece of glass into a custom ring. The jewelry vendors were extremely crowded, making it clear that many people who visited the festival were interested in sea glass adornment. She questioned a couple of vendors about custom work. Most people weren't interested. One vendor was interested, but the prices for her pieces were exorbitant. Beth had no doubt that the pieces were worth the cost, but it was too much for her pocketbook.

She rounded a corner and was stopped by a group of mostly women hovering around a small booth. It was jewelry, and it was almost a catfight with the women buying the rings on display. Beth could see why. The prices of the small stack rings were extremely reasonable. She saw other pieces of jewelry in acrylic cases artfully set up on small pieces of driftwood. These cases were filled with cuff bracelets adorned with sea glass, bezel-set sea glass necklaces, jewelry sets, and beautiful pendants with carved back designs. The vendor had placed a light behind the pendants, and the carved design showed through the glass.

The crowd thinned, and Beth was finally able to get to the front of the booth. The vendor was a man busy swiping credit cards and putting jewelry in bags. He was working his booth on his own, and it was clearly a juggle for him. He turned, and she nearly gasped. It was the young man with brown eyes and long golden-brown hair.

He noticed Beth, and it was as if time stood still for a moment, as if a large, invisible rope connected them.

"You," they both said at the same time, not even acknowledging the people vying to pay for their purchases.

Someone cleared their throat. A man yelled near her ear with a question about a price, and the moment of reverie was gone. The crowd jostled Beth. Someone called to the man and handed over a credit card and a couple of rings. Beth spied a business card and took one. She would come back when it wasn't so crowded.

The man's booth was near doors that led out onto the balcony. A few people were leaning on the balcony, looking at the bay. A couple more were smoking cigarettes. Beth found a chair near a small, wide, concrete cylinder that Beth guessed was a table in an ultra-modern sense. She took a breath, happy to be away from the crowd. The sun was still rising in the east, and the balcony remained shaded as the convention center blocked the sun. She wasn't cold but shivered a little.

Beth could barely believe that the golden-brown haired man was here at the ASGS Festival. She still held his card in her hand and turned it over. "Heart of the Bay," it read. *Fine, artisan-crafted jewelry from the heart of the Chesapeake Bay.* It listed a website and phone number. At the bottom of the card, there was a name, Matthew Jacobson, artisan jeweler.

Matthew. Beth said the name softly, trying it out. The address said North Bay, Maryland. She had wondered where he lived. It was quite possible that he lived directly across the bay from her. She looked inside. The crowd was still there. She loved his work, and it seemed many others did as well. So that's what he had meant when he'd said he was a glasser, too. He didn't just pick up sea glass. He created beautiful jewelry from the pieces he found on the beach. Beth reached inside her purse and pulled out the small Ziplock with the coffee-bean-shaped cobalt blue piece of glass. Maybe he would make a ring or something for her. She liked the many stack rings he had on display. Or perhaps he could set the piece in a small pendant. Beth wanted to talk with him about the possibilities. She loved his carved pieces. They were exquisite. She particularly loved the chrysanthemum on the white piece of glass. The glass had a pearly quality to it, and the chrysanthemum was delicately carved.

Her cell phone rang. It was Marsha.

"Beth!" Marsha cried. "Where are you? We said we going to meet up after the lecture. I've been texting and texting you!"

"Oh! Sorry, Marsha!" Beth told her friend apologetically. "I'm on the balcony. I'll be right in. See you soon."

Beth hurried to the door and noticed that Matthew's booth was still crowded. She went to the front of the vendor area where Marsha stood, impatiently tapping her foot.

"Sorry, Marsha," Beth apologized again.

"It's okay," Marsha assured her. "Did you find some good stuff?"

"Yes! And I've only been through about a third of the vendors. I started over there," Beth told her, pointing.

"Then, let's start in the middle. I can catch that side later," Marsha assured her.

Thirty-Three

MATTHEW

Rare colors of sea glass come from tableware.

She was here! Matthew couldn't believe it. The woman with the beautiful, long braid and soulful eyes. She had disappeared, and he hoped she would return. He didn't have much time to think about her, however. The festival was packed, and his booth was surrounded by

customers. His phone gave a satisfying ping each time a credit card transaction went through. This was one time he wished he didn't vend by himself. He could really use another person to help with the sales and to restock. But he was happy. He had already made up his vendor's fees and was on his way to covering his hotel and travel expenses and moving toward some profit.

The crowd was handing him cash and credit cards, and it was all he could do to keep up. He hoped Molly and Noah came. He could bribe them with dinner or something if they helped him out at his booth. He wondered if he would have a minute to text them, then remembered the situation with Molly's dad and the likelihood that they wouldn't make it to the show. He had vended at shows solo all of his life, so he just needed to soldier on.

Finally, at lunchtime, the crowd thinned. Hungry shoppers were on their way to find something to eat. Matthew had placed his lunch order with volunteers earlier that morning before the festival doors opened. He suspected they would be bringing his lunch by soon, but he needed a short break. He asked his vendor neighbors if they would keep an eye on his booth for about fifteen minutes, and they agreed. Matthew left to stretch his legs for a few minutes.

Thirty-Four

BETH

Thick, gray sea glass is usually over 100 years old.

Matthew had just gone when Marsha and Beth came around the row. When Beth and Marsha reached Matthew's booth was empty, and disappointment showed on Beth's face.

"He'll be back in just a couple of minutes," the lady at the next booth said. "He just needed to take a quick break. It's tough vending by yourself. I'm lucky to drag my husband along to these things. A mini honeymoon, you might say." She winked as she said it.

Her husband grunted. Beth wasn't so sure that he agreed with his wife.

"A honeymoon where you work," he said gruffly. But still, he smiled fondly at his wife.

Marsha and Beth looked around her booth. There were sea glass Christmas ornaments, garden décor, and house décor. Beth liked the angel ornaments. They were simple yet cleverly made with sea glass, seashells, raffia, and bits of lace. Beth wondered if she could make something like this at home with her burgeoning collection gracing the bowls and jars in her cottage. She bought two of the angel ornaments so that she could have one to display and one for a pattern.

"There, he is. There's Matthew," the vendor told her.

Beth turned to see that Matthew had returned to his booth. He was like a magnet. People started coming up right away. Beth nearly rolled her eyes at the new crowd starting to gather.

"Oh, Matthew!" Beth heard a voice. She looked up to see a tall, very thin woman about her age greet Matthew with a light hug and a kiss on his cheek. The woman had lots of freckles, a wide, friendly smile, red hair in two braids, and looked, to Beth, like an attractive, grown-up Pippi Longstocking. She and Matthew obviously knew one another.

"Let me help," the woman said, jumping behind the booth. She smiled up at Matthew and shoulder-bumped him, then started bagging the items as Matthew ran the credit cards on his phone.

The red-haired woman who had joined Matthew at his booth looked very friendly. Beth's first reaction was that she looked like somebody she could be friends with. Then she wondered about her relationship with the man. Was she a friend to him or a girlfriend? They looked as though they knew each other very well by the way they interacted. They seemed to get along easily with each other. Disappointed, Beth tried not to show any emotion. Suddenly, she doubted the reaction she'd had to him. Did she only imagine the connection she'd felt when their eyes had met? Lost in thought, she turned away from the booth.

"Beth?" Marsha asked. "Aren't you going to look here? This guy has those stack rings you were talking about. Maybe he would do a custom order with your coffee-bean-shaped piece."

"I thought so, too, but it's so crowded!" Beth complained to Marsha. "I'll come back."

"If you say so," Marsha told her friend. Marsha looked longingly at Matthew's wares. "I just love his jewelry!"

"It's gorgeous," she agreed with Marsha. "I would like to look more closely."

"Well, I hope he doesn't sell out," Marsha warned.

"Come on, Marsha," Beth said to her friend as she pulled her away from Matthew's booth. "You don't need another piece of sea glass jewelry!"

"Did my husband put you up to saying this?"

"Harry had nothing to do with it," she insisted.

"But he'll love you for saying so!"

Marsha was wearing part of her "collection" of sea glass jewelry. She had multiple stack rings on each finger, bracelets, earrings, and a couple of necklaces. Marsha insisted that she supported small craftsmen with her purchases, but Beth and Harry knew that she loved collecting any sea glass jewelry.

"Come on," Marsha said, "let's go to the lecture on mud-larking. This guy came over from England to talk about the treasures he's found in the mud on the Thames."

Marsha linked arms with Beth, and they went toward the lecture halls.

The lecture was fascinating, and Marsha and Beth had snagged seats in the very front where no one likes to sit. Their seats gave them a good view of the screen as well as the collection of things the gentleman had brought with him from England.

Beth was awestruck at the variety of artifacts the lecturer, Colin, had found on the muddy banks of the Thames. Apparently, mud-larking was a popular pastime for people in the United Kingdom. They found ancient jewelry, pottery, buttons, trinkets, and a variety of many things. It struck Beth that she and Marsha, and everyone glassing, were picking up bits of history as they went about their treasure hunting. She began to think of the history behind the glass she had in jars and bowls around the cottage. She wondered about the history of the coffee-bean-shaped, cobalt blue piece of glass safely stored inside the small Ziplock bag in her purse and the funny, little bottleneck piece she'd found at Tolchester.

When the lecture was over, Beth and Marsha gawked at the artifacts on the tables. Marsha had a few questions for the presenter, which he graciously answered.

They left the lecture hall, and Marsha announced, "I'm starving! How about you?"

Beth nodded. Breakfast, indeed, had been quite a while ago.

"Why don't we go and find some lunch, check into our Airbnb, and then make plans to go to the Boardwalk for dinner and evening fun?"

Beth glanced longingly back at the vendor hall. She wanted to talk with Matthew and ask him about her small piece of glass for a custom ring, but she agreed with Marsha. She, too, was starving.

Marsha caught her glance. "Tomorrow," she said, "We'll be the two first people here. I want to pick up a sea glass Christmas tree, and maybe a wreath."

"No jewelry?" Beth teased.

"Well... you know I always need more sea glass jewelry," Marsha commented as the bracelets clinked on her arm while they walked.

"Right," Beth returned sarcastically.

Thirty-Five

MATTHEW

The variety of colors of green shards mostly come from various beverage bottles.

Molly had been a lifesaver when she'd walked up to Matthew's crowded booth. She came behind the booth, gave him a hug and kiss on the cheek, and went right to work, taking cash, packaging things, smiling at customers, and answering questions as best she could. Matthew didn't feel he could have made it through the afternoon without her.

When there was a lull, they restocked the jewelry.

"Whew!" Molly said, "That was something!"

"It's a good show," Matthew told her. "I owe you, by the way."

"Yes, you do! You owe me a night out on the town, with Noah in tow, of course," Molly grinned as Noah came to join them.

Molly threw her arms around her husband's neck. "You missed all the fun," she told him.

"Ahh," Noah answered, "I'm not sure you're truthful. I found us a hotel room at the same hotel you're staying at, Matthew," Noah told them.

"Cool! You were lucky to get a room there. By the way, how's your dad?" Matthew asked. "You said he was sick and probably wouldn't make it."

"Fortunately, it was a scare and not an emergency," Molly said.

"That's a relief," Matthew agreed and then asked, "Will you cover the booth for a couple of minutes while I take a little break?"

"Of course! I'm an old hand at this now," Molly insisted. "And I'll train the new guy." She grinned at Noah.

Matthew stepped out of the booth as a few people came up to make more purchases. He thought he had seen the woman with the braid earlier, but she'd disappeared again. Damn! He looked around the vendor area. It was still pretty crowded even though it was almost four o'clock. A lecture was dismissed, and a sea of people went into the hallway, most returning to the vendor area. He didn't see the woman with the braid anywhere and knew he should get back to his booth with the new deluge of customers. Hopefully, she would return tomorrow.

Molly and Noah went to look around at the other vendors and promised to return to Matthew near the closing time. The crowds were thinning out, and Matthew worked to restock his things for the next day. He was glad he had made so many stack rings. They were selling like crazy. His stores were depleting quickly. He would need to get busy if he wanted to vend at any of the other upcoming sea glass festivals. The Lewes, Delaware festival would be in seven weeks. The Cape May Festival was later in the summer, along with the Rehoboth, Delaware festival in the early fall. That didn't even take into account the festivals in Erie, Pennsylvania, Northern New Jersey, or all the festivals in New England. He would need to look at a calendar to make some plans and a schedule for creating jewelry around his work schedule. The profits from this festival would make purchasing more silver and solder much easier.

When the festival closed at five, he covered up his wares and headed to the front of the vendor area, making small talk with a few of the other vendors. Some of them were meeting up that night in the hotel bar. Matthew told them his friends were visiting, and he might pop in on the way back from their evening.

He met Molly and Noah in the expansive hallway outside the vendor area. They drove to the hotel, promising to meet in the lobby after they freshened up. It was a bit of a hike to the Boardwalk, so they piled into Molly and Noah's car as Matthew's was filled with empty totes. Molly had teased him, saying he needed a panel van with his company name on the side, which wasn't a bad idea.

They parked near the Boardwalk and began scouting for a restaurant. Some of the restaurants were open for the season, but those were crowded with tourists. The lovely, warm spring weekend had brought people in droves. The wait for most of the places was over an hour, so they finally decided on an Irish pub near the end of the Boardwalk, which had a shorter wait. Noah headed to the bar, returning with beers in plastic cups to tide them over while they waited. It was still light, and they walked over to the railing at the edge of the boardwalk to look out at the rolling Atlantic Ocean.

"That was something today, the festival," Molly began, but Noah received a text that their table was ready.

They hurried to the pub and were seated on the outside patio, overlooking the Boardwalk. They ordered another round of beers and some appetizers. Noah wanted seafood tater tots and Molly, hummus, and vegetables. Matthew ordered poutine.

Molly straightened in her seat and looked Matthew directly in the eye,

asked, "Are all of the festivals like this?"

"Pretty much," Matthew told her. "This is one of the biggest

Festivals that I attend. It's getting bigger and more popular every year."

"Then you need to hire an assistant!" Molly advised. "It was getting pretty crazy!"

"And you saved me," Matthew told her again. "Thank you again."

"Anytime," Molly told him. "But I can't be there for all the festivals. You need to start looking for someone to work with you."

"You're probably right, but I have no idea where to look. I've been okay up until now," Matthew said. "Today was extraordinarily busy. And that's a good thing. I'm finally making some profit. Wouldn't it be nice to make enough to quit my day job?"

"It would at that," his friends agreed. "Or at least, only work part-time."

"Someday," Matthew mused.

Matthew gazed at the people strolling the Boardwalk. Family groups, couples, and groups of friends wandered along, laughing and talking. And there was the woman again, with the friend he had seen her with at Tolchester. They were laughing and talking and sharing a large cup of Boardwalk Fries. He thought of leaving the restaurant to talk with her, but words left him. She likely would have thought him crazy if he had approached her.

"What's going on?" Molly asked him. "Earth to Matthew!"

"I thought I saw someone I know," Matthew said, not really knowing what other explanation to give.

"Oh?" Molly asked coyly, her eyebrows raising into the red bangs on her forehead. "A *special* someone?"

Matthew sighed. "No, not really. At least not yet."

"What does that mean?" Noah asked. "You're not making sense, bro."

He explained to Noah and Molly how he had seen this woman and her friend at Tolchester Beach, how they had run into each other at the café in the park, and then today, at the festival. "I don't even know her name!" Matthew expostulated in a strangled tone.

"My, oh, my! "Molly teased. "I've never seen you like this, Matthew."

Matthew looked sheepish. Their food came and ended the conversation for the moment as they ate dinner. Afterward, they wandered down the Boardwalk. Many of the stores were still closed, but some were open. The Amusement Park had a few rides.

Molly dragged Noah and Matthew into the building. "Come on," she insisted, "I can't wait to see this historical carousel. I've been reading about it."

They went inside the carousel building. It was brightly lit, and the carousel animals were magnificent. Molly went crazy.

"Ooh! Look at that! And that!" she cried as the carousel animals went round and round. "I know, I know I'm being childish, but I truly want to ride this carousel." She turned to them with pleading eyes. "You two will join me, won't you?"

Noah and Matthew looked at each other and then patiently at Molly, who was waiting anxiously.

"Yes!" they said together.

Molly was bossy as they stepped onto the carousel. "You should ride the tiger, Matthew. Noah, you should ride the sea dragon!"

"Can't we choose our own steeds?" Noah asked, acting offended at his wife's suggestion.

Matthew dutifully climbed astride the beautiful tiger carousel animal. There was a woman carved on the side with long, flowing hair. Noah had chosen a pelican and Molly, a beautiful, white steed with a sash of roses. The music began, and they rode around and around and around.

Matthew admired the artistry of the carousel and would need to read again how old it was. Molly had made a comment that it was the oldest carousel in the United States, but she hadn't mentioned its age. The artwork and carvings were impressive.

Matthew looked around at the crowd in the carousel house. There she was again, just leaving with her glassing friend. He had only seen her with her hair caught in a long braid. Now it flowed over her shoulders. It was beautiful. He caught her eye, and her mouth opened in an "O" of surprise as she recognized him. He lifted a hand to wave in her direction. As his tiger went around, he caught her small wave from the corner of his eye. He hoped she would return to the festival in the morning.

Thirty-Six

BETH

Two out of three pieces of sea glass are white. This glass comes from clear bottles.

Beth was somewhat reluctant to a big evening out. She was tired but tried hard not to be grumpy to Marsha. They checked into their Airbnb. It was a small apartment attached to a house a couple of blocks from the beach. It had a double bed and a pull-out couch in the living room. The kitchenette had a couple of pots and pans and a coffeemaker with a few coffee and tea pods. They settled in and had a cup of tea while they decided what to do next.

"Boardwalk?" Marsha asked.

Beth agreed. Getting outside and breathing in the ocean air sounded good.

"If we can combine that with a walk on the beach?" Beth asked.

"Sounds like a plan!"

It was warm enough that Beth wore her flip-flops, crop pants, and a t-shirt. She took a light jacket in case she needed it when the sun went down. Marsha followed suit. It was a good stretch of the legs. They walked the few blocks to the beach and then on the sand until they saw the Boardwalk begin. Beth enjoyed the sea breeze even though it played havoc with her braided hair. She looked out at the sky and water for a while but naturally turned her attention to the sand—she couldn't help herself. She picked up a few small scallop shells, a razor clam, a slipper shell, and her favorite, a moon snail shell, and put them in the pockets of her pants. Marsha, too, was picking things up. She liked the purple pieces of clam shells that the Native Americans called Wampum. Beth thought if she were cleverer, she could make jewelry from the pieces of shells. She couldn't imagine fitting that into her schedule. Perhaps if she worked a normal nine-to-five job and had evenings and weekends off, she might be able to do it. Or so she thought. She didn't feel she was very creative, but that feeling was a leftover from Mike. She used to sew many of her own clothes until the ridicule from Mike had made her stop. Now her sewing machine was in the closet, hidden away since that day he'd teased her. Maybe she would bring it out and dust it off. Sewing again would be one step further from Mike's abuse.

She thought again about creating jewelry. She wished she knew how to drill sea glass. Some of the flat pieces she'd picked up on her beach would make great buttons. Lost in her daydream of creating pieces and selling them at the sea glass festivals, she wandered too close to the waves. A large wave came up and smacked her calves, drenching her legs and part of her pants. Beth shrieked in surprise, causing Marsha to turn to see her. Marsha laughed.

"That'll be a lesson to you for daydreaming," she teased.

"I guess so," answered Beth.

Beth moved away from the water and brushed the excess water and sand from her legs.

"Ready for some food?" Marsha asked. "I just remembered, we forgot to get lunch when we left!"

"Absolutely," Beth agreed. "I'm starving."

They walked to the Boardwalk and rinsed off at the public faucet, pushing sand off their legs and feet. Beth released her hair from its braid and finger-combed It so that it flowed over her shoulders.

"Do you want to sit down for food or grab something we can walk and talk with?" Marsha asked.

Beth eyed the lines at the restaurants. "Let's get something to go, or we might pass out waiting for a table."

"Sounds perfect," Marsha said.

They found a seafood sandwich place where Marsha ordered a deep-fried, soft-shell crab sandwich, and Beth ordered a crab cake sandwich. With their food, they made their way to a bench that looked out over the ocean. They ate their sandwiches, and although they were satisfied, Marsha had a suggestion.

"Do you want to be really bad?" Marsha asked.

Beth cocked her head at her friend and asked coyly, "What do you have in mind?"

"A big, overflowing cup of Boardwalk Fries with vinegar!" Marsha suggested.

"I'm in," Beth told Marsha eagerly.

They went to the French fry kiosk and ordered a large cup of French fries to share, dowsed them in vinegar, added more salt, and walked, blowing on their fingers as they downed the hot French fries, talking and laughing.

"I'm glad we walked tonight," Beth said as they finished up their fries. They were nearing the end of the Boardwalk and had arrived at the Amusement Park. Marsha told Beth of the vintage carousel and led her inside, where she read the history with interest as Marsha bought their tickets. Marsha insisted on riding the ostrich, and Beth chose a nearby, handsome black steed. They rode and laughed like little kids.

"I'm done!" Marsha moaned when they left the ride. "We have that long walk back to the Airbnb. Ugh!"

"We could call an Uber or a taxi," Beth suggested.

But Marsha was already on her way out the door. Beth glanced back at the carousel for one last look. It truly was a beauty. She was surprised when she saw Matthew sitting astride a tiger. He seemed to see her at the same time. Her mouth opened in surprise. Matthew waved. She gave a little wave back to him, but she wasn't sure if he saw it.

She found it odd that they kept seeing each other but never had the chance to talk. She still felt the connection and wondered if he felt the same. It was different from a lightning bolt, love-at-first-sight kind of thing. It was simply some sort of connection. And in her heart, it wasn't something to question. It just "was."

Thirty-Seven

MATTHEW

Two out of three pieces of glass are deep brown. They were commonly used in medicines, cleaners, and beverage bottles.

Matthew had been shocked to see the beautiful, young woman at the carousel house. What was it with her? When he'd seen her, he'd felt a sense of euphoria. It wasn't the lightning bolt thing they talked about in movies. It was more of a sense of relaxation and of warmth. It simply was "there" like a feeling of synchronicity.

They returned to the hotel after the carousel ride. Noah and Molly joined him for a quick drink with some of the ASGS Festival vendors before they turned in.

The next morning, Matthew met Noah and Molly for breakfast before they checked out of the hotel and headed toward Chincoteague to see the miniature ponies. After seeing them off, Matthew went to the beach to take a walk before returning to the convention center for the day.

It was a gorgeous day. People were already populating the beach. Matthew picked up a few shells and some of the purple wampum. He noticed that one vendor had prong set a shell along with a bezel set piece of sea glass to make a long pendant. He wanted to try mixing sea glass with shells, too and was hoping he could stop by their booth later that day to take a closer look. He had some lavender pieces of glass that would look lovely with the purple and white wampum. The multitude of white glass he'd found on his beach would look nice with the wampum. He thought of adding some Swarovski crystal beads to make the piece sparkle and give it a high polish. He was starting to see the designs come to life in his head. He could also bezel set the wampum and some sea glass pieces, join them with hand-forged links and make a striking, ultra-modern piece. He bent down to pick up more wampum, thinking he might have to come back at a later date to collect more. His pockets were heavy with shells and jingled as he jogged to his car. It was time to get to the Convention Center, and he was running late. He liked being an hour early to make sure everything was in place and ready to go.

At the vendors' area, he talked shop with other jewelers. They were discussing what was selling this year and what was not. The higher-priced items were slow. Matthew enjoyed making the creations, but it took a particular person with a decent bank account to purchase something that took days to create, large amounts of detailed construction, and a lot of silver and some-times gold. Matthew thought his prices were very fair.

It was close to the starting time for the second day. It was a tradition that everyone joined in a countdown with good wishes for a successful day. After the countdown, the doors opened, and the guests poured in. Word among the vendors was that people were lined up waiting to enter. There were more lectures today and a contest for the most interesting piece of sea glass. It, too, was an event that drew people in. Most came from the east coast, but some people came from hundreds of miles away to enter their favorite piece of sea glass in the contest.

Matthew double and triple-checked that his stock was as full as possible, checked his fanny pack for change, and that he had a battery pack to keep his cell phone juiced up for credit card sales. He turned to look under that table where he stored extra pieces and took out a couple of additional floral pendants to go in the cases. When he stood up, he met the eyes of the beautiful woman who was now standing in front of him.

"Hi," he stammered his greeting. His heart began to beat faster, and he didn't know what to do with his hands.

He fumbled with the pieces for the cases and almost dropped them. Feeling gauche, he set them down a little harder than he had intended where they nearly toppled from his display. One fell, and he caught it deftly.

"Good catch!" she said, smiling at him.

"Thanks, you can catch more moves when I start playing with the Orioles," he joked and grinned at her.

They both laughed, and the ice was broken.

"I'm Beth," she introduced herself.

"Matthew," he said, nodding at his name along with his business, "Heart of the Bay."

"Matthew," she said as if trying the name out on her tongue.

He liked how she said his name.

"Do you do custom work?"

"Sure. What are you looking for?"

Beth reached into her purse and pulled out a small Ziplock bag.

"You live in North Bay, right?"

Matthew nodded.

"I'm across the bay in Carpenter's Point. I found this the other week, and I would love to have it in a piece of jewelry."

Matthew took the little bag, admiring the small piece of cobalt blue glass.

He looked at Beth and told her, "I've always wanted to glass at Carpenter's Point, but I don't know anyone there. This is a nice piece. What were you thinking of?"

"I guess I was looking for a ring, like your stack rings," Beth told him.

"Easy enough," he said. "Do you want to leave the piece with me? I'll need your contact information and your ring size."

"Sure," she answered.

Matthew pulled out a notepad and pen. He handed it to Beth, who wrote down her contact information. He took her hand to look at the size of her fingers and stopped himself from lifting her hand to his lips. He cleared his throat awkwardly as touching her lit him up inside. It was the same as when their eyes had met, time seemed to stop for a minute. He wasn't sure how long he stood, holding her hand, but a customer said, "excuse me," and Matthew dropped Beth's hand guiltily. He took care of the customer and suggested to Beth to try on some of his stack rings to see which style and size she liked best.

He surreptitiously looked at Beth as she tried on the rings and noticed the mix of blond and brown strands of her hair. It reminded him of the different shades of gold he used in making jewelry. She was bent over the rings, and he had a glimpse of the curve of her neck. He thought he would like to kiss her there. His breath hitched, and she looked up. Their eyes met. Matthew felt he could happily drown in her eyes.

"I – I think this is the size I need," Beth stammered, holding up one of the stack rings. "And I like this style of band."

He took the ring from her, and their fingers brushed. Did she make a sound? Or was it him? It was probably him. He couldn't breathe, and he felt like he was in eighth grade. Awkwardly, he took the ring from her, wrote down the size, and took a photo of the type of ring she wanted with his phone.

"Okay," he said. "I'll be in touch. It will probably be a week or possibly two. Will that be all right?"

"That will be fine. Thanks!" Beth told him.

And there it was. Luck of the gods, serendipity, trusting the Universe, it had all come crashing to the little bit of paper with

Beth's name, address, phone, and email. A perfect segue to get to know her a little better.

Matthew stood, bemused, with the pad of paper until a customer said loudly, "Can I pay for this now?"

Jolted out of his contemplation, Matthew put the pad of paper with the little piece of cobalt blue glass in a small box under the table and took the customer's credit card. The day passed extremely fast. Matthew never got a break until the last convention guest left the area. He was happy. His stores were depleted, but his bank account was full. Matthew began to pack up his things before he said goodbye to his vendor friends. He returned to his booth and packed up, then waited his turn to load up his car and head home.

Thirty-Eight

JOSIAH – 1860

Many glassers use a kayak or canoe to get to their 'secret' beach for glassing.

The oyster season was well underway, and it was November before Josiah felt comfortable leaving the warehouse to go to Philadelphia. He found the list of mercantile his father used to visit. He hoped beyond hope that one of them belonged to Anna Grace's father. But that didn't matter. He would search the city until he found her.

Tyrone had mentioned to Josiah that Anna Grace had feelings for him. That was a hope he clung to, and he hoped she still shared those feelings. Throughout the experience of meeting her, recuperating from his accident, and losing her, he still felt there was a strong connection to Anna Grace. It didn't make any sense. They barely knew one another, but there it was.

Josiah thought constantly of Anna Grace. It was as if part of her lived inside of him. They had a strong, invisible, and invincible connection. He wanted to touch her honey-gold hair, look into her beautiful eyes, and hold her hand. The shred of hope that

Tyrone had given Josiah, the fact that Anna Grace had feelings for him, made his heart swell with love and desire. He held onto the hope that she felt the same.

The two of them set off on their journey on a blustery, cold November day. Josiah was eager to share the adventure of riding the railroad with Tyrone. Tyrone couldn't imagine traversing the distance between Baltimore and Philadelphia in under six hours. Josiah told him they would be riding an iron horse and finally, after seeing Tyrone's confusion, explained to him it was a passenger train that would take them to Havre de Grace, Maryland where they would transfer the train to a ferry to go across the Susquehanna River, and then onto Philadelphia from Perryville, Maryland. Tyrone didn't believe they would travel at a great speed of thirty miles per hour.

Josiah enjoyed sharing new things with Tyrone and laughed with pleasure as the man's eyes grew huge when the train whistle blew and steam poured out from the stack. It was an amazing machine. They settled into a rail car of plush upholstery and lacquered wood that was noisy and crowded. Body heat and a small wood-burning stove kept the car toasty, the but windows leaked the chilly air as the train sped along the track. Both men were fascinated as the train was placed on the ferry to cross the Susquehanna River in Havre de Grace. Josiah wondered aloud at the innovation and great achievement in recent years. The ferry was steel and connected to the train track to take them across the wide river. Perhaps in the future, there would be a bridge to traverse the Susquehanna. That would be an amazing achievement!

They were tired and hungry when they arrived in Philadelphia and checked in at an inn before finding somewhere to sup, too tired to begin their search. They would begin in the morning and as Josiah laid his head down to sleep that night, Anna Grace was on his mind. The memory of her became crystal clear in his dreams where she was so very happy to see him when he finally found her. He awoke the next day with a fervor he had not had in months, determined to find Anna Grace.

Thirty-Nine

BETH

Hanapepe on Kauai, Hawaii, is a popular Hawaiian sea glass beach.

There. Beth had met Matthew. She still couldn't figure out their connection. Perhaps when he completed the ring, she could talk with him at length. The ASGS Festival venue didn't work for a conversation while people were vying for his jewelry.

After she talked with Matthew, Beth met Marsha in the lecture hall. They listened raptly to a lecture on sea glass marbles, then returned to the vendor hall, where Marsha purchased sea glass Christmas trees and a sea glass wreath.

"I promised myself these this year," Marsha commented to Beth.

Marsha had been through the vendor area three or four times, looking for her favorite trees and wreath while comparing prices. After the lecture, Beth strolled around, carefully avoiding Matthew's corner. She ended up purchasing a small sea glass stained window. Marsha approved, telling Beth it would look lovely at her cottage. They stayed at the festival for the sea glass of the year contest, oohing and aahing with other festival-goers on shards of glass found all over the world. Beth was in awe of the dragon egg glass from northern England, and glass colors from Puerto Rico and the Mediterranean. One of the vendors created jewelry from Greek sea glass, and the thick, turquoise pieces were stunning. She talked with another vendor about cobalt blue glass, and they corroborated that likely, her piece was from a poison bottle, perhaps in the 18th or 19th century. When they left that evening, Beth felt her brain was full to the brim.

"Wow," she said to Marsha as they walked to the parking lot in a daze near the ending time of the festival. "That was something!"

"A yearly girls' weekend?" Marsha asked Beth.

"Definitely!" Beth agreed. "And now, back to reality. Do you know that I forgot to call the shelter and talk with Mrs. Jones?"

"You're off tomorrow, and you have your work cut out for you," Marsha told Beth.

"I know. I'm trying not to think about all of this," Beth told her.

Marsha drove back to Maryland as the sun was going down. It seemed to Beth that it was taking its time, and that was all right. She wasn't sure she wanted to go home. She'd left the feeling that everything was all right at the festival, and the fear was returning the closer she came to the cottage. Beth was terrified Mike might find her. She wasn't sure what to do.

As if Marsha had read her mind, she offered her couch to Beth again.

"I don't know," Beth almost whined. "I really need to get home, but I am a little scared."

Mike's subtle threats had a way of playing in Beth's mind. She kept telling herself in a mantra that she would not let him win. At this point, it wasn't working very well. Marsha followed her home and came into the house with her. They turned on all of the lights and checked the closets and bathroom. Mike was nowhere to be found. Beth sighed in relief. Marsha offered her couch a second time, and Beth thought long and hard about the offer before declining.

"No, I think I'll be okay," she finally told Marsha.

Marsha nodded and leaned over to give her a hug.

"Call me any time, day or night. I mean it!" Marsha told her, waggling her blond curls at Beth.

"Thank you for the distractions this weekend. I needed it," Beth told Marsha gratefully.

Marsha nodded and gave her another hug. Marsha left, and Beth locked the doors and propped chairs up against the knobs. She had seen people do this in movies to stop intruders. She wondered if it really had any deterring effects on someone. It made her feel only slightly safer, and she wished she had a big, black dog with a loud bark.

She was tired but wired and nervous, so she turned on her laptop and logged into her email. As she suspected, Mike had emailed her.

When you lose your job, don't expect to crawl back to me, the email from Mike read.

Beth's stomach froze into a lump. Here it was again. Beth forwarded this email and the others to her supervisor as proof of what was happening with Mike. Since the threats were not specific, Beth didn't know if she had a leg to stand on. She printed the emails and hoped she could get a consult with an attorney the next day.

Exhausted from the stress with Mike and the busy weekend with Marsha, Beth went to bed early. She didn't sleep well and seemed to wake up every hour on the hour to stop and to listen. It made for an uncomfortable night. Finally, she got up at five after having a nightmare that Mike was trying to kill her. She made coffee, then dozed over the cup as she looked out the window, waiting for dawn to come.

Beth felt disheartened. Why was Mike out to ruin her life? He must really, really hate her. What happened to the love that had once been between them? Had it been love? When she'd told the story of Mike to Marsha and to Pat, it had seemed all about control. It was at that moment that she realized Mike hadn't loved her. Even with the abuse, Beth had clung to the hope that he'd loved her at least a little. She had loved him. She'd stayed with him through all the criticism and threats, thinking that somehow, some way, it would get better. *She* would get better at making him happy. He had brainwashed her into thinking she was an imbecile, and now, she certainly felt like one.

Beth stared at her cell phone in her hand. It was time. She called the attorneys that Harry had recommended. One of the attorneys had an appointment available in an hour. Beth accepted the time immediately and scurried to get ready.

Attorney Kevin Hampton's office was in an old, stately home. Beth parked her car nearby and stepped onto the porch that was supported by tall pillars. The heavy, carved, polished wood of the doors looked imposing and, to Beth, about twenty feet high. In reality, they were likely twelve feet. She was surprised when the heavy door opened and swung on its hinges easily. It was so well balanced, it was deceiving. Beth entered the attorney's office with trepidation. She had never been to an attorney before in her life. The lobby area had more polished wood, and there was an office, with a woman sitting at a computer to the right.

"May I help you?" she asked Beth.

Beth found her voice. "Yes, I'm Beth, Beth Finnegan. I have an appointment?" she asked, rather than stated. "An appointment with Kevin Hampton."

The secretary looked at the appointment calendar on her computer, double-checking for Beth's name and appointment time.

"Have a seat," she said, nodding to the chairs in the lobby area, "I'll let him know that you're here."

Beth stepped back out of the office to sit in one of the tall, leather, wing-back chairs. It squeaked when she sat down, and she winced at the noise. She crossed her legs and then uncrossed them in a nervous fashion.

A tall man came from the office area across from where she was seated. He looked to Beth to be well over six feet tall, and like a combination between Abraham Lincoln and Steve Jobs. He was lithe and lean. Beth wondered if he was a long-distance runner as she stood, and he shook her hand.

"Kevin Hampton," he introduced himself.

"Beth Finnegan," she returned.

"Follow me and have a seat in my office," Mr. Hampton said.

And Beth followed, thinking, *said the spider to the fly*. She was so nervous that her throat was dry.

Mr. Hampton led her to an office with glass bookshelves stuffed with large tomes. He sat behind a beautiful, antique, mahogany desk. She sat in a tall, spindle chair with low arms.

"How can I help you?" Mr. Hampton asked.

Beth wasn't sure what to say at first. She plunged into her story of the possible allegations coming from Pennsylvania about her nursing. She told him she was advised to get an attorney but didn't know what the false accusations were about. She also told him about Mike, their relationship, and the recent threats.

Kevin Hampton was a good listener. He took an occasional note or two on a legal pad. He kept his eyes on her, watching as she told her story. When she was finished, he sat back in his chair, steepled his fingers, putting them up to his lips. He looked thoughtful and was quiet.

Finally, he spoke, "So, you're really asking me two things."

Beth looked quizzically at him. "Two?" she asked.

"Yes, you're asking me to look into the possible personnel issue, and to see if information from your old position has been tampered with. Secondly, you are proposing that you are being threatened by your old boyfriend."

Beth thought for a moment. "Yes," she replied.

Kevin Hampton nodded thoughtfully before he said, "I'll

SHARON BRUBAKER

need additional information from you about your previous employment. Also, I'll need you to sign a waiver so that I can obtain your personnel records. Regarding your ex-boyfriend, please print out the threatening emails and forward any information you can. The emotional abuse area can be muddy waters, but you definitely have a leg to stand on with his threats. Until he really does something, we can't get a restraining order. As you mentioned, he's a smart man, so he's likely to know the boundaries of what he can and cannot do. That, in itself, is concerning. We have to be smarter than Mike and keep a step ahead."

Beth handed Kevin Hampton a folder with the emails.

"Ahh," he said, "the game is afoot."

Beth smiled at this. It was a wan smile, but it was a smile.

"My secretary will get you the paperwork that you need to complete. Also, she'll give you a list of our fees. It's been a pleasure, Ms. Finnegan. I'll be in touch," he said as he stood to shake her hand.

She was dismissed. Beth left the office and went to the secretary. The secretary, in turn, handed her a packet of papers.

"Would you like to leave a deposit to retain Attorney Hampton's services?" she asked Beth.

"Oh!" Beth replied in surprise. "Certainly."

She handed over her credit card, thinking she might need to dip into her 401K for this. She had drained the bulk of her savings when she ran away from Pennsylvania and moved to Maryland. Beth completed the paperwork and gave it to the secretary. Donna Thomas was her name. She seemed very, very efficient. Beth thanked her and left, stepping out into the spring sunshine.

Back in her car, Beth texted Marsha about the events of the morning before returning home.

Forty

MATTHEW

One in 200 pieces of sea glass will be cobalt blue.

It was not quite back to business as usual for Matthew when he returned home from the ASGS Festival. Instead of listening to soulful folk music on the way home, he was quiet, and he thought of Beth. He thought of her beautiful eyes and how he longed to touch the thick braid and kiss her creamy neck. He then chided himself for being unrealistic. He didn't know anything about her. He would make her ring and, hopefully, be able to drop it off in Carpenter's Point. Maybe he'd even snag an invitation for glassing there.

He unloaded his exceedingly lighter boxes of stock and his booth set up when he got home. Matthew would need to take inventory, order more supplies, do more glassing, and make a lot more jewelry in the next eight weeks before the Lewes, Delaware sea glass Festival. He would be burning the midnight oil.

But first, he would need to make Beth's ring. It wouldn't take him long at all. He set up for a bunch of the stacker rings, figuring he could create them in an assembly line style. Picking up the little cobalt-blue, coffee-bean piece of glass, he ran his finger over it and felt the ridge. He found it fascinating. It looked like it could be from the same bottle as the piece he had found and from which he was creating the carved heron. His piece was much larger and obviously the bottom of a small bottle. Her piece? A minuscule piece of a ridge bottle of some kind, perhaps a poison bottle. He ran his fingernail over the ridge. It would be a one-in-a-million chance that they came from the same bottle. They certainly looked the same, however, and Matthew had to wonder as he began to work.

He created the bezel by tracing the glass and cutting the back of the bezel. After that, he measured the bezel strip around the stone, cut it cleanly, filed it, and soldered it together and then onto the bezel. Next, he created the ring shank. He soldered the half-round, half-hard sterling to the bezel. Matthew made sure the seams were tight, and he polished the ring. Using dental floss that he rested inside the bezel, Matthew set the glass inside the bezel. It was nice and snug. He removed the floss and pushed the bezel wire around the glass, tucking the silver over the top. Next, he polished it using a special tip on his Foredom drill until it shone. The deep cobalt blue looked beautiful with the shining silver. He looked at his work, admiring it. He packaged it neatly in a box, put his card in the box, and the sticker that read "Heart of the Bay." Next, he texted Beth, *Your ring is completed. LMK how I can get it to you.* Now he had to wait.

Forty-One

BETH

Sometimes you'll find a glass with patterns on it. These shards are usually from decorative ware.

When she returned from the attorney's office, Beth wasn't certain what to do next. She called the hospital and left a message with Pat, updating her on the day's events, but she still had not called the women's shelter. She couldn't remember the director's name, or the name of the shelter, and knew she would need to ask Pat again. She had lost the small bit of paper Pat had given her earlier on her trip to ASGS. Beth wasn't sure if the woman from the shelter could help. As the attorney had stated, Mike needed to be more threatening to warrant a restraining order. She was pretty much sunk until he made his next move. It was like watching a rattlesnake in slow motion, wondering if it would strike and bite you or if you could shoot it dead first. Beth hoped Mike would give up on harassing her. In her heart, she knew it probably wouldn't happen. He seemed to be hell-bent on ruining her life.

She changed into yoga pants and a long-sleeved t-shirt, then checked her garden before wandering to the water to look out and admire the blue and gold colors. The day settled into eventide when the cool evenings and nights stole the heat of the early spring day.

Beth sat in a very old Adirondack chair. The paint had mostly peeled off, and the chair itself was falling to bits, but Beth could sit on it without collapsing, which she did, pulling her legs up and wrapping her arms around her knees to keep warm. She stared at the water, thinking about Mike.

Beth felt very, very stupid and berated herself over and over again. She should have moved further away. She should have changed her name. She should have applied to work in private practice. She should have known better about Mike's connections as a hospital administrator. How had he found her? There had to be some sort of database between hospitals. That had to be how he'd found her. She had left Eagle Heights six months ago. It was like he was a hunter out for the kill.

Round and round, her thoughts went. The sun started to dip behind her, and colors seemed to surround Beth and her little cottage with their muted yet bright hues. She hugged her knees harder and then rubbed her arms.

Why was Mike so vindictive and frightening? She had left him. That was a fact. But he liked to be in control. He liked to have all of his ducks in a row, no questions asked, and no one bucking his decisions. She had seen first-hand what his anger could do when his plans were questioned or thwarted. She had cleaned up plenty of broken glass and called plasterers to repair punches in walls when things didn't go his way. The only consolation Beth had had while living with Mike was that the broken items and punches in the wall were not something caused by her. As the frequency of his violence had increased, so had her fear of him. Now Beth had taken his control of her away when she'd left him. His threats were a response to his anger. Would he turn to violence? She couldn't even think of what his next steps might be, other than to get her fired from her job. She was worried. The unknown from Mike was frightening.

Beth thought back on her relationship with Mike, wondering why she had been so naive to let him gain control over her as he had. Had she been that desperate? At first, she'd been in love with him. Had he ever been in love with her, or had it all been some kind of sick game? If the mind games were this bad, Beth couldn't even imagine living with the physical abuse that may have come if she'd stayed with him. Beth was convinced part of it had been her upbringing. She remembered the many tears her mother had cried before and after her father had left them. He'd left Beth's mother years ago when Beth had been young, disappearing from their lives. Still, she loved her dad and would probably welcome him back with open arms. She wondered now if he had verbally or physically abused her mother. Had she subconsciously known that and relationship with Mike was history repeating itself? It was almost sick to think about.

Beth's phone pinged, distracting her from her thoughts. There was a text message from Matthew saying her ring was completed. She was surprised as she had seen him only a few days ago. She finally texted back, asking if they could meet at the café at the park. For Beth, it was a neutral, safe place. And right now, even though she trusted no man, her heart raced at the thought of seeing him again. She thought of Matthew's eyes and of his long, curly hair. Part of her wanted to run her hands through his hair while he looked into her eyes.

And then, she berated herself. How could she think of such a thing? But, there was something about Mathew...

She continued to daydream and wondered if it would be a quick exchange or if they would have a chance to have coffee, or even possibly lunch? She was curious about the connection she felt to Matthew. Still feeling burnt by Mike, it didn't seem possible for her to entertain feelings for someone else. Did she even have a chance at happiness after the ugliness of Mike?

Forty-Two

ANNA GRACE – 1860

Winter is said to be the best time to go glassing.

Anna Grace was despondent when she pondered her future. She was happy to be home in Philadelphia and with her father. But, she wondered what would happen to her. She knew the expectation would be to marry again, but she didn't want to marry anyone but Josiah. And, he was gone. Her mourning garb was more for him than for Augustus. Augustus's death had emancipated her from the marriage, but not societal norms.

Anna Grace noticed that widowhood, or death for that matter, brought out two kinds of behavior in people. One sort would avoid her like the plague. Others wanted to simper around her and smother her. Some of the ladies at Meeting were like that. Anna Grace preferred the ones that avoided her.

She was more fortunate than most widows. Anna Grace had the opportunity of working in her father's store forced her to be convivial and social. In many ways, Anna Grace was grateful for the work in the store. It kept her busy.

Forty-Three

MATTHEW

Prior to the 1960s, most household products were packaged in glass and not in plastic. The glass was dumped into rivers, bays, and seas and eventually became prized sea glass.

Matthew was disappointed in receiving Beth's reply to his text. He wanted to visit the beach in Carpenter's Point. He reluctantly agreed to meet her at the café for coffee and brunch the next day. He thought about her. What was it about her? He thought of the schmaltzy musical *South Pacific* that his great-grandmother had forced him to sit and watch. Perhaps schmaltzy wasn't the right word, the romanticization of the Pacific end of World War II. His great-grandmother had been a nurse. She had served in World War II stationed in Hawaii. She'd had a fondness for the South Pacific and told him some horror stories. He remembered how his mom had always hushed his grandmother when she came to the more graphic events. His great-grandmother would sing the songs from the musical over and over. Perhaps that's why the lyrics to "Some Enchanted Evening" stuck in his head.

With Beth, something like the song affected him. When he

saw Beth, there was some sort of connection. True love? He wasn't sure he believed in true love, but he did know they had a bond that couldn't be disputed. He wondered if she felt it, too.

Matthew and Beth decided on meeting at eleven to exchange the ring and cash. He hoped he could talk her into lunch, brunch, or coffee. He could come home directly from work, snag a good nap, and be at the café in under fifteen minutes. He was looking forward to seeing her again.

He looked at the time and jerked to attention. He didn't want to be late, especially since he wanted to leave on time in the morning.

Matthew's work time passed quickly enough. He noticed that he glanced at the clock more often and that his pick rate was lower as he was distracted. At seven, he clocked out immediately and went home. He tried to sleep but found it difficult. He tossed and turned. Finally, at nine-thirty, he got up. He showered, dressed, and was ready to go to the park in no time. Matthew decided to drive to the park and walk before he met Beth. He put the ring in his pocket and jumped into his car.

It was a glorious spring day. In this part of the world, spring was long and incredibly beautiful. The bright, fuchsia-colored buds of the native redbud tree were brilliant against the still brown trunks of trees. Daffodils danced in yards, and the weather had taken a soft turn. There was something about spring, he thought. Perhaps it was the change in seasons, the new life, and new beginnings. He couldn't help but hope that was true for him. Matthew didn't understand his urge to rush to get to know Beth. It was completely out of character for him. He wasn't a love "em and leave em" sort of guy, but he was hard-pressed to think of a long-term relationship in the past few years. He hadn't met anyone who could deal with his schedule, his art, and him. It was slim picking for dates, let alone relationships.

The park was full of walkers, dog walkers, fishermen, and kayakers. Matthew parked, gazed about, and then got out of his car to stroll. The sun was blazing, but not hot. Just bright as a fiery lemon in the deep blue sky. The water looked like a million diamonds. And everyone was happy. Matthew couldn't help but smile. He strolled the walking loop and returned to the café to get coffee and a table outside. Beth was due in just a few minutes. Tables outside were prized on this fine of a day. Matthew checked his phone. It was ten fifty-five. He still had a couple of minutes. Not thinking, he took a large swig of his piping hot coffee, burning his tongue, the inside of his mouth, and his throat with the searing hot liquid. He wanted to spit it out, spewing it, but Beth came up to him.

"Are you all right?" she asked him.

Matthew had to swallow, and he did, feeling the fiery liquid now boil in his stomach. He looked up at Beth and stood up halfway to greet her.

"Oh, sit! Please sit!" she said, blushing. "Let me go inside and get some coffee. Do you need anything?"

Matthew could only shake his head. He sat back down, and Beth went inside. She returned a few minutes later with a coffee and a glass of ice water for Matthew.

He tried to stand again, but she shook her head in a minuscule shake and sat down with a smile.

"Here," she told Matthew, handing him the icy water, "I thought you could use this."

Matthew took a sip, then two, and then a gulp, relishing in the coolness of the ice water.

"Thanks," he said, finally able to use his voice.

"Not a problem. I am a nurse, you know. But I've never had the opportunity to work on a burn ward." Beth paused. "Oh! You probably didn't know I was a nurse!" Then she looked at her hands in her lap. "I'm sorry. I'm babbling."

Matthew threw back his head and laughed. "You can babble all you want," he told her.

Still, she looked embarrassed. She sipped at her coffee for a minute.

"Did you enjoy the ASGS Festival?" Matthew asked.

"Oh, yes! I loved it! I'm pretty new to glassing. My friend, Marsha, is more of an expert. She's the one who asked me to come to the show. I think it will be a regular girls' weekend from now on."

"There are a lot of festivals," he said. "I really like the folks at the ASGS Festival. We're sort of a family. Some of us meet up at a few other shows, but the ASGS Festival is our big show of the year."

"Did you have a successful show? Your booth always seemed crowded," she commented.

"It was terrific. Now I need to burn the midnight oil and get ready for the Lewes, Delaware festival in about eight weeks."

"Lewes, Delaware?" she asked, "That's pretty close, isn't it?"

"About ninety minutes away," Matthew told her. "It's an outdoor show, and usually, the weather is perfect for June. I love that show, too. Do you think you'll try to make it to that?"

Beth shrugged, "I don't know. I'll have to check the dates and check my work schedule. An entire weekend off is somewhat of an anomaly. But it seems close enough to drive down for the day."

"Absolutely," Matthew said. "Easily done."

They both sat quietly for a moment or two, sipping their drinks.

"Did you bring the ring?" Beth eventually asked.

"What? Oh! Oh, yes!" Matthew said, embarrassed. He felt around in his pocket and pulled out a little box. Inside was the ring with the cobalt blue, coffee-bean shaped glass. He handed it to Beth.

She pulled it out of the box and looked at it. She took in a breath in wonder.

"It's beautiful! Thank you so much!" she told him.

She held the ring in the sunlight, seeing the flash of the deep cobalt blue.

"Thank you!" she said again, awe in her voice at the beauty of the ring.

Beth reached into the pocket of her jeans, pulled out the cash, and handed it to Matthew, who put it in his pocket while she tried on the ring. It fit the middle finger on her left hand perfectly.

"It's perfect," she stated, a bit dreamily.

"I'm glad you like it. You said you live in Carpenter's Point?" he asked.

"Yes," Beth paused a moment, "yes, I'm renting a small cottage there."

"How's the glassing?" Matthew asked.

"I don't know if I have anything to compare it to. I feel I do get a fair amount of glass. I've been filling up some bowls since I moved there about six months ago. How about you? You said you live in North Bay?"

Matthew nodded and pointed south. "If you took a kayak when the tide is going out, you could be there in less than an hour. If you're fighting the tide, it would be a couple of hours," he told her with a grin.

"Do you have a good beach?" Beth asked. "My beach is minuscule."

"Only one part of the beach in Bayside has good sea glass.," he told her. "There are some cool rock formations, called concretions, that are on the rest of the beach."

"What are concretions?"

"They come from the late Cretaceous era," Matthew explained. "They're rock tubes, balls, and little bowl-like rocks. Apparently, the native Americans used the iron oxide in the enclosed ones, the ones that look like geodes, to paint their faces."

"That's fascinating! I would love to see them sometime," she told him.

"You're welcome any time. Text me when you're off next, and we can set up a time with the tide table," he offered.

"Really?"

"Sure. I could use some time away from the jeweler's bench."

"Do you make jewelry full time?" she asked.

"Nah," he answered. "I work nights at a warehouse to pay the rent and the bills. The jewelry is the job of my heart, and I do it every spare moment. Glassing is part of it, and it's fun."

"I was just off for a few days, so I won't know my schedule until tonight or maybe tomorrow," Beth said. "I can text you."

"That would be good," Matthew said. "I'm not off for at least a week due to being off for the show last weekend. If the company holds true to their schedule, then I should be off next Monday and Tuesday."

Beth nodded and said, "I'll text you when I get my schedule. I really need to run today to get ready to get to work in a couple of hours. Thank you for making the ring and meeting with me to pick it up."

"Of course," he answered.

Beth stood to go, and Matthew rose, too. They stood, awkwardly looking at one another for a minute.

"I'll talk to you soon," Matthew finally said, breaking the silence.

Beth nodded. She took a moment and glanced into Matthew's eyes, smiled, and turned to go. He stared after her. His mouth was almost agape.

Forty-Four

BETH

*In addition to sea glass, sea pottery is another popular thing to
search for and collect. Also, toys and bits of ephemera.*

Beth left Matthew standing in the bright sunshine. She
took a moment to turn back to look at him and smiled
involuntarily. There was something about Matthew that
pulled her to him like a moth to a flame. But it wasn't a quick
flutter of interest. It was something deep, almost primal. It was
almost as if their souls had some sort of karmic connection. That
was silly, or so Beth thought. It came to her in a brief blip through
her thoughts. She didn't consider herself cosmic, psychic, or in
any way sensitive. But his smile filled her from within, like a small
fire of joy that spread throughout her body. She had never felt like
this before. Not even in the good days with Mike. It was a new
feeling.

But her feelings toward Matthew surprised her. They pleased
her. The joy that welled in a small bubble seemed to light her
insides. Was she ready to trust again? Was it a good idea to get
involved, even in a friendship, with the current situation with
Mike? Beth wasn't sure. She wanted to see Matthew again. She

wanted to see him and get to know him, at least as a friend. And that was something.

When Beth put her hand on her car's steering wheel, she looked at the ring on her finger. Her small cobalt blue coffee bean of sea glass felt right. She loved the simple lines of the ring. The noonday sun lit it from within, showing the bright, blue internal flame inside. She couldn't wait to show it to Marsha.

Beth arrived at the hospital a little early. She wanted to stop to see Pat and update her in person, but when she got to Pat's office, she felt a wave of disappointment. The office was dark and locked. She thought Pat was in her corner, even though Pat hadn't told her the allegations. Not knowing drove Beth to distraction. What had Mike done? She remembered what his most recent email had said, *When you lose your job, don't come crawling back to me.*

Again, Beth wondered why she had ever trusted Mike. Why had she forgiven him so many times, justifying his actions with the fact that he hadn't hit her? As if that was enough to forgive his shoddy treatment of her? And, she'd believed him when he'd apologized and pleaded for her forgiveness, more than once. Was the fact that he'd never hit her part of the reason it had taken so long for her to leave him? Why had it taken her so long to say, "enough is enough?" With all the questions swirling through her mind, Beth thought maybe she should call the shelter after all. Perhaps the director could recommend a counselor or someone to help her answer the questions and assuage her doubts.

When she arrived at the floor, she discovered that Marsha was early too, and she followed her to the break room, putting away her coat and the dinner she'd packed for later in the evening. When she was settled, Marsha gave her a big hug.

"How are you doing?" Marsha asked.

"I really don't know," she sighed. "I have no idea what allegations Pat was alluding to. I just tried to stop by her office, but she wasn't in."

"Hmm," Marsha mused. "And what about the attorney?"

"He was very nice. Everything takes time—time and money," she said bitterly.

"Trust the *friendly* universe," Marsha crowed, pointing her finger into the air. She gave Beth a long look.

Beth laughed despite herself.

"Our new motto, TTFU," Marsha intoned to Beth.

"TTFU," Beth muttered, thinking it might be good advice.

Beth put a hand on Marsha's arm, stopping her briefly from leaving the break room.

"On a happier note, look at this!" Beth proudly showed Marsha the ring.

"Oh, Beth! It's gorgeous!" Marsha crowed excitedly. "I love the simple lines. It's just perfect!"

"I think so," Beth said and looked at the little ring lovingly.

They walked out to the nursing station to hear about the latest patients and begin reviewing charts for the evening.

Worried and stressed about the unknown allegations, Beth was even more meticulous than usual in her interactions with patients and updating their charts. Often, especially after busy days on the ward, the day shift left the night shift empty carts to refill. Beth made sure everything was in tip-top shape. She entered patients' rooms quietly and restocked the cabinets with the necessary items. It made the night pass a bit more quickly. Fortunately, it was a quiet night with no acute cases.

On her break, Beth checked her upcoming work schedule. She was off next Monday and Tuesday, like Matthew. She texted Matthew about her days off.

Matthew confirmed glassing the next Monday and suggested they meet at his house for breakfast, glassing, and a studio tour. Low tide was about nine in the morning, so they could meet after their night at work, have caffeine, and walk the beach. Beth agreed and asked for his address.

That settled, she moved through a very slow and stressful week. At the start of one shift, Marsha informed her that Pat had been asking many questions about Beth, her work, and her work ethic.

"I stood my ground and stood up for you!" Marsha told her stoutly.

Beth was worried. It had only been a few days, but Mike was silent, the lawyer was silent, and Pat was silent. She continued to work meticulously so that they couldn't find any fault with her patient care or records.

And so, the week dragged. Beth spent her awake time during the day in her garden and strolling the beach. It helped to center her. Often, she looked across the water, wondering where Matthew lived. She had his address, and he'd indicated she lived directly across the water, but she didn't know which house or neighborhood.

At the end of the week, Pat came onto the floor when Beth arrived. Beth hadn't seen her approach, but Marsha had given her arm a squeeze, and Beth looked up from her computer. She studied Pat as she walked, wondering if her face would reveal something. Nothing. She asked to see Beth, and they walked to a small consultation room.

"Sit down," Pat offered.

Beth sat, her stomach in knots.

Pat sat, too. She briefly looked at her hands but then looked Beth straight in the eye before clearing her throat. Beth felt she could jump straight from her skin.

"Beth, I wanted to touch base with you and let you know that we've found no fault in your work at the hospital, despite Mr. Masterson's frequent attempts to communicate otherwise."

"Mike," Beth murmured.

"Yes, Mike," Pat said drily.

"You need to know that he has contacted the hospital requesting your work schedule," Pat said.

Beth blanched.

"Of course, we can't give out that information, but it is my understanding that he has called frequently," she told Beth. "There's something…" she trailed off.

"Something not, quite, right?" Beth asked.

"Yes, that's it," Pat answered, "and it's worrisome. I'm not sure how to advise you, except to tell you to be careful."

"Thank you," Beth replied, her voice barely above a whisper.

At first, relief washed over her. The hospital had found no fault with her work. Then the worry and fear returned.

"I don't know what to do about Mike," Beth confessed. "It's all been on the fringes as if he's poking at me with pins to see how I'll react."

"I suspect that's the case," Pat replied, and then she asked, "Did you ever contact the shelter?"

Beth flushed, "No, I misplaced the number," she confessed.

"I'll get it for you. Mrs. Jones might have some answers. And, you have a couple of days off coming up. Perhaps you can meet with her?"

Beth nodded.

"I'm going to let you get back to work. I wanted to let you know that you do a wonderful job, and the hospital values you. You'll get through this," Pat said. "Let me know if I can be of further assistance."

"And the attorney? I have retained one," Beth commented.

"There's no need on our end," Pat assured her. "I'm not sure with Mr. Masterson. He made some serious allegations. That's up to you if you want to pursue a lawsuit for slander. If he falsified records, that's a criminal offense."

Beth digested this information. "Could I ask the attorney to contact you? I'm really not sure what to do."

Pat nodded, "Not a problem. I'll be happy to speak with your attorney."

Beth stood and let out a sigh of relief. "This is a nightmare," she admitted to Pat. "I can't thank you enough for your support."

Pat stood as well. "Not a problem," she told Beth.

Beth returned to the floor. The evening's activities had begun, and Beth scurried to do the meet and greet of her patients as well as a round of vitals. After most of the patients were settled for the night, she had a chance to catch Marsha up on what was happening.

Marsha was thrilled for Beth that the hospital had not found fault with Beth's performance. She was, however, worried about Mike.

"Beth, this is like something from one of those crime mysteries on television. It's not quite stalking, but Mike's definitely up to no good," Marsha said worriedly, "Maybe you should reply to the email. Stand up to him. Tell him to go to hell!" Marsha suggested.

"I know I'm a wimp about this. He definitely scares me. I'm waiting for the other shoe to drop. When we were together, it took me a long time to understand that I was not the problem. He had these crazy, irrational mood swings. It was like he didn't know what he was doing sometimes. And, when he did, he was profusely apologetic. I believed he would change and that it would never happen again, over and over, and over. I just couldn't please him, no matter what I did. He even told me that I did things to purposefully upset him, and I believed him!" Beth told Marsha. "But something's changed since then. He's like a stalker now, always on the fringe of things, threatening and pushing buttons. It's like he knows he's getting pleasure from scaring me."

"That's very messed up, but with the hospital supporting you, hopefully, this will all disappear. Unless you want to pursue a slander lawsuit?" Marsha asked, waiting for Beth to react.

Beth wouldn't meet Marsha's eyes. She shrugged.

"Let's change the subject. Do you want to go glassing on Monday?" Marsha asked.

Beth blushed and glanced at the cobalt blue sea glass ring on her finger.

"What? Hot date?" she teased.

"I'm meeting Matthew after work to go glassing Monday morning,"

"How long have you been keeping this from me?"

Beth smiled and shook her head. "We've been texting back and forth. We finally set a time," she admitted. "He asked me to go glassing in his neighborhood and have breakfast."

"Woot! Woot!" Marsha crowed. "That sounds like a date."

Beth smiled. "I guess it does," she admitted. "I'm pretty excited. He wants to come to Carpenter's Point, too. So, I guess I'll be returning the favor."

"This is just what you need, hon," Marsha said. "He seems really nice."

"I'm feeling sort of numb. I'm interested, but you know the old saying, "Once bitten...""

A patient light came on.

"I'll go," Beth told Marsha. She glanced at the time. "It's time to start morning vitals and meds, anyway."

Forty-Five

MATTHEW

It's the PH of the water that creates the corrosion of sea glass. The PH is higher in the ocean and lower on the bays and rivers. So, the smooth, sanded sea glass is caused by weather and chemical corrosion by the water's PH.

When Matthew received Beth's affirmation that she was coming on Monday to go glassing, he cleaned and tidied his apartment and his studio. He honestly could not remember the last time he'd had a woman over to his apartment. The night shift had definitely squashed many romantic intentions. And now, here was Beth, someone who had his schedule and understood.

He spent the week working on items for the upcoming sea glass festival, creating more sea glass stack rings. He also forged several copper cuff bracelets. He found the rhythmic pounding of the metal soothing. The bracelets sold well and were fairly quick to make. Once he forged a bracelet, he could embellish it with wrapped or bezel set sea glass. The copper was fun to work with, and he liked learning new fold-form techniques.

With each day that had passed, he was having difficulty focusing. His impatience led to a few pieces that didn't solder correctly and a couple of others that he melted. Finally, he gave up and put the ruined silver in a jar to be recycled by his favorite supplier. They would trade his scraps for newly recycled silver wire and silver sheet.

Sunday morning dawned. He worried slightly about cooking Beth's breakfast but settled on the idea of having scrambling eggs, toast, and fresh fruit. How could that go wrong? He picked up the food after work. The weather was fine, and spring was burgeoning. Boats were beginning to fill up the bay. Matthew opened the windows of his apartment and studio to let the warm breezes in, then headed outside. He had just purchased a Mayan hammock and strung it between two trees near the beach. He tested it out, letting the hammock settle into his circadian rhythms. His body relaxed, and he felt happily drowsy. The hammock was built for two, and Matthew couldn't help but think of holding Beth in his arms in the early mornings after work or watching the pearly moon rise over the water or the stars dance across the sky. As his mind drifted, he thought of making love to her in the hammock under a starry night sky.

He had it bad. No one had affected him like this since high school. His high school girlfriend, Debbie, had gone off with another guy as soon as they'd graduated. That had burned him. Since then, his relationships had been brief and shallow. But with Beth, it felt different. He anticipated it would be different. They had texted each other throughout the week. Just little things, but it was nice. The vibe between them was good. He could barely wait to get this relationship started, and his imagination swelled with possibilities.

Matthew stared dreamily into the blue sky through the filigree of newly minted leaves. There was a pale, green haze that softly lit the foliage all around. He lazily looked out to the water. Sailboats had caught a bit of wind and blew around the bay on the soft, gentle breeze. Matthew permitted his body to slip into a doze.

Waking hours later, he felt more refreshed than he had in weeks. At first, he didn't know where he was, but as he turned over, catching himself as he almost fell, he quickly remembered he was in the hammock.

Matthew rubbed his eyes and put his two feet on the ground. He checked his phone and found it was late in the afternoon. The weather wasn't cold, but the air was cooler than it had been earlier. The sun had turned. Matthew went inside to get ready for work and take a last look around his apartment and studio. He straightened a few things but mostly worked on packing his lunch before he grabbed a shower and changed for work. He reminded himself that Beth would be here the next morning.

His night stretched long before he motivated himself to keep up his speed, hoping if he kept pushing himself, the night would go by faster. It wasn't working as he had hoped, but time marched on as it usually did. *Funny thing, time,* Matthew thought. *The faster you want it to go, the slower it seems, and vice versa.*

At the stroke of seven in the morning, Matthew clocked out and raced home to prepare for Beth's visit. The sun was shining, and it portended to be a beautiful day.

Forty-Six

BETH

Cobalt blue, light blue, lime green, aqua, and lavender are rare sea glass colors.

Beth was relieved after speaking with Pat. At least she knew that her job was secure. She tried not to think of Mike and wonder where he was and what he was planning. Heeding Pat's advice, Beth called Ms. Jones at the women's shelter and made an appointment to speak with her on Tuesday. Monday morning was reserved for glassing with Matthew. It was her beacon of light in the week.

As she worked through the extremely slow week, Beth noticed that Mike was eerily quiet once again. Perhaps, he'd learned from the hospital administration that his threats had come to naught. Beth was certain this would anger him, and part of her was waiting for the other shoe to drop.

Finally, it was Sunday night. Marsha was off, and Beth worked with a new nurse, Shannon. They got along all right, but the night didn't have the same vibe as it did with Marsha. Beth missed Marsha but knew she would see her later in the week, and it helped that she was distracted thinking about Matthew. At the shift change, she rushed through the information briefing to the next crew and shot out of the hospital to head home for a quick shower and change before she went to see Matthew.

Beth celebrated the warm spring weather by donning capri pants and a T-shirt, taking along a lightweight, cotton cardigan in case it got breezy. She wore flip-flops so that she could step into the water if needed. She was a little nervous. After all, this really was a first date. Their texts this past week were light, and Beth felt comfortable with Matthew, but she was still a little nervous.

Sunday, Beth had picked up some breakfast treats at the local bakery in North Bay. She'd picked up a couple of sugar-crusted muffins for something sweet and luscious-looking individual focaccia bread topped with a variety of olives, peppers, onions, and herbs for a savory treat. The bakery had put them in old-fashioned bakery boxes and tied them with string.

At eight-thirty, Beth hopped into her car with the bakery boxes and put Matthew's address into her GPS. The directions took her through North Bay, and then she veered off on a side road that led past a marina near town. The slips were filling up with boats, masts tall and pointing toward the sky. Beth thought they looked like an eager herd of meerkats stretching up to look out to the bay. She continued down the road, past an orchard, a store with alcohol, and a deli that Beth wanted to check out soon. The road was twisty on the last leg of her journey, which took her through a bevy of trees. There were a few homes nestled in the woods. The road led her to a large open space where sunshine filled her vision, and the bay sparkled beyond. Beth's mouth dropped open, and she felt she was driving up a long drive to a plantation through tall trees on either side of the road. The road came to a "T," and her GPS told her to turn left instead of right toward more marinas. Matthew had said his place was just ahead on the right-hand side.

And there he was, sitting on a bench by an outbuilding, enjoying the sun. Beth pulled in, nervous but happy to be there.

Matthew opened his eyes when her car pulled in, and he hopped up, giving her a grin.

"Welcome to Bayside!" he greeted her.

"It's gorgeous here!" she exclaimed.

"Yeah, it is that," he agreed. "Come in."

Beth took the bakery boxes from the passenger seat.

"Here," she told Matthew, "A little something to go with breakfast."

He took the boxes from her with a delighted thank you, then led her inside. He pointed out that his studio was on the first floor, where a traditional garage area would be. She followed him up the stairs, and he opened the door to his apartment. Beth gasped a little when she saw the vista from his windows.

"Wow," she said.

"Here, you sit and relax," Matthew said, "and I'll get us some coffee. How do you take it?"

Beth told him that coffee would be a godsend and that she liked to drink it black. She perched a little nervously on the couch and looked out at the water and the sky. A few minutes later, Matthew brought her a large, handmade mug filled with coffee. He sat in the chair next to the couch. There was an awkward silence for a long pause. Beth sipped at her coffee.

"Thank you," Beth said. "I need this."

Matthew nodded, cleared his throat, and took a sip of his coffee. His voice cracked when he replied, "good."

After another awkward pause, he asked, "How was work last night?"

She sipped more coffee and answered, "Fortunately, it was fairly calm. You worked last night, too, didn't you?"

"Yup," he admitted. "It's an odd life, isn't it? Working at night, I mean."

"Yes, it's odd, but I'm coping."

"Me too. It's working for me right now. I really look forward to my days off when I can get on a normal schedule for a couple of days."

"Me too," Beth sighed.

"Well, we probably need some food. I'll scramble up some eggs. We can eat and then go onto the beach," Matthew suggested.

"Sounds great. Can I help you with anything?"

"Nope. Scrambling eggs is easy. You brought the baked treats, and I have some fruit. Will that do?" he asked.

"It sounds lovely."

Matthew went out to the small kitchen while Beth looked around. The seating pointed toward the view. There was an extremely small table with two chairs. Matthew had put out dishes of fruit and silverware. He'd put up a tray table to hold the focaccia, muffins, and some butter. His kitchen was compact and efficient, a little like the kitchen in her cottage, but with less cupboard space. Beth craned her neck to look behind her and noticed two doors. She assumed one went to a bathroom and the other to a bedroom. The apartment was bright and light, thanks to the huge windows facing the bay. She noticed a door that led to a small balcony and two chairs. Matthew was busily stirring eggs on the stove as she took in the space.

"I think we're ready. Are you ready for more java?" he asked.

"Absolutely!" Beth said.

Beth stood up and went to the kitchen, where Matthew poured her a cup of coffee from a French press. He picked up the plates, and they sat down at the table.

"This is lovely," Beth told him. "And it looks delicious! Do you find that you get hungrier working at night?"

He nodded, his mouth full of focaccia.

"This is yummy, by the way. Where's the bakery?" Matthew asked.

Beth laughed. "In North Bay, right in town. They have meals, too."

"I'll have to check it out," he commented around bites of the delicious baked goods.

When they finished their breakfast, Beth helped him clear the table and placed the dishes in the sink, where Matthew insisted, he would get to them later. He handed her a small Ziplock bag, and a full cup of coffee before heading down the stairs. He led her down the steps to a small walkway that passed around the house in front of his apartment and led straight to the beach.

"Does someone live here?" Beth asked, feeling a little self-conscious about going to the beach on someone else's property.

"The owner is in Florida 99% of the time," Matthew explained.

Beth put her hand up to her eyes. She wished she had binoculars but pointed and told him that she thought her house was directly across the water.

"We could have a signaling system," he suggested.

"Maybe," Beth agreed, then smiled at him. "It might be fun. We could set up smoke signals or those flashing things."

He grinned in return.

Matthew waved his hand at the small cove in front of them. It startled a blue heron scanning for fish nearby. Beth gasped in delight when she heard the rush of the bird's wings. They both watched as the large bird lifted off with an annoyed squawk and flew off toward Carpenter's Point.

"You know, I saw a heron right before I found my little shard of cobalt blue," she told Matthew.

"Interesting. I saw a heron before I found the cobalt blue rectangular shard I was telling
you about. This is where I find the bulk of my glass," Matthew said.

The tide was out, and there were layers of pebbles and large rocks near the waterline. Matthew started walking the beach, looking down in concentration. He was near the waterline, so Beth walked down the beach at the tideline. Almost immediately, she found some white pieces and a green piece. Two of the three white pieces were too young and quite shiny. Matthew was reaching down, examining a piece, and tossed most of the glass back into the bay.

"They're not quite 'done' yet," he explained, showing Beth the shininess under the frosting. "I throw them back so they can cook a little more in the bay. I have to trust the universe that they'll come back to me if they're supposed to."

"Hmm, trusting the universe," Beth murmured.

"What's that?" Matthew asked as a speedboat raced past them with a loud roar.

"Trusting the universe," Beth said, then shared the story Marsha had told her about trusting the universe.

Matthew threw back his head and laughed and laughed. He wiped a finger at his eyes. "I need to remember that," he said. "It's so true."

She agreed.

The sun was rising, and it was getting warm. Beth vacillated on taking off her cardigan. Matthew was in a t-shirt and shorts, so, finally, she took it off and tied the arms around her slim waist. She watched as he dove into the small waves to grab something.

"Look at this, Beth!" he called to her.

Beth hurried over to see what he had. It was a rock, but a rock tube.

"This is a tubular concretion," Matthew explained. "This is what I was telling you about in the café. I need to hollow out the sand in the tube, but this might make a nice jewelry piece. I can see something with silver wrapped around it or maybe copper. Something with vines, maybe."

Matthew had a dreamy look in his eye. Beth looked at the small rock tube, but she didn't see what he saw in terms of a finished jewelry piece. She was in awe of his visual thinking, how he knew exactly what he wanted from a piece.

"Do you always do that?" she asked.

"Do what?"

"Visualize a piece of jewelry from the rock or glass."

Matthew paused and thought a minute or two before he looked back at her.

"Yup," he admitted. "I can see the piece of jewelry I want to make from the pieces each time I find one."

"That's amazing!" she exclaimed.

Matthew shrugged his shoulders. "No, not really."

"Yes, really," Beth insisted before a yawn escaped her.

"Your night catching up with you?"

She blushed and confessed, "Yes, I'm pretty tired. Even after three or four cups of this." She raised her coffee mug in a salute.

"I hear you. Let's go back. You have a good haul," he said as he looked at her little bag.

Beth nodded, then turned and walked with Matthew back to his home.

"Let me show you the studio before you go," Matthew suggested.

"That would be nice," she replied, yawning again. "Sorry!"

"No problem," he said with a yawn of his own. "I understand."

She laughed as she followed him into the studio. As Matthew gave Beth a tour, she couldn't help but be impressed with the work he was creating for the Lewes show. She was especially impressed with the cobalt blue piece he had on the bench with a square of silver and sketches nearby.

"I found that on the beach a few weeks ago. Wouldn't it be cool if it was from the same bottle that your ring is from?" Matthew asked.

"Wouldn't it!" she agreed, glancing at her ring and then looking at the piece again. "What are you trying to create?"

"I'm planning on carving out a heron on the silver. It will show through, and then I'll knit a Viking chain to hold it. Things have been so busy with the ASGS Festival and now the Lewes festival that I haven't had the time to work on it. It's pretty intricate."

Beth took a moment to digest what he'd said. She couldn't imagine creating a piece of jewelry. She looked at the sketches.

"Which one have you chosen to carve from the silver?" she asked.

Matthew sighed with a little frustration, "I haven't decided whether to have the heron standing or flying," he told her.

Beth studied the illustrations again before she said, "I like both, but I think I like the flying heron the best. They remind me of pterodactyls."

"Yeah! Me, too," he said.

There were a few heartbeats of silence.

"Did I ask you before? Have you been?" he asked a minute later. "To the Lewes festival?"

Beth shook her head.

"Do you want to come with me?" he asked Beth. "I might ask you to sell a piece of jewelry or two if I need a bathroom break or something."

"That might be fun, but I don't know if I can get off work. Let me know the dates, and I can check," Beth agreed, thinking Pat would be happy to give her the time after what she was going through with Mike. "When do you want to come to Carpenter's Point?"

"Is tomorrow too soon?" Matthew asked hopefully. "I've wanted to go there since I moved here."

She laughed. "Sorry, I have an appointment tomorrow. Why don't I text you about next week? We can check to see if we have mutual days off and check the tide tables."

"That would be fine," Matthew said, but Beth detected a little disappointment in his voice.

Beth yawned again and said, "Thank you so much for breakfast and the glassing. It was wonderful."

"Wonderful for me, too," Matthew admitted, rather softly.

He opened the door to her car. His face was close to hers, and his eyes were intent. For a brief moment, she thought he was going to kiss her, but he didn't.

She climbed into the car, saying, "Thank you."

"It was great," he insisted. "Until next week at Carpenter's point. Go home and get some rest."

"You too," she advised.

She pulled out of his driveway and waved goodbye, while he watched her drive away.

Forty-Seven

MATTHEW

*In the 1970s, soda producers went from glass to aluminum cans.
Beer companies, too, changed from glass bottles to metal. This cut
down on the glass tossed into the water and sea glass production.*

There's something about her, Matthew thought as he watched her car turn onto his road and then drive through the line of trees that led to Bayside. Their interaction had been so natural that he felt he had known her for years. It was almost eerie. He was sad to see her go. He wished she could have stayed longer, but he knew it was much too soon to ask her to lie in the hammock or share his bed with her, so he waved cheerily before he turned back to his house. He made his way to the hammock and fell asleep, thinking of Beth. He woke sometime later, thinking she was next to him and feeling disappointed to find she wasn't.

Matthew poured his heart and soul into working on pieces for the Lewes show, forging copper and pounding out his frustrations. He wished he could speed up this relationship somehow. He worked until late in the day as his body was used to working through the night. Finally, in the wee hours, he retired, exhausted, still thinking of Beth. When he awoke the next day, he continued with fervor on melting and forging silver into several pieces. He used his Foredom drill and his tumbler to polish the pieces to a brilliant, shiny hue. Others, he turned black with oxidation to highlight a brilliant jewel of sea glass or form it in contrast to a highly polished piece of silver. By the end of his two days off, Matthew had a handful of striking pieces of jewelry to take to the Lewes show.

Dog tired, and eyes weary from staring into the flame of his torch, he sat on his deck to gaze at the sunset forming at the edge of the shore across the bay. Beth had mentioned she lived almost directly across the bay from where he sat. He took a swig of his beer and set the bottle down to go inside and rifle through his closet, looking for binoculars. He knew he had a pair somewhere. Finally, in the last place he looked, he found them and returned outside to his chair. He peered through the binoculars, but the setting sun was close to blinding him. Matthew cursed.

His phone pinged. Reluctantly, he set the binoculars down and picked the phone up to see who was messaging him. It was Beth! She inquired about his next day off and invited him to Carpenter's Point to go glassing.

He texted back that he would be off the next Wednesday and Thursday. Beth returned the text inquiring if he would like to come over Wednesday afternoon and have some dinner, adding a warning that she wasn't a good cook.

He laughed and offered to bring a pizza, to which she agreed.

"Until then," Beth ended the text along with her address in Carpenter's Point.

Matthew pumped his fist in the air and shouted "Yes!" to the world. He looked around, a little guilty at the noise in his very quiet neighborhood, but no one was about. Matthew smiled. He could do this.

Forty-Eight

JOSIAH – 1860

Cornflower blue is a coveted sea glass color.

J osiah and Tyrone scoured the city of Philadelphia looking for Anna Grace with no luck. He had visited his father's clients and introduced himself. Most of the mercantile were amenable to doing business with Josiah. At each mercantile, he would ask if they knew of a Widow Cadwallader. The answer had been no at each store. Josiah didn't know Anna Grace's maiden name, nor did Tyrone. So, they continued to search as the November weather turned colder.

Philadelphia, like Baltimore, was in a state of political flux. Parties for and against secession from the Union battled verbally. But tensions were high. Whispers of Civil War were discussed in many parts of the city, in drawing rooms, at drinking establishments, and in some mercantile. Josiah remained neutral when speaking. And, he wondered what war would mean to his business. Naval blockades were a possibility at the ports.

He couldn't worry about it now. He needed to find Anna Grace.

Forty-Nine

BETH

Most of the teal shards of sea glass are from glass produced before 1950.

Beth was dazzled by Matthew. She'd loved having breakfast with him in his cozy apartment and was in awe of his artisanship. She'd felt perfectly at home and comfortable with him, her nervous jitters disappearing when he first smiled and greeted her. If she hadn't been so tired, she would have stayed a bit longer, but they'd discussed glassing next week at her house, which made her feel good.

Beth went home to take a nap and then puttered around her house, beginning to clean some to prepare for Matthew's visit next week. She texted him, and they set the date of a week from Wednesday. She warned him that she wasn't a good cook and was relieved when he offered to bring a pizza. She would need to stock up on beer and wine, not knowing what his preference was, or maybe she would text him between now and that time to find out. It would give her an excuse to talk to him again.

The next morning, after a good night's rest, she prepared to see Ms. Jones at the shelter. She was a little nervous, doubting whether or not it was a good thing to do. Before she left, she checked her email, something she had begun to loath to do in recent weeks.

There it was, like an eyesore staring at her. A message from Mike. She clicked to open it to see what it said.

Don't think you can get away with your lies. You know you're not good enough to work at that hospital. They'll find out soon enough, even if they don't believe it now.

Beth trembled and slammed the lid of her laptop shut. It was so unfair the way he got under her skin, even three hundred miles away. She grabbed her purse and car keys and left, slamming the door for good measure. She drove almost blindly to the women's shelter, traversing the narrow, curving road faster than she usually did. A camper pulled out from the campground north of her development, and Beth had to slam on her brakes. It took her by surprise and knocked some sense into her. The camper moved slowly up the road. Worried she might be late, she tapped her frustration on the steering wheel.

Beth was surprised that the women's shelter was only a few blocks from the hospital in a nice area of town. It was a large, old, Victorian home nestled in the trees. A few spritely daffodils fought to bloom in the shade of the trees planted in the yard by the house. She parked in the small parking lot, then went up to the door and rang the bell. Ms. Jones had told her it would be locked, and she would need to wait for entry.

Someone peered at her before opening the door. A young woman opened the door and asked, "May I help you?"

"I have an appointment with Ms. Jones," Beth told her.

The young lady motioned her inside, introducing herself as Talia. She led Beth through. There was a clothing exchange or thrift shop type of area on the sun porch. They took two steps up and walked through a foyer to a small office. Talia knocked, and Beth heard a rich voice answer, "Come in."

"Go ahead," Talia urged Beth.

"Thanks," Beth told her and pushed the door open.

Ms. Jones stood when Beth entered the office. She was a tall, stately woman with beautifully coiffed hair and deep, brown eyes. She held out her hand to Beth and held her hand warmly, asking Beth to sit down.

"How can I help you?" Ms. Jones asked. "You said Pat Collins sent you."

Beth nodded, then told her, "I'm not sure where to begin. I... I..." She hesitated and looked helplessly at Ms. Jones.

"You have to start from somewhere," Ms. Jones advised.

Beth swallowed once and then again. She twisted her hands in her lap.

Quietly, she said, "I have, or rather, I had a boyfriend who is pretty horrible." The story spilled out of her, and when it was finished, she tried to hold back tears, coughing slightly.

Ms. Jones handed her a tissue, and the tears began to flow. Beth felt she couldn't stop. Ms. Jones waited patiently, handing her tissues as needed.

When Beth was spent, Ms. Jones spoke again. "My dear, you are not alone." Her eyes were soft and concerned. "Emotional abuse is at epidemic levels in our country. It's invisible. It deeply affects lives."

Beth hiccoughed and blew her nose as ladylike as she could.

"Do you feel safe?" Ms. Jones asked when Beth calmed down a little.

Beth shrugged. "I don't know how to answer you. I was feeling safe, tucked away here in Maryland, but now that he knows where I work..." she trailed off.

"Do you think he knows where you live?" Ms. Jones asked, looking Beth straight in the eye.

"I have no idea," she said. "I really don't."

"You were right to retain an attorney. You said he wasn't violent before, but it gave you pause to think he might get violent before leaving. You were brave, and you did take the first step, but this Mike sounds like a wily one. You still need to be on your toes." She paused. "I'm full to the brim, right now. I may have an opening in a couple of weeks if you need safe shelter. I can recommend some counselors for you, and I highly suggest that you call and talk with someone. The effects of emotional abuse can last for years. And please don't go back to him. Abuse is like suicide on the installment plan."

Beth sat, quiet as a mouse, as she took in Ms. Jones' advice. Suddenly, her fear ended, and Beth seethed with anger. "Ms. Jones, I have never been so scared in my life. I left him to stop the fear and to be able to live! That's why I came to this area. I don't want him to scare me from my life here! Everything is in limbo until he actually makes a move. I can print out the emails, but nothing will happen until he comes after me. That's when I can get a restraining order. So, I feel stuck. He's threatened my job. I've made it over that hurdle, but I don't know if he knows where I live. It's a cat and mouse game, and I really don't know what to do. Now his threats are just making me angry! How dare he go after my job!" Beth said in a vehement voice. "I'm so tired of his head games. He's ruined my relationship with my mom. Now, he's trying to control my life here from Eagle Heights. I will not let him win!"

"Good girl," Ms. Jones told Beth, "But, I'm here if you need me. Keep me apprised of your situation. Program this number into your phone in case you need help, day or night. And here are the names of the counselors."

Beth took the cards from Ms. Jones. She dutifully added the shelter's emergency line to her list of contacts and made it a favorite under Ms. Jones' watchful eye. Beth glanced at the cards of counselors before standing up.

"I can't thank you enough," Beth told Ms. Jones.

"You'll be all right, I think," Ms. Jones told Beth, "as long as we can get a handle on this Mike character."

Beth nodded. She left the shelter but sat in her car for a few minutes, sorting everything out. Ms. Jones had said she needed to get a handle on Mike. Beth had no idea how to do this. Mike was clever. She didn't know if or how she could trip him up. When she got home, she would need to forward the newest email to the attorney. And then what? She didn't know his plan, except that he was out to humiliate her. Anger and frustration boiled inside of her.

Fifty

MATTHEW

Finding a piece of orange glass is extremely rare. Only one in 10,000 shards might be orange.

Matthew's heart was light at the thought of spending more time with Beth. He worked steadily at the warehouse and at home in his studio with a new, lighter step. His supervisor commented on his increased numbers at work, and Matthew grinned at him. His supervisor didn't know that each piece picked, or every jewelry piece created made time go a bit faster and brought him closer to the time he would see Beth.

He received a text from Beth asking what type of beverage he liked. He smiled as he replied that he liked craft beers and red wine, then he asked how she liked her pizza. Beth returned, saying thin and crispy with black olives and mushrooms, which was his favorite as well. Was liking the same pizza a happy accident, or something more?

The week was in a strange time warp of speeding up and bringing him closer to the date, then crawling infinitesimally toward his day off. He hammered out his frustrations forging cuff bracelets in hammered or fold-formed copper. He added sea glass accents, soldering them carefully to the cuff.

Matthew began to tackle the carving of the heron on the silver bezel back. Several saw blades later and curse words turning the air blue, Matthew took a break to walk on the shore. Spring had officially sprung, and boats filled the bay. His neighbors' grandchildren and families shouted with delight as they swam and played. People fished from docks, and he saw families leaving the moorings at their homes to spend the day on the water. The neighborhood had taken on a festive air.

Many of the neighbors were intrepid gardeners. The ending of winter, with its unseasonable warmth, led to trees and flowers blooming profusely. While he walked, Matthew marveled at the beauty of the place where he lived. The flowers he'd seen were an inspiration for a new series of jewelry. Matthew had a vendor friend who created gorgeous, glued sea glass flowers. He had seen a few artisans use metal clay or the lost wax to create flowers with silver and sea glass. Now it was his turn to put his own spin on things. If he drilled through the glass, he could use silver wire and rivets to create a flower and green sea glass with silver wire for the leaves.

When he returned to his studio, Matthew drew sketches and wrote directions in his journal, and sifted through his jars of sea glass for pieces to create the flowers. Neatly he laid the shards on the bench in the shape of a flower with leaves and set up his drill press with a small dish with water and a sponge to drill the glass. Drilling was a little tricky. He marked the spot on the glass with a sharpie where he wanted to drill and inserted a diamond bit into the drill press. Slowly and carefully, he drilled through the pieces. He held his breath, silently praying the shards wouldn't break under pressure. In two of the pieces, he drilled second holes where the necklace would be attached to the silver chain.

Next, he soldered a circle of wire to provide a solid base for the stamens that would go through the drilled pieces. He didn't want the flower pendant to flop around, so he added an armature to the prong set for support. He also soldered tiny wires to add crystals or pearls to the center of the flower. In his journal, Matthew drew rough drafts of forged and soldered filigree wire links to accompany the necklace.

He was so excited about completing it that he neglected to sleep. It wasn't quite finished when he was forced to stop, but it was a stunning piece. At work, he found himself fatigued to the point that he could barely work. The massive amount of creative energy, too much caffeine, and lack of sleep caught up with him.

A pallet broke, spilling pickle jars everywhere. The smell of dill and vinegar filled the air, and his supervisor came rushing over.

"Are you okay?" she asked Matthew. "This isn't like you. That pallet almost landed on your foot! Are you feeling all right?"

Matthew rubbed a hand over his eyes and his forehead.

"Sorry," he told his supervisor. "I'm not at the top of my game tonight. Actually," he told her, "I'm not feeling one hundred percent. I think I need to go home." He spoke his words slowly, his fatigue making his speech thick.

His supervisor looked at him sharply and nodded her agreement.

"Are you going to be all right driving?" she asked.

"I'll take it slow," he assured her. "Thanks."

He sat in his car and fell asleep for almost an hour. When he woke, it was dark, and he was disoriented. After a moment, he remembered the earlier evening. He had never taken a day from work, but he knew he couldn't keep working in this fatigued state. He drove home slowly, noticing the restaurants and bars in North Bay still had patrons spilling from their doors. They were lounging contentedly on the decks of the restaurants that faced the street. People were walking back and forth, not really caring to cross at the crosswalk. Matthew crawled through the town, driving carefully so that he wouldn't hit anyone. Twice he had to come to an abrupt halt while a group of laughing tourists crossed directly in front of him without looking. He was never so happy to get through the town in his life. Usually, when he drove home in the morning, the coffee shop and bakery had their usual patrons, and sometimes he saw a store proprietor sweeping the walk in preparation for the day, but he never had people crossing the street at random intervals.

He was happy to drive out of the crowds in town and to the quieter streets to his neighborhood. His only hazard here were deer. He was careful to drive slowly to avoid their glowing blue eyes. He sighed with relief when he arrived home and stumbled up the steps to his apartment. Matthew lay, spread-eagled on his bed, fully dressed, and slept until noon the next day. He awoke, refreshed, and ready to begin work on the necklace again.

Showered and filled with coffee, he returned to his studio to complete the necklace, forging the swirled, filigree links and creating a clever clasp. He wanted to give it Beth. It would be his first gift of flowers for her. He hoped, the first of many sea glass and real flowers in their future. Time flew by that afternoon, but he finished the necklace before he headed to work that night. He would be seeing Beth the next day. He knew he could rest after work and then polish it before he headed out to get pizza.

The necklace was exquisite. Matthew grinned at the thought of seeing it around Beth's neck. It would be lovely.

His supervisor checked on him as he went on the floor. He assured her that he felt much better and proceeded to exceed some of his previous nights' picking in numbers. He was on fire to speed through the night.

When he went home that morning, it was difficult to sleep. Matthew eventually got up, polished the necklace, and placed it in an organza bag, which he then put inside one of his boxes and tied with narrow teal and green ribbons.

He lay in the hammock for a few hours, dozing off and on until his phone alarm beeped at him, rousing him from his slumber. Matthew showered and put on an ASGS Festival t-shirt, khaki Carpenter's shorts, and flip-flops. It was his glassing outfit for the summer, ensuring he had many pockets for sea glass treasures. He picked up the wrapped necklace and went to pick up the pizza.

Matthew had been to Kingstown briefly in the past. He had stopped at the public beach area where a historical sign told of the town's part in the Revolutionary War. He had found a couple of pieces of glass there, but not what he'd wanted. He'd also heard there were arrowheads to be found.

This time, he drove through the town and, following his GPS's directions, turned down a wooded road. Like his area across the bay, houses were nestled in the trees, and some roads looked as though they went to the water. The woods mostly ended, and a couple of farms were to his right. On his left was a campground that looked interesting. The road twisted and turned. He could see the water through the trees and assumed he must be at the end of the small peninsula. Beth's home must be nearby.

Stately homes perched on the cliff above the bay at the end of the peninsula as Matthew bore left with the road. The road swung around the end of the peninsula, where he saw the small beach community nestled at the water's edge. At one point, there must have been a community park as an abandoned swimming pool and lifeguard's chair were overgrown with weeds behind a fence with an aging strip of barbed wire at the top. He turned right and then left and followed the road until it ended. Beth's cottage was small and squat, sitting off on its own from the rest of the community. Matthew recognized her car and pulled in behind her.

He stepped from the car, grabbed the pizza boxes and the small gift, and went around the cottage to the front door that faced the bay. He noticed the small raised-bed garden with a protective arch of chicken wire over it to the side of the house.

Rather rickety-looking Adirondack chairs were on the lawn closer to the water. It was a gorgeous little place.

Matthew knocked on the door. He heard a startled "Oh!" from the house and footsteps hurrying to the screen door. And there was Beth. Her hair was lusciously loose, falling about her shoulders, and she was wearing a t-shirt and cut-off shorts. She was barefoot. She was perfect.

"Hi! Let me help you," she greeted as she reached for the pizza boxes. "Did you find this place all right?"

He was still a little stunned, taking in her prettiness.

"Yeah," he said, recovering. "It was easy. You either stay on the road or go into the bay."

Beth laughed. "That's true. Please come in. And I will apologize in advance. The cottage came furnished, and it's simply nowhere near House Beautiful standards."

"It's comfortable," Matthew said, ducking a little to get through the door. Right away, he noticed the bowls of sea glass and some driftwood on the windowsills. There were enough windows to keep the cottage bright.

"Thanks. I like it. Look out the window. Your place is almost directly across the water. We really could signal," she told him. "After dinner, I'll show you." She gestured to binoculars on the small occasional table beside the mission-style rocking chair at the window.

Beth had put the pizza down on the kitchen counter. The boxes filled the small, narrow countertop, but it was larger than the kitchen table which was painted white pine. The paint was peeling, and the accompanying chairs were yellow, white, and aqua. The table was set with silverware, salad bowls, and a fresh green salad in the center. There was an open bottle of red wine and two stemless wine glasses on the table.

"It's a testament to shabby chic," Beth told Matthew.

"Like I said, comfortable," he told her. He handed the box to

Beth. "I know it's appropriate to bring flowers, but I made a flower for you instead."

Beth gave him a puzzled look and took the box. She opened the ribbons carefully and peered inside the organza bag. Her eyes widened when she saw the necklace, and her mouth formed an "O" of wonderment.

"Oh, Matthew! It's exquisite! I've never seen anything like it! Thank you!" she exclaimed softly, her voice reverent as she took the necklace from the pouch. "Will you help me put it on?"

"Sure." Matthew agreed, but he was a little nervous.

Beth handed him the necklace, and she turned from him, pulling up her long hair so that he could fasten the necklace around her neck. Her neck was beautifully creamy, and there was a small mole southeast of her left ear. Again, he felt the urge to kiss her neck but stopped himself. He was taking too long to fasten it, and his fingers fumbled. When the necklace was around her neck, she patted the pendant and went over to a mirror to admire it.

"I'm stunned," she told him. "I don't think I've ever had anything this beautiful. Thank you so much."

"You're welcome," he replied. "I may make some more now that I've created this one."

"Oh! You should!" Beth insisted. "It's just perfect! You'll sell out if you make these."

She turned to look in the mirror again. She caught him staring at her and blushed prettily.

"Our pizza must be getting cold," she said as she turned back to him.

She handed him a plate and opened the pizza boxes. There was a pizza smothered in black olives and mushrooms, and another, white pizza with mozzarella and fresh tomato and basil leaves.

When she turned, her hair swung in a swirl. Matthew wanted to gather it into his hands. Instead, he took the offered plate and filled it with two slices of pizza, then waited for her to get her pizza.

"Yum," she said as she took a slice of each.

They sat at the table, and Beth pushed the salad a little bit toward him.

"Do you like salad?" she asked. "I picked it fresh from the garden this morning."

"I do, thank you," Matthew said.

It was filled with tender lettuces, arugula, and spinach. Something white was chopped into the salad, but Matthew didn't know what it was. He guessed jicama. Beth had added small tomatoes and a little onion. He wanted to take a small bite of Beth's lower lip, but instead took a bite of salad dressed in a light herb and lemon dressing.

"I thought you said you couldn't cook?" he asked her rhetorically.

"Umm...a salad isn't cooking," she said. "And the garden provided."

"It's delicious. Did you make the dressing? I've never tasted anything out of a bottle like this. And, what's this white vegetable? I don't recognize it."

"Yes, I made the dressing. More stuff from the garden," Beth answered, "and the white vegetable is a Japanese white turnip. They're really delicious."

"I'll say. They're almost sweet, and I like the crunch. I think it has more taste than Jicama, and it's a nice change from cucumber."

He helped himself to a second bowl of salad before biting into his pizza.

"How long have you lived here?" Matthew asked. "This is a prime spot on the bay."

"About eight months," she answered. "I moved in the fall of last year. I like that I'm a little away from the neighbors since I work the night shift."

"I hear you. My community is warming up to the summer frenzy of family visiting. I think I need to get earplugs from the noise of the people and the speed boats."

"That's a great idea!" she said. "I love to watch the boats zooming down the bay, but they don't allow for good sleeping."

Matthew nodded in agreement.

They finished their pizza, and Beth showed Matthew some of the sea glass in her bowls before leading him down to the small beach.

He poked through the jars and bowls, fingering a few thoughtfully.

"Would you consider selling me a couple of these?" Matthew asked.

Stunned, Beth stammered, "Just take them. When we're done glassing, we can have another glass of wine, and you can rifle through the jars. You're welcome to anything you want except for a few pieces that might make good buttons."

"Buttons?" Matthew asked, puzzled. "Why buttons?"

Beth told him she used to sew a lot and that she'd been thinking of sewing some simply constructed clothes and adorning them with sea glass buttons.

"I can help you with that," Matthew said. "I drill all the time. I can teach you."

"That would be fabulous! Thanks!" Beth responded enthusiastically, pushing open her door, so they could get to the beach. "As you can see, it's not a very big beach, but I do find a decent amount of glass on this small crescent," Beth told him as they sipped their wine and strolled along the beach.

Matthew looked down for shards but found himself watching Beth strolling along, instead of finding glass. She picked up a piece or two, threw a couple back into the bay, and tucked a few into her pocket. She stopped where the beach ended at a grassy hillock. Another property was just beyond, with an aging pier stretching out into the bay.

"I usually stop here," she confessed to him. "I don't really know those neighbors. I understand they're summer people. The older guy is kind of grumpy. He doesn't like people on his beach. One time, when I ventured onto it, he growled that it was private property, so I stay on my side now."

"Too bad," Matthew said, pointing at the neighbor's beach. "It looks like a really nice piece of green over there."

Beth looked to where he was pointing, a mischievous gleam filling her eye.

"I don't think he's home today," she mentioned. "Maybe we could sneak over and get that shard?"

They giggled and snuck over as if they couldn't be seen, grabbed the deep, green shard, and ran back to Beth's beach. They doubled over laughing when they reached her property.

"Why do I feel like I just stole a piece of candy from the candy store?" she gasped between gales of laughter.

Matthew laughed, nodding in agreement. "But we certainly got the prize!" He put the piece of dark green glass in Beth's palm. "This piece is a winner. Probably a piece from a 19th-century bottle."

"Wow!" Beth exclaimed. "I'm so amazed at the history behind the glass. It's like living someone's life a little vicariously. You could make hundreds of stories up about the glass, couldn't you? Like the blue glass of my ring." She held it out to catch the sun. "You and my friend Marsha said that it could be from a poison bottle. I love it, but I hope that it didn't bring about anyone's demise."

"I know. I love the history behind the shards, too. I think that's one of the reasons I like to work with sea glass. Gemstones are cool, but the glass is so unique. It's like stepping back into time sometimes," Matthew said.

They went back to Beth's yard to sit in the Adirondack chairs and look out at the water. Matthew thought he could spend many a day sitting here with Beth, looking at her and the view.

Fifty-One

BETH

Flat pieces of light blue glass are likely from windowpanes or car windows.

The seething anger that had been building in Beth about Mike dissipated when she was with Matthew. She was astonished that he'd made a custom piece of jewelry for her. He told her about the flowers blooming in his neighbors' garden that had been the impetus for the new jewelry.

Even though they had not communicated much during the week, things were comfortable with Matthew. It was like they had known one another forever. They picked up their conversation easily, like a cozy sweater slipping over her head. Beth didn't want to entertain *meant to be* thoughts, especially since she felt gun shy from her relationship with Mike. But there was definitely something special about Matthew. Something that was beautiful and strong.

Perhaps it's simply the second glass of wine talking, Beth thought. They had both been silent, watching the water and the sky, each lost in their own thoughts.

"More wine?" she asked him.

"Sure," he said. "Let me get it."

He leaped up from his chair, went into her cottage, and brought out the open wine bottle as well as the second bottle, and the wine opener. Beth's eyes widened.

Matthew split the remainder of the bottle between their two glasses, and Beth settled into the Adirondack like melted butter, sighing in contentment.

"Aren't we lucky," he said softly, looking out at the water.

"Absolutely," she agreed.

"You know, I see the sunset from my home," he said, glancing at the sky behind him, "but you must see some gorgeous sunrises."

"True," Beth said. "When I'm home to see them. I enjoyed seeing the later sunrises when I would get home from work in the winter. I have that mission rocking chair by the window that provides the perfect view."

She waved her arm back toward the cottage to indicate where the chair sat. The movement made her realize she may have had a bit too much to drink. "I think I need another piece of pizza to absorb some of the wine," she confessed to Matthew.

He nodded.

"My turn," she said, feeling a little unsteady as she stood. "Do you want me to heat it up?"

"No, it's fine as it is," he assured her.

She nodded and walked back to the cottage door, swaying a little bit. She placed two pieces of pizza on each place and took the plates back to the chairs.

"This is a good idea since I'll be driving in a bit," Matthew said.

For some reason, this information disappointed Beth. The wine had loosened her emotions and her attraction to Matthew as well. The fire in her belly wasn't just due to the wine she had imbibed. Beth sighed a little, the sound drawing Matthew's attention. She took a bite of pizza and asked him where he had picked it up.

"Yeah, I got it at the plaza, just north of town. It's a pizza shop that's been around forever in this area. Their other food is great, too. Sometimes I grab a sub sandwich on my way to work," Matthew confessed.

"It's delicious," Beth agreed as she finished a slice. I can't decide which one I like better."

"Next time, we'll have to split a calzone. Should we save this bottle for another time?" Matthew asked, holding up the still-closed bottle of red wine. "I should be getting home."

Beth nodded, but she didn't speak. She stood, feeling much less tipsy, and turned toward the cottage with their plates and her wine glass. Matthew followed with the bottle, wine opener, and his glass.

They stood, a little strained, in the kitchen. Beth ran hot water into the sink and squirted in a bit of dish soap before putting the dishes in the warm water. She turned to face Matthew.

"I'm glad you came today," she told him. "Thank you for the pizza and," her hand rose to her throat where the sea glass flower pendant was nestled in the hollow of her neck, "there aren't enough words to thank you for this."

Matthew stepped closer to her. He lifted up her chin and kissed her. Beth felt her body melt. She moaned. His kiss held the promise of many good things. She put her arms around his neck and returned the kiss, then he wrapped his arms around her, pulling her closer. Finally, she pulled back. She didn't want to, but the nightmare of Mike hovered in the back of her brain, disrupting the kiss that had filled her.

"I'm, I'm sorry," she said huskily, taking a step back. "I can't do this."

"Why?" Matthew asked, concern in his eyes.

"Maybe you should sit down. Maybe we should open the other bottle of wine," Beth suggested.

Beth went to sit in the chair by the woodstove. Matthew opened the wine and sat nearby. He handed her a glass.

"I'm sorry," she said.

"I don't understand—" Matthew began.

"There isn't any reason why you should understand," Beth said. She took a fortifying sip of the wine.

"I'm a mess," she confessed, looking at Matthew. "I'm not sure you want to get involved with me."

Matthew looked puzzled. He didn't reply but urged her to continue with his eyes.

Beth gave a bitter, little laugh. "You know, I didn't want anyone to know this when I got here. Now, I am spilling my story to everyone."

"What story?" Matthew finally asked.

Beth felt a little embarrassed, but she forged ahead and told Matthew about Mike and all that was going on. He listened. He didn't say anything. When she was finished, Beth drained the wine in her glass. She had sipped occasionally as she told Matthew about Mike, and now it was almost gone. Matthew refilled her glass before responding.

"Beth, I don't really care about Mike. I care about you. I..." he hesitated, "I think I'm falling in love with you, as odd as that may sound since we're just getting to know one another and every-thing. It's much too soon. There's something..." He trailed off words failing him.

Beth met his eyes. "I know just what you mean," she said softly. "I don't understand it, but I feel the same."

Matthew sighed with relief.

"Look," he said, "we can play this out any way you want. I'm a pretty patient guy. I don't know how I can help you with this Mike thing. I can listen and be supportive. I'm not really the violent type." He grinned at her. "Unless it came to defending the fair lady."

Beth smiled at this, grateful. Matthew reached for her hand and took it. His hand was warm and strong and felt to Beth like an anchor. There it was again, that feeling of a thick rope between them, invisible, but the strength of the braided rope that held large ships to a bollard on a wharf. They sat like that for several minutes, just looking at one another.

Matthew broke the moment. "I should be going," he told Beth. "I don't want to push you into anything."

"Thank you," Beth replied.

And this time, when he kissed her, it held the promise of more.

Fifty-Two

MATTHEW

Thick, aqua shards of glass are likely from old electrical insulators.

Matthew had gone and done it. He had confessed his feelings to Beth. He felt like he was caught up in some sort of strange love triangle with her ex-boyfriend, though. The guy sounded like a piece of work. How could he be abusive to Beth? Matthew didn't know her very well, but he felt that he could read her character. She was a wonderful person. Jesus! Now, he sounded like something out of a bad Romcom. He would need to be patient with Beth. And he could be patient. They could take this slowly. He coached himself with this mantra on his drive home.

The next day, Matthew texted his thanks to her for the great afternoon and asked her if she wanted to get together on their next day off. And then he texted her again, to see if she wanted to go out for dinner that evening. They were both off work, right? Beth agreed, making his day. He promised to pick her up at six.

He spent the rest of the day working on the heron pendant. He completed it late in the afternoon and polished it to a bright finish with his Foredom drill, buffing it carefully with the polishing wheels and paste polish. The blue glowed through the polished silver, and the flying heron took on a life of its own. Matthew held it up to the light, satisfied with his work. He found a Viking knit chain he had previously made and strung it through the sturdy bail on the top of the pendant. He couldn't wait to show it to Beth.

He dressed more carefully for their evening out, putting on a black polo shirt and khaki pants. He placed the heron pendant around his neck—the black shirt complimenting the blue and silver pendant. Matthew tied back his curly, light brown hair in black elastic. He would pick up real flowers for her tonight. He left early so that he could stop by the florist for a bunch.

With a light step, Matthew left to spend the evening with Beth.

Fifty-Three

BETH

Cobalt blue may not be the rarest of sea glass shards, but it continues to be one of the most popular.

Beth hummed happily as she blew her hair dry. She thought she heard something and turned off the hairdryer for a moment. A boat whizzed down the bay. Shrugging, she turned the blow dryer back on and finished drying her hair. Next, she applied some light make-up. She was looking forward to going out with Matthew that night. She felt a hundred pounds lighter since she had told him about Mike. Everyone she'd told had been understanding and supportive, especially Matthew. Mike hadn't sent any other emails, and Beth was hoping that the nightmare had ended, that he had given up. Maybe now she could really live her life again.

She brushed her hair until it shone, then padded into the bedroom to put on a short, floral dress before fastening the flower necklace around her throat. She had purchased a pair of white sea glass post earrings at the ASGS Festival and put those on as well. Satisfied, she put on a pair of high-heeled strappy sandals. She pulled a white, lacy shawl from her drawer to guard against the evening's chill and headed out to the living room to wait for Matthew, knowing he'd be there any minute. Beth went straight over to the window that looked out onto the bay. Then she heard a sound behind her that caused her to turn abruptly.

Shock was a small word for what Beth experienced when she saw Mike standing in her kitchen. His face was ugly, like a big dog snarling with a deadly growl.

Beth's voice trembled, "M-m-mike?"

"You, bitch!" he snarled, his voice in a low growl. "You think you can humiliate me and run away from me? You have another thing coming."

Beth's eyes grew wide. She fought to gain some control over her emotions. Her brain seemed sluggish. What was Mike doing in her kitchen? What was he holding?

"Mike!" she said more loudly, her voice finding itself. "Mike! What are you doing here?"

And then it registered, that Mike was holding a gun. It was a smaller gun. She remembered he had kept it in the bedside drawer in case of intruders. He had prided himself on owning that gun. He had told her it didn't have a hammer and that it could shoot someone easily by just pointing and aiming. Her eyes widened, her mouth dropped open, and she teetered a bit on her high heels.

"And what's this?" he sneered, waving the gun in a gesture to encompass her dress. "You're now whoring around?"

"I, I." Beth was bereft of words. "Mike, please," she pleaded. "Why do you have a gun?"

"Why?" Mike scoffed. He leered and gave a horrible-sounding, dangerous little laugh. "People don't humiliate me. You have this coming to you."

"Mike! No!" Beth screamed, trying to get him to make some sense of the situation. She wanted his attention. She vaguely remembered that it was best to keep someone in this state talking. He looked dangerously close to shooting her.

"Mike!" she said again, trying to gain control of her emotions and her shaking hands. The dainty lacy shawl was shredding under the twisting grip of her fingers.

"What, bitch?" he snarled again.

That's when Beth heard another sound. It was the sound of a car pulling into her driveway and a door slamming. It was Matthew. Beth knew it. He would be at her door any minute. How could she warn him? Mike had heard it, too, and an evil look crossed his face.

Beth knew she only had seconds, "Matthew! Don't come near! Call the police! Call the police!" Beth screamed.

But Matthew didn't hear her. He was happily heading toward the front door with flowers in his hand.

"Matthew, run! Call the police!" Beth screamed again.

This time he must have heard her. Beth heard his rushed footsteps then the door flew open. His hand was still on the door handle when the shot went off and Beth screamed as Matthew was knocked off his feet, flowers flying out of his hand.

Fifty-Four

BETH

Sea glass marbles are popular among collectors.

Beth turned on Mike, the anger that she'd carried over the past months joined with the adrenaline that filled her body the moment she saw Matthew fall. She took a heavy jar of sea glass and flung it at Mike. He ducked, and it crashed to the floor, cracking and breaking into a hundred pieces. It distracted Mike, giving Beth a moment to get to the kitchen and grab the first thing she could. There was a large cast-iron skillet on the stove. Mike had followed her into the kitchen and raised the gun to shoot her, but Beth had the pan handle in both hands and blindly swung the skillet like a bat, hitting Mike in the side of the head. He crumpled to the floor from the impact. She kicked the gun into the bedroom. Mike was still so she ran to Matthew.

"Oh, Matthew!" she cried. She reached for her phone and shakily dialed 911.

Matthew was bleeding heavily. Beth wadded up her shawl and put it on the ugly wound, applying steady pressure to it. She thought the bullet was still in Matthew's body, but she wasn't sure. She prayed it hadn't nicked his lung and caused respiratory failure. Beth answered the questions of the 911 operator as best she could. She continued to put pressure on the wound while also paying attention to Matthew's breathing. She wished she had a free hand to take his pulse, but suspected it was thready by the gray look on his face.

"Hurry!" she urged the operator. "Please! Hurry!"

Beth wasn't sure if Mike was alive or not. She had hit him pretty hard and he likely had a concussion. She hoped he would stay unconscious until the police arrived. If he was still alive. She realized then that she didn't care if he was dead. Her only concern was Matthew. She watched Mike out of the corner of her eye. His body was very, very still and she couldn't tell if he was breathing or not from where she sat with Matthew. The adrenaline left her body, and Beth felt herself wilt like an old piece of lettuce.

After what seemed like hours, she heard the sirens, the flashing lights of the police cars and an ambulance following shortly. Matthew started to wake, groaning in pain as he attempted to move. He had hit his head when he fell and had been unconscious for a few minutes.

"Shh," she whispered into his ear. "Help is here."

"Here!" she called to the first responders. "In here!"

The officers entered carefully; guns raised. Beth nodded at Mike.

"He shot Matthew. I kicked the gun in there," she explained, lifting one hand from the wound and pointing to the hallway toward the bedroom.

The police examined Mike. One of the police radioed that there were two victims, then the paramedics arrived. They split up, two running to Mike, two over to Matthew. She stood back as they moved Matthew onto a gurney. She saw the other supporting Mike's head and briefly wondered if she had broken his neck. They rolled Matthew out, and Beth went to follow them, but an officer stopped her

"I need to go, too," Beth insisted.

"You need to make a statement," he told her firmly.

Beth sat reluctantly, wishing she could be with Matthew. The officer sat across from her and waited. Here was the story again, but with a different ending.

She told the officer about Mike. She told her entire story about Mike, from his emotional abuse and controlling ways in Eagle Heights to how he'd worked to sabotage her job here and the threats she had received via email. She told the officer her attorney's name, as well as Pat's name and the name of Ms. Jones from the shelter. She provided their phone numbers and then told the officer about Matthew and the events that had transpired that day.

"When the gun went off, I think I went a little crazy," she said. "He hurt Matthew for no reason. He came after me and was turning the gun on me. I had to distract him. I had to do something, so I threw the glass jar of sea glass at him. And then, I just grabbed the first heavy thing I could." Beth nodded at the cast iron pan that now lay on the floor. Another officer had picked up the gun and put it in an evidence bag. "I wasn't thinking. I was just trying to save our lives."

The officers permitted Beth to wash the blood from her hands. She couldn't clean up until they processed the crime scene. All she wanted to do was to get to the hospital to see Matthew, she didn't care about the mess. After clearing her to leave, an officer escorted her to the hospital, driving so fast that she could barely keep up.

Matthew was in surgery when she arrived. Beth texted Marsha a little of what had occurred, and Marsha came down to the surgical waiting room to sit with her, holding her hand as she spilled out her story again. Beth was dry-eyed now, bereft of emotion outside of fear and worry and love for Matthew. The surgeon came to the waiting room, and Beth couldn't read his stoic face. He told her they had removed the bullet and that Matthew would be just fine. It had missed vital organs, but there was still the worry of infection and sepsis. Beth slumped in relief, and Marsha patted her back.

"Thank you, doctor," Marsha said.

Beth nodded at the surgeon, unable to speak.

Beth was waiting in the room they had assigned to Matthew when they brought in his gurney. He was barely conscious, slipping in and out with the pain medication. She stepped back, permitting the team of nurses to hook him up to all the monitors. And then she held his hands, willing him to heal.

The hours that followed were dream-like to Beth. Afterward, she remembered a police officer coming to tell her that Mike had been released from the emergency room to be taken to the county jail and processed for the shooting. The other crimes would need to wait until she could contact her attorney and talk to him about pressing additional charges.

When Matthew finally emerged from the cocoon of anesthesia and pain meds, he saw Beth and smiled.

"Some date," he said, his voice croaking from disuse.

"Yeah," Beth said drily. "It went off like a bang."

Matthew tried to laugh at the poor joke. "Don't!" he cried weakly. "It hurts to laugh."

"Sorry," Beth said. She leaned over and kissed his cheek softly.

They didn't say anything for several minutes, then Matthew remembered something. "Beth! The heron pendant! I finished it! I was wearing it. Where is it?" he asked.

Beth pulled the bag of personal belongings from under the gurney. She fished around and drew out the knitted silver chain with the pendant attached.

"Oh!" Beth took in a breath of wonder at seeing the pendant, "Matthew, it's stunning!"

There was a flash from the sun that raced through the cobalt blue pendant and her ring, joining them together with a bright flash of blue light. Beth gasped and cried out, "Oh!"

"They're meant to be together," Beth said, smiling. "Just like us."

Matthew smiled at her and held out his arm on his uninjured side. She climbed into the hospital bed, moving carefully, not wanting to hurt him. It didn't. Being in his arms felt like she had finally come home.

Fifty-Five

JOSIAH – 1860

"End of Day" sea glass can date back to the 18ᵗʰ century. It's glass that was tossed into the water at the end of the day of production.

It was a blustery, November day on the streets of Philadelphia. The wind had kicked up and blew in fierce, little gusts. Leaves swirled and eddied in the gutters and stuck to some of the cobblestones. Josiah pulled his coat tighter and buttoned the top button. He pulled the collar up around his neck. One gust almost blew his top hat off. Tyrone would be upset if he lost it. He was back at the inn, waiting for Josiah's return.

Tyrone had worked out well as a valet. Josiah was teaching him to read and do sums. Tyrone was proving to be helpful in his business as a secretary like Abraham had. Abraham's body had never been found, and Josiah still mourned his loss.

He had no room for melancholy thoughts today. He had been to nearly every mercantile in the city that he had not visited yet in his search for Anna Grace. Yesterday, he'd learned of another on Market Street, a bustling street with many stores.

And there it was, a large, brick store that towered three stories high. He opened the door to rich smells of wool, candles, and spices. There were a few people looking at wares and a tall man, with graying mutton chops greeted him from across the room.

At the counter for fabric, there was a blond head bent over fabric they were cutting for a customer. The lady finished cutting and her head rose. Josiah's heart nearly stopped. He was frozen as he watched Anna Grace fold the fabric and hand it to the customer with a smile.

As if his gaze was a magnet, she turned and saw him standing there. Her mouth formed a small "O," and she swayed in her spot, then grasped the counter for support.

"Josiah?" she breathed the question. "Josiah?"

Josiah was at the counter in three strides. He took Anna Grace's hand and murmured, "dear lady," over and over.

Tears rolled down Anna Grace's face, and she closed her hand over Josiah's, and there they stood, gazing at one another.

Fifty-Six

BETH

Cobalt blue glass has been a favorite worldwide since ancient times.

It had been nearly a year since the shooting at her house. Beth was vindicated by Mike's actions. He was in jail now for stalking, harassment, and intent to murder. He had also been charged in the shooting of Matthew.

Matthew had moved in with Beth, and they were renting to own a cottage in Matthew's neighborhood. It wasn't waterfront but was nestled in the woods and had access to the beach. Matthew had a larger space for his workshop in an outbuilding to which he'd added insulation and electricity to make it more livable.

Beth had unleashed her creative side and was creating simple, constructed clothes with sea glass buttons in a small loft inside the house. She had found a source of natural fabrics and loved working with wool, cotton, and linen combining the fabrics and textures to create shirts, kimonos, loose trousers, shawls, and poncho-like blouses.

They were attending sea glass and arts festivals together now to sell their wares. This weekend, they were headed to Baltimore for a juried arts festival. The booth space was outrageously priced, but it was good exposure for Matthew's jewelry and her clothing. Their businesses had taken off, and they'd both had cut their work hours to part-time in order to keep up with their online business and consignments at galleries in the area.

Beth was blissfully happy. She was looking forward to this show in Baltimore and had rented a historical townhouse in Fells Point for the weekend. The pictures of the space were gorgeous, with rich, wooden paneled walls, oriental carpets, and antique furniture. It dated back to the 19th century and had been lovingly restored. It was a splurge, but she thought it was worth it. There was something about the townhouse that drew her. She had ogled it on the website many times since booking and planned on packing champagne and romantic goodies for their time away from the show.

They arrived in Baltimore and set up their booth before heading to the rental. Beth and Matthew had their set-up well-orchestrated for the various shows, and it didn't take long once their car was unloaded to get their booth put together.

They weren't strangers to Baltimore. In fact, they'd taken many day trips exploring the city. They loved roaming the streets, shops, and museums of the Inner Harbor, Fells Point, and Little Italy. Beth's favorite was the Walters Art Gallery, and Matthew's the American Visionary Art Museum. They were both fascinated with the Baltimore Museum of Industry at the Inner Harbor and hoped to squeeze in one of their favorite museums on this trip.

Beth found the historic, restored home for rent in the Fells Point area. It was just a few blocks from the waterfront where warehouses had once stood. Now, the waterfront area was filled with a variety of restaurants, eclectic stores, and cobblestone streets.

The home was a stately, brick townhome on a cobblestone street. A brass historic building plaque was displayed by the door.

They unloaded their luggage and walked up to the door, where Beth used her hand to bring up a keypad. She typed in the code the host had sent her, and they opened the door.

They stepped into a wide hallway with a carved staircase about halfway down the hall. Doors to other rooms were off to the left and the air smelled of beeswax and lemon. The sounds of the city were muted by the heavy wooden door and thick walls. The house felt welcoming to Beth, and she was surprised at a sudden onset of emotion and déjà vu. She walked over to a small, narrow table just inside the front door. On it was a notebook welcoming the guests. Matthew had flipped it open to begin reading about the history of the house.

The house had been owned by Josiah and Anna Grace Bryant. They had been married in the house in 1863. Josiah owned a successful import and export business that withstood the rise and fall of economic fluctuations through the Civil War and beyond. Both Josiah and Anna Grace were fierce abolitionists who fought for the freedom of slaves before, during, and after the Civil War. The history noted Anna Grace's Quaker heritage.

As they read, Beth felt a shiver travel up her spine and the hairs on the back of her neck and arms stood up, but it wasn't from the cold. She took Matthew's hand and held on tightly.

"I feel so strange," Beth whispered. "It's like I've been here before."

She swayed a little, and Matthew gripped her elbow gently with his other hand and led her into the living room to find somewhere to sit. It was brightly lit from natural light and Victorian antiques lined the walls.

They sat together on a brocaded, Victorian settee where the afternoon sun streamed in the windows sending shafts of light to the walls and floor. On the opposite wall was a portrait of a man and a woman above the fireplace. The couple looked uncannily like Matthew and Beth in period dress from the Victorian era.

They were stunned. Beth put her hand up to her mouth. The

late afternoon sunshine poured in through the window and caught her ring and Matthew's pendant together in a blaze of light that lit up the portrait with an aura of cobalt blue.

About the Author

Sharon, born 1959, grew up in central Pennsylvania surrounded by the beautiful mountains. Writing has been a lifelong passion for Sharon. For Sharon, writing is like breathing. She says she has more stories in her head to write down than lifetimes to live. Sharon is a nationally award winning Librarian and the author of several educational publications. She is also an avid gardener and jewelry artist.

CPSIA information can be obtained
at www.ICGtesting.com
Printed in the USA
BVHW081941151022
649329BV00002B/7